A WARTIME WIFE

LIZZIE LANE

Boldwood

First published in 2014. This edition first published in Great Britain in 2022 by Boldwood Books Ltd.

Copyright © Lizzie Lane, 2014

Cover Design by Colin Thomas

Cover Photography: Colin Thomas

A CIP catalogue record for this book is available from the British Library.

Paperback ISBN 978-1-80415-904-0

Large Print ISBN 978-1-80415-905-7

Hardback ISBN 978-1-80415-903-3

Ebook ISBN 978-1-80415-906-4

Kindle ISBN 978-1-80415-907-1

Audio CD ISBN 978-1-80415-897-5

MP3 CD ISBN 978-1-80415-899-9

Digital audio download ISBN 978-1-80415-900-2

Boldwood Books Ltd
23 Bowerdean Street
London SW6 3TN
www.boldwoodbooks.com

1

It was two weeks following Prime Minister Chamberlain declaring war on Germany that Mary Anne Randall knew for certain she had a little problem.

Her neighbour Biddy Young crossed one knee over the other, puffing and wheezing in an attempt to straighten a stocking seam. 'Done the hot baths?'

They were sitting in Mary Anne's washhouse, a brick-built lean-to tacked on to the back wall. The house nestled in a squat terrace built in the nineteenth century and typical of many in the city of Bristol and way beyond. It had a door and a window and a hole in the pan tiles where the stack puffed steam from the boiling washing.

Mary Anne grimaced as Biddy tugged the grimy toe of her stocking through the hole of her peep-toed shoe. Biddy had a tinsel-bright glamour, face powder and lipstick applied after the briefest of washes and stockings worn until the toes were black or the legs laddered beyond repair.

Normally, Mary Anne wouldn't have taken much notice. Biddy was entertaining and usually made her laugh, but not today; her body was telling her things weren't quite the same and it worried her.

Fixing her mind on the subject of conversation helped overcome her queasy stomach. So did looking at the top of Biddy's peroxide-blonde head rather than her feet.

'I've tried Penny Royal and senna pods, plus half a bottle of gin; I even rode our Lizzie's bike over the cobbles, but that didn't work either.' Wincing at the memory, she rubbed her backside. 'And I've still got the bruises.'

Biddy chortled, her face reddening with the effort of laughing and still trying to straighten her seams.

Even now in the midst of her trouble, Mary Anne touched the moss-covered brickwork with something akin to reverence. The wash-house was far more than somewhere to boil the bed sheets. It was a sign of defiance, of independence. Its damp bricks made her fingers tingle like the high note of a chilly tune.

Biddy pursed her bright red lips. Even when she wasn't going anywhere, she never forgot her lipstick.

'Not a good time to get in the pudding club – not with a bloody war looming.'

'And not at my age,' added Mary Anne, trying hard not to stare at the bristles lining Biddy's upper lip. She shook her head in exasperation. 'It's just so... so.... *embarrassing.*'

Biddy looked at her as though she could well understand why her old man, Henry Randall, had found her hard to resist. Mary Anne hadn't run to fat like a lot of forty-plus women around, certainly not like Biddy whose belly sat like a blubbery doughnut on her equally flabby thighs. 'You're good fer yer age, Mary Anne.'

Mary Anne barely stopped herself turning bright red. The years had been kind. The reflection she saw every day in the mirror had wide-set greyish-green eyes, a neat chin and shoulder-length hair a few shades duskier than the gold of her youth, and a glorious complement to her smooth complexion. Her legs were long, her waist trim and she walked as though the best years were still ahead of her and ripe for the taking.

Reading the look in Biddy's eyes, Mary Anne touched the pinpoints of crimson erupting on her cheeks despite her attempts to control them. 'I didn't entice him, Biddy. I believe in acting my age, and so should he.'

Biddy mumbled as she placed her pudding of a foot back on the ground. 'Fat chance you got of getting him to do that. My Alf certainly don't act 'is age. He's just a bloody, big kid who thinks he's Kent Street's answer to Rudolf Valentino.'

Mary Anne smiled though her thoughts tapped like nervous fingers in her head. Snatches of conversation she'd had when counting out coins into a desperate hand in exchange for a pledged item – a nice piece of china, a clock, even a wedding ring; everyone was desperate at some time or another, some for the same reason as she.

'I hear there's a woman in Old Market...'

'Mrs Riley! Oh, yeah, she'll get rid of it for you all right, but mind,' said Biddy, one well-bitten finger held up in warning, 'she do know how to charge, by Christ if she don't!'

'I can pay.'

Biddy sniffed as her gaze wandered around their shabby surroundings. The bare bricks of the washhouse wall were green with moss and mould, natural in a place continually absorbing the steam from a wash load of boiling sheets. Her eyes finally came to rest on the set of cupboard doors set into one wall. They were big and bare of paint, but Biddy knew what was behind them. Mary Anne ran a thriving business – thanks in part to her.

Married to a bloke who put a third of his wages over the bar of the Red Cow didn't make for an easy life. For years, Mary Anne had scouted round for ways in which to make ends meet. At first she'd bought clothes at jumble sales, washed, pressed and sold them to needy neighbours in the area. From there it was a skip and a hop to pawnbroking.

The business had started three years ago. Biddy had been in need of money. The pawnbroker – a proper shop complete with the three balls hanging above the door – was shut.

'I need a shilling for Fred's tea and "uncle's" is shut,' she'd wailed, brandishing a pair of children's boots. 'The Sally Army gave 'em to me. They're almost new.'

Mary Anne had eyed the boots enviously, wishing the Salvation Army had given them to her. Not much chance of that, she thought with a mix of regret and pride. She wasn't as poor – or as careless – as Biddy, thank God.

Stanley, her youngest, had been without a pair at the time. Her thoughts had turned to the little bit of money inherited from a penny policy her mother had paid into all her life. So far she'd managed to keep the windfall secret from Henry, but had not quite decided what to do with it for the best. Biddy had given her an idea.

'I'll give you a shilling against them,' she'd said after a closer inspection. 'Your Cyril grown out of them already?'

Biddy had shrugged and held out her hand. 'He's used to going without boots.'

Biddy's youngest was eight years old, smoked butts he picked up from the gutter, and swore almost as much as his father. Alf Young worked on the docks when he could, weighing-on like a lot of men, sometimes working and most days not, depending on whether his face fitted with the foreman. In Mary Anne's opinion, quite understandable in a way: he had an ugly face. God knows what Biddy had ever seen in him.

And he drank too much!

Her own thoughts pulled her up short suddenly.

Well, that's the pot calling the kettle black!

She'd laughed at the thought and called herself a fool. Who was she to speak? Look at Henry. Look what he'd turned into, not that he'd always been that way. Their marriage might have been different if she'd kept her mouth shut and the truth to herself, but at the time he'd been overjoyed to have her. The First World War had taken the life of her sweetheart, Edward. Henry had been her parents' choice and she'd been happy to go along with it at the time, but she'd misjudged him badly. His character had changed after she'd told him she'd given birth to Edward's child before they were married. The child had been adopted, and she'd explained that Edward had been killed. It was then that he'd seen through her parents' collusion and felt duped, his pride hurt and his affection for her vanishing overnight.

Adjusting to the new circumstances of their relationship she had doted on her family, making sure they had the best of everything she could give them. Loving them helped compensate for Henry's shortcomings and eased her guilt.

In the process of paying for the boots, Mary Anne had rolled up her skirt and rummaged in the pocket sewn on the leg of her knickers.

Biddy had eyed the lace-edged pocket.

'I might sew on one of they meself. Keep my Alf's hands off it. Does it work with your Henry?'

'Safer than the Bank of England. It's not my knickers he's after – it's what they cover!'

Biddy laughed. 'Men! Like bloody animals they are!' Mary Anne handed her the money. 'I lend you a shilling, you pay me back one shilling and thruppence or I sell the boots.'

That was how it had started. Biddy never did pay back the money and Mary Anne kept the boots, only selling them once Stanley had grown out of them. But there were other times and other neighbours needing a loan to tide them over, and so her business had grown. She'd turned a good profit.

The whole neighbourhood – or at least the women in it – had got wind of what she was doing and as her rates were cheaper than the real pawnbroker and it wasn't so far to go, she didn't have a bad little trade.

'You've got a good business 'ere,' said Biddy. 'And yer kids are grown up. Love 'em as you may, babies can cramp yer lifestyle. They certainly did mine, and as we get older, well...'

'I'll send her a note,' said Mary Anne. 'I've got a stamp somewhere.'

'You could send a note with Muriel Harrison's husband,' suggested Biddy.

Mary Anne shook her head. Muriel's husband was a bus driver used to taking notes a bit wide of his route – not that Old Market was any problem. He was on that route – Knowle West to Eastville. All he'd have to do was pull up, say he was off to take a leak and nip round the back of Old Market to where Nellie Riley lived.

'I prefer to keep my business to myself.' She threw Biddy a warning look. 'And I'd prefer you to do the same if you don't mind.'

Biddy threw up her hands as though astonished that Mary Anne could possibly suspect her of doing otherwise.

'I won't breathe a word. Everything will be fine. Give it a fortnight and you'll be right as rain. Her concoctions don't taste all that grand, but they do work – I've heard hundreds say so, and anyway, even if it don't, she's got other methods, if you know what I mean.'

Mary Anne tried to ignore the last comment. The thought of having to resort to anything other than drinking one of Mrs Riley's brews was anathema and she shivered at the thought of it.

'I hear she's discreet,' she said thoughtfully, pulling on her boots so she could return to digging up potatoes from the garden for dinner. She liked gardening, was proud of her busy little plot, but only grew things that could be eaten. Rows of cabbages divided potatoes from peas, runner beans climbed up canes and raspberries, gooseberries and blackcurrant bushes stood shoulder to shoulder against the fence.

'She is, but don't hurt to give her directions. After all, you're the one paying. Up to you how you wants things done.'

'I've got Stanley to think of.'

'You mean if he has a good day, he might be wandering about.'

Mary Anne nodded. Stanley had a bad chest at the beginning of the year and she'd been sick with worry. He was puny for a ten-year-old and caught any coughs, colds and sneezes that were going around. So she protected him, some said too much.

'I'll send her it by post,' said Mary Anne. 'I want to keep it a secret. I don't want Henry to find out.'

Biddy sipped at the tea slowly going cold in the cup balanced on the boiler. 'Of course you don't, love.'

Before closing the cupboard door, Mary Anne glanced over her shoulder. Biddy was a gossip; a little bribery, she decided, wouldn't go amiss.

'No. Here,' she said, handing her a pair of silk stockings. 'I don't know who pledged these but it was over six months ago. Can you make use of them?'

Biddy's eyes grew round as she fingered the fine silk. 'Ooow! They're nice. If you're really sure...'

'Go on. You might as well have them.'

'Thanks, I will.' After rolling the stockings into a ball, Biddy shoved them down her cleavage.

Mary Anne shook her head. 'Haven't you got a pocket?'

'Not in this frock. It's like a second skin. Must 'ave shrunk in the wash. You know 'ow it is.'

Mary Anne moved a pile of washing from chair to boiler lid in order to hide her smile. Biddy had a good appetite; her body had got larger, not the dress smaller.

The rolls of fat resettled in different positions as she got up to leave. 'Well I 'ope I've been of some help. Best of luck with Mrs Riley. And thanks for the stockings.' She looked like the cat that got the cream.

Mary Anne smiled. 'What are friends for?'

Biddy sighed with satisfaction and swigged back the last of the cold tea.

If she knew the stockings were a bribe, she didn't let on. Biddy might be a friend, but she gathered and gave out gossip quicker than the milkman delivered two pints of gold top. Mary Anne hoped she had given her enough for her silence.

2

Michael Maurice handed his passport to Mr Abner Crombie of Crombie, Benson and Spyte, Attorneys at Law in Small Street. He sat rubbing his hands together, uncomfortable in alien surroundings in a building as dark as his thoughts.

The office walls were panelled in dark oak and the floorboards squealed underfoot as though being tortured. Lead-paned windows opened out over the cobbled street outside where costermongers sold fruit from barrows, and barrels from a brewery dray thundered into the cellar of the Assize Court pub next door.

Mr Crombie raised his eyebrows. 'A British passport?'

'I was born here.' Michael spoke slowly and precisely, anxious to impress by clear pronunciation that he had indeed been born in England.

'Mr Rosenburg was your mother's brother-in-law.'

'That is true.'

Mr Crombie nodded without taking his eyes from the black and white photograph of a serious-looking Michael taken three years previously.

'And you have lived in Amsterdam for most of your life.'

Michael nodded. 'That is true.'

The lie rolled easily off his tongue. He'd decided it was sensible not to mention having lived in Germany since he was twelve years old. He was in England now and anti-German feelings were running high.

Mr Crombie gave him a direct look, blinked and said, 'I see.'

It occurred to Michael that the solicitor knew the truth. He swallowed the fear that rolled into his throat like a ball of wire. He couldn't know. It wasn't possible. The letter had come to him via a cousin's address in Amsterdam. His cousin had known that the family had moved on from Holland but had not divulged the truth to this solicitor, a fact for which Michael was grateful.

The smell of dust and drains drifted through the window. Michael refrained from wrinkling his nose. He did not want to cause offence.

For his part, Mr Crombie, though not appearing to, studied Michael Maurice more intently than he would have before war was declared. He was not at all what he had expected, too young in his opinion to be left any business at all. His uncle had been swarthy, dark and very stout. The dark blond locks of the man sitting in front of him curled over his coat collar. No Englishman would wear his hair that long, thought Crombie, who had an inherent distrust of anyone who didn't conform to his own, musty and very old English style. Although he admitted Michael Maurice had an open face, such faces, in Crombie's experience, could be deceiving. On top of that, he didn't like being scrutinised quite so intensely. An Englishman wouldn't study another person to such an extent, certainly not until they'd met on a number of occasions. That didn't mean, however, that he couldn't do exactly the same thing and form an instant opinion. His opinion was that Michael Maurice had what he termed 'presence'. Deep-set blue eyes gazed steadily at each movement he took. His shoulders seemed tense, though perhaps they were just muscular; if so, they matched the strength in his face.

'Everything seems in order,' said Crombie, handing him back the passport plus a brown envelope containing a bundle of crisp five-pound notes. 'As I told you, there is only a small amount of cash.'

'Fifty pounds.'

The solicitor nodded. 'Times have changed. There's a lot of competition in the pawnbroking business nowadays. I've heard of people doing business from their front parlours.'

'Not proper shops?' Michael sounded surprised.

'No. Not really legal either.'

'I will make the shop better profitable.'

'*More* profitable,' Crombie corrected.

Michael flushed at his slip in grammar. 'That is right.'

'I have the keys here.' He reached into a desk drawer and brought out a bundle of keys. 'Thomas Routledge, the caretaker I placed in your uncle's shop following his demise, is still in situ. Morose would be the best word to describe him. Would you like me to come with you in case he takes to being surly?'

'I can manage,' said Michael, rising to his feet at the sametime as taking the bunch of keys from Mr Crombie's hand.

The two men shook hands. 'It won't be easy for you, especially seeing as you've never ran a business before.'

'I will learn.'

'I'm reminded of an old saying that there's no sentiment in business. I'm afraid your uncle did not adhere to those words. He had a soft heart.'

Michael blinked but said no more. He didn't want to say that his heart was dead or that ruthlessness could easily override sentiment if survival was involved. He didn't want to mention anything about his flight from Germany – nothing, nothing at all. At least, not yet: the memories were too painful.

The solicitor stayed behind his desk watching as Michael ducked beneath an overhead beam before gaining the door. It occurred to him that Michael had not smiled even once: a grim man for one so young.

* * *

Three brass balls hung above the shop door. Wooden shutters hid the windows and the door was firmly shut, the paintwork faded and peeling like burned skin.

Shielding his eyes from the bright September sunlight, Michael took a step back into the road and regarded his inheritance: at least one room on the ground floor, plus the shop, perhaps two above that and perhaps one or two attic rooms at the very top.

There was no sign of the caretaker, so he took it upon himself to enter. The key grated in the lock. An overhead bell jangled as he pushed the door open into a small porch enclosed by wire screens. Another bell hung beside a hatch arrangement. The notice above the hatch said that in the interests of privacy, only two people at any one time would be dealt with. The rest must wait outside.

He wasn't sure whether this was more to do with security than privacy.

No one came in answer to the bell. He looked around for a door into the rest of the premises but could see nothing. The wire screens finished about two feet from the ceiling, blocking his view. Taking hold as far up the screen as he could, he laced his fingers into the holes, placed one foot on the polished counter, and heaved himself up and over.

He found himself surrounded by glass-fronted cupboards filled with all manner of china, cameras, scientific and navigation instruments, musical instruments and, in barred and locked cupboards, an assortment of guns, sabres and assegais. Labels sprouted from brown paper parcels heaped along the shelving at the back. There were also drawers marked 'gold', 'silver', 'wedding' and 'engagement'. A pile of ledgers sat in a corner on the counter.

He'd expected to see the caretaker, but no one appeared.

The living room at the back of the shop was exactly how he'd imagined it would be. Sepia photographs of family ancestors in stiff poses hung from the walls. The paintwork was dark, the wallpaper from the previous century unbearably ornate and furry beneath his fingertips. A chenille pelmet hung from the high mantelpiece and a tea caddy made to celebrate the diamond jubilee of Queen Victoria sat next to a black onyx clock.

There was a kitchen beyond the living room where a teapot and two cups and saucers sat on the table. He reached out and touched the teapot. It was still warm and there were dregs of tea at the bottoms of the cups, a trace of lipstick around the rim of one. Someone was in the house. He listened intently, heard a small noise and looked up at the ceiling.

If Thomas Routledge was up there, why hadn't he heard him? What was he doing that distracted his attention?

The stairs were so narrow that his shoulders grazed the walls. The landing at the top was surprisingly wide and there was an arched window at one end. He paused as the heavy lace curtain billowed inwards in the breeze. The window, attractive as it was, looked out on a backyard and a tree vivid with red leaves.

A floorboard squeaked beneath his foot and brought an exclamation from behind a bedroom door followed by frenzied muttering.

Without preamble, Michael opened the door. The room smelled of sweaty bodies and recent sex. The man was naked. The girl was young, possibly no more than fourteen, though she had a worldly face.

The man pulled the bedclothes over his lean shanks. 'We're closed!' he barked, but looked nervous.

The girl giggled, her small breasts jiggling in sympathy. 'No. It is open,' said Michael. 'You were supposed to be running the business not lying in bed.'

Realising who he was talking to, the man adopted a nervous grin. 'I can explain—'

Michael stayed his tongue but made his feelings very obvious. The curtains tore as he pulled them back, the window jamming then squealing as he pushed it open. Fresh air funnelled in.

''Ere, just a minute...'

Michael pointed at him. 'Get out of my shop, and take the girl with you.'

The girl opened and closed her legs, giving him an unobstructed view of what was on offer. 'I only charge ten shillings, mister,' she said, her rouged lips smiling invitingly as though she were the most glamorous woman he'd ever set eyes on.

She aroused no desire, but only memories of beds once slept in and events he'd prefer to forget.

'Out,' he said, his words as controlled as in the solicitor's office. 'Out,' he said again, his fingers tightly gripping the door handle.

Routledge shuffled his trousers before putting one hairy leg inside the brown, cheap material, closely followed by the other. 'I'm still owed five pounds,' he grumbled.

Michael regarded Routledge with contempt. He'd met plenty of his sort, the coarse exterior hiding a matching though cowardly inner soul. His inclination was to take hold of the man by the scruff of the neck and the seat of his pants and throw him out through the window, glass, shutters and all, but he couldn't. He mustn't. He had to tread carefully in a country where foreigners were viewed with more suspicion than they'd ever been.

Although it grieved him, he peeled off a fiver from the pile in the envelope.

'And then there's expenses...' Michael hardened his look.

Routledge was wily enough to know when he was pushing his luck. He rubbed at the three-day growth of stubble sprouting from his cheeks and chin. 'I can see you think I've had more than a fair share.' He glanced at the girl. 'Maybe you're right, sir, maybe you're right.'

The girl squealed as he took her elbow and pushed her out of the door in front of him, even though she was only half dressed.

'You owes me,' she whined.

'Let's go down the pub. I'll pay you there.'

Michael followed them out to the door, where he wrenched the spare set of keys from Routledge's hand, then locked and bolted the door behind them.

Once it was closed, he sighed with relief, glad to be inside the shuttered building even though the smell of neglect was strong and the sound of water dripping from a faulty tap echoed like halting footsteps.

Out in the meagre kitchen, he found a larder containing tins of food, some cheese, ham and bread. He also found a bottle of Camp Coffee, made himself a thick, black cupful, and winced as the bite of chicory crawled along his tongue.

The living room was comfortable though dark. After eating and half finishing the coffee, he settled down to doze, the tiring journey, the fear of what the future held finally catching up with him – except he didn't sleep. Something caught his eye.

In the corner of the room, he saw – wooden, old-fashioned, but compelling – a gramophone. Next to it was a pile of records. Like a man starved, he slid one after another off the pile, his eyes widening and his heart lifting. Jazz, popular songs of the day and classical; the latter were in the majority.

Lovingly, he caressed the works of Hoagy Carmichael, Ella Fitzgerald and Caruso. Amongst them all he found a performance of *Cavalleria Rusticana*.

The music wafted over him, salve to a tormented soul. The memories returned. Fearing to face them and blaming the music for their resurgence, he went to bed, but even there he could not escape. The past was too recent, too raw.

Behind his closed eyelids he was back there, in 1929, pledging allegiance to the Nazi Party. To do otherwise would have isolated him completely from his friends, the young men he'd known for most of his life.

The dream was pleasant enough, but unfortunately led into the later nightmares. He wasn't ready to face them, and wasn't sure he ever would be.

* * *

In the morning, Michael checked his inheritance. The pledges – so he had found them named in his uncle's ledger – were stacked on shelves, in cupboards and drawers, each labelled as to their content: watches; gold, watches; silver, bracelets, necklaces, rings; miscellaneous silver;

miscellaneous gold – the latter, he discovered, included a number of gold teeth. He wondered what misfortune had occurred to necessitate the obvious discomfort of having a filling ripped from one's mouth.

Furniture was stacked and labelled in a back room, clothes parcelled and placed on myriad shelves.

Some of the items pledged saddened him; a child's clothes – pledged to pay for a funeral, it said in scrawled writing. So Crombie was right. His uncle had been too sentimental for his own good. The clothes were shabby, never likely to be sold on or reclaimed. He threw them into the pile he was making of items to be disposed of. It was growing swiftly.

Other items almost made him laugh out loud or certainly raise his spirits.

Combinations. New.

A glass eye?

A pair of black lace garters. Never worn.

He didn't hazard a guess as to the reasons why any of them had been pledged. After checking the dates – years ago – he threw the items onto the pile, had second thoughts about the black lace garters and retrieved them.

The next thing he did was to destroy the family photographs. He didn't want them staring down at him. He didn't want to remember who and what they were because in doing so he would be reminded of what he had done.

3

One week later, Mrs Riley came in response to Mary Anne's letter, sneaking along the back lane like a thief in the night, just as instructed.

Mary Anne looked up as the back gate creaked open, the sound making her stomach churn. As she eyed the quick, thin figure scurrying up the garden path, her instinct was to curl her hand over her stomach. God knows, every mother's first instinct was to protect the new life within.

But you can't keep it. Harry will hate you being pregnant just as he did the other times. And you have to live with him – if you can call it that.

The formalities were quickly dispensed with. Mary Anne wanted no friendship with this woman. The bottle was as small and brown as the person who brought it. She clenched her jaw as she handed over the two pounds she was being charged. Two pounds! She didn't doubt that the canny old woman had made enquiries first to see how much she could afford. She had a shrewd face and small, quick eyes, the sort that eyed up everything in order to weigh up its worth.

Mary Anne did a few sums in her head. With a bit of luck, she should make that amount up within the next week or so with a few hocked items from women wanting to give their men a good send-off, or provide extra winter clothes before the war economy really started to bite. And even if she didn't... well... the final outcome had to be worth it... if it worked, that is.

Mrs Riley spat on the pound notes before folding them in quarters and sliding them into the large bag she carried. Mary Anne tried to avoid studying the bag, but its purpose drew her more so than its details. Made of thick tapestry fabric with wooden handles heavily soiled with sweat and other stains she didn't want to think about, the base bulged with what could have been balls of wool. The tip of a bone knitting needle pierced the tight bud of a stylised square rose. Along with the brown bottle, the needle was one of the tools of Mrs Riley's trade.

'Will it work?' Mary Anne asked, carefully averting her eyes from the tip of the knitting needle. She wasn't a fool and knew well what else it was used for. Pray God she wouldn't need it to end her predicament.

Mrs Riley, infamous for helping women out when they were in that 'certain' predicament, jerked her chin high and nodded like a braying donkey. 'Oh aye. A dollop in the morning, a dollop at noon and a dollop at night should shift it, me darling. There's a good bit of Penny Royal in that, liquorice, senna and some old gypsy herbs that you wouldn't know about.'

Mary Anne felt her stomach tightening as she nodded an acknowledgement. Her mouth was too dry for words. Penny Royal was one of the best things going for passing the unwanted from the body. It hadn't worked so far, but perhaps the secret gypsy herbs might make a difference. Despite the feelings of guilt and shame, it was something she had to do. You're too old to be expecting, she'd told herself after two months' bleeding had been missed. A third month and the old familiar feelings of bloat, painful breasts and instinct confirmed that she was.

The liquid in the bottle glugged and gurgled as she rolled it around in her palm. Her thoughts were so involved with her 'little problem' that she hardly noticed the Riley woman was slow in leaving.

'There's one other thing before I go,' Mrs Riley said, sniffing back a nostril of snuff while delving into the depths of her copious bag. 'What will you give me on this?'

A snow-white tablecloth shone like the moon in the dim coldness of the washhouse.

Mary Anne's eyes widened as she fingered the gleaming fabric as a thought came to her. The whiteness was dazzling; too white for the likes of Mrs Riley to have laundered and ironed.

'It's damask. Where did you get it?'

Mrs Riley's smile revealed yellow, irregular teeth in a face as round as a suet dumpling. 'You could say it was a gift – for services rendered.' Her grin widened. 'Even the toffs need my services; they did in the past, and they will now we're at war with Germany again. There'll be a lot of women enjoying themselves too much, their men away fighting and the few left behind able and willing to do them a service. Women gets lonely being left trying to make do with what the rations allowed, and I ain't just referring to the food. Sometimes they're left with a little problem, so they call for old Mrs Riley. So there you are! Best damask there is. Will you give me five bob for it?'

Mary Anne couldn't take her eyes off it. She imagined it covering her table with a Sunday tea laid out on best china. Five shillings! It was worth far more.

Only rarely did she hope that someone never came back for the item they'd hocked. She'd lent money against everything from a tanner for a tin of pre-war sardines to two pounds for a wedding ring. But this was an exception. Mary Anne loved the look and feel of good quality linens – and five shillings was such a tiny pledge. It had to be worth more than that.

'It's very fine...'

She couldn't help hesitating. Her visitor didn't look rich enough to possess such a fine cloth and she didn't entirely believe it to be a gift. It was on the tip of her tongue to say so. Seeing her hesitation and guessing at the reason, Nellie Riley made a smacking sound with her lips and went on to explain. 'It belonged to a lady's maid up in Clifton. She 'ad a problem, you see. The master of the 'ouse was a bit too free and easy with her. Poor cow was beside 'erself and the dirty old sod denied all knowledge. Threatened to throw 'er out on the streets if she kept on accusing 'im. Wouldn't pay a penny towards what 'ad to be done, so me dear, I took payment in kind plus five shillings he finally gave her when she threatened to tell 'is wife. But just look at it! What in the name of the Blessed Virgin am I going to do with a white tablecloth that size in my place in Old Market? It's big enough to cover me place twice over. And it's a shame to waste it, though it's not that I'm that 'ard up, but seein' as I don't have no use for it...'

Mary Anne fingered the soft whiteness while fighting the urge to bury her face in the crisply beautiful fabric, just like her own washing after a day of blowing in a stiff breeze. The prospect of turning a shilling couldn't be overlooked, though there was nothing to gain by appearing too keen.

She decided that Mrs Riley was as hard up as anyone and would do anything for an extra shilling; hence the damask cloth... and the dark liquid in the small brown bottle.

Mary Anne pushed her personal worries to the back of her mind, hid how she really felt about the tablecloth and adopted the shrewdness for which she was famous thereabouts. 'I can't give you much.'

'I'll trust you to give me what it's worth, and if you don't then I can take it down Uncle Bob's.'

'Uncle Bob's dead,' said Mary Anne, referring to the foreign owner of the proper pawnbroker's at the bottom of Bottle Lane off East Street where the three ball sign swung above a lop-sided door. She didn't know what his real name was. Everyone called him 'Uncle Bob'. 'His shop's closed until one of his family takes over. I hear it's a family member from abroad.'

Mrs Riley made the sign of the cross over her scrawny breasts. 'God rest his soul, poor heathen that he was. It won't be easy for them to come quickly, foreign as they are. Polish or some such like and still over in them parts. There is a war on, though saying that, I can't be waiting until someone turns up and I knew of your reputation. I know you won't fleece me. Besides, who knows... if the syrup don't work, you may be needing some closer attention so a bit of generosity won't go amiss.'

Mary Anne stiffened at the thought of the same needle that knitted a woolly hat or gloves also being used to terminate a pregnancy. She'd go down on her knees before sleeping tonight and pray the contents of the brown bottle worked. It took a lot of effort, but she swallowed her revulsion.

'Five shillings,' she murmured, taking her notebook and pencil from its home beneath the boiler. 'I'll need your details for my register.'

'If you could hurry. It's almost six.'

Mary Anne jerked up from what she was writing. 'Six? It can't be!'

It was, and her shrewdness turned to panic as a sudden hammering echoed through the house and out into the backyard.

Mrs Riley nodded squirrel-like at the crack in the door towards the back of the house.

'Sounds like yer old man's home. Been down the Red Cow no doubt and now wantin' feedin'.'

Mary Anne bristled and pursed her lips. Henry was her problem. She wanted to say 'Mind your own business,' but she wanted Mrs Riley to leave and quickly. 'Here's your receipt.'

A slim slip torn from the bottom of the notebook, the bottom corner numbered to coincide with the top corner, was swiftly exchanged for the five shillings.

'You'd better go now.' If she sounded rude, she didn't care. She didn't like Mrs Riley. She didn't like her sort. She was only here on sufferance because she was in a pickle.

Thrusting two half-crowns into Mrs Riley's podgy palm, Mary Anne bundled the woman out of the door, pointing her towards the back gate. 'Get out that way. I don't want my husband to see you.'

Mrs Riley waved a hand as though she were swatting a fly. 'I knows what you means. That five bob 'uld be over the bar of the nearest pub. I used to 'ave one like that – drunk before dinner and sozzled before supper... Powdered glass – put that in his grub. That'll calm 'im down,' said Mrs Riley. 'Killed mine stone dead.'

'Be on yer way. I'll mark you down and trust you without yer signature. You've got the five bob, now it's five and six if you want the table-cloth back. You've got a week.'

She wondered whether Mrs Riley really had used powdered glass to do away with her husband.

'You know where to find me, Mrs Randall. Every woman around here knows where to find me...' Hesitating, she grinned as though there was a secret bond between them that would forever remain that way – if she chose it to be so. 'You might be needin' to see me again, specially if the stuff don't work.'

Mary Anne replied through gritted teeth. 'Well, let's hope it do.' Mentally, she promised herself she'd do all in her power not to allow the situation to arise again, though how she'd keep Henry Randall from claiming his 'rights' would be far from easy. He sulked if she refused him, his temper building up like a spoiled child about to throw a tantrum, although in his case it was normally a fist.

The hammering at the front door intensified. He never came round to the back door – thank God. Slamming the ledger shut she hurriedly put it back into its hiding place.

'All right, all right,' she shouted, safe in the knowledge that he couldn't possibly hear. 'That door will be off its hinges going on like that.'

She threw the tablecloth in the cupboard above the boiler. She had a sneaking suspicion Mrs Riley wouldn't be back for it. She certainly hoped not. The vision of it sparkling on her parlour table wouldn't go away.

She hid the bottle behind the boiler with the ledger. No one must know she had it, and no one would. It was rare for her girls to help her with the washing, and then only under duress and later in the day when her clients had all done their business. Some husbands worked shifts. Few wives were inclined to let their other halves know that their wages had to be supplemented; men had pride. Still others didn't want their husbands to know that they had vices. It was amazing what went on in Kent Street - some women drank, some couldn't resist a flutter on cards or on the horses and still others couldn't stop buying hats or shoes. Henry Albert Randall was still beating the hell out of the front door and singing in a deep baritone that must have all the neighbours hanging out of their windows. Her husband's efforts to find the keyhole when he was drunk always attracted an audience, and her face reddened at the prospect. Why did she put up with it? She knew why. For her children.

The sound of raucous singing...

'Onward Christian soldiers, Marching as to war...'

She pushed her hair back from her brow. At least she'd look respectable even if Henry were far from that.

Muttering disapproval under her breath and adding a small prayer that he wouldn't be too drunk but merely be merry, she pulled the door open.

Her heart sank. Her stomach tightened. The brim of Henry Randall's hat nestled around his neck, only the crown remaining on his fair wavy hair. Solemn-faced as a Sunday preacher, his hands were clasped before him as if in prayer.

'I'm callin' collectin' for the church, madam,' he pronounced, his voice sonorous though slurred.

Despite not wanting to rouse his temper, Mary Anne couldn't help feeling mortified. Just as she'd guessed, curtains were twitching up and down the street, and women gossiping in doorways watched silently or tittered behind their hands.

'Henry Randall!' she hissed, grabbing his coat lapel and dragging him over the polished brass doorstep. 'Get in here!'

She glanced up and down the street as she bundled him past her, through the doorway and into the passageway.

Two gossiping neighbours, huddled against an open door immediately opposite, were staring boldly, grinning as though Henry were providing a comedy turn purely for their benefit.

Mary Anne glared at them, dabbing her finger on the tip of her nose. 'Had your eyeful or want your penny back,' she shouted, tapping the end of her nose with her finger once more before slamming the door hard enough to set the whole house shuddering.

She imagined them talking about her, calling her a stuck-up cow because she didn't talk like them, didn't look like them and hadn't come from the same district or class. She was different and would always be set apart.

Once the door was closed, her embarrassment got the better of her judgement. Why couldn't he be different? Why did he have to get drunk? Why couldn't he be like Edward, the man she should have married?

Nothing – not even fear – could stop her from lashing out.

Standing with her hands braced on her hips, her eyes blazed with anger.

'You certainly have not been to any church, that's for sure, unless the Red Cow has had a pulpit installed!'

Edward wouldn't have behaved like this. Edward had been upright, brave and kind to everyone. Why did he have to die? Why had there been that other war?

By way of supporting himself, Henry spread his palms on one wall of the narrow hallway, his heels against the skirting on the opposite wall, as though laughing were too much for his body.

He tilted forwards, face close to hers. She winced as the smell of stale stout wafted over her.

There was contempt in her eyes and a grim set to her chin that wasn't there when he was just coming out of his drunken state. When he was like this, in the heart of his drunkenness, she could say and do whatever she wanted.

'Good God, you stink as though you've been swimming in it. Now get upstairs and sleep it off.'

A strong whiff of carbolic from her own hands mixed with the stink of stout as she gripped him by the scruff of his collar and the seat of his pants and frogmarched him along the passage, their heavy footsteps thundering over the uneven floorboards.

The front door opened – Lizzie, her eldest daughter, choosing that moment to come home from work. She looked amused when she saw her father. 'Oh, Dad. Drunk again?'

He grinned at her. 'My sweet little bird. You know I loves you, don't you, my darling. You knows I loves you.'

'Yes, I do,' Lizzie answered, laughing and pressing herself against the wall as he tumbled back to within a few feet of the front door before her mother pushed him towards the narrow stairs.

'What a state,' said Mary Anne, the sour expression replaced with one of amiable toleration now that Lizzie was home. Lizzie would not see how it really was between them; none of her children would. She'd vowed from the day their firstborn had entered the world that this would be a happy house, that no matter her regrets, no hint of unhappiness would ever touch her children's lives. 'I told him it might be a good idea if he takes his bed down there.'

'Just enjoying meself, but yer mother don't like me doing that,' he called over his shoulder. 'You can tell that. Look at yer mother's face. She don't like me to enjoy meself.'

Mary Anne adopted the usual smile reserved for such a situation.

'You go on and put the kettle on, Lizzie. I'll be right back down once I've settled yer dad. And if you could nip out into the scullery and bring in that pot of potatoes. Put it straight on the gas stove. The salt's already in them.'

She said it in a very matter-of-fact way, as though that's all it would be: settling him down so he'd sleep it off and they'd all have dinner together, just one happy family.

In truth every muscle in her body tensed at the thought of what would truly come once he awoke.

Burdened bedsprings squealed in protest as he fell onto the bed in the front bedroom they'd shared since the day they were married. Mary Anne eased off his boots and placed them neatly at the foot of the bed. He was snoring fit to wake the devil even before she'd straightened up, rubbing at the ache in her lower back. She stared at him as she would a stranger.

This was her husband, the man that had been *chosen* for her to marry. His mouth hung wide open. A sliver of spittle trailed from the corner of his mouth to the tip of his moustache.

Was it her imagination or were the walls of the room closing in on her, the air stale although she could see a curtain blowing in the draught from an ill-fitting window? She didn't recognise her discomfort as resentment, but only knew that something threatened to suffocate her.

He was too big and ugly for the tiny room that she had tried so hard to make pretty. Tiny mauve flowers, painted with gay abandon by virtue of a small set of watercolours someone had pledged and never redeemed, decorated the whitewashed walls. Amongst the smaller, scattered buds, she'd painted bouquets of similar blooms, but larger and bordered with other colours of paint to look like frames. Other pictures in real frames had once hung on the walls, hurled and smashed when Henry had one of his moods. These events never happened when the children were there. Violence was the provenance between man and wife and occurred only when they were alone.

Was this the same man as the one who used to make her laugh and took her dancing? Had he really been any different than Edward?

Edward had been from the same background as she; his father had been a manager at a rope-making company. Her father had owned a grocery shop. They'd been heralded as the ideal couple. A few years and they would have been married. Unfortunately, the shooting of the Austrian emperor in 1914 had heralded the Great War.

Edward hadn't joined up until 1916, so they'd had a few years together. Only a few months into the conflict, in the depths of winter, he had died, not shot or gassed by the enemy but taken by pneumonia.

Six months before his death and convinced they would always be together, that he would somehow survive the war, they'd made love before his departure. A child had been conceived.

The child had been adopted and only six months later she'd met Henry. He'd lifted her spirits and, encouraged by her parents, they'd married without him ever knowing that there'd been someone else and that she wasn't a virgin.

That first year had been idyllic; it seemed that nothing could come between them, so Mary Anne had confessed her sin.

'There was Edward before you,' she'd told him. 'Three months after he got killed I gave birth to his child. At my parents' insistence, the child was adopted. And then I met you. And my parents said...'

Simple facts uttered in innocence but received with a darkening countenance by a man who never forgave her.

Everything changed.

The considerate husband, who had been proud to serve his country, had considered himself cheated. His mood had changed. No longer attentive and kind, he'd turned jealous and quick to anger. No matter what she did, he'd never changed back to the man she'd married.

Memories of the time before her marriage and romantic dreams of Edward were what kept her sane. She had transferred her love to her children and they were what kept the marriage going.

But Edward was her solace. Unknown to Henry, she still had his letters.

At the thought of them, she eyed the walnut dressing table that had once belonged to her mother. There was a drawer on either side beneath the mirror. Inside of each was another drawer tucked back out of the way and unseen unless you knew they were there.

Sometimes, when her spirits were low and she was in the house alone, she retrieved those letters, sadness stabbing at her heart as her fingers touched the crisp paper, reading and remembering the hopes and dreams that had come to nothing. Henry worked as hard as anyone driving one of the city's blue cabs, his permanent pitch being outside Temple Meads Station. The tips could be decent if he was lucky enough to pick up some 'big pot' fares. When it wasn't in use, he kept the vehicle in a garage in South Street. Unfortunately, there were a number of pubs between South Street and Kent Street and by the looks of his clothes and the smell of his breath he'd been in every one. With Henry it was a case of grab the housekeeping whenever possible, though you wouldn't think so to hear him. 'You should all be grateful to me for keeping you fed and warm; not like when I was a young whippersnapper, out to work at five in the morning earning two bob a week looking after the milkman's horse. Ten years old I was, just ten years old.' Harry, Daw and Lizzie adopted an attitude of smiling forbearance, telling him that of course they knew, and of course they were grateful. Young Stanley was oblivious to it all.

The reality was different, though unacknowledged by Henry.

After a good rummage, she went back down the stairs, the coins she'd lifted from his coat pocket swiftly counted from one hand to the other.

Lizzie looked up from unbuckling her shoes and rubbing at her toes.

Mary Anne noticed, her face buckling with concern. 'Are those shoes pinching you?'

Lizzie grimaced. 'Just a bit. Still, they're fine for work.' She steeled herself for what was coming. Just as she expected, a slight frown creased her mother's brows.

'Here,' said Mary Anne, fishing under her skirt and taking out a pound note then a ten shilling note. 'Get yourself a new pair.'

Even as a child, Lizzie had noticed that her mother couldn't bear for her children to suffer any discomfort or misfortune in their lives. She'd always insisted on making things better. As children they'd appreciated her indulgence; as adults Lizzie was beginning to regard her selflessness as interference.

'Ma! I've just told you. There's no need. They'll be okay for work.'

Mary Anne turned huffy. 'Okay What does that mean? Why can't you say something English?'

Lizzie immediately felt guilty. She hadn't meant to hurt her mother. Mary Anne's intentions were good, but sometimes Lizzie felt smothered.

'Everyone says it in the pictures. It's American. You know it is.'

Her mother pounced on cushions, beating them into shape before crushing them back into their respective chairs, putting things away in drawers, slamming them so hard that the cups hanging from hooks on the dresser tinkled like bells.

'Well, this isn't the pictures and it isn't America!'

Lizzie deliberately massaged her toes again, her hair falling around her face and hiding her expression. She would say nothing until her mother had worked her disappointment out of her system.

No word was spoken until the crashing and slamming of dresser doors and drawers had slowed; until in effect there was nothing more to put away.

Her mother had never been much good at taking 'no' for an answer. Lizzie waited for what she was certain would come next.

The one pound and ten shilling note appeared beneath her bent head.

'Go on. Take it. Buy yourself something nice.'

Lizzie sighed, stood up and covered her mother's hand with her own.

'*You* buy yourself something nice, Ma. Do something special with it. I earn me own wage now. Spend it on yerself. You deserve it.'

'Me?' The tone of her voice and the look on her face said it all. She wasn't used to spending on herself. Her children were her world. 'What in the world do I need?' Her smile was hesitant and accompanied by a shrug.

'Oh, Ma,' she said, throwing her arms around her mother's neck. 'You deserve all the best things money can buy.'

'It can't buy me love,' she said, her voice muffled against Lizzie's hair.

'No,' said Lizzie, cupping her mother's face in her hands. 'It can't. You've got my love, Ma, and you always will no matter what you do.'

There were tears in her mother's eyes when she smiled. 'You are a good daughter,' she said softly.

'And you are a good mother, but we're not babies any more. You deserve something for yourself.'

Unless they really knew her well, or were like everyone else in the family, took her too much for granted, they wouldn't have noticed that her smile stiffened and that her eye colour changed with the thoughts behind them.

Lizzie had always been more observant than her siblings and wondered at the feelings behind the changed expression.

Perhaps she regrets us not being babies any more, she thought. There couldn't be any other explanation.

'And how was work today?' asked Mary Anne.

'Fine,' said Lizzie brightly, brushing her skirt as she stepped away from her mother.

'Just fine?'

'Of course. I'll go and hang my coat up.'

She felt her mother's eyes following her out and wondered just how much she had guessed about her job, especially with regard to Wednesdays.

4

Wednesday morning: half-day closing for every shopkeeper in the city and her favourite day of the week. Lizzie took a deep breath, tucked a stray sliver of hair behind her ear and mentally rehearsed what she was going to say before knocking on the parlour door.

'Come in.'

Mrs Selwyn, her employer, was sitting in an armchair, the light from the window falling over her, adding much-needed pallor to a face prone to pinkness. Lizzie had originally been employed as a maid. In time, once Mrs Selwyn noticed she was a passable cook and excellent organiser, she found herself housekeeper at eighteen years of age.

'I'm sorry to disturb you, Mrs Selwyn, but I'm going to have to stock up on meat and greengrocery. We've run out of essentials,' said Lizzie, her hands clasped deferentially in front of her.

Frowning, Mrs Selwyn looked up from the book she was reading. She always read a little after lunch before she took an afternoon nap, claiming it settled her digestion. So far she hadn't cottoned on to Lizzie's strategy.

'Oh, how annoying! You really should have words with both of them,' she said, sliding her spectacles down her nose and peering over them as though to scrutinise Lizzie that much more closely. When she spoke the sound of her voice reminded Lizzie of a scoop slicing through butter. 'This happens every week. Do you think they are short changing our supplies?'

Lizzie adopted a suitably contrite expression. 'It's my fault, not theirs. I was determined to keep expenses down, what with food rationing likely to come in. Luckily, I've got my bicycle so it's no great inconvenience to cycle into Bedminster and get what's needed.' If the truth were known, she'd purposely been under-ordering, just so she and Peter could get together on a Wednesday afternoon.

Looking pleased at the prospect of saving money, Mrs Selwyn pushed the glasses back up to the bridge of her nose and beamed. 'What a very clever girl you are. Of course you must go. What would we do if you didn't have a bicycle?'

'There's no point me coming back here with the groceries and then cycling home again. Do you mind if I go straight home afterwards?' said Lizzie.

Mrs Selwyn pursed her lips as she thought it over. 'I don't see why not. I shall cook a little something for myself this evening and Peter will probably join me.'

'And you can you manage to make your afternoon tea without me?'

Her chin raised higher, her manner loftier. 'If I can cook dinner for two, I can certainly make tea for one. I shall read my book until teatime. I'm quite enjoying it.'

Lizzie knew she would be snoring her head off just minutes after she left the room and not waking until Peter got home; in fact she was counting on it.

Leaving the house made her feel like a canary fleeing its cage. On leaving school, she'd expressed a wish not to join Daw and Harry in the tobacco factory. Going into service was a slightly old-fashioned career, and even she had had doubts about sticking the dull domestic routine; that had been until she'd met Peter.

Peter Selwyn knew how to charm women of all ages. He'd certainly charmed her with his winning ways, hazel eyes and the way his chin jutted forwards when he was determining what exactly he wanted from life, his mother or her.

She laughed with joy as she rode her bicycle towards St John's Lane and Clancy's Farm. The day was crisp with autumn smells, leaves crunching like broken biscuits beneath her wheels. Her whole body tingled with anticipation and her face turned pink with the exertion of cycling.

Peter's Austin Seven was already there, parked on the grass verge outside the gateway leading into Clancy's Farm and their secret field.

After parking her bicycle against a hawthorn hedge, she climbed over the gate, pausing halfway up so she could see over the expanse of Golden Rod and early Michaelmas daisies bordering Clancy's pond.

Stretching her neck, she thought she saw a dent amongst the feathery heads of grass. She thought about calling him to come and meet her. Sometimes there were cows in the field; she hoped they weren't in here now. However, wouldn't it be better to surprise him, regardless of their meeting being prearranged?

Taking a second sweep of the field, she took her courage in both hands and climbed down from the gate and into the field. The wet grass tickled her legs and the path was slick with mud. She was glad she was wearing her sensible shoes even though they pinched her toes. They'd never used to pinch so much until she'd taken to walking through damp fields to meet Peter without his mother knowing. The dampness had shrunk the leather, but they served their purpose. She'd never have stayed upright in boggy ground wearing court shoes.

Peter was lying on a blanket, his eyes closed, his arms folded beneath his head, and he was wearing his sports jacket, brown trousers and tie; smart clothes he wore to work.

He was snoring as though asleep. Her heart leaped to her mouth. He looked so beautiful lying there, his cheeks slightly pink, a kiss curl of damp hair plastered to his forehead.

Her first inclination was to bend down and kiss his lips. A resonant snore changed her mind. They were both pretending: he to be asleep, and she that he hadn't heard her, but of course he had.

Smiling and treading softly, she picked a long piece of grass, and carefully brushed its feathery seed head down his nose and into his mouth.

Snorting suddenly, he grabbed her legs. 'Who's been eating my porridge?'

Laughing, she tumbled down beside him on the blanket. 'You cheat! You were only pretending.'

'And you fell for it. And fancy calling me a cheat!' He sounded genuinely surprised. He even adopted a petulant expression, though she knew he was only funning.

'But you are a cheat. Your mother thinks you're still at the shop.'

Peter grinned. 'And she thinks you've gone to buy sausages and cabbages.'

Lizzie smiled triumphantly. 'It was a good little plan.'

'I totally agree with you,' he said before kissing so hard she had to push him off in order to catch her breath. 'Aren't I lucky to have such a doting mother.'

Between nibbling her ear and kissing her throat, he mumbled something about his mother having always had an eye for good financial management.

'My father loved being in the shop. He loved it very much. My mother loved accumulating money. In fact, it was my mother who was responsible for Selwyns' growing from a shop into a store. Father was more into the hands-on aspect of the business.'

'What your father did... hands-on... is that the same as what you're doing?' she gasped in a broken sentence, half-closing her eyes in ecstasy as the thumb and fingers of one of his hands drew steadily decreasing circles around her nipple.

'I don't know,' he murmured, his head falling to her breast. 'Wouldn't be surprised though...'

Lizzie stared up at the deep blue sky. If it were water she'd be tempted to dive into it. Such a beautiful day; if only Peter would make it perfect. If only she could find the courage to ask him if there was anything in particular that he loved very much, but she couldn't.

It's not the right time, counselled the more needy side of her brain.

Have it out now, counselled the more rational side.

As usual, she did nothing. He loves me, she told herself. He wants me.

It certainly seemed that way. He was unbuttoning her dress, pulling out her breasts and kissing each nipple, tracing his thumb around the sensitive tip.

She lay back, her breathing coming in short, sharp gasps and interspersed with trembling words that meant nothing, and yet meant everything.

'What did you say?' he asked.

'Nothing. Just noises.'

'I like those noises,' he whispered.

'It's your fault I'm making them.'

One hand either side of his head, she ran her fingers through his hair as he licked at her breast, studying the top of his head, wanting to savour this moment to memory. His hair was pale brown, lighter at the temples, thinner on top. No doubt he would lose his hair early in life, but she didn't care. No matter his physical faults, she badly wanted him to tell her 'I love you.'

All in good time, she told herself, but still ached inside. His breathing intensified. The hardness of his penis throbbing against her thigh excited her, though she was sure the pressure was causing a bruise to form.

This was the moment she dreaded. It was like standing raging with fever on a cliff top, longing to fall into the cool sea many feet below, knowing that there were rocks beneath the surface, that she could be dashed to pieces, and yet it was so enticing.

As his hands swept down her stomach, a finger tentatively stroking between her thighs, she sat bolt upright, pushing his hands and the hem of her dress back towards her knees.

'Don't!'

'Damn!'

Peter rolled onto his back, putting inches between them, his hands returning to the back of his head. He stared up at the sky, features grim as granite.

Immediately regretting her reaction, Lizzie bit her lip. This was the moment she hated. The pressure to give in was enormous, but the consequences formed a brick wall that she was unwilling to smash through.

'We can't, Peter. You know we can't.'

His face remained rigid and his voice was scornful. 'Then you can't have much affection for me. If you did you'd show it.'

Lizzie frowned. They'd had this conversation before. 'So you keep saying. But we can't. I wouldn't want to get into trouble...'

He rolled onto his side, his head propped on one hand. 'Then you can't care for me too much.'

She knew he was baiting her, and she badly wanted to please him. Her emotions were having a war of their own. 'That isn't true. You know I do, but you have to understand—'

'But things have changed, Elizabeth. I could get my call-up papers any day now, and then where we would be? I could be sent anywhere and we wouldn't see each other for weeks, perhaps months, perhaps even years.' He said it haltingly, softly, purposely stirring her emotions.

And yet she sensed that the irritation in his voice was more pronounced than usual, and he'd resorted to calling her Elizabeth in that same tone his mother used. Reminding her that he could be called up to fight before very long made her feel guilty.

Hugging her legs, she frowned and hid her face against her knees. Suddenly the clear blue sky didn't seem quite so beautiful. A cloud hid the sun. Very shortly it could turn into a battleground between wind and rain.

The needs of her body and of him battled with her common sense. She tried to think of a way she could put into words exactly how she felt without giving in. But no words came. What if he did go away to fight? What if he did die? She'd forever regret not sharing the sweetest moment of all.

When his hand came across and fondled her breast, she lay still.

When it travelled further, sliding down over her stomach, lifting the hem of her dress and caressing the soft expanse of flesh between stocking top and lace-edged knickers, she did not protest.

'Lie down.'

She did exactly as he wanted, feeling as though her body were no longer hers to command, but leaving it to follow its own inclinations.

First there was pain, exactly as she'd expected. In dreams of this moment, she'd imagined the pain turning to pleasure and was surprised when it didn't. In fact she felt as though something very dear had been taken from her and nothing given in return.

Regret for her actions would have been total but was lessened when he said the three little words she had always wanted to hear.

'I love you,' he whispered, and she almost cried with happiness.

'I love you too,' she murmured, throwing her arms around him, wanting to lie there for the rest of the afternoon despite the gilt-edged clouds now hiding the sun.

'Come on,' he said, pulling her to her feet. 'I have to get back to the shop and you've got sausages to buy.'

'I wish we didn't have to do anything,' she said, pressing herself against him and gazing up into his face.

Wrinkling his nose, he glanced up at the sky. 'Stay here by yourself, old fruit, but I warn you, it's going to rain.'

She sighed. For one moment in time her spirits had soared.

Now it was back to normal.

They bundled the bicycle onto the car roof so that Lizzie could get into Bedminster quicker than she could by bicycle.

The traffic was light until they got into East Street, the main thoroughfare lined with shops, pubs and the police station.

'Better get out here,' said Peter, frowning as a convoy of trucks carrying stacks of corrugated iron pushed their way past buses and trams. 'Looks like the war is catching up with us.'

Lizzie stared at the coldly frightening sheets. 'Anderson shelters,' she said in a disinterested way. Preoccupied with what she had just done, she couldn't harbour any enthusiasm for anything to do with the war – except as it might affect her or, more especially, Peter.

This afternoon she'd given in to him and he'd rewarded her with those three little words, but in the aftermath she wasn't feeling quite as she'd expected.

'Do you think anyone will notice?' she blurted, tugging the hem of her dress more firmly over her knees.

Peter, anxiously tapping the steering wheel while glancing from traffic to wristwatch and back again, frowned as though he hadn't really been listening. 'Notice what?'

'I feel as though I've grown an extra head.'

'What?'

'I mean, do I... do I look any different... I mean... after what we've just...'

It hurt when he looked at her askance. 'What the bloody hell are you talking about?'

She frowned and pursed her lips. 'Don't look like that! I'm not stupid, for goodness sake, it's just that I feel... different.'

A sudden flash of temper made his good looks ugly.

'Oh for goodness sake! Come on. You're not the first and you won't be the last to get her fair share before tying the knot. Get out. Come on. I've got work to do.'

Clouting the driver's side door with the heel of his hand, he got out his side and, without offering to open the door on her side, proceeded to unload the bicycle. He looked stiff and unyielding, as though nothing of any great importance had taken place, whereas she...

Resolved that he didn't want to talk about it and that she should somehow try to make amends, she got out of the car.

'That was silly,' she said, lowering her eyes as he passed the bicycle to her. She shrugged. 'Why would anyone notice? They can't really *see* what we did.'

He sighed impatiently. 'Don't worry about it. I won't. I know girls can be silly.'

The quick peck he gave her on the forehead was disappointing.

She'd hoped for a more passionate embrace even though they were in the middle of East Street.

'So no one will know that I've done it.'

He smirked. 'Not unless they were lurking in the hedges,' he said, his surliness tempered with amusement. 'Now come on. I've got to get back to the store and you've got some shopping to do.'

There was something more important than shopping playing on her mind. She couldn't let him go without somehow reliving that wonderful moment.

'Did you mean what you said?' she asked as she mounted her bike and followed him around to the driver's side of the car.

Peter climbed in and started the car. 'Mean what?' Lizzie positively glowed. 'That you love me, of course.'

'Of course,' he said, and stroked the hand she rested on the car door. 'Now I must be off. I'll see you next Wednesday and I can love you some more then. Hope the weather stays dry or I'll get a wet bum, won't I?'

The last of the heavily loaded trucks passed and he pulled away, heading towards the far end of East Street and Redcliffe Hill.

Feeling terribly alone, Lizzie watched until he was just one more car in the traffic. It would have been nice if he'd stayed and showed that it was as momentous an occasion to him as it was to her. Where was the boyish young man who'd been tongue-tied when he'd first come across her in his mother's kitchen? They had met only once before she'd started work and that was on the occasion of Lizzie being interviewed for the job. He had been there at his mother's request so had spoken politely and generally only at his mother's behest.

All the sighing in the world won't alter things, she thought to herself.

She started to push off from the kerb, but stopped, her attention diverted to a young woman with a pram. She was fresh-faced and hardly looked old enough to have a child. Two older women were bending over the pram, peering at the tiny bundle nestled beneath the hood. Their voices were as thick and sweet as syrup of figs.

'How old is the dear little mite?'

'Two months.'

Though they smiled, their lips were taut, as if they were clenching their jaws in order to keep their insincerity at bay.

'Two months! Now ain't that lovely, God bless 'im, though what a time to be born into.'

Once the woman with the pram had moved off, the older two watched her go, their heads coming closer together, as though plotting something too dire to be overheard.

'Shame the father wouldn't marry her,' said the first.

'Ruined for life,' said the other, folding her hands one over the other and the handles of a square, no-nonsense shopping bag. 'No one's going to want her now. She's soiled goods.'

The other woman nodded dolefully. 'You're right there, Gladys. If only these young girls knew what they were getting themselves into they wouldn't give in as easily as they do. But there, give it away once they'll give it away again. Sluts, all of them. Not like in our day. In our day—'

Face reddening, Lizzie didn't wait to hear any more but shoved off, peddling like mad towards the pork butcher in North Street, glad of the breeze cooling her hot cheeks.

A group of boys were playing marbles in the gutter outside the shop where fresh rabbits and chickens hung from a rack in front of the window.

'Knocked your niner!' shouted one of them.

Lizzie wouldn't have given them a second glance, if she hadn't heard a thin, crackling kind of voice protest that it just wasn't so.

'You cheated. And if you don't give me my niner back, I'm goin' to knock your bloody block off.'

'Stanley!'

Her youngest brother spun round in boots that looked too big for his skinny legs, a look of surprise on his face.

Swiftly leaning her bike against the drainpipe dividing the butcher's shop window from the cobbler's next door, she made straight for him, grabbing his arm before he could run away.

'Does Ma know you're out?'

Stanley coughed then screwed up his face. 'She said I could go out if I feels all right.'

'But she likes to know first, and you didn't tell her, did you?'

He squirmed and twisted his features, but the truth was obvious by the way he jerked his jaw as though he might speak, but only if he was really forced to.

The scruffy group of kids he was with gathered round. 'She's me sister,' Stanley explained, wiping his snotty nose on the back of his sleeve.

'Yer sister!'

The news was passed from one boy to another. 'She's only his sister!' Derisive scowls appeared on each face.

'Just 'is bloody sister!'

Lizzie gave a long drawn out sigh. 'I take it you're not impressed. Not that I care. He's still got to come home.'

'Leave 'im alone.'

'Come on back and play marbles, Stanley.'

'Tell 'er to sod off,' said one lanky soul, his grey flannel trousers flapping around straight, spidery legs. 'She's only yer bloody sister. Tell 'er to sod off!'

The others, beaming with admiration that their chum had uttered a forbidden word and got away with it, took up the anthem.

'Yeah! Sod off!'

'Sod off!'

'Sod off!'

Though they gathered round, threatening to push her towards the butcher's shop, Lizzie ignored them. She wasn't the type to be intimidated, certainly not by a group of children.

'Come on,' she said, still gripping Stanley's arm. 'You're staying with me.'

Under pressure from the chanting boys, she made for the shop door more hurriedly than usual, having to take the route immediately beneath a row of dead rabbits, ducks and hare.

Somehow, the boys sensed her aversion to all things dead. 'Look,' said the most vocal, a boy who could have passed for fourteen, though must have been only ten if his clothes and cherubic features were anything to go by. He pointed upwards. 'They're all looking at you, and there's blood dripping from their mouths.'

'Ughhh! Blood.'

'And brains.'

'And innards.'

Lizzie pushed Stanley through the door. 'Don't be so disgusting. And clear off,' she shouted before slamming the door so hard that the closed sign fell off its nail.

Averting her gaze from the rows of glassy-eyed rabbits and chickens hanging from hooks above their heads, and after replacing the sign, Lizzie pushed her brother towards the blue and white tiled counter on which a plaster pig sat holding a sign saying:

Pork Sosages – 3d a pound.
  Pigs Trotters – 1d each Pork
  Driping – 1d a corter

'He can't spell,' Stanley murmured, scuffing his button-up boots on the sawdust floor.

Lizzie nudged him. 'Stop doing that.'

'No! I like the sound it makes.'

Lizzie saw the smirk on his face and the cheeky grin he exchanged with his friends outside, whose faces were now pressed against the window, their features distorted and their breath misting the glass.

'Just wait till I get you home,' Lizzie whispered. 'Or I might clip your ear before then.'

'I'll tell Ma and she'll tell you off.'

He was right there. Mary Anne spoiled him, and that was a fact.

'I don't care. I'll still give you a clip around the ear.'

In response, Stanley proceeded to scuff the toes of his boots against the counter. It seemed to Lizzie that he was enjoying annoying her.

She glanced down at him, just to make sure it was the little brother who had lain sick in the front parlour, ever since his chest infection back in January. He'd always had bad days and good days, but wasn't normally so badly behaved in those moments when his health improved.

'I don't know what's up with you. You never used to be so badly behaved. What's brought this on?'

'Cos I'm a man, that's why.'

'And what's that supposed to mean?' She shook her head. 'I don't understand.'

Stanley continued to scuff his toes against the sawdust, piling it in small drifts against the counter.

Lizzie sighed. Don't let him see you're annoyed, she said to herself, and purposely looked overhead at the hanging game rather than the boys making faces at the window.

The sights and smells of the pies were so delicious that she soon forgot the glassy-eyed corpses hanging overhead.

Stanley, whose appetite tended to come and go, forgot about goading his sister; his eyes opened wide at the sight of thick strings of sausages hanging from overhead hooks and draped like a cloak around a plaster pig sitting on the counter clutching the blackboard on which the price list was chalked. Crusty pies and home-cured hams sat in wooden trays on the counter, blending their fragrance with the irresistible aroma of succulent faggots, juicy pork dripping and freshly made Bath chaps. Lizzie eyed them too. Sampsons' was the best butcher in Bedminster according to her mother. Judging by smell alone, Lizzie had to agree.

The door between the shop and the area to the rear opened, and the butcher came in. Standing six feet three in his boots, Fred Sampson peered down at them, his curly black moustache quivering as he spoke.

'Well now. What 'ave we got 'ere then?' he bellowed, the timbre of his voice a direct result of being deafened in the artillery when serving on the Somme.

Compassionate eyes peered over round cheeks and his rubbery jowls quivered with unspoken sympathy as his eyes rested on young Stanley.

'And how are you, young man?'

Stanley gazed up at him wide-eyed and muttered, 'All right.'

It was apparent to Lizzie that Mr Sampson must seem like a giant to him and his voice reverberated like cannon fire.

'Now what you need in order to grow bigger is to eat more of yer mother's suet puddings and boiled potatoes.'

Stanley had a sour expression on his face. 'I'm big enough, mister, and don't you say any different.'

Mr Sampson turned to Lizzie. 'Not too well tempered is he, your little brother.'

The look Lizzie gave her brother was just as sour as the look he was giving her.

'He's not usually like this. It's the company he's mixing with,' she said, jerking her chin at the faces being pulled against the window.

The butcher leaned over the window display towards the flattened noses and gargoyle mouths. 'Hop it!'

The boys jumped back, regrouping in the gutter, their dirty knees pulled up to their chins.

'Now,' said Mr Sampson, his voice still loud but not enough to break eardrums. 'Something for yer mother?'

'No. It's for the lady I work for. I'd like one pound of sausages, one pound of back bacon and a large pork pie. I have the money here.'

The butcher twirled the end of his moustache with fingers the thickness of his own pork sausages.

'Certainly, my dear.'

The door that led to the living quarters of the shop and was immediately behind the counter opened suddenly. A woman with protruding eyes and fleshy jowls appeared.

'Frederick! Frederick! Have you cut my chops yet?'

The butcher half turned. He looked surprised. 'Frederick! My word, me dear, what's brought you on so that you're calling me Frederick?'

'As soon as you've finished. Will you be long?'

'As long as it takes, me dear. As long as it takes.'

The door closed. Lizzie got the impression that Mrs Sampson was loitering on the other side, waiting to pounce the moment they left.

Mr Sampson, perhaps noticing the look of curiosity on her face, began to explain even though she hadn't queried Mrs Sampson's interruption.

'My Beatrice is a little worried. Every bit of news about the war, and she's reporting it to me word for word, terrified that I'm going to get called up. As if,' he said, pointing at his ears. 'The sergeant major would 'ave to use sign language to get me marching. But still she comes out 'ere to tell me snippets of news, but if there's customers 'ere, makes the excuse she wants some chops for our tea.'

After wrapping the bundle again in newspaper, Lizzie paid him.

'Ah!' he said. 'Hang on there. Yer mother wanted a pig's cheek. Can you manage to carry all of it 'ome with you?'

'Yes. I've got my bike – and Stanley,' she added as an afterthought, throwing her brother a warning grimace in case he dared dash off once her arms were full.

'Good.'

He disappeared into his storeroom and came back in with a pig's head, chopped it in half then chopped each cheek again before this too was wrapped in the same way and slammed onto the counter.

'There you are, me dears, and tell your mother I've left the eyes in. They'll see her through the week.' He snorted then burst into loud chuckles at his own joke.

Lizzie managed a smile. He always said the same thing to anyone who wanted a pig's head, and always laughed loudly at his oft-repeated joke.

'Tell 'er she'll make a good bit of brawn from that one. No one can say that I don't breed the best pigs in North Somerset, and, 'angs 'em proper before I cuts them up. Now. Can you manage? Right! That'll be ten pence, please.'

Following a quick glance at the coins, he took them to his little wooden drawer that passed as a cash register and counted out the change into Lizzie's outstretched hand.

'And take this,' he added. 'A piece for you and a piece for his lord-ship, 'ere. A ham bone – cut in half.'

Another parcel, smaller this time, was placed on the counter. 'And if that lady you works for wants to open an account, you let me know.'

'I'll ask Mrs Selwyn tomorrow morning.'

He turned swiftly at the mention of her name, a serious look firming up his broad face and layers of chin.

'Mrs Selwyn? 'Er that lives in Ashton? Opposite the park? Used to know 'er 'usband, I did. Officer and a gent, if ever there was. Died a few years back... left a son, if I remember rightly. Bit of a lad about town. Want to watch him, my girl. He's the sort that would lead any respectable girl astray, from what I hear.'

'I'd better be going.' Lizzie sucked in her breath and felt her cheeks reddening. She didn't want to hear this, and she certainly didn't want the butcher to read the obvious into her blushing cheeks. Would he guess what she'd done that afternoon? Plucking absentmindedly at imagined grass stalks stuck to her clothes, she made for the door, sausages, pies and pig's cheek tucked beneath her arm, and one hand gripping Stanley's shoulder.

She needn't have worried. Stanley's attention was fixed on the juicy ham bone.

'Thank you, Mr Sampson.'

The hand he waved at them was patterned with patches of dried blood. Lizzie grimaced.

It was going to be difficult holding on to Stanley and pushing her bike because the little monster was squirming like a tadpole. His mates were standing at a distance making faces and taunting him with cries of 'sissy, sissy, sister,' urging him to join them.

'They murders people in that shop and minces 'em into faggots,' shouted one of them.

'That's disgusting,' said Lizzie.

Stanley grinned and his eyes shone up at Lizzie with such enthusiasm for the idea that she shivered.

'And in pies,' he added, gloating when Lizzie visibly paled.

'Come on. Home,' she said, pushing him in front of her having given up trying to hold on to him while pushing the bike. 'You just stay where I can see you...'

The moment her hand left Stanley's shoulder, he was off, his friends crowing in delight as he joined them, whooping like a group of Indians surrounding a wagon train.

Before she had chance to park the bike and grab him, they were gone.

'Little sod!'

She wasn't usually easily angered and rarely swore, but today could have progressed more smoothly. Recalling the events of the afternoon soon drove her anger away, though she did have some misgivings. Even though he'd declared his love for her – or it had seemed that way – Peter's attitude seemed frankly casual. If it had been the first time for him as it had for her, why hadn't he reacted in a similar way?

She pushed Mr Sampson's comments that hinted at Peter being a bit of a playboy to the back of her mind. In time they'd marry, she told herself; she had no doubt about that. It was the thing to do, and they would do it.

Dusk was deepening into darkness. Squares of bright amber fell from shop windows onto damp pavements.

Trams and trolley buses trundled past bringing the workers home from the tobacco factory. The factory was in East Street, the building red-brick mock Gothic; pretty little arches above square, blank windows. Behind those windows, a vast array of production machines clanked and jangled, men and women labouring like workers in a hive. At the end of the week, they'd be delving in their wage packets, spending and puffing on the products they spent all day making.

Brewery drays thundered in and around the trams, the great shires snorting steamy breath as they made their way with their lightened load back to George's Brewery, a warm stable and fresh hay.

Lizzie surveyed the scene through screwed-up eyes, her nose wrinkling at the dusty air. Sometimes she saw a car and immediately thought of Peter. It was the first time she'd been in love and she was sure no one or nothing could ever equal what she was feeling right now.

At last she turned into Kent Street. 'Lizzie!'

Wearing trousers that he'd long grown out of, his jacket so big that the cuffs covered his hands, Patrick Kelly leaned against the corner shop window. He had square shoulders and long legs, his hair the colour of corn and his eyes as blue as the trees on willow pattern china.

Lizzie pulled the bike to a standstill. Tilting her chin upwards, she smiled directly into his eyes and his naturally wary expression melted.

'No work today?'

'Mr Shellard ain't well.'

'Oh.'

'Been on the scrumpy again,' Patrick explained on seeing the knowing look on Lizzie's face.

Patrick's mother had a bad name and he had no father, a fact that had puzzled Lizzie when she'd been younger. Her curiosity aroused, she had questioned her Sunday school teacher why that was so. Miss Pamplew, a spinster of sixty with the physique of a malnourished sparrow, had assured her that everyone did indeed have a father. The bird-like face had puckered up with Christian kindness when she'd asked why she wanted to know. Lizzie had explained to her about Patrick Kelly.

'He's got a lot of uncles and a mother, but no father. I heard someone call him a bastard. Is that the name for people with no father?'

Miss Pamplew, a born nun if ever there was, had coloured up and dragged her to the tap in the outside yard where she'd pushed a piece of soap between her teeth, held her mouth open beneath the water pump and told her never to utter such a wicked word again.

'I'm going to join the army. I'm going away from here,' Patrick blurted.

Lizzie's face froze as she took in the news, and then she laughed. 'Don't be silly. You're too young.'

'I'm eighteen... and a half,' he said, sloping his shoulders back as though he were already wearing a uniform and required to stand to attention. 'Every able-bodied man is being called up, but some of us are off to the recruiting centre soon as we can.'

Lizzie eyed his lean frame sceptically. 'You need feeding up if you're going to do that,' she said, and immediately delved into the parcels loaded into the pannier at the front of her bike. She got out the pie she'd bought for Mrs Selwyn and thrust the package into his hands. 'It's a pie. I've heard an army marches on its stomach. You'll need it more than me or my family.' Or Mrs Selwyn for that matter.

It was a well-known fact that Patrick fended for himself. His mother never cooked. Half his life he'd lived on charity. His fingers curled over the small package and his jaw moved as though he were already savouring the taste of it. Pride stopped him from licking his lips but his voice broke with emotion.

'At least the army will feed me.'

It started to rain. Lizzie brushed at the fine drops speckling her hair. 'It'll seem funny... you not being here any more.'

His face cracked into a smile. 'Better get used to it. There's going to be a lot of us. Most of us will be going to France according to the newspaper, and some to Belgium, p'raps even Turkey like men did in the first lot.'

'Such faraway places.' She thought of all the boys and young men in the street not being there any more, all off to fight a war. She'd been at school with a lot of them.

The rain became heavier. They stood there, the gathering gloom more like January than October, appropriate weather for the man-made storm presently gathering momentum.

Patrick spoke first. He looked sheepish but sounded brave. 'Will you come with me to the recruiting office? There's no one else I can ask.'

'Yes. Of course I will.'

'Will you write to me – if I write to you and let you know where I am?'

'Oh! Yes. Why not?'

She shrugged off her surprise and smiled warmly. For some reason, it had never occurred to her that Patrick could write. He was good with mechanical things, wooden things; in fact anything that broke, he could put back together. He'd mended her bike enough times, fixed her punctures and fitted a bell.

'Yes,' she said quickly before he detected her disbelief. 'I'd love for you to write to me. And I'll write back. I promise I will.'

Just before reaching the front door of the house she'd been born in, she glanced back in time to see Patrick biting into the pie. She wondered when he'd last eaten and was glad she'd given him something.

5

Mary Anne had almost gone out of her mind on finding Stanley missing, looking for him in the streets running parallel with Kent Street, and finally coming across him sitting on top the cannon in the park and coughing between shouts of 'Load the shot!' and 'Fire!'

'Home!'

He came begrudgingly, dragging his feet, his new friends at first jeering him, then shouting that they'd see him tomorrow.

'Down the Malago,' they shouted.

'Down the Malago,' he shouted back.

Mary Anne jerked him so hard forwards that he covered the same length of ground with two steps that usually took three. 'Oh no you won't. You're to keep away from that smelly stream.'

Once he'd eaten, he was packed off to bed, coughing and grumbling, his face slick with sweat and his cheeks pink as apples.

Earlier in the year, he'd gone down with a fierce chest infection and at one stage it had seemed she might lose him. She'd never quite got over it, watching him for the slightest sign of the infection returning.

Frantic with worry, she'd slept most nights in the front parlour where his bed had been placed when things had seemed at their worse. The bed was still there – just in case.

'When's our Stanley going to join Harry – all boys together?' Lizzie had queried.

'When I say so,' she'd answered, not trusting to anyone else's judgement except her own.

She was still wary about letting him out to play or go to school. That night he'd slept well and, following a morning dose of medicine and his plea that he was still too ill to go to school, she let him stay in bed.

A tap on the back door heralded the arrival of Aggie Hill. She was one of her regulars, always wanting a bit of extra money for something. Her ginger curls fought to escape a thin hairnet and formed corkscrews of colour like small springs around her face.

'Joe's off!' she said abruptly. She pulled out a chair, slumped firmly into it and promptly burst into tears.

Guessing she had a lot of listening to do, Mary Anne lit the gas beneath the kettle, fetched the teacups from the dresser and spooned tea into a shiny brown pot that she placed on the kitchen table beside the milk jug and sugar bowl.

Affectionately shaking her next-door neighbour's shoulder, she said, 'Come on, Aggie. Tell me about it while the kettle boils.'

Aggie dabbed at her eyes. 'You know our Joe's in the Territorials?'

'Yes.'

'Some bigwig from the army went into Wills' and said all them that are in the Territorials are to go home, fetch their kit and report to Temple Meads railway station by eight o'clock this evening.' Aggie leaned across the table, her face wet and her eyes brimming with tears. 'When am I going to see him again, Mary Anne? When?'

Mary Anne declined to answer such a question. 'Let's get this tea made.'

The gas made a popping sound as she turned it off. Normally, she didn't give it much notice. Today it made her jump. Usually, she only gave six stirs of the pot, plenty enough to mash the tea. On this occasion, she gave it double that while she considered the best thing to say to a woman whose son was off to war.

She placed both cups and saucers on the table, pushing Aggie's close so that the lip of the saucer touched her arm. The woman's eyes were brimming with tears and she was staring at the wall.

'Help yerself to sugar and milk, then take a good gulp of it.' Aggie did as she was told.

Mary Anne sipped at her own cup.

Aggie blew her nose in a man-sized handkerchief that looked as though it might once have been the tail of a shirt.

'He's me only son, Mary Anne. If he gets killed...'

Mary Anne patted her shoulder. 'You can't think that, Aggie. He wouldn't want you to think that either. You've got to send him off with a smile on your face and tell him it won't be long before he's home on leave.'

'It's not easy.'

'Of course it's not easy, but he's got to go and be brave, and you've got to stay behind and be brave. You've got to put on a brave face even though you're frightened of what might happen. But just because it might happen, doesn't mean to say it will. And anyway, they're saying it's all going to be over by Christmas.'

Aggie sniffed; her eyes, naturally bulging and brown, now became as big as saucers. 'Do they?'

Mary Anne patted her hand. 'I think Chamberlain said so, and he should know. He's been to Germany.'

It wasn't a lie. She'd heard it from someone. At the time she'd recalled hearing the same thing said about the Great War, and that had lasted four years. Over a million men were dead at the end of it. But Aggie didn't want facts, only reassurance.

Aggie blew her nose again and wiped the last of the wetness from her bloated cheeks. 'And Chamberlain didn't want this war, so he'll probably still be trying to stop it,' she said, her back stiffening as though she'd just breathed in a lungful of courage. 'Me spirits is lifted, and talking of spirits...'

Mary Anne braced herself for what was coming. Aggie Hill was a spiritualist; she believed in it all, even the charlatans who asked for a shilling before going into a trance and speaking in what passed for the voice of the departed. She was also keen on telling the future from reading the tea leaves.

'I'll do mine first,' she said, draining her cup, tipping it upside down and turning it three times in its saucer.

Taking the cup in both hands, she held it close to her face, her bulging eyes threatening to come out on stalks as she peered at its contents.

'I can see birds, a lot of birds flying in the sky.'

'What sort of birds?'

'Well. They could be any sort. Big birds.'

'Like seagulls?'

Aggie's face brightened. 'Yes, I think they're seagulls. Now there's a thing. Joe said he'd probably end up down on the south coast.'

Mary Anne smiled to herself. 'Well there you are then.'

Tea leaves just looked like – well – tea leaves to her, but if it made Aggie happy, then what did it matter.

Aggie's whole body sighed with relief. 'Hope the weather holds. The fresh air will do him good.'

Her good spirits continued. 'It don't say here that any harm will come to him, and the tea leaves do speak for up to two years ahead at least.'

'No dark stranger then?'

Aggie had been a widow for years, her only income a widow's pension, and Joe's contribution from his job in the tobacco factory. She also cleaned the doctor's surgery in the next street along with some of the posh houses down in Ashton where Mary Anne's daughter Lizzie worked.

Aggie sighed. 'Nobody could replace my Reggie. Nobody at all.'

Glad to see her happy again, Mary Anne drew the moment out, nudging Aggie's arm. 'You never know yer luck, Aggie!'

Aggie chortled with merriment, the broken veins of her cheeks turning even redder.

'Is there anything else?'

Aggie narrowed her eyes, the tip of her nose almost meeting the rim of her cup. 'I can see a new job coming, but not the same kind of thing that I've done before, something where I've got a lot of responsibility, and even a uniform!' She glanced at Mary Anne. 'Ooow! I've always wanted to be a nurse.'

'Fancy letting you loose with all them doctors.'

'I works with one now.'

Mary Anne laughed. 'Never in a month of Sundays could you describe Doctor Sneed as tall, dark and handsome.'

'Oooow, no!' Aggie hooted, her laughter enough to rattle the pans hanging from their hooks. 'Now your cup,' she said, once their laughter had died.

Mary Anne dutifully drained her cup and Aggie repeated the same procedure she'd carried out with her own.

'Oooow! There's a lot of changes.' Frowning, she peered closer. 'Something's going to happen to make you feel young again.'

Mary Anne thought of her present condition. Babies had always brought her joy, but she'd been younger then. Was that what Aggie was seeing? 'That would take a miracle.'

'There's them seagulls again as well.' She looked up. 'P'raps you're going to the coast as well. Not thinking of evacuating, are you?'

Mary Anne shook her head. 'Henry wouldn't allow it.'

'I would have thought the sea air would do your Stanley some good.'

Mary Anne studied her hands, which were presently folded in her lap. 'Henry won't hear of it. He reckons moving him would do more harm than good.'

If Aggie could have read her mind as easily as she read the teacups, she would have seen her defending herself against Henry's assertion that she was too soft on the boy.

'Well, there's definitely seagulls, and what's this? Look here, Mary Anne Randall, I see a tall dark stranger. Now who might he be?'

'You've found me out!' said Mary Anne, slamming her palms down on the table and setting the spoons rattling in their saucers. 'In fact I'm expecting him tomorrow morning at ten.'

'You are?' Aggie's mouth dropped open.

'Yes,' said Mary Anne, gathering up the crockery. 'I've got a new coalman coming with half a ton of Welsh steam coal and you can't get much darker than that!'

Aggie Hill rocked with laughter, her plump hands holding on to her jiggling stomach. 'About the only dark stranger we're likely to get at our time of life! Or at least for me, but you've still got yer looks, Mary Anne. It's a wonder Henry don't lock you up in case that tall dark stranger do chance to call.'

Mary Anne stood over the sink, turning the tap then swilling the cups one at a time. She was smiling, but couldn't find it in herself to laugh with the same exuberance as her friend, Aggie.

The moment was too silent for too long. Aggie came and stood beside her, picking up the tea towel from off the draining board.

'Is anything wrong, Mary Anne? You seem a bit – well – quieter than usual.'

Mary Anne shook her head vigorously. 'Nothing!'

'Where's Henry?'

'Upstairs. Asleep. He did the night shift last night.'

Aggie took the last cup from her hand. Mary Anne saw her knowing look and dropped her eyes.

'I saw him come home. The whole street saw him come home.'

Mary Anne snatched the tea towel from Aggie's hand. 'It's no one else's business.'

Unlike her own family, living in ignorance of their father's true character, the women of Kent Street were more circumspect.

'I don't know how you put up with it,' said Aggie.

Mary Anne spun round on her. 'At least I have a husband. There's plenty who ain't and plenty who entertain the husbands of other women!'

She could see from Aggie's face that the barb had hit home. It was a well-known fact that Aggie had been 'carrying on' with the husband of a woman in the next street, the poor wife prone to intermittent fits.

Aggie headed for the door.

Mary Anne instantly regretted her remark. 'Aggie!'

Aggie paused. Her merry expression was replaced with hurt.

Mary Anne wiped her hands over her hips and attempted to make amends. Her smile was weak but her sentiments were genuine. 'I hope everything goes well for your Joe. I hope he doesn't travel any further than the south coast.'

Aggie's hardened expression softened. 'Thank you.'

Only minutes after Aggie had left, the sound of movement came from upstairs.

Mary Anne raised her eyes to the ceiling, fear prickling her flesh. She tried reassuring herself, though it wasn't easy. Perhaps he'd fall back into bed and not surface until the girls got back. He kept his hands to himself when the family were around. It was only when they were alone that his temper and physical demands seized him, no matter what she did or said. It was worse after a night shift. Henry Randall with the drink inside him was bad enough. Henry Randall when sobriety was enforced on him – there were no pubs open at that time in the morning – was something else.

She tried to dull her fears by peeling potatoes, one of the little household chores that dulled her sensitivities. Carrying out simple tasks left her mind free to wander, sometimes in sheer fantasy, sometimes to a past that might have been different if it hadn't been for the Great War. The best thing about her past was Edward's lips on hers, the pale pink beauty of the child she had borne. There were a number of worse things: the news of his death, giving the child up for adoption—A dull thud came from the room above, shaking the ceiling and shattering her thoughts. The potato knife clattered into the sink and the colour drained from her face.

'Woman! Woman!'

He was calling down for her to come up. He was in *that* mood. She knew what was coming and her mouth turned dry. She had to swallow before shouting back. 'I'm coming.'

Climbing the stairs was a slow and painful process, her legs heavy with reluctance. When she opened the door, he looked up at her, his eyes glassy and red-rimmed, his face flushed and his jaw hanging so low, it seemed to be resting on his chest.

'Where the bloody hell have you been?'

Smiling weakly, she leaned against the closed door, her hands behind her, fingers clinging to the doorknob. She found her voice. 'I was peeling the potatoes.'

'You was peeling the potatoes.' He mimicked her voice in a high, squeaky tone. His eyes dropped to her breasts then her belly. 'You're getting a fat belly. Not expectin', are you? I'll kick it back in if you bloody well are.'

'Course not,' she said. She tried to laugh it off. 'At our age?'

His eyes stared, though his face clouded. 'Why not at my age? Do you think I'm not capable, eh? Think I'm any less of a man, do you?'

He stood up, his fingers dropping to his belt buckle.

'I didn't mean...' said Mary Anne, her knees weakening because she knew what was coming.

'You didn't mean,' he muttered winding the belt around his hand. 'You insult me, and then say you didn't mean it? Well, I'll show you, my fine lady!'

Mary Anne winced as his hand cupped the nape of her neck, the hand holding the belt raised high as he bent her over the bed. 'I'm still the man I always was!'

He repeated the same words with each rise and fall of the belt. Mary Anne bore the pain, gritting her teeth so she wouldn't cry out. The fact that Henry was shouting so loudly troubled her.

'Henry, keep your voice down. You'll disturb our Stanley.' On this occasion, her rebuke only added to his anger.

His fingers, strong from pulling triggers and lifting pints, groped at her blouse, tearing the material and sending buttons popping. 'Tell me when to be quiet, would you? I'm not a boy. I'm a man. Do you hear me? A man! It's just you ain't the woman you were. You're fat, ugly and got too much to say for yerself!'

She winced as one hand folded around her neck, the other digging inside her clothes, squeezing her breast, pinching her nipple.

'Please, Henry... No...'

'No? No?' He sounded surprised. His black brows knitted together, a strange, puzzled expression, as though he was aggrieved or insulted. This was his idea of enjoyment. He gave the orders, enjoyed the power he had over her and revelled in the torture. 'You're me wife, Annie, me lawfully wedded wife and I've needs...'

The cloth of her brassiere did not give so easily, unlike her breast. She gritted her teeth as he yanked a crescent of whiteness over the top of her blouse. Without looking, she knew her flesh was dappled with redness, the marks of his fingers.

God knows, she didn't want this, but from experience knew it was best to submit. 'On the bed then, Henry.'

The hand that had held her neck fell to her skirt.

He mimicked her voice. '"On the bed then, Henry."'

She cringed at the stink of his breath, warm and moist. His spittle sprayed her face.

'I'll have you on the bed all right.'

He pushed her. She fell face down, his weight on top of her, pulling her blouse back, baring her chest and pinning her arms to her side.

She closed her eyes, praying Stanley wouldn't hear, praying it would all be over as quickly as possible, or perhaps he'd fall asleep on top of her. It wouldn't be the first time.

But he wasn't drunk, he'd been working all night, and that angered him. Not today, she thought, inwardly screaming as he hoisted her skirt up to her waist, pushing her onto her knees, her head and shoulders buried in the eiderdown, unable to get up on her hands.

There was a ripping sound as he tore her underwear down to the tops of her stockings. He was quick unbuttoning his flies. Burying his fingers in the waistband of her corset, and without the benefit of preliminaries, he pushed himself into her. The pain was terrible. Squeezing her hands into tight fists she sucked in her breath and bit her lip – anything to stop from screaming.

Face pushed into the eiderdown, she saw nothing but felt a sudden draught and heard the sharp squeal of rusty hinges as the bedroom door swung open. With a sinking heart and a mix of horror and embarrassment, she knew that Stanley had heard.

Henry also had noticed and slackened his grip.

Mary Anne tried to rise, but only succeeded in turning her head.

Stanley stood at the door, his eyes like saucers; lips pink and moist like a painted angel. He saw his mother's predicament and there was pain in his eyes. His flickering gaze shifted to his father and turned to hatred.

She escaped Henry's weakened grasp, swiftly rearranged her clothes and ran to her youngest son. 'Stanley, Stanley! Come along. You shouldn't be here.'

Stanley was like a statue, stiff in her arms, though unlike something made of marble or clay, his eyes were not unseeing. He'd seen it all, and although he was not knowledgeable about what bestial act his father had been committing, he saw and reacted to his mother's distress.

Fixing his eyes on his father's face he addressed his mother. 'Why is he hurting you? Why is he hurting you?'

'It was nothing,' she said, her tongue flicking across her lip where a droplet of blood had burst through the bitten skin. 'Just a game,' she said, her heart racing at the incongruity of her lot. 'Just a game.'

With her son weighing heavy on her arms, she made her way back downstairs to the front bedroom.

'I'll kill him when I grow up,' said Stanley.

Mary Anne wrapped him in her arms, tears squeezing from the corners of her eyes. She kissed his forehead, her voice faltering and her vision blurred as she attempted to reassure him. 'You were having a nightmare and it woke you up.'

She felt him tense as her tears turned into sobs.

'He hurt you. I know he hurt you. I hates him, Ma. I hates him.'

Mary Anne held her child more tightly to her chest, narrowing her eyes against the anger brooding there.

'So do I,' she whispered softly against Stanley's hair. 'So do I.'

6

For days afterwards, Lizzie felt mortified for even considering that anyone could tell by just looking at her that she'd committed 'original sin'. As if she were wearing a placard around her neck! Eventually, she gave herself a good talking to.

Are you the first? she asked herself. Hardly. It was Eve that started it all in the Garden of Eden.

There was small comfort from that fact. Eve wasn't her and Kent Street was far from being the Garden of bloody Eden! She was Elizabeth Anne Randall and there was only one of her – at least as far as she knew.

Her gaze kept wandering to her sister Daw. Had she done it with John?

'What are you staring at?' asked Daw as she undressed for bed in the room they shared.

'Oh, I was just thinking how different your side of the bedroom looks to mine. All those toys and dolls you've kept.'

Smugly, Daw took in her collection of every toy she'd ever been given. The teddy bears and the golliwogs were handmade by their mother when they were children in the wee small hours after they'd gone to bed. The dolls were bought and dressed; every bit as good as the ones she could have bought in the shop. They all sat in a row on the chest of drawers on Daw's side of the bed.

Lizzie also had a chest of drawers on top of which there was only a mirror, a hairbrush and a photograph of Lizzie as a baby, taken at a Christmas bazaar. In the photograph she was chuckling, yet she distinctly remembered being determined not to laugh, until someone had made funny faces. Funny what you remember, she thought.

When they were children they had willingly shared secrets. Lizzie was still willing, telling Daw about Peter and how they sneaked out to see each other under Mrs Selwyn's nose. So far she hadn't told her about giving in to him. It was like crossing a bridge, but only wanting to go halfway, wanting Daw to admit to the same sin; sharing it would make her feel better.

'Don't fiddle with them,' said a frowning Daw, snatching a small golliwog from her sister's hands. 'You know I don't like you touching my things.'

Lizzie swallowed a sharp retort. She didn't want to send Daw into one of her sulks. Finding out whether she'd surrendered to John's urgings was more important. She had mentioned John wanting to, but so far there had been no sign of her giving in. Perhaps in time she might, but Lizzie was desperate to know.

'Will you miss John if he gets called up?'

Daw looked hurt, as though her sister had implied something quite insulting. 'Of course I will. And he'll miss me.'

'No doubt.' Lizzie sat on the bed, one leg crossed over the other as she unsnapped the suspenders that held up her stockings. The real question still hadn't been answered.

Now! How best could she put this?

'Will you... you know... do anything before he goes?' Daw had inherited the dark hair and white skin of her father.

Two round patches of pink appeared on her cheeks when she blushed, making her even prettier than she was. Lizzie smoothed her own honey-coloured locks back from her face. The same grey eyes as those of her mother fixed on Daw.

Daw flushed. 'What a question! I don't know what you mean.'

'Oh yes you do,' said Lizzie in a low, even voice. 'You know exactly what I mean. I can see it in your eyes so there's no point denying it.'

Daw's dark eyes fluttered nervously as she swiftly rolled her stockings up into a tight little ball. 'He wants to,' she said in a hushed voice, sucking in her lower lip and glancing over her shoulder on the off chance someone was listening.

The house had only two bedrooms. A curtain divided Harry's sleeping area from their own where they shared a double bed.

'Harry won't be back yet,' said Lizzie interpreting Daw's cautious glance. 'He's rarely back before midnight – you should know that by now.'

Chin almost touching her chest, Daw sat down on the bed. 'I don't know what to do. I can't bear the thought of him going away. We talked about getting married, or at least engaged.' She smiled shyly when she said the last bit.

Lizzie swallowed a pang of jealousy. 'Daw, that's marvellous!'

'Don't tell anyone.'

'Of course I won't.'

Something of the old intimacy swept over them. Their eyes met.

'Should I give in?' said Daw, chewing her lip, a nervous habit she'd acquired in childhood. 'I mean, we've been together practically all our lives and we are going to get married. Would you do it if you knew Peter was going to marry you?'

Lizzie sucked in her breath. 'Yes,' she blurted. 'I would... I would.'

Later, she lay in bed with her eyes wide open, wishing she hadn't sounded so encouraging. It was for Daw to make her own mind up, just as she had, though she hadn't had the courage to tell her sister that.

It will keep, she thought to herself. She turned onto her side and fell into a deep sleep disturbed only by the sound of Harry getting into bed on the other side of the dividing curtain as the clock on St John's church struck three.

7

There was something on the wireless about gas masks and not throwing potato rinds away but keeping them in a bin for pigswill or chicken feed. Mary Anne only caught snatches of the plummy voice waxing forth on something a bloke with a cut-glass accent couldn't possibly know anything about.

Smug sod.

What did he know about running a home and being a woman?

Her thoughts drifted to a more important matter. Mrs Riley's mixture hadn't worked. Straightening her stocking seams, she composed her face and headed for the lavatory, a small brick-built blot at the end of the garden.

She'd checked herself again and again – perhaps three times in the past hour. There was still no sign of bleeding. Desperation makes you do silly things, she thought to herself before pulling up her underwear and emerging from the lavatory.

Three gardens down, Vi Partridge waved her podgy arm at her from behind a billowing line of washing. Mary Anne waved back and forced a smile. Vi had the figure of a cottage loaf – two big round bits, one on top the other – and her hairstyle matched her body. She sighed. What a boon it would be if she was as stout as Vi; at least her belly wouldn't show for a while. As it was she'd kept a decent figure; not as svelte as in her youth, but slim-hipped enough for a swelling belly to show.

Vi's voice was as big as her body. 'Your boy called up to this bleedin' war yet?'

Mary Anne collected herself. 'No. Not yet. Any of yours?'

Vi's voice bounced over the garden fences. 'My Roger's signed up for the bleedin' navy, stupid sod. Says he ain't getting stuck in any bloody trench like 'is father was.'

Vi's colourful language was well known. So was the fact that house-work wasn't her favourite pastime and that grass grew in her back porch. Still, thought Mary Anne, keeping a tidy house didn't neces-sarily make a loving marriage so what did it matter?

She nodded her assent. 'Give him my best regards.'

'I will. You heard about them shelters – them tin things that's supposed to keep us safe from bombs. I don't fancy 'avin' one of the soddin' things in my garden. I'm stayin' in me bed. If Hitler comes along and bombs me ass off, well, I got plenty to go round!' She jiggled from her cheeks down, rivulets of movement falling like water over her body as she laughed. 'You 'avin' one of them?'

'I haven't given it much thought. I think I'd prefer to use the big ones they're putting up in Melvin Square.'

The voice of Vi's husband sounded from the house. 'Vi! Vi!'

'I'm coming, I'm coming,' she shouted back.

The conversation at an end, Mary Anne went back inside.

The kitchen was warm and steamy from the suet pudding bubbling away on the stove.

Henry was rolling a cigarette from a tin he balanced on his knees. He was sitting in the armchair next to the fireplace. He looked up as she walked in.

'You got diarrhoea or something?'

'No,' she said, instantly making a big thing of checking the suet pudding. 'Whatever makes you think that?'

Henry turned back to the task of filling the flimsy white paper with just enough tobacco. 'Well, you been in and out to that lavatory like a seaside donkey all bloody week.'

'Just a bit of a stomach bug,' she said, thankful that the steam could be blamed for the flush spreading over her face. She couldn't bring herself to tell him the truth and hoped she wouldn't live to regret it.

Dinner was on the table by the time Harry, her son and his father's namesake, came home from the tobacco factory.

Harry was handsome, in his mother's opinion, the best-looking young man in the whole city. He was dark-haired like his father, his skin clear and his eyes the colour of Bournvita chocolate.

He was also unbending as far as his father was concerned and not easily intimidated.

As Mary Anne laid the table, Lizzie and Daw came in and sat down, while Henry filled the kitchen with cigarette smoke, his body still sprawled in the only armchair at the side of the fireplace. He looked up, throwing his son an accusing glance even before he'd taken his boots off.

'You were a bit bloody late getting in last night.'

'So what? I'm over twenty-one.'

Mary Anne felt the contents of her stomach curdling. Why couldn't Harry be more respectful to his father?

'Go somewhere nice did you?' she interjected in an effort to smooth things over.

'I did indeed. Met up with friends, had a drink. It was good,' Harry replied.

'At that time?' blared his father. 'What pub round 'ere stays open all hours?'

'I didn't go to a pub. I went to a club.'

'A nightclub?' his father said incredulously.

Harry concentrated on hanging up his coat. 'A nightclub.'

'Well, just you remember whose house this is,' said his father, cigarette trembling at the corner of his mouth. 'As long as you're under my roof you obey my laws, and I says you should be in by midnight or get your own place.'

'Give me time and I will,' said Harry, slumping into a chair beside his sisters at the table and taking a few deep breaths before bending down to loosen his bootlaces.

'Is she pretty?' Lizzie asked, totally ignoring her father's chill expression and putting it down to plain old-fashioned worry.

Harry concentrated on rubbing his feet, frowning as he massaged his toes. 'Is who pretty?'

'The girl,' said Lizzie.

'Anyone we know?' added his mother, gladly steering the conversation away from Henry's critical disdain.

He smiled disarmingly. 'That's for me to know and you to find out, and knowing you women I dare say you'll go snooping around and find out eventually.'

'So?' said Lizzie.

'Yes, come on, Harry,' added his mother.

Both women wore the most intense expressions. Both were bursting to know who it was.

Harry merely smirked, closed his eyes and leaned his head against the back of the chair. 'So it's up to you to find out. I'm certainly not telling you.'

At first his sleep was only feigned, but it wasn't long before he was dozing.

After putting his work shoes away in the cupboard, Mary Anne dished up dinner. Every so often she glanced at her son, pleased to see him so completely at peace. And long may it be, she thought, praying to God that he wouldn't be called up, that by some miracle he would be overlooked.

She put the cruet set on the table just as the news was read on the BBC. The sonorous voice was sharp and the words well defined. When the newsreader started reporting planes called Stukas screaming like banshees as they dived at civilian targets leaving hundreds dead, she turned it off.

'Let's at least eat in peace,' she said.

For once Henry didn't command her to turn it back on although he loved all this talk of fighting and killing. Residual threads of the BBC news flickered in the eyes of those sitting around the table. Only their father still wanted to talk about it. 'Every man over the age of twenty is being called up,' said Henry Randall, who was due to work the night shift. In preparation he had slept for two hours after a session at the Red Cow. His eyes were bright and his face animated with enthusiasm. 'Tommy England will do his duty, never fear, though in my opinion, this country is going to need experienced commanders to see this through, though God knows if we've got any left worth their salt.'

'John said it's the air force that will win this war,' said Daw, her voice faltering at the prospect of her beloved John shooting at the enemy and being shot at in return. 'He's dead keen on joining.'

'Now, now, Daw, there's nothing for you to fear. Aircraft are only used for reconnaissance, or were in my day. It's still the Tommy on the ground that wins the war. Hand-to-hand combat; see the whites of their eyes and fire. Warfare ain't changed that much, I can tell you.'

Lizzie eyed each member of her family in turn, wondered what would happen if England too was invaded like Poland and the other countries. She barely resisted the urge to shiver as she made what she considered a sensible comment. 'They said on the wireless that people in Poland are being killed by Stukas – aren't they aeroplanes?'

Her father threw her a withering look. 'They're not British. What we do and what they do are two different things. We still have a sense of honour.'

'I do hope so,' said Mary Anne, unable to resist glancing up at the ceiling. 'Imagine hearing planes overhead and a bomb dropping through the roof.'

Henry threw her a contemptuous glare. 'Then stop imagining. They won't get this far.'

'Come on then, Dad,' said a smiling Harry in a voice Mary Anne recognised as the one he always used to goad his father. 'Tell us how the generals won the last war.'

Mary Anne noticed the faraway look in her husband's eyes. She knew what was coming. He started as he always did. 'I remember how it was...'

Using the cruet set, the bread knife and a tin of golden syrup, plus three sets of cutlery, he explained the situation as he remembered it.

Mary Anne raised her eyes to heaven. *Not all this again.*

Harry hid a grin behind his hand, pretending to wipe his mouth. Their son had his own opinions along with his own style. He preferred good clothes to drinking, a regular haircut and wore a trilby, even to work.

'Now this was the Belgian frontier,' Henry said laying out the bread knife and three forks into a ragged line on the tablecloth. 'This was the Kaiser's army.' The cruet set was manoeuvred into position directly opposite the bread knife. 'And here,' he said placing the butter dish in the centre of the table, 'this is Sarajevo where the Archduke Frederick—'

Mary Anne broke her silence and corrected him. 'Franz Ferdinand. His name was Franz Ferdinand.'

Henry Randall frowned at her. 'Are you sure, woman?'

'Very sure. I read it in the newspaper at the time.'

Henry grumbled a low guttural sound. He made the same sound when he was about to eject phlegm from his lungs.

Due to her condition, the bile rose to her throat. Swallowing it was hard.

'That may be, woman. But as I said, it happened in Austria, not Germany. That's where the two differ. One was Austrian. One German.'

'Hitler is Austrian.'

Henry shot her a warning look.

There were times when she couldn't help but stick up for herself. This was one of them, though there was more than one reason for doing so. Being contentious helped her overcome the queasiness in her stomach.

She repeated what she'd already said. 'Hitler is Austrian. I read it in the newspaper.'

'That don't mean they was right. Some big pot I 'ad in the back of the cab, who reckoned he worked for a newspaper, insisted that Hitler was Austrian, yet how can he be if he's Chancellor of Germany, tell me that, eh?'

'I told you. I read it in the newspaper.'

'So you say,' he muttered and looked away, not daring to meet her eyes.

Mary Anne exchanged a swift look with her son. Henry's embarrassment pleased her. He had never learned to read. His father, of the same mind as his son, had not held with working men knowing how to read. In his opinion, being hard was all that counted.

'I knows my place,' he'd said, 'and you should know yours.'

Henry had never voiced any regret about his lack of literacy in their courting days and although he'd initially succumbed to her lessons, pride and his father's influence had eventually got the better of him. The army hadn't helped. All men together back then, but nowadays his lack of learning festered like a hidden wound.

His face clouded. 'What do women know?' Shaking his head, he turned his attention back to the battle lines between the butter dish and the cruet stand. 'Now! As I was saying.'

The cruet set advanced on the bread knife. 'And this is that devil, Kaiser William—'

'Wilhelm,' Mary Anne corrected. 'His name was Kaiser Wilhelm. And Hitler is Austrian. It says so in the paper.'

'She's right, Dad.'

There was an earnest rustle as her eldest son, having once again completed the crossword in record time, waved the stark headlines in front of his father's face. Henry peered at the paper as though he could understand every word. The truth was that except for a few simple words, he was lost.

Harry, as keen a reader as his mother, was as different from his father as it was possible to be. He'd inherited his father's colouring, a leaner frame and had an agile mind.

Mary Anne was adamant. 'Adolf Hitler is an Austrian and also a painter, a house painter so I understand.'

Harry grinned. 'Front doors and window frames a speciality!'

His mother laughed. 'Not that kind of house painter. At least, I don't think so.'

Henry's clenched fist hit the table. 'I don't care who he bloody is or what he bloody well does! The Boche is no match for the British Tommy. We'll whip them we will! Whip them fast and be home again by Christmas.'

'That's what was said last time,' Mary Anne said quietly, as she dished potatoes onto separate plates. 'A lot of our boys will meet their maker before this war's over.'

Henry glowered. 'Pah! You're just a bloody woman. What do you know?'

'Only what I read and hear on the wireless.'

'Then stop listening and stop reading. It's nothing to do with women. Get back to yer sink and yer stove.'

Mary Anne slammed the saucepan onto the table. 'Don't you dare say that, Henry Randall. Of course it concerns women. It's women's sons, sweethearts and husbands who'll be going off to fight.'

'That's right. Women are joining up too,' said Lizzie, chin resting on her hand, gazing at her mother and thinking how beautiful she looked and how glad she was to look like her. And I'll look just like her when I'm forty, she thought wistfully.

'And there's more than one way of fighting a war,' added Harry, as he scribbled grids of letters and numbers on a piece of scrap paper. No one quite understood these grids and when asked what they stood for, Harry had tapped his nose and said, 'Secret.'

'I agree with John. I think air power will win the wars of the future.'

His father spat into the fireplace. 'Pah! Airpower indeed. Never mind that. Joining up will be the making of most of the milksops we've got around here! Mark my words!'

'My John's not a milksop!' Daw retorted. 'He'll be going. He's told me so.'

Thinking there was enough war going on in her own family, Mary Anne sighed and turned out the gas under the potatoes. 'Roger Partridge has joined the navy. His mother told me out back. She seems to be coping. Roger didn't want to get stuck in trenches like they did in the last war. Can't say I blame him.'

Harry nodded grimly. 'They came into the factory and ordered everyone in the Territorials to go home, get their kit and report to the station. Poor sods.'

'Poor sods, be damned! Now that's what I call patriotism!' Henry beamed.

'That's what I call bad luck,' muttered Harry, the strength of his cynicism seeming to light up his face, although at no time did he smile.

Trembling with patriotic fervour, Henry rose to his feet. 'For King and Country!' He saluted.

None of them dared laugh no matter how ridiculous he looked with his braces hanging around his hips, the top buttons of his shirt undone and a piece of tobacco trembling on the end of his moustache. War, whatever the circumstances, was a serious matter.

Only Harry made comment. 'Cannon fodder required. Enquire within.'

Mary Anne adored her eldest son, perhaps more so than her other children though, heaven forbid, she'd never admit such a thing. He looked like his father when he'd been younger, but did not share his unwavering patriotism.

Thankfully, Henry hadn't heard his son's last comment. For a while he seemed lost in thought before sighing resignedly. 'It's a great pity that I'm too old to serve,' he said in a muted tone and sighed again, his eyes sparkling with nostalgia. 'Though I'd love to, of course. I'd really love to. There's nothing like serving your country in the company of others of like mind – fine young men, all like yerself.'

He looked directly at Harry.

Mary Anne heard the yearning in her husband's voice and saw the expression in his eyes, totally at odds with that of his son. The army and the adventures of his youth were all gone, but still she could tell how her husband hankered after the chance to live it all over again. So did she, but for different reasons. As for her son...? Fear clutched at her heart as she eyed his dark hair curling towards the nape of his neck, the melting brown eyes... he never blinked, or at least, it seemed that way... now... now she was making a great effort to memorise every single feature, to remember... just in case... but she didn't see patriotism in her son's eyes. His eyelids flickered and his dark lashes fluttered over his high cheekbones in response to his thoughts. Like his speed when doing a crossword, each thought was perused and quickly done with and he was on to the next one, his expression remaining one of unguarded cynicism.

Unable to read his son's expression and swelling with pride, Henry slapped his namesake on the back. 'So off to war, eh, me boy? And never fear, I shall be proud of you.'

Harry's eyes met those of his mother. She saw the contempt, the bristling indignation and in that moment she knew exactly what he was going to do. The knowledge sent a shiver down her back. He was clasping his hands tightly together, his knuckles looking fit to burst through his skin. He clenched his jaw while avoiding his father's flushed gaze.

'I'm not enlisting,' he said in a quiet voice.

His father's jaw dropped to his chest, his eyes staring in disbelief. 'What? What was that you said?'

Silence fell around those eating, Lizzie's fork pausing halfway to her mouth. Mary Anne sat with her hands folded in her lap, her attention fixed on husband and son. Only Daw, immersed in her own thoughts, continued to eat.

'I'm not enlisting,' Harry said again in a firm, even tone. His chin jutted forwards, his look as challenging as throwing a gauntlet between them.

Mary Anne sucked in her breath and, although she said a silent thanks to God that her son would not rush to fight, she knew her husband would not be pleased.

The look in his eyes hardened. The room fell to silence.

Henry Randall clenched his fists, causing the hairs on his arms to stand on end. He looked at his son as though he wasn't sure he was his.

'What are you talking about? You have to enlist!'

Harry shook his head. 'No. No, I don't. If they call me up to fight for my country, I'll go. I will have to or go to prison, or worse... But I will not wilfully march to kill. Someone will have to make me. Besides, there's more than one way to fight a war.'

Henry didn't seem to take in the last few words. Refusing to fight was enough to send him mad.

'Make you?' His voice screeched to the ceiling and his face turned puce. 'Make you? This is your country we're talking about here, Harry. And what about Poland? That bloke Hitler walked in there as though he owned the place.'

Harry kept his eyes fixed on his hands. 'He does now. Anyway, as I said, I'm not rushing to do anything. I'm going to see how things turn out and do what suits me.'

'So we leave the French to build the trenches?' said Henry Senior, pounding the table with his clenched fist in order to emphasise the point.

Harry almost laughed. 'Don't be ridiculous, Dad. There won't be any trenches. Not this time. Even the civilians will be in the front line, just like they were in Spain a few years back. They'll be bombing us, Dad, and no amount of trench-building by blokes armed with only a Lee Enfield is going to save us. That's all of a bygone age! As I said, I will not go blowing trumpets and beating drums. I don't think modern warfare is in any way glorious. In fact, I don't think war ever was, though it's always been a money spinner – for some, that is.'

'I'll disown you! I swear I'll disown you if you don't do your duty!'

Mary Anne pushed her two daughters through the door, ordering them to start washing the pots. Harry's raised voice followed them out.

'I've never seen Dad so angry,' said Lizzie.

'Don't worry. I'll calm him down.'

Mary Anne went back into the kitchen, hovering over the table.

Father and son held each other's gaze, immovable objects on either side of the table.

Mary Anne bustled between them, snatching up the bread knife like a housewife whose world was confined to her home and knew nothing of the wider world. Inside, she cursed men for their crass stupidity, but she was there for a purpose. She made an attempt to calm the situation.

'Well, you can't go yourself, Henry Randall. The days when you and Lewis Allen went over the top are long gone. It's time for a new set of brave young men.'

Henry's glower flickered, his eyes switching to the collection of photographs on the mantelpiece, and one in particular of Henry and his pal, Lewis Allen.

'Aye,' he said, sighing deeply. 'Me and Lewis would 'ave showed 'em. Give us a sharp bayonet and we'd 'ave pig-sticked the lot of 'em!'

The thought of anyone pig-sticking any other human being, enemy or ally, filled her with disgust and a powerful urge to back her son, to do anything to stop him going to war. She lived for her children. It was all that kept her going and made life worth living. She didn't want him to go. She didn't want him to die.

She turned to Harry. 'I think you're right, Harry. This war will be different and there'll be more than one way to fight it.' Henry looked as though he was about to burst a blood vessel, but she knew he would keep his temper – at least for now. Her expression was as stern as that of her husband. 'If you men stop playing at soldiers, I can refill this cruet set and put some fresh bread on the board.'

Her heart beat like a drum. Already she could see the anger smouldering in Henry's eyes. No doubt she'd pay for it later, but even if it meant a slap or two, she would do all she could to keep her son from being sent away to fight. After snatching up the necessary utensils, she retreated back to the scullery where the two girls were whispering together.

Lizzie eyed her over the top of a saucepan she was wiping. 'Is Dad still angry?'

Mary Anne didn't want to discuss the matter. She gave orders instead. 'Being busy will keep our minds off things. Lizzie, go scrub the pig's head.'

Daw was trembling. 'Ma! I've got something to tell you.'

'What's that then?'

A deep flush rushed over Daw's cheeks. 'It's something to ask you really – seeing as I'm not twenty-one yet.'

Mary Anne had been about to open the outside larder where the dairy products and eggs were kept. She paused, fear clutching her heart. She thought she knew what was coming. She could see the intensity on Daw's face; the fear of what she presently had being wiped out before she could really enjoy it. Hadn't she been there herself over twenty years ago?

'John and I... well... seeing as there's going to be a war and it's pretty sure that he'll be called up... we want... he's asked me—'

Lizzie interrupted. 'For goodness sake, Daw. Don't blush about it. It's perfectly normal.' She turned to her mother. 'They want to get married, Ma. Just in case...'

Mary Anne finished her sentence. '...just in case he doesn't come back.' She knew the words well. She'd known them years ago in the days before Henry, before Edward had gone marching to war. He'd asked, she'd accepted, but her parents hadn't allowed it. 'You're too young. You're both too young.' He hadn't been too young to fight. Off he'd marched and never came back. There was a hole in her heart that had never been filled, even by the young, dashing Henry who'd been flattered, surprised in fact, when she'd agreed to marry him. It was only later he found out the reason why, and had turned on her like an animal caught in a trap.

Mary Anne turned the tap, the water dribbling over the pale meat. 'You're not twenty-one. You'll need your father's permission.'

Daw bit her lip. 'He will say yes, won't he, Ma?'

The sound of arguing still filtered out from the other room. Lizzie put her arm around her sister. Her eyes stayed fixed on her mother. 'Of course he will,' she said, shaking her sister's shoulders as she hugged her. 'Of course he will. Won't he, Ma?'

'You're under twenty-one. There's a form to be signed.'

'Should she ask him now?' pressed Lizzie.

'Oh, no!' Daw looked fit to faint at the prospect.

Mary Anne pushed her hair back from her face and half closed her eyes. 'Get the paperwork. We'll wait for the right moment.'

'Will you sign it, Ma?'

Mary Anne thought of Edward and nodded. 'Yes. I will.' She shrugged. 'Unfortunately, it's not up to me. It's your father that has to sign. You know that.'

Daw exchanged a nervous look with her sister.

'Never mind, Daw,' said Lizzie. 'Go and get yourself ready to meet John. You can borrow that nice new red scarf of mine if you like. I'll help you tie it into a turban once I've helped Ma clear the dishes.'

Once Daw was gone, Lizzie silently piled the last of the dishes on the draining board.

Mary Anne sensed she had something to say.

The silence was pregnant with questions. Mary Anne waited, wondering what was on Lizzie's mind.

'What was it like? The Great War.'

'Extremely bloody.'

'Did Dad enjoy it? It sounds as though he did.'

'Why don't you ask him?'

'Because you're easier to talk to. Besides, I don't want to know about big battles, I'm more interested how it affected people's lives. Nothing was ever the same afterwards, was it?'

Mary Anne shook her head and looked at her daughter with interest. She certainly had hidden depths, and her looks... well, it was almost like looking in a mirror and seeing a reflection of herself twenty years ago. She touched her daughter's face with her wet fingers. 'You look so much like me, or rather how I used to look.'

Lizzie laughed, catching her mother's fingers with her own. 'You said it right first time. You don't look that much older than me. You look more like my sister than my mother.'

Mary Anne laughed and pushed a luxuriant lock of hair back inside her hairnet.

Lizzie cocked her head, sending her own lengthy locks tumbling over her shoulder. 'I saw the baker watching you from his van the other day. You were talking to Mrs Young and he was staring at you.'

'I didn't notice. If I had, I might have slapped his face.'

Dimples appeared at the side of Lizzie's mouth. 'No you wouldn't, and you did notice him. I know you did. I saw you purposely turn your back on him.'

Mary Anne remembered doing exactly that, and for exactly the reason Lizzie had suggested.

'Now why would I do that?'

'He's just a baker, not a knight in shining armour.'

'I think they're all dead.'

'Bakers or knights?' Mary Anne laughed.

Lizzie wiped the draining board down. 'There will be knights in this war, but they won't be wearing shining armour or riding horses. Some will be flying. Some will even be women.'

Mary Anne eyed her daughter warily. Having a son in uniform was something she knew might happen. It hadn't occurred to her that daughters might be called up too. Her fear that her family might disintegrate before her eyes intensified.

Later, once the dishes were put away and the men were smoking, Mary Anne stood alone in the scullery considering the future.

A droplet of condensation fell on her head. She shivered. The scullery was built of wood and glass, no more than a lean-to leading off the kitchen, housing a brown clay sink next to the water pump. Beyond that, and only reached by an outside door, was the washhouse, a place of soapsuds, piles of laundry and locked cupboards.

Scrubbing hard at the pig's head and scraping its bristles off with a knife kept her hands occupied. Narrowing her eyes, the triangle of pink flesh became Adolf Hitler. Her knife zipped faster over the bristled surface. War had come to the world and danger to her children. A cold blue eye stared mockingly up at her, for all the world as cold as the ones she'd seen staring out at her from the newsreels at the picture house.

Firmly gripping the handle of her knife, she stabbed at it. The inner fluid spurted out, a mush made misty by the tears running silently down her cheeks and into her mouth.

8

By teatime the next day, the pig's head was in a saucepan, the snout sticking up through the water, and Mary Anne's tears were under control when Doreen came out. She'd washed and changed ready to meet John. Usually she smelled of tobacco dust. The air in the tobacco factory was like a choking fog and everyone ended up smelling the same, the dust getting into pockets, around collars and even into the turn-ups on men's trousers.

Her eyes were downcast and she kept fiddling with her hair, her ear lobes and the buttons of her high-necked blouse.

'When are you seeing John?' Mary Anne asked in as calm a manner as possible.

'About half past eight. He has to do his stint in the shop first.'

John worked in one of the bonded warehouses where the tobacco was stored and weighed by customs before being delivered to the tobacco factory. His working day didn't stop on arriving home. He was still expected to help out in the corner shop run by his aunt and uncle, who had brought him up since the death of his parents.

'Here,' said Mary Anne, passing her a ten shilling note. 'Go out and enjoy yourselves.'

When Daw's face broke into a smile, her mother thought she

looked beautiful. 'Oh, thanks, Ma.' She had dark eyes and luxurious hair formed into an exuberant cottage-loaf style, which framed her face and rested on the nape of her neck. Her cheeks were pink and her complexion a creamy white. Men tripped over pavements when she walked by, though her daughter rarely noticed. All her life she'd seemed blissfully unaware of the effect she had on people. John was the only man who mattered.

'Are you sure he'll enlist?' asked Mary Anne, but thought she already knew the answer.

'Of course he will. You know what John's like. He would have joined the air force long ago if it hadn't been for his Aunt Maude and Uncle Jim. He gave in then, but now... well... he might not have a choice.'

Daw fiddled with her fingers as she spoke. She and John had been childhood sweethearts. It was only natural that they would get married one day.

Mary Anne threw her arms around her daughter. 'Damn! Damn war and damn men for making war!'

She stepped back, holding her daughter at arm's length and giving her a reassuring smile.

'Don't worry, Daw. This will all blow over and you'll be married with three little 'uns before you know it.'

She felt Daw's shoulders shake and a muffled sob break against her ear.

'I don't like this talk of war. I don't like it at all. It frightens me.'

Mary Anne patted her back as though she were eight not eighteen. 'None of us do, but cheer up. Have a talk with John later. Get yerselves a fish and chip supper. Everything will be all right, you see if it won't.'

She looked up to see Henry staring at her from the doorway, eyeing the ten-shilling note fluttering in Daw's fingers.

'You giving good money away?' He said it breezily for Daw's benefit, as though he were only joking. Mary Anne knew otherwise, but went along with what Daw would view as a joke.

'For her and John to have a fish and chip supper seeing as he's joining up. They have to say their goodbyes.'

'Enjoy yerself, our Daw,' he said, adopting the benevolent expression of the doting father, not once betraying the other man reserved for his wife alone.

Once Daw was gone his attitude changed. He pointed an accusing finger and raised his voice. 'That money's for house-keeping and from my wages. I'll have words with you about that.'

She knew what he meant. Inside, she trembled. Outside, she remained calm. He never showed his brutish side in front of the children. He saved that for her.

Turning his back, he left her there and for once the anticipation of what he would do later faded away and somewhat surprised her. After considering this new response, she counselled that England was sticking up for itself, and perhaps it was time she did so too.

Back in the kitchen, the atmosphere was damp and steamy, warm though a little more subdued than normal.

'Come on,' she said, with a wave of her wooden spoon. 'I'll have no glum faces around this table. Hitler ain't invited to dinner. He can get his own!'

'Wouldn't dare,' muttered Harry, disappearing behind another newspaper and another crossword.

His father still glared at him, disdain flaring his nostrils and like flints in his eyes.

Lizzie was attempting to open a drawer of the painted green dresser which stood, packed with crockery, against one wall. It was scuffed and scraped and painted pale green. Its handles were brass and its drawers and doors sagged slightly. It was stuck.

Lizzie was exasperated. 'It won't open.'

Mary Anne elbowed her aside. 'Let me.' She tugged.

Begrudgingly, it opened. Lizzie put the cutlery away.

'Better tell our Stanley that there's suet pudding and custard left.'

'I'll go.'

'No. I'd better. I asked him earlier and he said no, but his stomach might be feeling emptier now.'

'Has he been out again?'

Mary Anne sighed. 'Yes, the little devil. He's tired himself out.' She frowned. 'I wish he wouldn't. He's too sick. He doesn't seem to realise...'

'Mum, he seems so much better,' said Lizzie. 'He's not really so sick.'

Mary Anne was indignant. 'Yes he is! I'm his mother. I know him better than you do.'

Her snappy response made Lizzie jump. 'What's up with her?' asked Harry.

'She's only got one child left and she's making the most of it.'

Mary Anne went along the passageway and into the front room where a bed had been put up when Stanley had first became ill. So far, Mary Anne had resisted all attempts to put the bed back upstairs behind the curtain dividing the boys' sleeping area from the girls'.

'Hello, Stanley,' she said brightly as she peered round the door.

Stanley did not reply. He lay very still, his big blue eyes sunken and ringed with dark circles. His fair hair stuck out from his head in delicate sweaty pikes, framing his face like a fragile halo against the white pillow.

He was far better than he had been, but not so strong as they'd like. Her heart lurched in her chest. It always did on every occasion she entered the room, half expecting the inevitable, which was why she rarely sent her other children to see if he was all right – in case he was not, in case he was no longer breathing, though the doctor had stated that the worse was over. A tremendous relief flowed over her body as his eyes flickered open.

'I was tired,' he said.

'Do you want something to eat?' she asked, her smile truly reflecting a sudden surge of joy. She licked her lips hoping that her action might whet his appetite. 'I've made spotted dick and custard.'

For a moment he said nothing, his eyes regarding her impassively, almost as though he had not heard or was not sure whether she was real or if he was dreaming.

Sitting on the bed, stroking his hair away from his face, she fought to control her expression. His skin was clammy.

Mary Anne's smile became fixed. 'You've been out running about with those boys. Our Lizzie told me. You'll tire yourself out.'

He stared at her almost accusingly. Was he angry with her for not allowing him out? He'd come home sweating and worn out on the day Lizzie had seen him at the butcher's.

She began plumping up his pillows and tucking in his bedclothes.

'You know I only want the best for you, Stanley. I want you to get better and stay better. You do know that, don't you?'

Her cheeks grew hot in response to his steady gaze and the strange look in his eyes. Deep down she knew why; no other member of the family had ever witnessed the violent Henry. No other member of the family had ever given their father anything but respect. She pushed the truth away, just as she'd always done, and adopted her 'all is well' smile.

'So what about some pudding?'

He shook his head. 'No.'

'Perhaps later. I'll come in again.'

He said nothing, but she felt almost naked in the intensity of his gaze. He knew the truth that she did not want to admit to. She couldn't talk about it, not with him, not with anyone.

'Your cough's better,' she said brightly.

'Yes.'

'Are you sure you're not hungry?'

'I'm sure.'

'Never mind. You rest for now and I'll tell you a story.' She told him one of the stories she had made up just for him: tales to cheer him up and take him far away to a land where there was no illness, no pain, a land she said was like paradise.

'Who lives in Paradise?' he asked when she'd finished the story.

'Fairies, elves, kind people, magic people, Jesus and God and all the angels.'

'Dad won't be there, will he, because he'll be going to hell,' he said, his voice heavy with feeling.

Mary Anne swallowed the well of emotion that rose up inside her.

Again she avoided the real issue, putting his comment down to tiredness.

'Are you sure you don't want anything?' she asked again once she'd regained her self-control. 'Spotted dick is your favourite.'

He shook his head, his fearsomely bright blue eyes following her to the door.

'I'll see you later, Stanley,' she promised, giving him a little wave as she left the room.

'Does our Stanley want anything?' Lizzie asked on her mother's return.

'No, but I said I'd ask again later before I go to bed.'

Mary Anne paused for a moment before plunging the bread knife into the steaming pudding now unwrapped before them in all its glory.

At first she didn't notice that the atmosphere in the kitchen had changed. Pen in hand, Harry stayed behind his newspaper.

Lizzie's eyes were flitting to everyone in turn. Mary Anne noticed her trying to catch her eye, jerking her chin towards where their father sat, his jaw clenched firm enough to break. He was glaring at Harry, who stayed behind the newspaper.

Mary Anne sucked in her breath. She knew her husband well as all women do after a long marriage. He sat rigidly as he ate, his mouth chomping and chewing at the food; oh, how that sound filled her with revulsion. She hated that sound. Hated the man who made it and wished he wasn't sitting at her table. Once his belly was full, the dam would break. The sound of eating would give way to anger.

The pig's head rumbled around in the boiling water. Steam turned to water and hissed as it dropped on the gas ring.

Cutlery clattered onto an empty plate. The voice of Henry Randall also rumbled, like a dark cloud about to burst with thunder.

'I'll have no son of mine called a coward – me, who fought the Boche in Picardy. How will I ever hold up my head.' He wagged a yellow finger, stained by years and years of smoking. 'Never mind all this gallivanting half the night. You'll join up, mark my words if you don't!'

War, screamed the headlines on the front page of the newspaper. The word itself quivered and the paper rustled before Harry came out from behind it, making a clicking noise by running the top of his pen along his teeth.

'I will not.'

'I insist.'

Harry held his father's gaze as he shook his head. They were so alike, thought his mother, but she loved one so much more than the other. She loved all her children.

'No. I will not.'

Slowly, stiffly, Henry Randall got to his feet, his knuckles resting on the table.

'I'm warning you, my boy. You'll present yourself for duty, or you're out of this house!'

'Then I'll be out of here,' said the younger man without raising his voice, without any sign of aggression at all.

Henry Randall clenched his fist, kicked his chair behind him and moved towards his son. Harry did the same, but with mockery rather than anger in his eyes.

Mary Anne reacted instantly and ferociously, standing in between them, the top of her head barely reaching their shoulders.

'There'll be no more talk of war,' she proclaimed, the bread knife pointing at husband and son in turn.

Both men stayed glaring at each other, one angrily, the other smirking his contempt.

Mary Anne raised her eyes to heaven and said in a voice soaked with emotion, 'Can we at least have some peace until tomorrow?'

The two men bristled then sat down. Mary Anne sighed with relief.

Eyeing both of them with a mix of misgiving and anger, she put a second helping of spotted dick and custard before each of them. Food led to contentment, and hopefully, peace.

Lizzie, her expression fearful, made an announcement that she trusted to change the subject. 'Patrick Kelly is joining up tomorrow.'

Retrieving his chair, her father sat down and dug his spoon into his pudding. 'Is he now. Well there's a brave lad. Imagine! He could end up in Belgium, or even France. I'd be proud to call him son if he were mine.'

'Well, he'd better not be your son,' warned Mary Anne, her fixed stare conveying her hidden meaning.

Lizzie's intake of breath captured Harry's attention. Both looked surprised, as though they didn't expect their mother to know anything of Molly Kelly's reputation.

Henry Randall took a moment to understand her meaning. Once he did, he bowed his head. 'Don't be so daft, woman.'

Head bowed and using his spoon like a spade, Henry shovelled spoonful after spoonful into his mouth.

Lizzie and Harry exchanged knowing looks. Patrick's mother was a slut. Everyone knew it, and some men just couldn't resist.

Mary Anne looked in the mirror above the sink, smoothing her hair away from her face and feeling faintly surprised, even quite satisfied, that she looked as good as she did. What did the likes of Molly Kelly have compared to her? Certainly not looks, but then, what did she care? The world had turned darker. Worrying about her children outweighed any worry about her husband's fidelity.

Harry left his pudding and headed for the back door. 'I'm off out back for a smoke, and then I'm going out.'

Mary Anne followed her son out into the backyard where vegetables pushed bravely up through the dark soil. A host of gladioli, bright orange and red, stood in regal battalions against the end wall, clinging on despite the descent into late autumn. An alley ran between the end wall and the soap factory. At this time of night, the gate was bolted. Mary Anne never allowed her family to use it. They were ordered to go round the front. Only her customers used the back, willing to pick their way through the puddles and chance meeting a rat running from the holes in the bottom of the factory wall.

The tip of Harry's cigarette glowed red in the darkness. He was staring up at the sky.

Mary Anne rubbed her hands together before wrapping her arms around herself. The night was turning chilly.

'You mustn't take too much notice of your father. He's upset that he can't go himself.'

'It don't make no difference, Ma. I ain't going,' he said, flicking his cigarette into the cabbage patch.

'But you're not afraid.' She said it as a statement, not a question, patting his arm affectionately as she admired the firm contours of his face.

He thought about it before replying, his gaze still fixed on the stars.

'Look at them stars,' he said and pointed to the brightest in the sky. 'How many lives have them stars seen slaughtered in pursuit of a cause? How many blokes have been told that they're fighting for freedom, their country or whatever, and that God was on their side? Well, God can't be on everyone's side, can He, and some of those wars that were fought now seem bloody stupid; pointless in fact. So, Ma, I'll bide me time. I won't rush into the recruitment office on the spur of the moment. Besides, like I say, there's more than one way to fight a war. I'll think about it, and if in the meantime I get called up, then that's a different matter, but until then...'

'Here,' she said, her hand closing over his in order to hide the pound note she was slipping into his palm. 'Spend it on yerself. Have a pint or two with the boys.'

He looked at the money in his palm. 'That's more than a few pints, Ma.'

'Then take a nice girl dancing.'

He grinned. 'I don't know any *nice* girls.'

Mary Anne laughed with him. 'You cheeky bugger.' Her mood turned more serious. 'I don't care how you spend it. Just enjoy yourself.'

'One day I'll pay you back for all you've given me, Ma. I've got prospects. You know that, don't you?'

'Of course I do. I know that one day you'll make me very proud, but you don't need to pay me back every ten shillings I've ever given you.'

'But I will. In fact, I'll pay you back a hundredfold. I promise. I'll make sure you're taken care of, Ma. You see if I don't.'

Mary Anne laughed. 'Ooow, I could get expensive if I really tried. You'd have to be really rich.'

The side of Harry's mouth lifted in that wicked way of his. 'I will be rich some day, Ma. You wait and see if I ain't.'

'I believe you.'

They stood holding hands and looking into each other's eyes. Love flowed between them and needed no words, but a look came to Harry's eyes, as though he'd come to an agreement with himself, perhaps as a man heading for the confessional.

'There's something else I've got to tell you.' His thumbs massaged her knuckles and the look in his eyes made her feel nervous. 'It's something that I can't tell anyone else, something that's become something of a burden. I need to share it with someone. I need someone to understand.'

She frowned. 'If you want me to understand, you have to tell me what it is.'

A host of worries ran through her mind. What disease was he suffering from? Was he going to die? Or could it be something not life threatening at all, in fact quite commonplace if the truth was known.

'Have you got a girl pregnant? I wouldn't force you into marrying her, not if you don't love her. I wouldn't do that, Harry. It can cause more problems than it solves.'

Shaking his head, his mouth lifted in that half-smile she loved so much. 'No. That isn't it. You're the only girl in my life, Ma. You always will be.'

Laughingly, she punched her fist against his broad chest. 'You big softie!'

He sort of laughed with her, but half seriously, as though she'd almost hit on the truth.

'Just as long as you remember how important you are no matter what I do and where I go. I'm going to get myself my own place, Ma, a little flat somewhere along Coronation Road. I've also a mind to go into business for myself. Those with a way of turning a pound could make a fortune if they put their minds to it, and that's what I intend to do. But I don't want you to be upset when I leave. Is that clear?'

She hid her true feelings, smiling broadly, though her eyes were misty, relieved that he hadn't put into words what she'd thought he was going to say. Deep down the fear of no longer being wanted, which had come into existence on the day her eldest had started work, began to grow, faster now because soon they would all be gone.

'What else?' she asked, sensing he'd been about to tell her of this burden he was carrying.

He shrugged his broad shoulders. 'Nothing much. Nothing that can't wait.'

She sensed there was more, but didn't press him, leaving him to tell her in his own good time.

He kissed her on the cheek before going back inside to get ready to go out. Later in the evening, Mary Anne watched him saunter off down the street, whistling nonchalantly, his hands tucked into the pockets of his raincoat.

She smiled. She imagined the girls being drawn to him like a moth to a flame. How could they resist? He was her son.

* * *

It started raining around eleven that night when Henry pushed her into their bedroom. The curtains remained open, the street light two doors down lending enough light to see each other by.

The walls were thin. His voice was low.

'Give my money away, would you? Well, don't ask me for any more housekeeping this week. If there ain't enough food in the 'ouse, it's you that's to go without, not me. Get that?'

She didn't answer. She wouldn't tell him that the money was nothing to do with the meagre housekeeping he gave her, but earned from her business, her dearly beloved business that compensated in a very small way for the rest of her life. The money it earned was for her children, not for him and the landlords of the Red Cow, the White Lion, and the Admiral Nelson.

Henry was crafty. She'd found that out years ago. He enjoyed his children's respect. He wouldn't want them to know how he really was. His voice would remain low. Only Mary Anne would hear his threats. Only she would feel any pain.

Once they were in bed, he took her savagely, thrusting into her as though his penis was a knife and he was stabbing at her very soul, trying to kill the part of her she kept from him. She gritted her teeth, not daring to cry out, but praying for him to fall asleep. At last, he pushed her away from beneath him as though his need and her availability were disgusting. Within minutes of rolling onto his side, his back to her, he began to snore.

The clock in the tower of St John's struck midnight and a full moon threw shadows through the small washhouse window.

After making sure she was alone, Mary Anne retrieved the brown bottle and gulped down what she considered a suitable amount. The seriousness of her predicament, the shame it would attract, caused her to pause and consider whether she'd taken enough. She thought of the forthcoming war and all the lives likely to be lost. The world was becoming crueller. That's what she told herself before taking a second gulp, closing the cap, and putting it back in the cupboard.

'Please God,' she whispered, 'let it work.'

9

The air inside the Ship on Redcliffe Hill was thick enough to cut with a knife. Bodies were packed tightly against each other all the way to the bar, and those seated leaned over tables in the squash of people trying to pass by and also to hear their companions' conversation.

Harry leaned on the bar next to the flap that opened to allow the landlord and other staff in and out to collect glasses. The brim of his hat threw a shadow over his features, and his collar stood up around his ears. He looked too poised and well turned out to be a tobacco worker and knew it.

'Got a light?'

Harry automatically offered the end of his own cigarette. His eyes slid sidelong, casing the room, searching the crowd for anyone who didn't fit in.

'How many do you want?'

Charlie Knowles, a thief and a fence and well known in the area, kept his voice low and spoke out of the side of his mouth. 'How many have you got?' he asked, his hand cupped around the burning glow of Harry's cigarette.

'Two hundred.'

'Packets of ten?'

'Of course.'

'What you asking?'

'Sixpence a packet.'

Charlie made a tutting sound. 'That's a bit pricey, ain't it? You ought to be hung.'

'There's a war on. Think how much you're likely to make once the rationing starts. Tobacco comes from America and suchlike, remember?'

After delving into his inside pocket, a crisp fiver was handed over, peeled from a wedge that looked to be at least an inch thick. Harry took it and tucked it inside the grey suit jacket he wore beneath his raincoat.

'Better do the deed outside,' said Charlie. 'Too many tea leaves in 'ere.'

Harry grinned at the comment. Wasn't Charlie one himself? He followed him outside, glad to escape the stink of bodies, booze, cigarettes and cheap face powder.

The lane at the side of the pub led around the back of the building and into an area where empty bottles clinked together in wooden crates.

A woman of robust proportions, her head wreathed in cigarette smoke, stepped out from the shadows.

Harry winced at the sight of her. She might have been reasonably good-looking at one time, but at some point she'd fallen foul of someone with a very bad temper and a knife with a serrated blade, judging by the cuts on her face.

Harry wondered at the shadowy world she inhabited, a world he was entering at his own volition because he wanted the good things in life, and also because using his mind to combat danger excited him.

'Gladys will take them,' said Charlie.

The named woman grinned, revealing a gap in her teeth that did nothing to complement her features. Her hair was greasy and clung in thin tendrils around her face. She had big breasts, but from there down her body seemed to fall away, making her seem cone-shaped, not normal womanly at all.

Harry began unloading the cigarettes from his person and into a pouch Gladys had sewn into her skirt.

Harry congratulated himself. It was so easy: an oversize raincoat lined with pockets could take as many as two hundred and fifty packets of Woodbines. Charging sixpence for ten brought in five pounds. Wills, the tobacco giant he worked for, wouldn't notice a few packets going amiss. After all, he thought to himself, they could afford it.

'You know where to take them,' Charlie said to Gladys once the transfer was done.

She nodded. 'All right, Charlie.'

Looking as though she were pregnant with twins rather than with two hundred packets of Woodbines, she trundled off, her body tilted backwards, her belly thrust forwards.

Charlie stubbed out his cigarette, grinding it into the dirt. 'Fancy a pint?'

'You buying?'

Charlie clenched his chin and gave Harry a warning look. 'You're a cocky little sod, Harry. Could get you in trouble one day.'

Harry smiled. 'No offence intended, Mr Knowles.'

It didn't do to push the likes of Charlie Knowles, a right bad, mad case if ever there was one.

It took a split second for his face to change. His smile was as crooked as his reputation. 'None taken. And call me Charlie. You strikes me as a bright boy, Harry Randall.'

'I try to be.'

Once back at the bar, two pints of bitter in front of them, their conversation turned naturally enough to the war.

Charlie was squinting. Anyone who knew him well, including his family, knew he was doing some serious thinking if he was squinting.

He addressed Harry. 'You remember I said a bloke with a bit of savvy about him could make a few bob from this war?'

Harry nodded. 'Just a few bob? I was hoping to make a few quid, and I don't mean just from cigarettes.'

Charlie shook his head and waved one hand as though dismissing

Harry from his vicinity. 'You're a greedy little bastard, Harry, and you ain't thinking straight. You're only just starting out on your chosen career, and I ain't referring to making the bloody stuff you sell. But you still got a lot to learn, and everybody got to do an apprenticeship, don't they?'

'I'm in a hurry.'

'Not when you're working for me you ain't. I like things done properly so I believes in training my people to do a good job.'

'So what would I be training for?'

'Everything I know. Ain't got no son of me own and I'm gettin' on. I fancies passing on me knowledge, though I have to say, I ain't quite sure what we're going to be dealin' in, though I think food at first. This rationing they're on about ain't gonna be well received. So I'm sorting out some contacts in the food line. Then there's all these foreigners coming in from abroad. Not all of 'em are kosher if you know what I mean and them that ain't are going to be without passports and other important paperwork. And petrol! That's another thing going to be rationed. So what do you want to do? Are you in, or out?'

Harry locked eyes with a face in the crowd. The eyes were blue, the nose straight above a Cupid's bow of a mouth.

He dragged his attention back to Charlie. His mind was agile enough to deal with two trains of thought at once. *You should have been a ballet dancer*, his mother had said. This had been on the basis that a dancer counts beats while whirling across a dance floor.

'It sounds interesting. Do you think it will pay well?'

Charlie smiled. 'Once it really gets going, we could make a real packet. Do you want to shake on it?'

Harry shook his head. 'No. Anyone watching will guess we're doing a bit of business, and the Ship's got a bit of a reputation.'

Charlie opened his eyes wide, pulled his hat more tightly down on his head and looked around him. 'Yeah,' he said. 'So I hear.'

'By the way,' said Harry as Charlie prepared to leave, 'what happened to Gladys's face?'

Charlie turned up his coat collar and tightened his belt. 'Didn't do 'er training right. Made a stupid mistake and paid the price.'

Harry didn't ask who'd cut her face; he could guess. Lingering over his beer once Charlie was gone, he searched the bar for the blue eyes and Cupid's bow lips. Just as he'd anticipated, the face he'd seen in the crowd made his way over.

Slowly and without saying a word, they looked each other up and down.

Harry introduced himself. 'Harry.'

The pink lips smiled. 'I'm Mark. Pleased to meet you.'

10

Michael washed the pawnshop windows with warm water and a soft chamois, scrubbed the handsome black and white tiles of the porch and polished the brass door handle. Once the shutters were put away, he criss-crossed the windows with tape as advised by the War Department.

After that he stood back and surveyed what he'd done. He was particularly proud of the tiles; they shone, a handsome welcome to potential customers, but something else. They also reminded him of the hallway of the house he'd grown up in, filling him with a nostalgic longing to turn back the years, to make things better than they had been.

To feel such affection for a few old tiles, he thought. He shook his head and smiled at his foolishness.

A group of boys, no more than ten years old by the look of them, came running past kicking a tin can.

They were noisy, shouting, laughing and diving around all over the pavement. In the throes of tackling for the tin can, they danced into the doorway and over the black and white tiles leaving dirty footprints in the residual wetness.

Preoccupied with his personal thoughts, Michael spun round on them too quickly, too angrily.

'*Verboten!* Get out of there!'

At first he didn't understand why their jaws dropped and their eyes widened in surprise, until he realised that, in his haste, he had shouted at them in German!

An icy shiver trickled down his spine. He'd warned himself to think in English so he would automatically speak in English, just as he'd done before his mother had married the pastor. The thought of what might happen could upset all his plans. He'd be interrogated, most likely flung into prison or incarcerated in one of the detention centres for enemy aliens he'd heard about.

Inside he cringed, but common sense kicked in and he attempted to make amends.

'I did not mean to shout,' he said, attempting to smile and taking a step towards them.

The boys eyed him warily. There were three of them and definitely not from the best side of town. Their hair was stiff with the dried remnants of carbolic soap. Their sleeveless pullovers of multicoloured Fair Isle were baggy around the bottom from constant washing and the armholes sagged as though the garment had originally been knitted for someone bigger.

One of the boys, the eldest if his size was anything to go by, leaned across to one of his friends, whispering in his ear.

A kind of enlightenment appeared on their faces coupled with a mischievous gleam in their eyes.

'Gerry!' shouted the biggest, half turning to make good his escape.

'Gerry! Gerry! Gerry!' shouted the others, all in unison now, yelling their loudest at the same time as running backwards away from him.

'I am Dutch,' he called to them, but doubted they heard, or even if they had done, if they would understand. A foreigner was a foreigner and likely to arouse suspicion in the present climate, no matter what.

The boys ran off towards the main road.

Michael eyed the windows of the houses opposite with guarded apprehension, searching for the tell-tale sign of a twitching curtain. He knew they watched, but wondered if they had heard. Perhaps not. The day was cold and all sensible people were keeping their windows closed.

It helped calm his nerves to do more scrubbing and cleaning: sweeping the shop floor, polishing the trembling glass of the display cabinets where gold rings and watches jostled for space alongside silver cruet sets and glass paperweights.

At last he was satisfied, so satisfied that his slip of the tongue and the catcalls of the street kids were, at least, partially forgotten.

Everything in the shop was ready for business, which turned out to be slow in coming.

He didn't know why he had expected people to come trooping in with their valuables once they saw the shutters were off and someone new was in residence. He'd even accepted that some would come in just for a glimpse of the new owner; they'd obviously seen him working. But the strange thing was *no one* came in to do business; *everyone* came in to stare.

As it was a Wednesday, he'd done the same as he'd seen the other shops in the rank do and closed at one o'clock. He'd noticed they never opened on a Wednesday afternoon and resolved to do the same. After all, he wanted to fit in so must do as everyone else.

Two women came in around midday, supposedly to survey what was on offer. He could see from the moment they entered that *he* was the object of their curiosity.

'Can I help you with anything, ladies?' he asked, the deep timbre of his melodious voice causing one of the women to raise her hand to her breast as befitted a maiden rather than a maiden aunt.

'Thank you! But we're just looking.' She sounded breathless, even a little excited, and the way she looked him up and down was really quite shameless.

Her friend, a wide woman with the jowls of a bloodhound, was not so taken aback. Her eyes were like black beetles burrowing into his soul.

'We have to see if we can trade here. There's a lot of foreigners about and a war on. Who knows who's who and what's what? It don't hurt to be careful.'

'Yes,' he said, and dropped his gaze. For a moment he was back there – the place where it was all happening.

'You don't sound from round here. Foreign are you?' asked the first woman.

'I was born here.'

'Don't sound like it.'

'I've lived abroad for a while.'

Beetle Eyes asked, 'So where are you from?'

The strident enquiry had been answered a dozen times already that morning. He gave the same answer.

'I was born here but have recently lived in Holland. My parents live in Holland. My father is a minister of the church.' It was a lie, but a convenient one. His father was his step-father and was a minister. Michael had despised him for it. The country was Germany not Holland. Lying gets easier and easier the more you did of it, and Michael had done a lot – a terrible amount.

The sour-faced woman tossed her head in an exaggerated nod. He'd won her approval.

'How much for this salt shaker?'

Michael took it out from the cabinet. The shaker was an electro-plated imitation of an eighteenth-century silver original. Anyone with taste would not have bought it. He sold it to her for two shillings and sixpence. He didn't know whether it was a fair price, it was just the first figure to come into his head.

They left shortly after. Michael stared at the open door. They were long gone by the time he closed it. He told himself there would be busier days once he made sure they believed he was from Holland. Tomorrow would be better.

That night he made himself a meal and listened to the fine strains coming from the wind-up gramophone. He had chosen Schubert – something soft and gentle to ease his troubled soul. By the end of the week, the little cash drawer behind the counter held only a little silver and about two pounds' worth of copper coins.

A typical customer was a man who called in wanting to retrieve a set of silver spoons given to him as a wedding present by his mother.

'What with this war going on, she's coming to live with us. Frightened to death she is. Couldn't tell her I put her spoons in hock because a greyhound that should have won stayed at the back of the pack.'

It wasn't much money, but better than nothing. Michael looked at it in the palm of his hand and mused about why he wasn't making more.

'Make the most of it,' said the man. 'Go out and have a few drinks before you gets called up.'

'I am not quite physically fit.'

The man looked him up and down. 'You seems healthy enough. Takes one hell of an injury not to present as A1.'

'Looks are deceiving.'

Looks are deceiving. He'd learned that phrase back in Germany and well knew its worth. Looks, indeed, were deceiving. So also were actions.

A woman came in later. She was looking for a wristwatch as a going away present for her husband.

'One he can count the minutes on until he gets back,' she said, her eyes misted, her head drooping like a damp flower. 'I tried the other pawnbroker in Kent Street, but she didn't have anything.'

Michael frowned. When the shop was shut he'd taken the opportunity to get to know the area better, walking around and around, noting shops, houses, bus stops and likely competition. He did not recollect seeing a pawnshop.

'I did not see any shops in Kent Street.'

'Oh. There's not. It's just a woman. She runs a bit of a business from the back of her house. Nothing much, mind you, just little things for the neighbours.'

She bought a watch. Fifteen shillings – his biggest transaction so far, but it wouldn't be enough for what he had in mind. He needed more customers, he thought, gritting his teeth as the truth suddenly dawned. There was competition: unfair, illegal competition. He slammed the door shut behind the woman who'd bought the watch.

* * *

Another Wednesday: after shutting up shop at one o'clock, he put on his good suit and made for Kent Street, a cul-de-sac not too far away. The terraced houses looked flat and bland, the surface of the pavements shining bright and brittle in the autumn sunlight.

A communal shelter was being erected at the end of the street. There was a shop on one corner, an ARP station being erected on the other. The sight of shelters and suchlike filled him with despair. Already, before hardly a shot had been fired between Britain and Germany, the war was taking over people's lives.

Nobody paid any attention to the tall man whose careworn expression belied his years. They too would look older if they'd gone through what he had, but they wouldn't know and he wouldn't tell them. Secrets, trials and tribulations were not meant for sharing.

It was two o'clock. Women standing at doorways watched what was going on, exchanging comments with their neighbours. Some jiggled babies on their hips. Being careful not to betray his accent, pronouncing every word with care, he asked one of them where he could find the pawnbroker.

A woman stopped wiping the snot from her baby's nose and eyed him suspiciously, as though considering whether she could trust him with such important information. She made up her mind that she could. 'Number ten, but you'll have to go round the back. She doesn't do business at the front. There's an alley...' She pointed. 'That way.'

Stepping over piles of sandbags and skirting pools of newly poured cement, he made his way through an archway running beneath and between the end houses. The alley was narrow and made narrower by yellow flowering weeds and nettles and hummed with the sound of machinery from a soap factory whose wall ran along the back of the lane.

On the other side, chicken coops, garden sheds and ramshackle greenhouses crowded the long narrow gardens, the homemade greenhouses only big enough to hold a tribe of tomatoes and a few boxes of seedlings.

The houses were not numbered at the rear, so he relied on memory to count each house from the archway and thus reach the right one. His hand closed over a green iron gate. A narrow path wound between a fence and a line of washing. There was no shed or greenhouse, just an upright oblong of bricks that he guessed was a lavatory.

He made his way up the path, dodging the billowing sheets as he went. The building described to him was no more than a shed tacked on to the back of a Victorian terraced house. The door was closed. He tried the handle. It was locked so he went to the back door of the main house and knocked at the door with his bare fist.

As he waited he eyed the level garden, the rows of peas, cabbages and beans – some little more than seedlings, some coming near the end of their time. That was when he saw her. She was leaning on a spade above a row of potatoes watching him, her hair tossed by the breeze, like a fiery halo around her face. He realised that the billowing sheets had prevented him from seeing her.

Her puzzled expression lessened as she straightened and brushed unseen dirt from her palms. He judged her to be older than him, but not plump like most women of a certain age. She was rangy and gave the impression that she could move quickly if she needed to. In some other time or place she might have been an athlete. She had that look about her.

Tucking a strand of honey-coloured hair behind her ear and using her spade like a walking stick, she approached him.

'Are you a friend of my husband?'

'No. If you are the pawnbroker, I think I am looking for you.'

A flash of suspicion passed over her face at the sound of his voice. He warned himself not to let his anger affect his pronunciation.

She frowned. 'Do I know you?'

'No. But you knew my uncle.'

She frowned and shook her head. 'I'm sorry...'

'I have come to take over my uncle's pawnshop.'

'Oh!' She sounded like a girl surprised by her sweetheart. She *was* girlish. Despite himself and the reason for his visit, he found himself admiring her. She had strength and purpose, characteristics he'd always appreciated.

The suspicious look was replaced by a warm smile, which lit up her face and made her eyes sparkle. He squirmed beneath its intensity. He'd prefer her to eye him suspiciously; mutual distrust made betrayal or aggression so much easier.

'I'm sorry. How do you do?'

She held out her hand. He took it and clicked his heels. She looked at him askance.

He immediately realised his mistake. His mind worked quickly in order to allay her suspicions. He repeated his action, but this time also kissed her fingers.

'My father had relatives in the army,' he lied. 'This is what they used to do in more elegant times. I fear clicking heels are now associated with Germany alone, though the kissing of hands is not.'

The lie was plausible enough, at least it seemed so by the look on her face, though the puzzlement returned.

'Was there something in particular...?'

Michael was consternated. The sudden familiarity had caused him to remember that he had to tread carefully. The heat of his anger was less now. He could deal with her coldly, though as politely as necessary. He was a stranger in this country and an outcast in his own.

'Your husband – he provides for you?'

That frown again. 'Yes.'

'So why do you take my business from me? Do you realise the damage you are doing? You must not do this any more. If you do then I will report you to the authorities.'

Now it was she who was angry. Pleasant creases appeared around her eyes, intensifying their blueness. 'You will do what?' Mary Anne had been surprised when the stranger appeared, though he looked pleasant and she even thought back to Lizzie's talk of knights in shining armour. Her curiosity had turned to anger the moment he threatened her little sideline. He could not possibly comprehend how important the business was to her, so was totally unprepared for her swift response.

The spade made a whooshing sound as she swung it over one shoulder.

'Get out! Get out now!'

Earth crumbled and fell as she made a cursory sweep of the spade.

Michael backed off down the path, the sheets mockingly wrapping around him as sheets do, as they had done once before when he had seen his destiny – or thought he had.

* * *

'Not so noisy. Your father is writing a sermon,' his mother had warned. He'd been thirteen years old and sitting next to the garden fence, blowing his trumpet. His mother had been hanging out the washing on a clear, bright day. The sheets billowed – like clouds cut from paper – brilliant white against the crisp colours of late spring. He'd not exactly noted the crispness of the day back then. It only came back to him now. What had mattered was that his friends were about to march by. They all belonged to the Scouts. Michael's mouth had watered at the sight of their parcel-coloured uniforms, the braid, the badges sewn like military medals over proud pubescent chests. Oh, how he'd longed to march with them. Oh, how he'd begged to join, to be a member, to be as they were, all boys doing the same things.

Pastor Heinz Deller had made it clear that he did not approve of uniforms. His voice had boomed down from his great height onto Michael's head, just as it did from the pulpit and onto the heads of the congregation.

'Thou shalt not kill.'

'But it's only the Scouts.'

'They wear a uniform. Uniforms make a mob of mere men.' He'd asked to join many times. He'd been refused many times. It had rankled, stewed like an old broth over a dying fire. The troop containing so many of his friends had marched on. He'd followed the sight of their heads bobbing, their arms swinging until they'd disappeared and he was alone; without friends, with only his mother and the man she had married.

His mother had attempted to placate him. 'Your father is a pastor. He has a lot to live up to.'

Michael had been defiant. 'He is not my father.'

She had gripped his shoulders and shook him until he felt his eyes would fall out. 'You must never say that. It is better for you – for both of us – that you recognise him as being your natural father. Do you understand?'

He didn't understand because it had never been explained to him. He didn't find out the truth – or what he thought was the truth – until later, much later.

In the meantime, on that bright spring day, he had blown his trumpet as his friends marched by. One of them, Carl, was the group's bugler and blew his in response.

Pastor Deller came out of the house in a temper. 'Can I get no peace around here?'

The trumpet was confiscated and Michael's feeling of isolation intensified. The pastor did not like him mixing with militaristic types and that included the seemingly inoffensive Scout movement. His mother had supported her husband even when Michael implored to be allowed to do the things his peers did. As his isolation intensified, so did his resentment. Sometimes it boiled over.

'One day I will do exactly as I please,' he'd shouted. 'Then you'll be sorry.'

How he wished he could turn the clock back.

11

Mary Anne looked down at the street from her bedroom window to a world of grey wetness. Slate tiles dripped rain into gurgling gutters and on the other side of the road the milkman's horse shook excess moisture from his mane.

Henry stirred in the nest-like warmth of the bed. He wasn't due to get up for another hour and held the bedclothes tightly to his head; a barrier between what he had to do and his preference for doing nothing.

'It's raining,' she said.

'Get back to bed, woman,' he grumbled, diving deeper beneath the blankets.

She stared at the spot where she'd lain beside him. The greyness seeping in at the window made the sheets look grubby. She consoled herself they'd look better as the day brightened, but she might wash them anyway. Last night ached in her belly.

'I can't sleep.'

The milk cart moved off, the wet road softening the thud of the horse's hooves. The milkman saw her and waved.

Mary Anne waved back and watched until the cart disappeared

behind the corner shop at the end of the street just as the lights in the broad window flooded the road with light.

The shop bell jangled preceding the emergence of John and his uncle armed with newspaper billboards, tin buckets, baths and brooms.

Thoughtfully, she patted her stomach, wishing the brown liquid would do its work before the day was out. Her belly was barely lifting her apron, but her breasts were swelling against her blouse buttons.

She tried to imagine what Henry would say if she lost the baby and didn't tell him. He'll kill me, she thought. He'd want to know my reasons and jump to an untrue conclusion. The unwanted pregnancy was not the only thing on her mind.

She thought about the foreigner, nephew of Uncle Bob, and swallowed hard. What if he were to report her to the authorities? Could they do anything? Worse still, what if he came to the house when Henry was home? What would Henry do?

Tight-lipped, her gaze fell on the iron-grey streaks in the dark hair sprouting above the bedclothes. To her mind it blemished the whiteness of the pillow. She was proud of her linen, confident that her washing was the whitest in the street. Vigorous scrubbing, hot water, a nub of blue and a handful of soda made her hands red, but at least the end results were something to be proud of, just like the business she ran from her laundry room, about which her husband knew nothing.

'I think I'll make a start on the washing.'

He didn't respond, but then she hadn't expected him to.

The washhouse was chilly at first but warmed up once the copper was boiling. Mary Anne skimmed the scum from the surface of the hot water and pushed the laundry down into the bubbles with her boiler stick. The steam clung to the walls. The smoke from the fire escaped through the small stack at the end of the lean-to. To those of her neighbours in need of a loan, it was a signal that she was open for business. The best time was always before Henry was up or once he and the rest of the family had left the house.

Satisfied that the hard yellow block of Sunlight soap had softened enough, she attacked a sheet laid over the draining board, and followed it up with the scrubbing brush. Her stomach ached, the muscles knotting and cramping and giving her hope. Suds seeped between her fingers; hopefully something similar would happen between her legs, blood, not water.

Absorbed in the task, she didn't at first realise that she was no longer alone.

'Mrs Randall?'

Mary Anne jumped at the sound of a man's voice. Surely it was too early for customers. They knew better than to call before Henry had left for work.

'John!' The sudden quickening of her heartbeat thudded beneath her hand. 'You gave me a fright!'

'Sorry about that.'

He looked nervous, shifting from one foot to another like a schoolboy who's been caught scrumping apples.

'Daw said you were joining up today. I s'pose you've come to say goodbye.'

'Well, that and... Sorry, I'm forgettin' me manners.'

Mary Anne hid a smile as he took his cap from his head and folded his arms, tucking his cap into his armpit. Daw was going to wind this soft-centred young man around her little finger.

'The thing is... you know that me and your Daw... I mean Doreen...'

Mary Anne held up a hand. 'We all call her Daw, John. No sense in you calling her anything else.'

He nodded, the dark hair he'd inherited from his Italian mother spilling over his forehead. His eyes too were dark and he had a steady, mature look about him as though he'd turned wise at a very young age.

'Thing is, I want to do things right. I'm proud to be off to serve me country, and me only worry is that Daw might get snapped up by somebody else while I'm gone, so I've decided to ask her to marry me.'

Mary Anne controlled her amusement. John could be so intense, though passionate was probably the right word. As an orphan, he'd arrived in Kent Street just as news broke out that Lindbergh had circumnavigated the globe. John had collected every newspaper cutting about flying ever since. He'd also walked out to Filton, a green suburb to the north of Bristol where a flying school and a small factory had sprung into existence. He hadn't been able to afford to fly, but he'd watched from beyond the perimeter fence, fascinated as prototypes built by both the factory and local enthusiasts had bounced along the ground, flying in short, sharp bursts before bumping along the ground again. He'd told everyone who would listen about it.

'So why are you asking me?'

He looked down at the ground and cleared his throat. 'I want to buy her a ring.'

'Ah!'

Mary Anne knew immediately where this was leading. 'And you don't have the money.'

He shook his head. 'Not for a really decent one. She's worth a decent one.'

His sincerity touched her heart. 'Of course. You're a decent man, John Smith.'

'I've got this,' he said, rummaging in his pocket. He brought out a silver crucifix set on a wooden mount. To one side of the cross was a picture of the Virgin Mary. On the other was Joseph. 'It was my mother's. I think it's valuable. How much can you lend me against it?'

It was beautiful and obviously Italian. Mary Anne stroked the intricately worked silver feet with her thumb and swallowed the lump that came to her throat. He must love her daughter a lot to be hocking this.

'How much do you need?'

She sensed his hesitation, his fear of feeling foolish or worse, greedy.

'Would four guineas be too much?'

Mary Anne bit her lip. She'd had a few bits of silver come through her hands, but mostly gold, wedding rings put in hock until next payday. But silver such as this? She'd never seen its like before and sensed it was very valuable indeed.

She smiled. 'Four guineas is no problem, John. Do you mind turning your back?'

He looked askance.

'I keep my money in my underwear,' she explained.

'Oh!'

Cheeks reddening, he turned his back.

She still did keep money in her knickers, but not guineas. The boiler was set on bricks so that the rim came to waist level. There was a gap at one side where she kept the bulk of her money, a cash sum she'd saved up over the past three years. Beneath the sink was a meat safe where she kept some of the stuff brought in to be pledged against money lent. Behind that was a gap in the wall for bigger items.

'There's five guineas. It's worth that.'

'I don't think...'

She cocked her head to one side and eyed him reproachfully. 'Would you buy my daughter something cheap?'

He shook his head and looked bashfully down at his feet.

Mary Anne picked up the boiler stick and stabbed again at the washing. She had thought of suggesting that he take one of the wedding rings left with her, but none of them were at the end of their hock yet. Besides, it would be nice for her Daw to have something that was not second-hand.

If a young woman wanted to marry, she couldn't pick a better man than John. That was why she wanted to hide her expression. He mustn't see the envy there. It's wrong to feel like this at your age, she thought. But wouldn't it be wonderful to do it all again, only with love and passion this time.

'You don't think Mr Randall will object to us gettin' married?'

Mary Anne stabbed more vigorously at the boiling washing. 'Not if I've got anythin' to do with it.'

* * *

There was toast and dripping for breakfast. A big brown teapot stood on a stand in the middle of the table, steam curling from its spout. Lizzie was first down, her gloves and dark-green beret tucked beneath her arm, ready to cycle to her job in Ashton. The bicycle meant she didn't have to live in at the Selwyn household, so every day, at around six thirty, she set off to cycle to her employment.

'I don't want anything to eat.'

'You'll have a cup of tea.'

'Aw, Ma!'

'You're not leaving this house until you've had breakfast.'

Mary Anne took hold of her daughter's shoulder and pressed her into a chair. Lizzie resigned herself to the fact that she would have to at least drink a cup of tea before leaving for work.

'You've a long day and Mrs Selwyn works you hard.'

'Well, she'd better remember that when I ask her for time off this morning. I've promised to go to the recruiting office with Patrick Kelly. He's got nobody else.'

Mary Anne nodded approvingly. Patrick worked at Shellard's Garage on Coronation Road. Mr Shellard had a reputation for drinking too much cider and left Patrick pretty much to his own devices. She felt sorry for Patrick. He'd been scruffy and neglected as a child. The holes in his socks had never seen a darning needle and his boots – if he happened to have any – would have uppers swiftly parting with the soles.

'That's very kind of you.'

'The least I can do—' Lizzie suddenly caught the expression on her mother's face. 'Ma, don't read anything into it. He's just a friend. I've got no intention of having the likes of him as my sweetheart.'

'Why not? He's had a bad start in life but has a good heart.' Lizzie eyed her mother over the rim of her cup. 'I want something better, Ma. I don't want a bloke from round here who comes home smelling of tobacco or oil or sweat. I want one that smells sweet and can buy me nice things.'

Mary Anne fixed her daughter with a knowing look. 'And don't think I don't know what that means. Times have not changed that much. Mr Selwyn is not for you, Lizzie. He'll dally and play with you, but when it comes to the crunch, he'll marry a girl from a similar background, now mark my words.'

Face flushed, Lizzie sprang to her feet. 'He's not like that!

He's really nice and he's got a motor car—'

'He's not for you!' The crockery rattled as she slammed her hands palms down on the table. 'Lizzie! Don't be a fool. I'm telling you. Fellas like that don't marry girls like you. I'm telling you the truth!'

Lizzie was defiant. 'What would you know about it? What would you know? You're old! All that's behind you now, and besides it was different in your day.'

The old memories, a similar scene, flooded over her – or so it seemed. Her physical state reminded her of another girl, another boy and another war.

The room swam and Mary Anne clutched the back of a chair. A button popped off her blouse. Her hand fell inside to her breast as she gasped for breath. The room swimming, she slumped onto a chair.

'Ma!'

Lizzie fell to her knees and stared up into her mother's face. 'Ma? Are you all right, Ma? Are you sick? What is it? What's the matter?'

Feeling the first effects of early morning sickness, Mary Anne heaved, bent almost double and brought her hand across her mouth. She mustn't be sick. She mustn't give herself away. 'It's all right.' It wasn't all right. Her chest was heaving.

She swallowed the threatening sickness. 'I'm just a bit tired. Our Stanley had me up during the night. His breathing wasn't right...'

Judging by Lizzie's expression, it seemed the lie was believed. She looked relieved and more than a little contrite. She was all apologies.

'I didn't mean to upset you, Ma.'

Mary Anne shook her head. 'You didn't upset me, Lizzie.

I just want the best for you.'

Lizzie reached for her cup of tea. 'Here. Drink this.' Mary Anne did as she was told. 'Just a bit faint.'

Lizzie slid the sugar bowl towards her. 'Here. Have some more sugar.'

Mary Anne put her hand over the cup. 'No. No sugar. I don't like sugar in my tea.' She noticed Lizzie's frown. 'I used to, but not any more. I suppose it's something to do with age.'

Lizzie blinked in a curious way, a little frown between her brows, a concerned tilt to one side of her mouth.

'I'll be all right,' Mary Anne repeated.

She felt her face alternate between the cold pallor of a faint and the heat of embarrassment. 'I'll see you off. The fresh air will do me good.'

She followed Lizzie and her bicycle to the front door. The fresh air was like a wet veil on her face. 'Keep your head, Lizzie, and give young Patrick my love.'

Lizzie smiled over her shoulder before mounting her bike and cycling off.

Mary Anne went back into the house. There were others needing to be fed before going off to work, but Lizzie would be her favourite – until the others came down. It had always been hard to favour one any more than another – although there were differences, there would always be differences.

Daw was pale and agitated when she came down to breakfast, flitting between table, dresser and mantelpiece like a butterfly, unsure of the best place to settle. Harry came down just after her.

'I'm only reporting in,' she said, picking up a piece of toast and dripping, raising it to her mouth, then putting it down again. 'I can't eat.' She rubbed her palms together as though they were cold or had something stuck to them. Suddenly, she was very still. The face she turned to her mother was stiff with fear. 'I'm so afraid for him, Ma.'

Mary Anne pursed her lips. She had promised John that she wouldn't whisper a word about the ring. Smiling, she shook her head and pushed a wisp of hair behind her right ear. When she was young it was honey coloured and had glinted in the sun. Now it was a few shades lighter than the gold of her youth and streaked with pale, unmanageable strands.

She addressed her daughter in a melancholy voice. 'It's all a big adventure to men. God knows, but it's nothing but a struggle and a worry for the women left behind.'

Sitting at the kitchen table behind them, Harry made no comment but concentrated on eating his breakfast and drinking his tea.

Mary Anne's feelings turned warm when she looked at her son. Like his father, the top of her head barely reached his shoulder, but there the likeness ended. Harry weighed everything up before forming an opinion. His father had branded him a coward, but he'd stuck to his beliefs and taken a stand. In his mother's eyes, that made him a brave man indeed.

She would dearly like to know who he had been out with until two o'clock this morning, but he still wasn't saying.

In time, she told herself, smiling, and hoped to meet her soon.

12

Streetlights glimmered and the road glistened beneath the wheels of Lizzie's bike. The morning mist was damp on her face, the air fresh as water. Houses, trees and people were without colour; varying shades of greyness in the early morning world.

She passed the milkman's cart at the end of Coronation Road and wondered whether she'd got the time wrong.

Outside the back gate of the Selwyn house stood a lorry heavy with sacks of coal.

Lizzie brought her bicycle to a halt, flustered because surely his arrival confirmed she was late.

'Mr Evans! I must have misread the time.' She pushed her bicycle through the wooden gate, left it leaning against the hedge and rushed up the garden path to open the door to the coal shed.

'You ain't done no such thing,' he replied, his back hunched beneath the first hundredweight of coal. 'It's me that's early. I'm off with me eldest boy to the recruiting office. I've got ar Archie, me other boy, helping me now.'

He said it proudly and nodded to where a lanky boy in dusty cords, no more than fourteen by the looks of him, was bent almost double beneath the weight of a sack. A rumble like thunder preceded the black cloud, piercing the morning air as the first sack was tumbled into the shed.

'I'm going there too,' said Lizzie, stepping back onto the lawn so she wouldn't breathe in the thick cloud of dust.

'They don't take girls, I think; they certainly didn't in the last war,' said Mr Evans, his grin marked by the cigarette at the corner of his mouth, his eyes like dabs of whitewash in a sooty black face.

She managed to smile. 'They don't have women soldiers in this one either, Mr Evans. But don't worry. I won't be wearing a tin hat and khaki trousers just yet. I've promised a friend I'd go with him.'

'Oh,' he said.

No comment was made about the friend being her sweetheart. She was glad of that. Admitting Patrick was only a friend seemed somehow disloyal. Patrick needed someone to support him, and there was no one else. Now all she had to do was convince Mrs Selwyn that it was an act of patriotism for her to take mid-morning leave.

'Be seein' you later then,' called Mr Evans once he'd finished his drop.

* * *

The kettle was singing, the porridge was thick and creamy and the smell of fish caused her empty stomach to rumble. The porridge was for herself and Mrs Selwyn. The piece of smoked haddock was for Peter.

She poked the fish down so it would cook better. As she watched it shift slightly, she wondered at how her mother had guessed about her and Peter. Although the advice was well intended, she had no intention of taking it. She couldn't. Her heart bounced every time Peter was near, but how could she explain her feelings to her mother? Unlike Daw, she did not believe that mothers and fathers were beyond such things and put on earth purely to cater to the whims and wishes of their children, but trying to explain was never going to be easy. She was so set against Peter, continually implying that he would only take advantage of her because she was of a different class. The image of her mother looking so pale popped into her mind. She felt guilty for being so disagreeable, but her comments about Peter had caused her to question both his motives and her own. It came to her then that it was not the first time she'd seen her looking pale, though she'd never actually fainted before. Was it just tiredness because of young Stanley? He'd been ill, but that was a while ago now and she hadn't heard him disturb during the night.

Her thoughts were interrupted when Mrs Selwyn came into the kitchen at seven o'clock as she did every day, including weekends. She was always down for breakfast at least an hour before her son and always made the same pronouncement.

'I'm ready for breakfast, Lizzie, and my son will be down in precisely one hour.'

'Keeps a clock in 'er bloomers,' remarked Ivy Smith, who came in to help now and again and covered on Lizzie's day off. But this morning was different. She came down early, taking Lizzie by surprise.

'Good morning, Lizzie. Peter and I are ready for breakfast.

Today we intend dining together.'

Lizzie ceased stirring the porridge with a large wooden spoon, but contained her surprise. Peter rarely rose before eight. She'd heard from the staff at the haberdasher's, the family business, which he'd inherited on his father's demise, that they never expected to see him until nine thirty.

It struck her that Mrs Selwyn didn't look quite herself. Her clothes were no different than usual: a dark-grey dress, the high collar fastened at the throat with a blue and white cameo brooch, her hair crimped into tight curls that dangled like seashells over her forehead. There was something furtive about her. The set of her jaw was at variance with her eyes. Her lids were lowered and she kept her face turned away, as though she did not want Lizzie to see them and perhaps read her thoughts. Overall, Lizzie got the impression of distraction. 'Mrs Selwyn, I wish to go to the recruiting office this morning...'

Her employer stiffened, as wooden as the door she held half-open.

'War! There will be no talk of war in this house!'

Lizzie frowned. How could she not talk of it? Everyone was talking of it. She determined to press on regardless.

'I'm sorry, Mrs Selwyn, but I have to. I came in early this morning because I've promised to go to the recruiting office. One of my friends... and my brother—' she knew Harry wasn't going, but it sounded better if he was included '—are going to the recruiting office. I've promised to go with him... them... to give them courage, if you know what I mean.'

She found herself curtseying as she said it and felt a fool. She didn't usually curtsey to Mrs Selwyn, who was merely the widow of one shopkeeper and mother of another.

'After all,' she added, watching as Mrs Selwyn simmered like the kettle boiling behind her, 'saying goodbye to those about to march off to war is much more important than black-leading the grate or pushing the laundry through the mangle. All young men over twenty who don't enlist will be called up anyway, so I hear. My father says that no one will be exempt unless they're cripples, lunatics or conscientious objectors, though he reckons some will hide and some go abroad to Canada and places like that.'

Mrs Selwyn's odd expression, the stiff face muscles and the hooded eyes, suddenly altered. In time Lizzie would remember that expression and realise its significance, but she was too preoccupied with thinking about her last meeting with Peter to take much notice.

It had rained so the grass had been too wet to lie down. They'd climbed into the back of the car, the leather cold against her naked thighs.

'We shouldn't be doing this,' she'd murmured against his neck.

'Of course we should.'

His words had been delivered in a hot breath against her cheek. His hands had been stroking between her legs, the tip of his penis nudging towards its destination.

'Do you love me?' she asked, desperate to hear again the words that would go some way to justifying her letting him have his way.

'Yes, yes, whatever you want, my darling, whatever you want.'

The loose flesh of Mrs Selwyn's throat seemed to tremble against the stiff collar, the words she spoke rumbling like the coal had done. 'Yes. Well, of course, Peter has plans about what to do. I mean, everyone does, don't they, but of course he'll only go in as an officer. A young man experienced in running a business and organising staff is bound to end up as an officer.'

Lizzie wasn't sure whether overseeing a dozen female shop assistants, two old storemen and a young apprentice counted as good officer experience, but it wasn't her place to say anything.

Determined to accompany her sister and the two young men, she found herself searching for reasons to justify her taking the morning off. 'The milkman... and the coalman... they're going too... their sons, you see...'

Mrs Selwyn's face paled. 'Well. Yes. I suppose they would. One couldn't expect anything else. Mr Evans is huge. A brute of a man. His sons take after him and will no doubt have their uses.'

Lizzie frowned and wrinkled her nose at the smell of burning.

'The porridge!'

By the time Lizzie had swept the pot from the hob to the draining board, Mrs Selwyn had gone. Usually she would have got a ticking-off for inattention, but today Mrs Selwyn was preoccupied and it didn't do to ask questions.

Her employer had trained as a schoolteacher, so she said, though the fact that she read trashy romance was a little out of character. Lizzie had peered into one or two of the more lurid paperbacks where the heroes pledged undying love and the action stopped at the bedroom door.

Wiping the dampness from her forehead with the back of her hand, she gritted her teeth. Regardless of what Mrs Selwyn might say, she was going to the recruitment office. Perhaps she could send Peter a message to meet him afterwards. Surely Mrs Selwyn could accept such an excuse?

'Yes,' she muttered to herself, as she dug the last of the porridge out with a wooden spoon. She'd have it out with her after breakfast, even though it might mean she'd have no job at the end of it. What did it matter, she told herself as she ladled the porridge into a serving dish. You have your bicycle. You can get a job anywhere because you can get to it better than most people. But there wouldn't be a Peter, she thought, and Peter was what kept her here. She could earn much more at the tobacco factory, much more at the munitions factories that were taking over the production lines in engineering firms and garages.

No. There would be no Peter. The thought of not seeing Peter, not being near him, not being...? Available? The meaning made her pause in the preparation of breakfast.

Available! She frowned. The job was convenient – for both of them.

Balancing the tray in the crook of her arm, she opened the kitchen door and headed for the breakfast room.

If the porridge was a little on the burned side, nobody mentioned it. Peter gave her a tight smile and wished her good morning as though they were nothing more than master and servant. Mother and son fell to silence. It struck her that whatever they'd been talking about was strictly confidential because she fancied the conversation resumed once she was out of earshot. When the service bell jangled, she presumed more tea was required and filled up a fresh pot.

Mrs Selwyn's face was upturned and smiling when she re-entered the room, and might almost have looked handsome if the curtains behind her hadn't coloured her complexion a sickly shade of pea green.

'Lizzie. Peter and I are off to the railway station, so you may go as soon as you've washed the breakfast things.'

Lizzie couldn't contain her delight, but hid her puzzlement.

Mrs Selwyn had seemed so brusque earlier.

'My dear son will also be leaving us,' she said, her pearl drop earrings bobbing around her cheeks as she turned to her son and patted his hand.

Lizzie froze. 'Leaving?'

One thought above all others raced around her head. Why hadn't he told her yesterday when he'd said again – or almost said – that he loved her?

His eyes didn't meet hers, but he smiled, reached for his cup and tapped it with his spoon. 'Let's have some more of that strong tea of yours. I might not be getting any for quite a while.'

He exchanged a strange look with his mother, a look she couldn't quite interpret.

'He's going to Canada,' said his mother. 'For training... for the sea. Yes. The sea.'

Lizzie's heart sank. There would be no more afternoons lying in the grass, staring up at the sky, no more stolen moments on the back seat of his car, no passionate words said in a rushed breath against her ear. He was going to Canada and then to sea. She couldn't show her feelings, certainly not in front of his mother. Keeping them inside was like forcing a stopper into a bottle of shaken lemonade.

'Yes, ma'am,' she said to Mrs Selwyn. 'And the best of luck, Mister Peter.'

It hurt when Peter thanked her for her good wishes without looking up from his food. Dazed, she washed the dishes, dried them, washed the tea towel and hung it above the warm hob to dry.

Peter was going. 'Well, of course he's going,' she muttered to herself. He was a man and men were needed in the army and on the sea. Her mood changed because it had to. She steeled herself to what was to happen. And what was it to her? What was she to him?

She rubbed at her eyes and blew her nose in a clean tea towel, which she immediately flung into the laundry basket. She thought back to her first days in the Selwyn household. The armchairs, the sofas, the carpets and the highly polished furniture, so different than the serviceable and well-worn furnishings at home in Kent Street, would have overawed most girls from her background. Instead, it was Peter that had impressed her. He was like a god, clean and well spoken, never uttering a swear word or stinking of drink like most of the men in Kent Street. Did the afternoons in the grass and on the back seat of the car mean nothing to him?

She wanted to cry, but something steelier took over. Her fingers were all thumbs as she buttoned up her coat. Mrs Selwyn had told her there was no need to come upstairs and say goodbye, but she couldn't go yet. She wanted to see Peter alone before he left.

Once she was ready to leave, she sat on a chair, glancing every so often up at the kitchen clock, promising herself that she would not leave until it had struck eleven o'clock, the hour when she *had* to leave.

She told herself that Peter would come before then to say goodbye. She was sure of it, but as the minutes ticked away, so did her hope.

The clock finally struck eleven and still he hadn't come.

She pulled open the coal-house door. Her bike rested against the wall. The air inside tasted gritty still and an oblong of light fell onto the black heap, making it glisten. Like stars, she thought. Small stars.

The stars vanished as a shadow fell through the doorway, blanking out the light.

'Were you going to go without saying goodbye?'

Peter smelled of cologne, hair cream and clean clothes, not like her father who smelled of dust, and her brother who smelled of tobacco. He didn't look like a haberdasher, a man in charge of selling ribbons, silks and Nottingham lace. Although his nose was straight and his chin receded slightly, he was broad shouldered as suited the merchant seaman he was setting out to be.

She felt a fluttering in her heart. 'I don't know what to say.' She said it in a small voice as though she had no business saying it at all.

He stepped onto the flagstone floor and, without a moment's hesitation, they fell together.

Above the gritty taste of coal, Lizzie smelled the seasonal dampness clinging to his clothes.

'I had to wait for Mother to go to the bathroom before I could get out. I had to kiss you goodbye before I go.'

She clamped her mouth to his, kissed him long and hard, then broke breathlessly away. 'I feel like Mary Pickford saying goodbye to Douglas Fairbanks in a film, not like real life at all. I can't believe you're going. Why didn't you tell me? Why so soon?'

His arms squeezed her tightly to his chest. 'It was sudden. Mother arranged it.'

'But I thought...'

She was going to say that even merchant seamen going abroad to Canada had to go through some form of call-up. His mother could hardly go there in his stead.

'Don't think,' he said, pressing his mouth against hers.

She felt like butter melting in the sun. She drank in his smell, the feel of his chin and cheeks. She wanted to remember his features, his feel and this moment for ever. Keeping her eyes open, she drank in the sight of his closed lids and the way his nostrils flared with each breath he took.

'Elizabeth,' he murmured against her ear as she fought for breath. 'Has anyone ever kissed you like that before?'

'No. You're the first.'

'The first to kiss you like that, or the first to kiss you?'

He studied her face as he awaited her answer, his fingers stroking the nape of her neck in ticklish, delicious strokes.

She thought about lying, boasting that he was not the only man in her life; she so badly wanted to hurt him just as his leaving was hurting her, but she couldn't lie, not to him.

'No one's ever kissed me before – except my mother.' A slow smile crossed his face.

'How delicious.' His hand ran down her arm. 'And no one's ever held you this close in a dirty coal house before?'

She shook her head. 'No,' she said, her voice now sounding so small that she could barely hear it herself.

'Or done this?'

She moaned as his hand closed over her breast. There was something daring about being this intimate so close to the house and his mother. And she couldn't stop him; in fact she didn't want to stop him. This was ecstasy and took her breath away. A tingle of pleasure spread out from her bosom and all over her body. A tinge of guilt came with it along with the chance that they might be discovered.

She pulled his hands away from her breasts. 'Peter, I don't think you should do that.'

He frowned. 'Don't you like it? I thought you did, or is that only in the back of the car or in the grass at Clancy's Farm?'

'Of course I like it.'

'Then say so,' he said, his hands going back inside her bodice. 'Oh, Lizzie, I'm going to want to remember this. We're going to be far apart, and who knows when or where we'll see each other again – or if at all.'

'Don't say that!'

He looked sad. 'It's the truth. Things are hotting up. Who knows where either of us will be a year from now.'

'You'll survive,' Lizzie blurted. 'You'll come home.'

'Damned right I will,' he said, his face brightening. 'And when I do, will you be waiting for me?'

Lizzie didn't hesitate. 'Of course I will. Anything you want.'

He nodded gratefully. 'Then can I ask you to look after Mother?'

She lowered her eyelashes. It had occurred to her that without Peter around she might just as well get a better-paid job in a factory. His request had changed all that and she immediately felt guilty because she'd said she would do anything he wanted.

'No... I mean yes... I mean... Oh, I don't know what I mean, except...'

'Except what?'

'My legs are like jelly. I won't be able to ride my bike.'

She thought about the recruiting office and Patrick's anxious face, Daw and John too.

Peter laughed. 'Surely I'm more important to you than a bicycle. I thought I was someone special to you.' His fine lips that only a moment before had been pressed firmly on hers, now pouted alarmingly, as though she'd stabbed him with something sharper than words.

Fearing she'd upset him, Lizzie's response was instant and heartfelt. 'You are, you are! I didn't mean to...'

'Never mind,' he said, and kissed her again.

'Of course I'll stay and look after your mother.'

She'd said it, all thoughts about bettering herself and earning more money sacrificed for the sake of Peter Selwyn.

You're mad, she told herself, then relented. His eyes were looking down into hers and he couldn't stop kissing her.

Yes, she really did feel like melting butter.

'I love you,' she said, and ran her hands over his face, his shoulders, touching the neat cleft in the centre of his chin, brushing his hair back from his face and feeling the hardness in his groin which on this particular meeting would remain unsatisfied. 'Lizzie,' he said in that hushed voice that made her whole body feel as though it were turning to jelly. His fingers brushed her breast as he undid the top two buttons on her dress. It was mauve and provided by Mrs Selwyn for weekdays and was worn beneath a sparkling white apron. She had blue for the weekends. The two colours seemed to float before her like an early morning mist. 'I'll remember this,' he said, bending his head and kissing her breast. 'And I'll remember this,' he said, running his fingers up the inside of her thigh and beneath her knickers to the soft hair between.

He could have taken her there. She would have given in willingly, but like a dream the magic was suddenly broken.

'Peter! Peter! Where are you? The taxi is here.'

At the sound of his mother's voice, he broke away. Lizzie was left gasping, tears springing to her eyes. Peter's attitude changed abruptly.

'Make yourself decent,' he said briskly, smoothing his own clothes and heading towards the door.

He paused, his face shiny with sweat. 'Shh,' he said, his finger against his lips. 'Mustn't tell Mother our secret now, must we?'

He winked and made a clicking sound from the corner of his mouth. Then he was gone and all she could see was the red-leafed creeper climbing the brick wall dividing this house from next door. The leaves were dripping with teardrops of rain, and Lizzie wiped one or two from her eyes.

* * *

Mrs Selwyn was grim-faced. 'She's just a servant, Peter.'

Peter grinned. 'That doesn't mean to say that I shouldn't be kind.'

'Just as you were to Ruth and to Hilary?'

Peter shrugged himself into his overcoat and reached for his hat.

'It was hardly my fault. They threw themselves at me. Goodness, Mother, I'm only just about holding Elizabeth off. The poor thing's besotted with me – and she's terribly sad that I'm going off to war, which is quite amusing really.'

A look of alarm crossed his mother's face. 'You didn't tell her the truth, did you?'

He patted her cheek and looked down into her face. 'Of course not.'

If anyone had studied their features more closely, they would have seen the resemblance despite the difference in years. They both had the same hard glint in their eyes and the spoiled pout of someone who always expects to get their own way.

Mrs Selwyn stroked her son's hair. 'As long as you're safe, my darling.'

Peter took hold of his mother's hand and kissed it. 'Don't worry, Mother. The war will soon be over and I shall keep my head down until it is.'

* * *

There was a smell in the air outside the recruiting office. Lizzie became aware of it the moment they became part of the excitable throng eddying like a freak wave around the open door. Although her thoughts were preoccupied with Peter, she couldn't help being carried along by the crowds and the atmosphere of fearful excitement.

Patrick saw the look on her face, presumed it was fear and dared to squeeze her hand – at least she thought he did. It was hard to gauge whose hand it was. Men determined to do their bit for their country pressed forwards, aided and abetted by screaming or fainting women. The world had gone mad.

Patrick bristled with excitement. 'Look at 'em, Lizzie. All these blokes not waiting to be called up but coming down here to enlist – it's unbelievable.'

'It is that all right,' Lizzie answered, her voice and expression betraying the reservations she felt. 'Don't they realise they could be killed?'

'We're off to do our duty,' Patrick replied, but Lizzie knew it was something more than that in his case. He was escaping from his past. Born illegitimate to a mother with the worst reputation in Bedminster, this was his chance to make something of himself.

'You can't blame Patrick for wanting to go, and you can't help admiring John being so brave,' she whispered to Daw.

Pale and tearful, Daw clenched her lips and nodded. She didn't want John to go, but on the other hand he was doing what was expected of him. She was proud of that.

'Kill the Hun,' one old man shouted. He was wearing a spiked German helmet from the Great War and his cheeks were as red as his jacket.

Despite the crush, Lizzie felt herself growing cold. If killing had a smell, then that's what she smelled now.

She glanced across at Daw and saw that John's arm was wound tightly around her shoulder as though he were trying to keep her from falling. Suddenly she felt lonely even though she was in the midst of a crowd. Daw had John, but although she tried to kid herself that she had Peter, he wasn't here was he, but off to Canada.

As the queue surged forwards, she was pushed into the gutter, her hat knocked sideways. Patrick grabbed her before she fell.

'Steady on there, Lizzie.'

John shouted at them both. 'Get back across the road, the pair of you. Patrick and me'll get over to you once we've signed up.'

He pushed Daw towards her and somehow, Lizzie didn't know how, Patrick swapped places with her so that he and John went forwards together.

Trams, cabs and tradesmen's carts and lorries pushed their way through the crowds along with a few double-decker buses. Crossing the road was only possible once they'd passed, the crowd dispersing long enough for them to get through.

'Look,' said Daw once they'd gained the other side. Lizzie admired the stone glinting on Daw's finger.

'He bought it for me last week and kept it a secret until he'd had a word with Dad. Fancy him keeping it secret from me. He reckons Mum already knows, but she ain't said nothing to me.' Her expression changed from anxiety to excitement in a matter of minutes.

'We're engaged, Lizzie. We're going to get married before he goes. I don't think Dad will say no, do you? I mean, does Dad ever say no to anything we want to do?'

''Course not. Dad's a big softy. He'll give in. He always does.'

Frightening moments stayed in Daw's mind. 'He wasn't too pleased with our Harry.'

'Ah!' said Lizzie, also surprised at their father's anger. They'd never seen him angry before, only drunk, and even then, he was always jovial. Nevertheless, she did her best to reassure her sister.

'That was different, Daw. Our dad loved the army and always did his duty for his country. He can't believe that anyone else wouldn't be keen too, just like he was. Our Harry surprised him. Men like to think their sons are as brave as they were. Anyway, you're nearly twenty-one so it won't matter much if he did say no. Leave it to Mum, she'll bring him round.'

She felt like adding that John was not twenty-one yet either and that he was old enough to get killed so why should there be a problem. Who was to say when the time was right?

It was half an hour before Patrick and John returned. Lizzie tried to read their expressions. Patrick looked exuberant. No surprise really. He was off on the biggest adventure of his life. Nothing could be worse than the childhood he'd endured, neglected by his mother and shunned by those who should know better.

John's face was a different matter. He looked stunned, almost miserable, as if he'd only just realised exactly what he'd done.

The air was humid, the bleak clouds of a gathering storm pressing uncomfortably down on them.

'Daw,' he said, the narrow gap between them somehow seeming a mile wide. 'I can't marry you. There's no time. We have to go home, gather our personal belongings and report to Temple Meads Station. We're being sent for training.'

Daw's pink cheeks paled. 'You're in the army already?'

He shook his head. 'No. The air force, just like I said I would.'

Head thudding onto his shoulder, Daw burst into tears. He held her tight, his face against her hair, his expression as heavy as the gathering storm. 'I'll be going away for training. They haven't said where. It's top secret.'

Lizzie felt her stomach heave. Daw had told her that John had only asked her that morning when he'd given her the ring.

Daw finally raised her head. 'So what do we do now?' She laughed, a nervous, alien sound hiding an underlying sob.

'We do as we're ordered,' said Patrick, who had stood patiently and quietly, watching the loving couple with a mix of embarrassment and envy. 'We've got no choice.' He looked at Lizzie and smiled ruefully. 'I've joined the air force too. I don't know whether I'll be doing any flying, but they want ground staff too. They're sending us away for training right away. It was that or the merchant navy. Freddie Hill's joining that.'

'So's—' Lizzie had been going to say that Peter Selwyn was also going into the merchant navy, and barely stopped herself. She didn't want any awkward questions.

Instead she smiled. 'Then we'd better head for home.'

Inside, she harboured deep concern for both boys. She hadn't expected to worry about either of them, especially Patrick. And yet seeing them clutching their recruitment papers, their faces tense with expectation, she shared their fears, the realisation that they had done something momentous, something they only now were coming to terms with.

Luckily, they'd packed everything they would need for leaving so swiftly.

Temple Meads Station was more packed than the recruiting office. Hundreds of men milled over the platform and the air here was as charged with apprehension and excitement as it had been at the recruitment office.

'You promise you'll answer my letters?' Patrick asked Lizzie.

'Of course I will.'

Patrick smiled. 'Thanks for that photograph. You don't mind if I tell blokes that you're my sweetheart, do you?'

Lizzie had given him the photograph earlier. Daw had brought it from home and it was too late to give it to Peter. Besides, it wasn't her best photo; she was about fifteen and still wearing a girl's dress with frills around the sleeves, a shapeless skirt, cotton socks and sandals.

'Yes, I do mind! It's an awful photo. You'd better tell them that I'm your best friend.'

He looked disappointed, but she couldn't help it. There was and always would be a stigma associated with Patrick Kelly. It was sad, but that was the way of things. If only she'd known that Peter was going away, she would have made a point of choosing her best photograph and giving it to him.

'There's three trains for troops,' the railway porter explained. 'They're going to three different training camps.'

'And where would they be?' asked Patrick.

'You'll find out when you get there,' the porter answered and disappeared into the crowd.

The fumes and noise of steam engines reverberated against the overhead roof.

'It's here! It's here,' shouted Patrick. 'Come on, John. This one's fer us.'

John barely had time to hug and kiss Daw before Patrick dragged him off, Daw's face smothered in tears as Lizzie pulled her away.

The crowd pressed into the gap left by the two men. It was a useless task, but Lizzie did her best to console her older sister.

'Wave goodbye, Daw. Wave goodbye. See? There they are... just over there.'

She pointed to where John and Patrick were hanging out of a carriage window, waving for all they were worth.

The two sisters waved back, Daw blowing kisses, as her nose began to run along with her tears.

'They'll be home in no time,' Lizzie assured her.

'By Christmas,' said a woman beside her, her hat tipping over her middle-aged face. 'My two boys are going to be home by Christmas. I told them to be sure of that.'

'Do you think they will be?' Daw asked.

Lizzie didn't hear the woman's reply. Her gaze had drifted to the opposite platform where Peter Selwyn stood waiting for the boat train, his arms around his mother, who was sobbing profusely against his chest.

She only turned away when she realised that Daw was whispering something against her ear.

'What was that you said?' she asked, her gaze still fixed on Peter Selwyn.

'I said, we did it,' said Daw, her face pink with embarrassment. 'We couldn't stop ourselves.'

Lizzie was dumbstruck. She saw her sister's dark eyes and bright red lips through a blur of guilty thoughts. Was it her fault she'd done it? Had she unwittingly encouraged her to give in to John?

Daw's bottom lip quivered. 'You don't think I'll get pregnant do you, not from just doing it the once? It was the first time, Lizzie, honestly it was.'

'I don't know.' Lizzie shook her head and turned her attention back to Peter and his mother. There was no sign of them and the boat train to Southampton was moving out of the station. He was gone and she didn't know when she would see him again.

13

The knocking at the front door was polite but persistent. 'I'm coming, I'm coming.'

Mary Anne muttered angrily to herself at the same time as climbing over a pile of blackout curtains that she'd not quite finished hemming to the right length for the front parlour. Her attention was riveted on the door and whoever was hammering on it.

'If it's not the doctor or the vicar, they'll get the sharp edge of my tongue.'

At the same time she untied her apron and flung it on the hall-stand. It was a rule that she never answered the front door wearing her apron, and few people used the front door. Customers wanting to pledge and borrow went round the back. Only important people like the doctor or someone from the taxi company to ask where Henry was, or Henry himself. Everyone else came in at the back door.

The last person she expected to see was Biddy all done up like a dog's dinner, smelling of Evening in Paris, a tawny red fox fur draped around her shoulders.

Biddy's face looked strangely tight, as though she had adopted a particularly singular expression that morning and was holding on to it for dear life.

Mary Anne frowned. 'What do you want? Is something wrong?'

Biddy shrugged one shoulder, dragging Mary Anne's attention to the snout of the long dead fox.

'I wanted to pledge me fur. Our Brian's joined the navy and I wanted to give him a good send off – so foxy here has to go.' Mary Anne folded her arms and adopted her own tight expression. 'Then you, of all people, should know better. Why didn't you go round the back as usual? Gone up in the world are we?'

Biddy looked taken aback. 'What? With him there?' She jerked her dimpled chin to the archway dissecting the terrace and the only way to the back alley.

A sense of foreboding swirled inside Mary Anne's stomach, which already ached in the aftermath of Henry's anger about Harry refusing to enlist. He couldn't have found out about her business, could he?

She followed Biddy's pointing finger.

'Him,' Biddy said, nodding to where a matt black shadow fell from the archway. 'He says he'll stop anyone from doing business with you. He says it's illegal. I told him I didn't care, and who was he anyway to tell me where I should pledge me valuables. He told me that he's a *real* pawnbroker and that you got no rights doing him out of business.'

Mary Anne stared at her dumbfounded, then back to the figure in the archway. 'Oh does he now!'

Bundling Biddy inside, she told her to find her own way to the washhouse and to put the kettle on the gas on her way through the kitchen. Pulling the door almost shut behind her, she took a deep breath and rolled up her sleeves like a boxer ready for a brawl. This was her street, her territory. Ready to face anything, she headed for the archway.

Although her knees trembled, her indignation kept her going. No one was going to stop her earning a shilling – legal or not.

She recognised the foreigner who had accosted her in the back garden, nephew to the old man who had died. He had a wary look in eyes half hidden by thick, straight hair that fell darkly across his brow.

Lines radiated from the corners of his mouth, surely too many for someone of his age? Surely he couldn't be much more than twenty-five, and yet what was it about him that made her think he'd have some tales to tell if she had a mind to listen.

None of your business! She forced herself to focus on the present problem. Never mind tales, what the bloody hell's he doing here?

The foreigner was taller than her, though not so tall as her husband or son, but he had a more hardened look, his brow throwing a shadow over his eyes.

She stood directly in front of him.

'Why are you doing this?' she asked, knuckles resting on her hips – they were small and not likely to do him much damage, but she did look battle ready.

'Why are *you* doing this?' he retaliated.

She felt trim and in control when she straightened herself to full height. 'You've got no rights stopping people going round the back lane.'

'I am not stopping anyone from passing as long as they are not doing business with you.'

'You have no right to do that!'

He jammed his knuckles on his hips, his stance echoing her own. 'And you have no right taking the bread out of my mouth. I have a shop to run, taxes to pay. You are affecting that.'

'How dare you! You, a foreigner here...'

His face darkened. 'I did not ask to be here. The war forced me to come here. You are not at war yet, not really. It is just words. You do not know how it is, what is happening. A few skirmishes at sea, an army sent over to France all sitting on their backsides waiting for the Germans to face them. Does no one in this country realise that the Nazis prefer to stab in the back?'

Although her chest heaved with indignation, something in the way he spoke filled her with fear. But she couldn't possibly relinquish what she did. Her family were the best dressed and fed in the street, but wouldn't be without the money brought in by the business. Even the blackout curtains had been bought with money she'd earned from her ramshackle pawnshop.

'Then if war is so terrible, why are we arguing? Surely there's room for a small operation such as mine?'

'I cannot allow it. I have responsibilities. I have a duty to my dead uncle to ensure that the business survives.'

A cold breeze lifted her hair, exposing an unlined throat. She wrapped her pale-blue cardigan more closely around herself, tucking her chin into the deep collar.

Michael had the impression she was hiding in it, trying hard to survive in her small domestic world, at the same time attempting to ignore the wider issues. People, especially women, did that, he'd noticed. His mother hadn't necessarily believed in what his stepfather had believed in, she'd merely appeared to. Living through those she loved was more important than living her own life.

Eyes unblinking, she studied his face, saw the hardness, but couldn't help sensing it was only a barrier between the world and the man within. He spoke eloquently and in other circumstances she might have enjoyed listening to the melodic precision of his voice. As it was...

She shook her head, her grey eyes dark with thought. 'No. You cannot do this. It's not fair. Not fair at all.'

'Not fair?' His voice raised an octave, echoing between the terraced houses lining both sides of the street.

The men putting the finishing touches to the air warden's hut at the end of the street stopped what they were doing and looked in their direction.

'This is England,' Mary Anne said. 'Foreigners can't just come here and tell us what to do.'

Her voice carried to the workmen, just as she'd intended it to. Shouldering shovels and pickaxes, they came in her direction.

'You all right there, luv?'

Arms folded across her chest, she smiled triumphantly up into the pawnbroker's face. 'You see? This is England. It's a free country and I can do what I want.'

He looked over her head at the advancing gang. The shadow of his brow receded and she saw the fear in his eyes, sweat bursting like dewdrops from his forehead and finally all over his face.

There was no way she could possibly know the secrets of his past, at least, not specifically, and yet she knew there were bad things. Could that be because there were bad things in her life too? The thought of them having something in common was alien, but would not go away.

'Did you say he was a foreigner, missus?' asked one of the men. 'Can't be too careful, you know.'

The others brought their tools down from their shoulders as they gathered round, as though ready to beat anyone not home grown.

The thought of it made her sick. The dizziness threatened to return. She looked over the heads of the grim-faced men to the women beyond – standing in doorways, cleaning windows, sweeping pavements – all still now and looking her way, wondering what the noise was about.

No! She mustn't faint. No one must suspect. No one.

Grabbing the pawnbroker's arm, she shouted at the workmen. 'Just a long-lost cousin – from Australia,' she added.

Judging by their expressions they didn't believe her.

Without a backwards glance, she pushed the eloquent young man through the archway and out into the alley.

'This way. You can go through the house and out the front door once they've cleared off, and pray that's before my old man comes home.'

'Your old man?'

'My husband.'

She pushed him through the garden gate, past the rows of potatoes, cabbages and carrots.

'I didn't mean for that with the workmen to happen,' she said. 'But there, they were only trying to protect a good, honest Englishwoman, weren't they?'

'I should think you are capable of protecting yourself. In fact, I know you are.'

Blushing, Mary Anne recalled their first meeting when he had surprised her hanging out the washing.

'You're right. I was going to brain you with a garden spade.'

'Brain me?'

'Hit you over the head. You did startle me.'

'I am sorry. I did not mean to. I only wished to tell you I was not happy that you were stealing my trade.'

'So you said,' she said with a grimace, pushing open the door to the washhouse.

Biddy had pulled up a stool and was sitting with her back against the copper, which still held heat from an early wash load. She looked up, her face radiant with welcome.

Biddy's jaw dropped as she suddenly recognised the pawnbroker, the man who'd been standing in the archway. 'Hello, young man.'

Michael nodded a casual greeting but looked wary.

Noticing his discomfort, Mary Anne hid her grin. Obviously he knew a tart when he saw one and had good reason to concern himself. The fact that she was married had no effect on Biddy's love life. She took it wherever and whenever it came.

Lizzie fancied that the glassy eyes of the fox fur eyed her accusingly as she entered.

'This is...' Mary Anne began.

'Michael. My name is Michael Maurice.'

Biddy tittered like a young girl. 'Pleased to meet you, I'm ever so sure.'

Mary Anne raised her eyes to heaven. 'Biddy doesn't get out much and meeting strangers is as good as meeting royalty to her.' She turned back to Biddy. 'Michael and I have business to discuss.' It was all she could say by way of explanation.

Michael's smile was like a warm glow melting a frozen pond, the cracks racing off in all directions. They exchanged a look of understanding.

'It was getting ugly out there,' she said. 'The workmen,' she added in response to Biddy's blank expression. 'They don't like foreigners.'

'Ooow. Where are you from?' asked Biddy, eyeing Michael with renewed interest.

Michael trotted out the same lie. 'Holland.'

'I quite like foreigners, especially them from Holland.' She grinned widely, like a cat about to pounce on a trapped mouse.

Michael responded by choosing the furthest corner to stand in.

It amused Mary Anne to see their behaviour. She doubted that Biddy had ever met a foreigner in her life, but made no comment, merely explaining what she intended to do.

'I'll take Mr Maurice through the house and out the front door as soon as they go to tea.'

'They go about four,' said Biddy, her pink cheeks bunching like roses. 'I've made it for them meself sometimes.' She blushed to the roots of her hair. 'Nothing in it, of course, just being friendly.'

'Yes,' said Mary Anne, 'and the whole street knows how friendly you can be.'

An alarm clock sitting on the top shelf chose that moment to chime four.

'It's later than I thought. Come on. I'll let you out the front door,' said Mary Anne, throwing Biddy a warning look to behave herself.

'You are pushing me around again,' said Michael, though he obediently allowed himself to be pushed.

'What about my fox fur?' Biddy wailed.

Mary Anne gritted her teeth. She'd hoped Biddy would wait until she'd got rid of Michael Maurice. But that was the way Biddy was. Her eyes and face were as round as her body and just as soft. Spaniel brown eyes looked innocently up into Mary Anne's face, like a child determined not to be overlooked.

'It's for my Brian,' she murmured, her bottom lip quivering. She turned to the pawnbroker. 'He's joining the navy. He's doing his bit for his country and he'll look a right picture in uniform, but I've got to give 'im a decent send-off. Poor lamb deserves it.'

Biddy's Brian was as far removed from a lamb as you could get, mused Mary Anne. He stood at six foot three in his socks and had shoulders as wide as a barn door.

Recognising there was no way Biddy was leaving until she had exchanged the fox fur for some money, Mary Anne resigned herself to fixing a price.

'Here,' she said taking her tin box from its hiding place behind the copper. 'Here's fifteen shillings.'

Biddy's eyes turned round as saucers as she took the money. 'Oooow. I never expected so much.'

'Well, there you are. You can never tell,' said Mary Anne. The truth was that the fox fur wasn't really worth that much, but Biddy loved her kids even though rumour had it she did a turn on a street corner now and again just to keep her head above water and, as a mother, Mary Anne understood her wanting to do her best by her son.

A couple of fleas jumped out when she gave the fur a shake. Michael noticed too, but Biddy was already billing and cooing at the money, listing the things she would buy in order to give her son a good send-off.

Mary Anne pointed at a nail close to the ceiling and way out of her reach.

'If you could hang it up there,' she said to Michael. 'A good airing over the steam will do it good.'

Michael's veiled smile echoed her own. 'I think so too.'

'I'll poke my nose out and make sure they're gone,' said Mary Anne, jerking a thumb towards the back of her house. 'I'll keep you company, dear,' said an effervescent Biddy to an alarmed Michael, her fingers fondling the sleeve of his jacket and her eyes glinting with more cunning than the fox hanging on the nail.

'No doubt,' said Mary Anne.

She whispered at Michael on the way out, 'I'll have to leave you to look out for yourself.'

She saw a glimmer of helplessness pass over his face before she left. Now who was the poor lamb?

Before going to the front door, she pressed her ear against the door to the front parlour where Stanley was sleeping, but heard nothing. The familiar panic set in. Was he still breathing? Fear spurred her towards the bed. He was her beloved son, her youngest, and although she'd been assured that he was better, she wasn't entirely trusting of anyone's diagnosis but her own.

'Stanley?' she called softly, fearing that he'd overexerted himself. 'Stanley?'

She felt for his head and found only the pillow.

'The little...' She swore under her breath. The bed was empty.

She'd have to go and look for him, but first she had to check that the workmen were gone for tea.

The blue and red of the upper glazed half of the front door made patterns on the lino. Pretty, she thought and smiled because the red reminded her of Biddy's cheeks – and how Michael's might end up if Biddy had her way.

Now, if she could just get him out of the house, she could search for Stanley before Henry came home. The November air was damp and bad for his chest and she had to stop him going out without telling her.

'Enough to give anyone a heart attack,' she said to herself. A heavy hammering at the door swiftly dispelled her thoughts and confirmed the worse. The patterns on the floor trembled, and so did Mary Anne. For the second time that day, she opened the front door, only this time it wasn't inoffensive Biddy Young wanting to flog her fox fur. It was Henry and he was full to the brim with drink.

'I'm collecting for the church,' he said, his speech slurred and the brim of his hat nestling around his shoulders.

Her heart lurched. 'You're early.'

He grinned and spread his arms so that his hands rested on either side of the doorway. It made it seem he was holding the house up.

'I wanted to come home and see me loving wife. I thought we could have a quiet ten minutes to ourselves before the tribe of bloody Israel get home from work.' A sudden thought seemed to strike him. 'Work? Work? They don't bloody know the meaning of the word.'

Pushing her to one side, he continued to mutter all the way along the passageway, then stopped by the stairs, the leer on his face and the glint in his eyes leaving her in no doubt of what he had in mind.

'Time to perform yer wifely duties,' he said, the leer spreading over his face in a series of deep furrows.

Mary Anne winced as his beery breath wafted over her face. She thought of Biddy and Michael out in the washhouse. They had to be warned. She attempted to push past him. 'I've got to hang out our Harry's shirts.'

His fingers dug into her shoulders and one shoe went flying off her foot as he spun her backwards, slamming her against the wall.

'Damn Harry's bloody shirts. Big nancy boy. That's what he is. Likes to look nice but don't want to fight for his country.'

His face reminded her of the gargoyles high up on the cathedral.

'Henry...'

She liked neither his attention nor his insinuation about her beloved Harry, and tried to wriggle free, but he held her tight.

'Get up them stairs.'

She fought to control her expression as her thoughts turned to Michael being kept company by the overblown Biddy. Stiff with protest, she closed her eyes. Pray God Biddy doesn't bring him through the house.

She didn't want to do this, but Henry must not discover that she was hiding a man in the washhouse. Adopting a smile and a smooth voice as though she really welcomed his amorous attention, she said, 'How about you go on up and I bring you a cup of tea.'

In her heart of hearts she knew damned well that unless she was there beside him, he'd be snoring once his boots were off and his head had hit the pillow.

'No. I've got a better idea. How about I have you here,' he muttered, his eyes bloodshot and yellow around the edges. 'How about that then – that I take you up against the wall like the slut you really are. Eh?'

His insults had no effect. He'd been hurling them at her for years. All she considered now was how best to take advantage of the situation. Her mind worked quickly. Here, she thought. Here would be quick and afterwards she could get out and warn Michael to stay put.

Yes. I'll play the tart if it gets you up them stairs when you've finished, she thought, her fixed smile barely hiding her disdain.

'If that's the way you want it,' she said, eyeing her husband of some twenty-odd years like a dirty little whore, or at least how she imagined a prostitute would look when propositioning a man. 'So let's see how big a man you are,' she said, hitching her skirt up above her stocking tops and rolling her knickers down to her knees. 'Let's see what the ale you've supped at the Red Cow has done for your performance.'

Goading had the required response. His nostrils flared. His pupils turned densely black and little flicks of spittle flared from the corners of his mouth.

She helped him undo his fly buttons, her stomach churning though she still smiled. The best thing Henry Randall had ever given her was her children. The acts of intercourse leading to their conception had left her feeling as though he were trying to take something from her and not give anything in return. There was no preamble, no kiss and no attempt to prepare her for his penetration. He did it like he always did, with loud grunts and swift thrusts that did nothing for her but was selfishly and entirely for his own satisfaction.

For better or worse...

She certainly knew which this was.

Chin stubble grazed her cheek and she almost vomited the beer fumes she was forced to breathe and swallow.

The walls were thin, the floorboards twisted with age, creaking beneath their weight. A faint echo of the sound came from the direction of the kitchen. She turned her head, saw only shadows.

She closed her eyes. *Let it be over swiftly.*

As is the way of men focused on their own goal, he reached his climax swiftly, breathing his satisfaction against her ear, the moisture from his mouth dampening her hair.

'Now I'll have that cup of tea,' he said, buttoning his fly. She willed him to look at her so she could search his eyes for some emotion, some hint of what had once been there. He didn't look. Without a further glance or a kind word, he turned his back on her and climbed the stairs.

14

Just minutes after Mary Anne left the washhouse, Biddy made her move.

The legs of the stool screeched in protest as she dragged it closer to the pawnbroker without totally removing her considerable bulk.

Before he could retreat he found his hand clasped in both of hers, big brown eyes gazing up at him from a moon-shaped face.

'You're a 'andsome bloke, Michael,' she cooed, clasping his hand to her powdered cheek and leaving a peach-coloured smear on the cuff of his jacket.

Words failed him. She mistook his lack of speech and action for admiration at best, arousal at worst.

'I won't charge,' she said, as if that would make a difference, her round face like an upturned dinner plate.

The back of his jacket scraped against the whitewashed walls as he felt for the door, his fingers taking on bits of moss and flakes of paint.

'Excuse me,' he said, just stopping himself from giving a stiff bow. 'I need to...' He jerked a thumb towards the outside.

'Pee,' said Biddy.

He nodded. 'Yes. Pee.'

Outside, he took great gulps of air. No matter his misfortune, he would still have lacked desire for a plump woman wearing too much make-up and smelling of bacon grease.

The back gate swinging gently on its hinges beckoned him, though he felt churlish to leave without saying goodbye. Surely he owed Mary Anne something for saving him despite their differences? At first she'd seemed no different than any other housewife, living in a world of housework and general homemaking. And yet he couldn't help admiring a woman who had done something to improve her lot even though the business threatened his own. It took intelligence; it also took inner strength.

You owe her nothing, said the cynical voice that had steered his life before coming to England.

He paused. The luxurious honey-coloured hair and the intelligence that he'd seen burning in her eyes swayed his judgement.

Turning on his heels but walking backwards, he looked up at the back of the terraced house thinking to glimpse her at the window and wave goodbye. There was no sign of movement, the windows reflecting nothing but sky, factory chimneys and a flock of circling pigeons.

The back door was open. He paused and eyed it thoughtfully, careful that his footfall should be as gentle as his presence. Of course he could ask Biddy to relay his thanks.

Biddy no doubt presumed he had gone outside to relieve himself. She'd be expecting him to come back. He shivered. Going back into the washhouse was not an option. He imagined her preparing herself for his return, her buttons undone and her bosoms ballooning like proved bread over the top of her underwear.

If he were wise he would leave right now. An old-fashioned sense of honour pricked his conscience. Mary Anne deserved a polite goodbye. He was a foreigner and, despite his hostile attitude, she had stepped in to save him being beaten, possibly marched off to a police station, and who knows what horrors that might hold. Hopefully she wouldn't come looking for him, but what if she did?

Quietly, he crept past the washhouse and the sound of humming. A full watering can lay against the corner of the building. In a desperate attempt to add authenticity to his excuse for leaving the washhouse, he nudged it over with the toe of his boot. A shower of water tinkled against a zinc bath. The humming from within paused, interspersed by a light giggle before resuming again. Michael headed for the open door.

Old habits of creeping around a silent house where prayer and contemplation lay as thick as dust motes stood him in good stead. He passed through a small room where root vegetables freshly picked from the garden lay with earth and leaf mould clinging to their roots.

The kitchen smelled of good things, was neat and clean, the table covered with a blue and white gingham tablecloth.

He heard noises that he presumed to be something cooking, but noticed the gas stove was not lit and neither was there anything to either side of the glowing hearth.

A curtain hung at the door between the kitchen and a passageway. It was tied back at the halfway mark with a length of green cord.

He still heard the noises, like a runner's deep breathing, or the hot breath of cattle in winter stalls.

Beyond the curtain... he saw them.

Her eyes were closed. The man who pumped at her like a dog on heat could not know that her lips were compressed into a tight line, that her fists were clenched and her whole demeanour was of a woman submitting to torture, not responding to love.

For a moment he could not move. An overwhelming urge to charge at the coupling was swiftly overcome once he realised that the man must be her husband. There was no passion, no love. She was not protesting, merely enduring what had to be, because that was her duty. Such a waste, he thought. She is reacting as though her passion has been dead for years, and yet she could be so much more...

Thinking of how she could be with the right man made his face hot. He imagined how it could be, shuddering at the beauty he saw in his mind.

It wasn't until he had regained the fresh air that he realised the extent of his own arousal. In a normal man it would have been an agony bordering on ecstasy. In him it was painful; ecstasy had been forfeited the day he had mutilated the physical badge that had singled him out as a Jew.

* * *

'We are Lutherans. Joseph is not.'

That was what his mother had said when he had asked her about Joseph Rosenburg, who had come to visit them from England.

His mother had never been one for elaborating on information. Even when amongst other women at the endless church gatherings, she never, ever, conveyed any additional gossip. Her companions gossiped; she merely listened, nodding where necessary and offering no comment except to question the truth and implications of what they said.

Joseph Rosenburg was a square-shouldered man with more hair on his face than on his head. His beard was black whereas his pate shone like a full moon on a dark night.

His warm, sweaty palms had engulfed Michael's hand like a whale swallowing a minnow.

'You look like your father,' he'd said.

'Do I?'

Michael could not argue with him. He had never even seen a photograph of his father. Following her husband's early death, his mother had moved in with relatives in Holland where she had met and married the pastor. Eventually they'd moved to Germany. Her new husband had resented her clinging on to old memories – photographs had remained in England.

'I should know, should I not? I am your uncle.'

They spoke of old times and relatives over a dining table of cold meats, garden vegetables, butter, and cheeses, brown, white and seeded bread.

Michael's eyes popped out of his head. 'So much food,' he'd said, patiently containing his glee until his stepfather had offered grace.

'Praise be to God,' his uncle had added.

Michael noticed his uncle did not eat any of the ham, which was quite the best meat on the table.

'You do a good spread,' Uncle Joseph had said.

'I do my best,' his mother had replied.

'Not easy in these times,' added his stepfather. 'I fear for the future. These bands of brigands, strutting about in their uniforms—'

'Hush!'

Michael had sensed there was plenty more his parents and their visitor wished to discuss, but not within his earshot.

Once the meal was finished and coffee served, Michael was dismissed, but he lingered, intrigued to hear more.

'Yes, yes,' said Uncle Joseph. 'A young man has better things to do than listen to his elders discuss times long past.'

'I don't mind staying,' Michael had said, curious to hear what this stranger had to say.

His stepfather had insisted. 'No. You go. We have serious matters to discuss that you will not understand. Go to your room.'

He had looked to his mother for help. Eyes downcast, she did not acknowledge him but continued to sip her coffee.

Simmering with rebellion, he did as he was told, his fists clenched at his side, his jaw set. But he didn't just leave the room, he left the house, marching down the path to the gate and the road beyond, where he could hear the sound of bugles and drums and knew his friends were marching by and that they were all wearing uniforms.

Pink-faced with annoyance and the warmth of the August day, he had made an instant decision, slammed the gate behind him and joined in the march.

He knew the boys from school; some of them even attended his stepfather's Sunday school but they were no longer in the Scouts. Their switch of allegiance had provoked condemnation from the pulpit. Pastor Deller had not been happy that they could come to church one day and wear the uniform of the Hitler Youth the next. 'Man cannot serve two masters,' he'd said in his sermon.

He'd had a visit from someone shortly following that and a large bruise had appeared beneath his right eye. His mother had been upset, but no word of what had happened came to Michael's youthful ears.

The young adolescents grinned as he stepped out beside them. 'Hey, Michael. Won't your father whip you for marching with us?'

'He is *not* my father,' he'd snapped defiantly, wishing he had their crisp uniform. He dreamed of smart uniforms, of marching with boys who would be friends, craving their acceptance and comradeship.

He fell into step, arms swinging enthusiastically to the marching beat, heart soaring because he was suddenly one of them – only he did not know then exactly what they were and what they stood for.

It was as if they knew where they were going and exactly what the world had to offer. They had not been sheltered from it as he had been.

Chest expanded, shoulders back, he kept step, proud to be associated with these boys from whom he had once felt so isolated. In the past they'd hurt his feelings; now his eyes brimmed with tears of happiness. The smell of the pine trees, the wildflowers girdling their trunks, was more pungent than ever before and through it all the sound of strong, marching feet, was like thunder rolling unstoppable across the earth. It would later prove true that the whole country was on the march.

The heat haze that had hung some distance ahead of them dissolved along with the road, running into the rough shingle bordering the Gros See, a lake surrounded by pine trees. Ripples of coolness tinkled against boulders and reeds trembled in the water-borne breeze as if they were singing in welcome.

The lieutenant, a pink-skinned young man, his hair sleek and pale as swan's down, gave the order to relax. If he noticed Michael, he didn't say anything. One more member was all to the good.

Boys who had once avoided the loner – the boy who wasn't allowed to mix with them – offered him bites of their lunch: sausage, strong cheese, apple cake and fresh bread. He could have cried with delight.

'Why did you join us today?' asked Johan, a boy he remembered from school as being very amiable – that was in the days before his stepfather had insisted on educating him at home.

Feeling uniquely privileged, he explained, 'They do not know I am here. They have a visitor from England.'

Eyebrows around him were raised. 'From England?'

Michael had nodded. 'He's my uncle.'

'Another Pastor Deller?' groaned Johan.

'No. He's not a pastor. I think he has a shop. His name is Joseph Rosenburg.'

He noticed one or two exchanged looks of surprise, but he gave it no account. They probably hadn't met many English people themselves and it made him feel good. No one he knew had English relatives.

'Let's swim,' ordered a boy he knew as Hans, a ringleader at school and apparently the same in uniform.

The conversation ended. Leaping and yelling, the boys stripped off, Michael with them, shouting louder than they, leaping higher and racing for the cool water with just as much joyous zeal.

That part of his memory – splashing, swimming, pushing each other beneath the cool water – was best of all. Better still was the feeling of being accepted by boys his own age.

Two blasts of a whistle and the shouted order of the lieutenant changed everything. Although still joyous, the boys obeyed, laughing, pinching and punching in fun, their naked bodies glistening as they filed out of the water.

And still Michael laughed with them as he stood in their circle, pulling underwear over his damp skin.

The beaming lieutenant, fists on hips, stood in the centre of the circle, nodding approvingly as his beady eyes swept over their bodies. There was lust in those eyes, though Michael didn't know that at the time. On that day Lieutenant Schwartz had singled him out, though certainly not for sex or favouritism.

His pink face visibly deepened in colour. His expression hardened and a fat finger pointed at Michael's loins.

'What is *that*?'

The boys about him fell to silence, their attention drawn to where the finger pointed.

A few frowned; some shrugged; most gave no response, unsure of what had been discovered.

Michael trembled, not sure why his penis should be of such interest to either the lieutenant or the boys. It differed little in size or colour from anyone else's, though he noticed the tip was shaped differently.

'This boy has been circumcised!'

The statement was shouted so loudly that a flock of crows in a nearby tree took flight, squawking disapproval as they climbed. There were intakes of breath. Michael was mortified.

'I don't understand...'

The lieutenant leaned close so the tip of his nose almost met that of Michael's.

'You're a Jew, aren't you? A filthy, stinking Jew.'

A gasp of horror, but also of surprise, swept among those gathered around him.

'Please, sir,' said Johan, stepping forwards and saluting smartly, though only half dressed. 'Michael is the son of Pastor Deller. He cannot be Jewish.'

The lieutenant's eyes narrowed.

Michael lowered his eyes, uncomfortable at having his penis so closely scrutinised by anyone, and especially here amongst his peers. His face reddened.

He winced as the lieutenant's square-ended finger stabbed at his shoulder.

'You have Jewish blood somewhere, don't you? That is why your penis has been cut. That,' he cried, his arm sweeping across his chest, 'is the sign of a Jew. Mark it well all of you.'

Trembling, Michael had shaken his head. 'I honestly do not...'

'He only has English blood,' blurted Johan defensively. 'His uncle is from England. He told me so himself.'

The lieutenant looked taken aback. This wasn't quite what he'd expected to hear. 'Is that so? And what is your uncle's name?'

'Rosenburg,' blurted the incredibly naive Johan. 'Joshua Rosenburg.'

Then he had known what it was to be Jewish; what his father was, what his mother had been. It all made sense, or at least as much as he knew made sense.

The lieutenant addressed the boys, hands clasped behind his back, head high and his eyes piercing into Michael as though pinning him to the ground.

'We do not want your kind here. Pure Aryans such as you do not mix with Jews.'

Something like a consensual tremble ran from one boy to another.

Michael opened his mouth, meaning to shout that he went to church just as some of them did, but the words would not come. In his heart of hearts he knew it would not matter whether he professed to be Christian or otherwise. They could see what he was – or rather what he had been born – for themselves.

The lieutenant's eyes blazed with a joy born of intimidation, the right of the strong over those weaker or different. 'Drive him from here! Drive him like the vermin he is.'

In the uncertain minutes that followed, when some boys hesitated while others picked up sticks and stones, Michael gathered up his clothes and ran.

Clothes bundled beneath his arm, boots swinging from their laces, he ran as fast as he could. At first the stones hurt his feet, but once he had gained the warm, smooth surface of the road, he sprinted away beneath a barrage of sticks and stones.

Some caught him on his back, his buttocks and legs. A sharp stone hit the back of his head. It hurt and soon he felt blood trickling onto his neck and down his spine.

He did not know the exact moment when they stopped pursuing

him. The road baked at the end of a hot day. His feet were blistered, his body bruised, but the tears in his eyes were of anger rather than pain.

Before they had perceived him as different because he was kept from their company, but now he was *physically* different and he didn't want to be. He vowed to do something to hide the mark of the Jew that they said he was.

The grown-ups had taken their drinks into the garden, their conversation buzzing like drowsy bees getting ready for sunset. He could see them through a gap in the bushes. He recalled his mother insisting the bushes be trimmed this summer. So far they hadn't been. Their leaves, big as a man's palm, tumbled in gleaming layers from a great height. They hid him well, their shadows falling over him and the blue and red tiles of the garden path soothing his blistered feet.

The house was cool and echoed with emptiness, but Michael heard only the cruel jeers of contempt.

Hot and red-faced, he ran through the kitchen where the smell of food lingered temptingly. Normally, he would have stopped and opened the pantry: food was expensive and scarce, though the Ministry of Propaganda insisted things would soon get better.

Today, he ignored temptation and left the warmth of the kitchen for the dark, dankness of the cellar. A previous pastor, an avid engineer and inventor, had left a few tools and bits of machinery down there.

He reached for the light switch and a single electric bulb threw a pool of light, beyond which everything was in shadow. Wooden shelves holding bottles of wine, preserves and pickles lined one wall. On the other side was a workbench. At one end was a lathe. At the other a press, for driving ball bearings into place, so he'd been told. It had a handle at the side and a gauge for selecting pressure.

Michael gave no measured thought to what he was about to do. Blinded by his need to belong, to be as everyone else, he selected what he thought was a suitable pressure. He'd seen it done; the old pastor, who had retired and lived fairly locally, had demonstrated the force and weight of the press with an apple; it had been smashed to a pulp.

He didn't need it to be as heavy as that, but just enough to right what he considered to be a very great wrong.

Pressure selected, he took out his penis and lay its tip off centre to where the apple had been. Taking a deep breath, he released the handle. The last thing he remembered was screaming in pain. After that, darkness...

15

The brown liquid still hadn't done its job. Mary Anne decided a little assistance was needed. It was Saturday, the larder needed restocking and she had a plan in mind.

She asked Lizzie to keep an eye on Stanley, who was kicking his heels against the dresser, aching to get out to play and sullen because he wasn't allowed.

Lizzie's reluctance showed on her face. 'Do I have to?'

'Well Daw can't. She's still sulking upstairs because John's leave wasn't as long as she'd hoped for, Harry's working and as for your father...'

'Lunchtime session down the pub,' said Lizzie, and looked up suddenly. 'Why do you put up with it?'

'Put up with what?'

'Dad being drunk so much. Why do you put up with it?'

Surprised at her daughter's insight, Mary Anne busied herself with her coat buttons. They were square-shaped and awkward to fasten. Today they were made more awkward by the question Lizzie had asked her.

'We're married. Until death do us part. That's the way it must be.'

Mary Anne tried to prevent her consternation from showing on her face. Why did Lizzie always make her feel so ineffectual?

From when she was small, Lizzie had always questioned the ways of the world, often the questions as disconcerting as this one.

'Why must it be that way? I mean, haven't you ever thought about leaving?'

Mary Anne fixed her with a steely gaze. 'Lizzie! How could you suggest such a thing?'

The truth was she *had* fantasised about living a different life; she'd imagined herself making the grand tour of Europe as they had in previous centuries. Florence, Rome, Paris and Pisa all beckoned from the books she'd read. In her imaginings, she was alone with her thoughts and the sheer exuberance of being able to indulge in history and books without having to worry about appearing too clever in front of her husband. In her mind, she wandered around cities that were vibrant with knowledge and culture, but the woman in her mind was not the dutiful wife and mother, but one who lived for herself, and Mary Anne found that very hard to do.

Lizzie was sitting in the comfortable armchair reserved for her father, her feet tucked under her, reading a book and sucking on a custard cream.

'I'd live alone rather than live with a man like Dad.'

'Not if you've got children you wouldn't. Children need a stable home.'

'Mother, you may not have noticed this, but soon it will be just you and Dad. Three of us are grown up and likely to fly the nest before long, and Stanley won't be that far behind.'

Lizzie's sharp observation struck a chord with them both. They looked to where Stanley was leaning against the back of a chair, a brooding, angry look on his face.

Alarmed by his disgruntled expression, Mary Anne immediately bent to him, looking closely into his face and stroking his hair back from his glistening forehead. 'Is something wrong, my darling? Are you feeling ill?'

Lizzie sighed in exasperation. 'Mother. He's fine. Stop fussing.'

Mary Anne's attention was firmly fixed on her son, her hands clasping his and her eyes full of apprehension.

Stanley shook his head and wrenched his hand from her grasp. 'Nope! Why can't I go out?'

'Because your chest is bad and this damp weather will make it worse.'

'He is better,' said Lizzie after he'd slumped off into the front parlour where his bed was still situated, slamming the door behind him.

Mary Anne was adamant. 'You can't be too careful.'

Lizzie didn't look convinced. 'Is he really still *that* ill?'

'Yes,' Mary Anne snapped. The worry of being told by the doctor sometime back that he had a fifty–fifty chance of recovery was still with her, and no matter how well he *might* seem she couldn't take the chance.

'Sometimes I think you feel guilty if you haven't got something to worry about,' Lizzie said, dropping her gaze back to her book.

* * *

East Street was busy with late shoppers, the shrewder of whom always left buying fresh fruit, vegetables and meat until late on a Saturday when the best bargains were to be had.

Mr Sampson wrapped her up a large piece of brisket and two breasts of lamb and from there she went to the greengrocer's for vegetables, Reynolds' for a bag of biscuits, and David Gregg for a hambone, a pint of cockles and two pounds of smoked haddock. Hearing on the wireless that bacon and butter would be rationed as from mid-December, she'd bought two pounds of collar and three pounds of butter, after waiting in a queue that had formed.

Usually after shopping for groceries, she took the bus back from East Street, but after two went by full to the platform, she decided to walk, even though the weight of shopping threatened to pull her arms from their sockets.

It was getting dark. In peacetime she wouldn't have minded this, but the pools of amber light thrown by shop windows were no more. The blackout had made the world a much duller place, and the gloom of evening started at around three in the afternoon. Ahead of her a group of small boys huddled against a blacked-out shop window and around an upturned orange box.

'Penny for the guy, missus?'

A host of grubby palms thrust forwards as Mary Anne walked past, her arms stretched with the weight of three bags of shopping.

Cheeky devils. Her lips curved just short of a smile. 'I can't give you anything. My arms are full.'

One of them she recognised as Paul Grant, a boy of around twelve, who lived in the next street and had a bad reputation. A dog-end of cigarette, no doubt picked up from the gutter, dangled from his mouth. Thumbs hooked in his braces, he stepped out in front of her, barring her way.

'We'll look after yer shopping while you get a tanner out of yer purse, or we can get the money out of yer purse for you, missus. Kind like that, we is.'

Mary Anne eyed the frayed pullover and the grey flannels skimming his dirty knees. Paul Grant was the sort likely to succeed in going to prison before he was much older. She gave him a jaundiced look. 'I bet you will!'

Unperturbed and cocky as you like, his top lip curled back to reveal his large, protruding teeth. 'Mean cow! Give us a penny!'

Like a pack of worrying dogs, his mates gathered round, full of bravado because they were all together and she was alone.

Finding her way barred, Mary Anne stopped dead in her tracks. 'You little devils. Let me pass.'

'No. Can't do that,' said Paul. 'Not until you give us a penny – no – thruppence for our guy.'

Mary Anne bristled. Bedminster was a tough area. She'd known that before she'd come to live here and she might have given in if it hadn't been for the fact that there was something about Paul that made her see red. Henry! That was it! He reminded her of Henry!

Swinging her shopping bags – one of which held ten pounds of King Edwards – she pinned him to the wall.

The look of surprise on his face was worth seeing. So was the fact that he couldn't wriggle free, the potatoes heavy against his chest.

'Don't go thinking you're too big to have your mouth washed out with soap and water or that I won't pull down your trousers and wallop your backside, Paul Grant!'

His bottom lip quivered. 'I'll tell my ma about you!'

Mary Anne was defiant. 'You do that. And you can also tell her that if she does take it into her head to come and see me, remind her to bring the three bob she still owes on that hat she bought off me for your granny's funeral. The old dear's been in Arnos' Vale Cemetery for six months now and I've not seen hide or hair of the money or the hat. Tell her that!'

At the first swing of her shopping bags, the other boys had ran off and now huddled around the guy sitting on the orange box. Initially, the ramshackle figure had seemed no more than a ragged jacket and oversize trousers stuffed into worn-out boots. Most of his face seemed composed of a beard made from horsehair pulled from an old sofa. A greasy trilby covered the upper half of his face including his eyes.

Now it sat upright, hat shoved back to reveal a pale face and defiant blue eyes. Her own son!

Like the others, he was open-mouthed, staring at a shamed leader pinned against the wall with pee dribbling down his leg.

'Stanley! Come here this minute!'

'Aw, Ma!'

Whispers ran from one boy to another. 'That's your ma?' asked one.

Stanley, his face like thunder, didn't answer but pulled off the smelly outfit, showing his temper by flinging each item onto the ground.

'What a bloody battleaxe,' commented another.

Mary Anne threw him a warning look. 'And you're another whose mouth could do with washing out,' she shouted.

Round-eyed, the boy clapped both hands over his mouth.

Mary Anne turned her attention to her son. 'And you're getting a good bath the minute we get home,' she scolded, eyeing the bits of straw sticking to his clothes. She didn't want to think of what else the old clothes had left on him; they'd been far from clean.

Stanley's face remained stiff with defiance. 'I don't want to go home. I want to stay out with my mates.'

His accusing look was disconcerting. It made her want to ask him what she had done wrong and the firm jutting of his chin was totally at odds with his cherubic features. Where was her little angel, and why was he acting like this? Deep down she knew the truth, but pushed it aside, still not able to face the fact that Stanley, the most innocent, the youngest of her family, knew the true state of her marriage. She hated Henry for that.

Stanley sloped along behind her and stayed in a foul mood all the way home. When they got back to Kent Street, she immediately put the wash boiler on and got Harry to get the zinc bath down from the back-yard wall.

But Stanley was still rebellious, and transferring hot water from the washhouse boiler into the bath would take time.

'Come here, you little blighter,' she said, as Stanley dived under the kitchen table.

'Nope!'

'Nope! That's his favourite word,' she said, too exasperated and tired to chase him any longer.

Sweeping her hair back from her face, she slumped onto a chair at the table, her tiredness washing over her in dizzying waves.

Lizzie noticed. 'Mum. Are you all right?'

Mary Anne nodded from behind the hand with which she shielded her face. Mum. Lizzie always called her that when she was worried.

'Don't worry,' said Harry, who had already stripped off his shirt, ready to wash before going out that evening. 'I'll deal with our Stanley.'

Harry dived under the table, crawling and scrabbling after his brother, who chuckled and laughed.

At last Harry pulled him out. 'Come on. I'm boiling you along with the sheets.'

Fists punching in fun against his brother's back and shouting words of protest, Stanley was carried out to the washhouse. 'I'm dumping him straight in,' Harry shouted over his shoulder.

Lizzie put the kettle on. 'You have a cup of tea, Ma, and I'll put the shopping away.'

Her mother did as she was told. Relief from taking the weight off her arms and feet flooded over her and gave her time to think.

Lizzie's comment about her children being grown up now had hit home, especially the fact that she would be left alone with Henry. When they were no longer at home he could only get worse.

At present Henry Randall was triumphant. Before John had gone back from leave, he was told of the marriage and had made no objection. On the contrary, he'd been over the moon, slapping John on the back, offering him a cigarette and telling him he was proud of him joining the RAF and that he was joining the family.

'Very glad we've such a brave chap in our street,' he'd said, while throwing an accusing glare in Harry's direction. 'We need more like you if this bloke Hitler is to be taught a lesson.' Harry had smiled in that disarming way of his, as though he knew secrets no one else was privy to. Casually, as though it wasn't him his father was referring to at all, he took up his pen to yet another crossword.

John had glowed in his praise, and Daw had thrown her arms around her father's neck and rained words of thanks against his ear, including the words her mother had asked her not to utter. 'Oh, Dad, I'm so glad you didn't mind us getting engaged before John joined up. Mum said it would be all right.'

Mary Anne perceived a tightening around his throat; the veins prominent like fine bones. The engagement had been kept secret until John came home on leave to ensure his acquiescence, Mary Anne taking the view that he couldn't refuse anyone in a uniform.

His tone was like treacle. His eyes were like lead. 'No, sweetheart. Of course not. You've got yerself a good man, a son-in-law any chap would be proud of.'

Mary Anne's stomach had tightened at the subtle change in his voice and eyes. Her children did not notice, but then that was the way their marriage had developed. To his children he was a firm but doting father who boasted to anyone who would listen that he never raised a hand to his children – and he didn't. His wife was another matter entirely.

Henry had been livid that she'd known about the engagement and hadn't told him. The storm clouds were most certainly gathering, but she'd kept up the pleasant facade. Years of practice had made it easy.

After everyone had drank the health of the happy couple with a small glass of Harveys Bristol Cream, Daw and John decided to go out and celebrate.

'Are you coming, Lizzie?'

Lizzie declined. She had kept her own secret that she was missing Peter. The only thing she was happy about – besides her sister's engagement – was that she'd had her monthlies, and so had Daw.

'I don't want to be a gooseberry,' she said, settling herself down at the table with a copy of *Picture Post* and a second cup of tea.

They'd laughed and Daw had blushed. 'You won't be. We're going to watch the film.'

'All right, then. I'll powder my nose and get my hat and coat. It's turning chilly.'

John had turned to their brother. 'What about you, Harry?' Harry was standing in front of the mirror above the mantelpiece smoothing his Brylcreemed hair. He was wearing a well-cut, navy-blue suit; his shirt was crisply white, and his tie a subdued mix of red and yellow stripes. His mother had commented how handsome he was, that she was proud of him. She also mentioned that the suit looked very expensive. 'Must have cost you a fortune.'

'Been doing a lot of overtime, Mother,' he'd said, and kissed her.

'No thanks,' said Harry in response to John's invitation to accompany them. 'I've got a previous engagement.'

'A date?' The girls said it in unison, their faces bright with curiosity.

Harry shook his head and went back to smoothing his hair. 'No. Just a mate.'

His father had scowled, his lips curling with distaste. 'Making yerself look nice for a mate, now if that ain't strange...'

Harry turned, the set of his broad shoulders and scowling face leaving his mother no option but to stand between father and son.

The girls and John were too wrapped up in their own plans to notice that anything was wrong.

'We'll be off then,' said Lizzie, linking arms with her sister's fiancé. 'Now we'll go in the back row if you like, John, but that does mean you'll have to share your kisses with both of us. Is that all right?'

John's pink and white complexion turned scarlet. 'Oh... um...'

'Only joking,' laughed Lizzie.

Mary Anne smiled. It was the first time that week she had heard her laugh. Why had everyone been so glum of late? The war, she thought, answering her own question. Just the war.

Once they'd gone, Henry had sat glaring at his son, his knuckles almost white because he was gripping the chair arms so fiercely.

His face was one big, angry scowl.

'Don't you feel ashamed not doing as John's done?'

Harry raised his eyebrows in pretended surprise. 'Going to the pictures?'

The blood vessels in Henry's neck pulsed with anger. 'You know damn well what I mean. You'd have more mates in the army, more worth bothering with, that is.'

A half-smile lifted the side of Harry's mouth as he buttoned his suit jacket and reached for his brown trilby. He skimmed its brim with his fingers so that one corner dipped over his right eye when he put it on.

Mary Anne thought how much he resembled a photo of Humphrey Bogart she'd seen in *Picture Post*. Her heart swelled with pride. Some might say he was more like Noël Coward, but she couldn't see it. Regardless of how they appeared to others, all her children were faultless in her eyes.

'You don't need to be in the army to have a lot of mates,' Harry said, sliding his arms into his overcoat. One side of his mouth twisted in contempt. 'Personally, I think a load of blokes being so close smacks a bit of left footers, if you know what I mean.'

Mary Anne balked at the insults flying back and forth between father and son.

Henry's face turned puce and puckered as he sprang to his feet. 'Us blokes in the army didn't smell like bloody pansies! We were men. Real men.'

Harry smirked. 'And stunk like it no doubt.' Henry leaped at him.

Mary Anne moved more quickly, standing between the husband she tolerated and the son she loved.

'Now stop it! Just stop it!'

Henry winced before her ferocious gaze. This fiery look was unfamiliar on the woman who kept the peace and had created as loving an environment as possible for the sake of her children; a rare glimpse of the woman beneath the dutiful exterior.

There was pleading in her voice. 'Leave him, Henry. Leave him to be what he wants to be.'

Henry raised a purposeful finger, his face still glowering with rage. He wagged his finger just inches from Harry's face.

'If he thinks—'

Mary Anne gripped his upper arm with both hands. 'Henry. Please. Who knows what's in the future. As he said himself, he might be one of the first to be called up, and if he is, so be it. All he's saying is that he will not rush to enlist. Remember all those in the last lot? Rushing to do their bit and certain all the fighting would be over by Christmas. Well, let's face it, they were wrong then and it looks as if they'll be wrong now. No one's even began fighting on a big scale just yet and

Christmas isn't far away. Remember,' she said again, the fierceness gone and a sad look on her face. 'Remember how it was, how many of your own comrades never came back.'

Fixing on the yellowing photograph of him and his friend Lewis, Henry blinked as the memories she'd provoked came flooding back, his whole body slack as though each and every one of those old pals were weights around his shoulders.

Terminating their conversation, Harry turned his back on his father, now slumped in his favourite armchair.

Harry kissed his mother on the cheek. 'Don't wait up for me, Ma.'

All might have been mended if he hadn't turned up the knob on the wireless as he passed it. 'Dance a bit. Enjoy yerselves.'

Memories shoved aside, Henry sprang to his feet. 'Don't you bloody treat me like—Ouch!'

In attempting to intercept him, Henry hit his knee on a chair. Mary Anne pretended not to notice. His mood would be foul enough without her making a comment about his clumsiness.

Once the sound of the front door being slammed reverberated above the sound of the wireless, she began gathering the last of the dinner things, moving swiftly to pile saucepans upon frying pan and plate on top of plate.

Out of the corner of her eye something moved; the prongs of a fork glinted beyond Henry's tight grip.

He was on her before she had time to pick up the plates and dash to the scullery, the fork digging into her cheek, just below her eye.

'Turn my family against me, would ye!'

She winced as the prongs dug into her face, enough to cause a red mark, but not enough to break the skin.

'Please Henry. Everyone will see. And I haven't turned anyone against you. Why do you say that?'

She bit her lip as he repositioned the fork against her throat. 'Like hell you didn't! Never told me about me own daughter getting engaged. What right have you got to do that, eh?

What right? They're my children. I've a right to know. The other...
the other don't matter... the other...'

His voice fell away and his brown pupils turned to black. 'It was a
long time ago, Henry. Why can't you forget it? It's all in the—'

His face leered closer. 'Because you never told me! That's why! You
never told me!'

Tears squeezed out from her eyes. 'But he died... he died.' Henry
sucked in his lips and raised his hand.

*'The opening bars of the Blue Danube waltz played by the BBC Light
Orchestra...'*

The wireless, its walnut case gleaming and smelling of beeswax,
sounded so sane, so ordinary.

He dug the fork into her side more deeply than her face or throat.

She screamed.

'I could easily kill you for what you did,' muttered Henry, his hands
around her throat, his face black as thunder. 'Had another man's baby
and didn't tell me.'

'Edward didn't come back. He died and the baby was adopted,
Henry. My parents wouldn't let me tell you. You know that very well—'

Her words were choked off. She had been going to say that it
happened before she'd met him. Her parents had thought it best for
her to marry, even though Henry was working class. They'd insisted
and at the time he'd been pleased to do so.

She was pretty and had brought money to the marriage. If only
Edward had come back. If only she had told him about the child. How
many times had she regretted not doing that? Perhaps he would have
been different – or perhaps he would have passed her by, too proud to
take on soiled goods.

'Stanley!'

She hadn't heard him come in, but there he was, standing round-
eyed in the doorway, his pink lips wet and shiny, and a bloom in his
cheeks.

His mouth moved, but no sound came out. He looked as though he had just opened his eyes from a nightmare that was still there before his eyes.

In that moment, she had never hated Henry so much as she did now.

As Henry's arms dropped to his side, the fork clattering to the floor, she ignored the soreness in her side, her own arms reaching out to enfold her son. Sinking her head against his, she enveloped him, smelled his hair and the slickness of his skin.

'Stanley. My dear love.'

She felt his eyes going beyond her, over her shoulder to where Henry stood, his arms lank at his sides.

Stanley's bottom lip trembled against her face. 'Why were you hurting my ma?'

'He wasn't really,' Mary Anne protested, managing a laugh though her side ached badly. 'Your father was showing me how he'd fought a German in the war...'

Henry's face seemed to shiver as though he were searching for the right emotions to make the necessary changes to his face. She braced herself for the change of countenance, the corners of the down-turned lips tilting up into a smile, the softening of the square jaw, and the veins of his neck receding into the tough skin.

He could do it so easily, she thought; charm the birds off the trees if he wanted to...

She watched, feeling a little sick as Henry's whole face beamed like the moon just coming out from behind a cloud. His voice was gruff.

'We was just playing. Just having a bit of fun.'

Mary Anne felt Stanley's eyes upon her, the tips of his fingers delicately tracing the redness around her neck. In that moment, she knew that he knew, that he had seen and heard too many times.

'No you weren't,' he said. 'You're always hurting my ma, and if you hurt her again, I'll kill you.'

Mary Anne shivered. The words were said with all the innocence of one without strength but with a great deal of endeavour. How could such a small boy speak so chillingly?

Henry's expression hardened and, for one dreadful moment, Mary Anne had wondered, Would there come a time when he would strike one of his children? He'd come close with Harry, but that one was too fly and strong enough to fight back, and Henry knew that. But Stanley...?

She had resolved to stay close to him, to guard him with her life. Judging by the look in Henry's eyes, she might very well need to.

16

The letterbox rattled and another letter from Patrick Kelly toppled onto the doormat.

'One for me and one for you,' said Daw, handing it to Lizzie.

'I'll read it later,' said Lizzie, placing it in one of the tiny drawers of the hallstand.

Daw, of course, ripped hers open immediately, her eyes filling with tears and her face reddening with emotion as she read John's letter.

'He's being transferred, but he doesn't say where.' She glanced at Lizzie. 'Hope it's somewhere in Wiltshire.'

They'd studied a map together, pinpointing airfields convenient for mainline train stations. At present both boys were in Suffolk – a fact they'd learned from John's last visit home.

Patrick, who was training to be an armourer on fighter air-craft, had come home only briefly, gone to the pictures with them, called in on his mother, and then promptly went back to base. He'd explained to Lizzie that there was someone else in his bed at home and only a pretty broken down chaise longue was available for him to sleep on.

'If only they were both closer.'

Lizzie echoed her sister's sentiments, though her heart didn't jump for Patrick as much as Daw's did for John. He was just a friend and always had been, but his letters were amusing. It had never occurred to her that he could write so eloquently; both his prose and his poetry had surprised her.

Unlike John's letters, Patrick's letters were passed around the family, an entertaining and enlightening read about what was happening. John's, of course, were far more personal and for Daw's eyes only.

Lizzie told herself that her relationship with Patrick could never be personal, but still she waited for the postman with just as much anticipation as her sister. So far she had not received one letter from Peter and it hurt.

The fact that it was Peter's mother who had told her he was leaving for Canada, on the very day he was leaving, still festered like an open wound. Why hadn't he told her himself? There'd certainly been enough opportunity. Only two days before, she'd been snuggled up with him on the back seat of his car, her eyes closed as she sniffed in the combined smells of the leather seats, his clothes and the scent of his hair.

'Even if you die tomorrow, I'll remember this moment for ever,' she'd said.

He'd sat bolt upright. 'Steady on. I wasn't intending to be bowled out just yet.'

Trying to persuade herself that perhaps he hadn't known he was about to leave was only partially successful and left her feeling disappointed. Another and quite unexpected side effect was that she kept analysing their relationship, comparing what she'd thought it had been to what it truly was.

Where did he actually take me?

Nowhere. They either made love in the grass, on the back seat of his car, or in his bed if his mother wasn't at home.

Did he really love me? Had he really said it?

She ticked off each answer from her mental list. Only after goading. Only in response to me saying I loved him.

Analysing spread through her thoughts just as a rash might spread over her body. Once she'd started working out the whys and where-fores of one subject, she couldn't stop.

It's about observation, she thought, and began observing other things, the results too worrying to face headlong. One of these was with regard to her family.

Lizzie had never noticed any problems in her parents' relationship. They were pretty typical of middle-aged couples in Kent Street. Her mother kept house, providing a warm environment for her family, ensuring there was plenty of food on the table, and clean underwear when needed. On the whole, regardless of her father's habitual drinking, they had a better standard of life than a lot of people. Now why was that, she wondered, and promptly did a few sums. After adding up the combined income of the household, it struck her that they must be living beyond their means. Her bike was new (bought by her mother), Harry dressed like a film star, and Mother was always slipping Daw a ten-shilling note 'as a little treat'. Where did all that come from?

Her mother giving money to her and her siblings also gave rise to another observation. Her father didn't like it. She had never studied his face at those times but now she saw the movement in his jaw, waves of dissatisfaction reverberating through his flesh from his clenched teeth. And sometimes there was an atmosphere – frostiness between her parents that she had never noticed before.

Working for Mrs Selwyn was not the same either. Peter wasn't there and, although she had made up her mind that despite the better money she would not work in a factory, she felt like a change.

The house in Ashton felt incredibly empty – Mrs Selwyn rattling around there all alone – and except for the casual help brought in to do extra cleaning, one day was very much like the next, rolling one on top of the other.

Somehow she had hoped Mrs Selwyn would confide in her, not quite taking her into her *total* confidence, but just enjoying her company, talking to her about Peter or her past life, but she didn't do that. The only time Lizzie got a response from her was when she remarked that she hadn't seen any letters arrive from Canada.

'Is Mr Peter well?' she asked.

His mother had flushed slightly. 'Of course. Why shouldn't he be?'

'I would have thought we might have heard something from him,' she said, dabbing a duster into a tin of beeswax and lavender polish and attacking the table as though it was her greatest quest in life.

She detected Mrs Selwyn's uneasiness, apparent in the way she pursed her lips and her teacup rattled as she put it back on the tray.

'Canada is a long way for the post to come, and you've surely heard about convoys being attacked. I expect the ship carrying it got sunk. I shall get one soon.'

And I'll look out for it, Lizzie told herself.

Being observant went on; weighing up the good in people and the bad, deciding that Mrs Selwyn was deceitful and that Patrick, whose letter writing was very prolific, was totally open, and very sentimental.

It was like a new world had been discovered. I'm not going mad, and I'm not imagining things. I'm just seeing things more clearly, she decided. Suddenly, there seemed no point in staying in service; her connection with Peter was all but severed; not even a letter.

She thought more about it as she cycled home, the place she'd regarded as warm and cosy all her life. What right did she have to condemn Peter for not writing? He was training to be a merchant seaman. Perhaps he was at sea at this very moment on one of the convoys bringing food from America to England.

No, said the more practical side of her character. She had every right to analyse, but no right to judge. He was doing his duty, and you, she decided, should be doing yours.

When she got home, bread, butter and jam were on the table, and neck of lamb stew bubbled on the stove.

Her mother slid the letter she'd put in the hallstand from her pocket.

'It's from Patrick,' she said, placing it on the table beside Lizzie's place.

Lizzie glanced at it before reaching for the bread. 'I know.'

'Aren't you going to read it?'

Lizzie shook her head and filled her mouth with a crust from the slice of bread she'd cut. 'I'm starving. You read it.'

Mary Anne sighed as she flattened the paper.

'My word, but he writes very beautifully. See?' She flashed it across the table.

Daw nodded. Henry grunted approvingly and Lizzie continued chewing her bread. Harry was absent, a bit later than usual getting home from the factory.

Lizzie noticed the avid interest in her mother's face as she silently read the letter, a slow smile gradually curving her lips.

As had become her habit, Lizzie eyed the other members of her family. Her father in particular was staring at his wife, impatience simmering in his eyes.

At last, unable to prevent himself, he demanded she read it. 'Well, come on. Let's be having it. Tell us what the brave young chap is up to.'

Her mother's eyes stayed fixed on the letter. Her voice was gentle, almost whimsical.

'It's censored. He's just saying that everything is going well and that he expects to be promoted because he was top of his class. As yet he hasn't got a posting, but will let us – you,' she said, correcting herself and nodding at Lizzie, 'know if he can.'

Her smile remained, still reading the letter.

'The rest is a poem,' she said in response to Henry's demand that she read on.

Lizzie had never been an avid reader of poetry, but the look of pleasure on her mother's face intrigued her. 'Yes. Go on. Read it, Ma.'

Mary Anne glanced at her, smiled and bent her head to the paper.

Remember me at dawn, when the grass shivers in an
    early breeze,
And is dappled by a shaded sun.

Remember me at midday, when shadows fall in black-
    ened squares,

On the ground I left behind.

Remember me at evening, when swallows dip and dive
    around the setting sun,
That once gilded my face.

Remember me in the blue blackness of an England in
    darkness,
Awaiting my return.

Lizzie stared blankly at the far wall where a picture hung of a great stag in a Scottish landscape, though she wasn't seeing the fine beast. Observation and analysis had suddenly come into its own. Was this letter really from the Patrick Kelly reviled by some because his mother was a tart? He was doing his bit, just like Peter.

And you should be doing yours.

She caught the rest of the family doing what she was doing: staring into space, suddenly blinking themselves back to reality.

'Beautiful,' said Mary Anne, folding the letter back up and passing it to her daughter.

Daw made a small sound, like a hiccup, though Lizzie knew it was really a sob. Daw was trying to control herself.

Lizzie sighed and patted her arm. 'It was sad, wasn't it, Daw? But don't upset yourself. John will be coming home, you just see if he won't.'

'At least he's doing his bit not like me own son,' snapped Henry, folding his paper, a precursor to making his way down to the privy at the bottom of the garden.

'And I'm going to do mine,' blurted Lizzie. 'I thought about joining the Wrens or something.'

Daw looked astounded. 'You can't.'

'Why not?'

The moment the words were out, she knew that now was not the right time. Daw burst into tears – only to be expected seeing as John had caught the train a few days before for pilot training, 'destination unknown'.

Mary Anne seemed as stiff as the salt block currently sitting on the table. 'Leaving home?'

Lizzie felt as though she were melting beneath her mother's gaze. She'd always been proud of the fact that her mother looked so much younger than many of her friends' mothers. A quick glance at her face now and she felt guilty. Worry and having a family certainly aged people, though she thought her ma was still lovely.

'Lots of girls are, Ma,' she said lightly, as she spread butter on a doorstep of bread. She couldn't see the problem. 'It'll be an adventure.' She didn't add that Peter Selwyn was doing his bit away in Canada and, in his absence, she felt obliged to do her bit too.

Her father's paper rustled as he got to his feet; he was certainly taking his time going out the back. His jaw moved from side to side as though he were chewing something. He did that when he was thinking things through.

'Women in the armed forces? It didn't happen in our day. Women stayed firmly at the rear.'

Lizzie leaned towards her father, her face shining with enthusiasm. 'Some Wrens are nurses. Some operate wirelesses or just do office work. They don't get to fire guns or anything like that.'

'I should hope not,' he said, going outside now forgotten. He rustled his paper again before disappearing behind it to look at the pictures and laboriously pick out the words he knew.

Lizzie smiled smugly to herself. If her father was going to object, he would have done so, but he hadn't.

Her mother's expression wiped the smile off her face. Mary Anne was cuddling the teapot against her chest, as though it might fly out of her hands if she dared relax her grip. 'I don't want you to go, Lizzie.'

She looked at her mother. She was standing looking at her side-long, her hands clasped at her chest, as slender and alluring as a painting she'd seen by Rossetti of a woman with reddish blonde hair and wearing a green robe.

'I might not have a choice in the matter. Women are being called up.'

'Then wait until you are.' Her mother's tone was strident and her worried look made her feel uncomfortable. She reached for the butter and jam and made a great show of slapping both onto a thick slice of bread.

'Why do you have to volunteer? What's the point of it?'

Lizzie felt herself colouring up. In her mind she recalled the feel of Peter's fingers unbuttoning her dress, the smell of him, the intense deliciousness of feeling his body, even his breath, falling on hers. She could hardly admit that she was doing it for his sake; it was her way of supporting him, and Patrick for that matter, though only at a distance.

'I just think I should,' she said finally.

'That's ridiculous – and don't put so much jam on that bread. Everything with sugar in is going on ration. You'll have to cut down.'

Lizzie slammed her knife down. 'Then I'll do without! What do you care if I starve!'

'Lizzie!'

The legs of Lizzie's chair squealed across the lino as she sprang to her feet. She was grown up. She didn't deserve to be treated like this, but neither was there any cause to behave as she was doing. It was all to do with how she felt inside.

Sucking in her lips, she considered how best to make amends, change the subject, do something useful, or better still, something good.

'I'll go and read Stanley a story.' A reasonable excuse, she thought, to leave the table and not have her plans questioned.

Her mother's mouth dropped open as though she was about to comment further. Lizzie didn't wait to hear reasons why she shouldn't leave home, though she could have dealt with them. It was the hurt in her mother's eyes that made her feel guilty.

Her father intervened. 'Stop trying to wrap the girl in cotton wool like you do that boy. At least someone in this 'ouse has got the guts to fight for their country.'

The cooler air of the passageway between kitchen and front parlour calmed her red cheeks.

'Oh, Peter,' she moaned softly to herself, rolling her head against the silky cold of the limewashed wall and closing her eyes.

The sound of the wireless followed her out. Her father had switched it on, waiting for the six o'clock news. At present a dance tune – a foxtrot, by the sound of it – drifted along the passageway, superseded by the news.

'This is the BBC news... threats of air raids have necessitated...'

Lizzie closed her eyes.

Air raids! Gas masks. Evacuation. Call-up papers... She clapped her hands over her ears, tried to shake the words away, and finally opened the door to what had been the parlour serving as Stanley's bedroom since he was first took sick.

Her little brother was sitting up on top of the coverlet reading a book. He hadn't come out for his meal, and had refused everything offered.

Lizzie made faces around the bedroom door until her young brother was in fits of giggles. He giggled even more when she sat beside him on the pale-blue eiderdown and tickled his ribs. 'No more,' he cried, 'No more,' already bent double and choking with laughter.

She cuddled him gently, bracing herself before feeling the thin arms and spare shoulders beneath his pyjama jacket.

'I thought you were feeling better,' she said. 'You certainly look it.'

He nodded. 'I am. And tomorrow I'm going out to play. Mum said I could if I went to bed early.'

'It's pretty cold out. You'll have to wrap up well.'

'I'm glad it's cold. I hope it snows.' His hair tickled her hand as he tipped his head back. 'Do you think it will snow?' he added, gazing up at her with eyes like crystal pools.

'It might at Christmas.'

'That would be nice,' he said, his smile wide enough to cut his face in half.

Her own spirits were lifted by his look of excited expectation. She couldn't help being infected by it.

'If you make a wish for snow at Christmas, it's bound to come true – at least, so I've been told.'

Stanley sucked in his bottom lip, his brow crumpling as he gave it some thought.

'Do all Christmas wishes come true?'

'Of course,' she answered, and promptly wished a few for herself: send Peter home for Christmas, have the war end and Mr Chamberlain announcing on the wireless that it was all a dreadful mistake, and mend the rift between her father and brother. The latter had surprised her. She'd never known them fall out before.

The new, analytical Lizzie perceived that the warm atmosphere she had taken for granted all these years had fractured, hairline cracks appearing where there had been only solid smoothness. The divisions between countries had grown wider, and so had those between people. Perhaps they had always been there; it took a war to bring them into focus.

But for now, Stanley's wishes were the most important. She sensed he had something else far more important to wish for than snow, or had more than one wish on his mind. She considered the obvious. Perhaps a toy train, a fort with lead soldiers or merely a book, or perhaps he really would wish that there would be no war. God knows enough people wished for that, but the blackout curtains were up and gas masks were hanging from their shoulders during the day and beside their beds at night. The future was frightening.

Stanley squeezed his eyes shut. 'I wish—'

Lizzie interrupted. 'For lots of snow.'

He shook his head.

Lizzie waited, marvelling that he looked so much better.

Lizzie prepared herself for happy Christmas wishes. 'I wish that my dad would stop hurting my mum.'

Lizzie froze. Surely she'd heard wrong. 'What was that you said?'

He repeated his wish word for word. His pale-blue eyes looked up into hers. It was like looking into a mirror, an image of what she had once looked like, though she'd never had his pale skin, had never been ill, but always a healthy, contented child. The picture in her mind of their happy home, the one she was always glad to come home to, threatened to crumble. She told herself that it couldn't be true, that despite the fraught atmosphere following her father's drinking sessions, her parents were happily married and had four wonderful children. That was the way it had always seemed. He's only a child, she thought, eyeing the startlingly white hair and the luminous eyes.

She cleared her throat while searching for the right words. When they finally came, it proved difficult to keep her voice from shaking.

'What makes you think he hurts Ma?'

He blinked as he thought some more. She tried telling herself that it wasn't hatred she saw there. It scared her too much in one so young, but his words scared her more.

'Because I've seen him – loads of times – when he thought I was asleep. I used to creep away, but I don't any more, and now he knows that I know. He's seen me watching and he knows I hate him, but I don't care... I don't care.'

17

The morning was busy. People were buying up the things likely to become scarce once the war was truly under way so everyone needed a little more cash to spend and the little washhouse was crammed with goods.

Aggie Hill had brought in a mother of pearl vase. 'These bloody ration books. The buggers in charge don't allow for a growing family, do they?' She spoke loudly, her voice barely restrained by the stout brick walls of the washhouse. 'Not that mine's going to be around, poor little sod. As I told you, he's already joined up. I just want a bit by me to buy what's going when he does come home,' she added, her voice taking on a kind of reverence when she spoke of her son.

'So I hear.'

Mary Anne folded one arm across her belly. Concentrating on the job in hand wasn't easy this morning. Aggie's son had been called up. How long before Harry was?

Barely noticing the finer details of the vase – if indeed it had any – Mary Anne shook her head. 'I haven't got room for this, Aggie. Normally, I would have, but there's just too many people bringing in stuff. I can't take it.'

Aggie pursed her lips, causing the hairs on her chin to point forwards. 'Well, that's a bloody nuisance.'

Mary Anne offered a solution. 'You can take it to Uncle's.'

Aggie's black eyebrows, totally at odds to her white hair, beetled like large caterpillars over her large nose. 'Has the nephew arrived then?'

'Apparently so,' said Mary Anne, deciding not to divulge that she'd met him.

'Jesus bloody Christ, thank God for that.'

Two other people had bits of silver to hock. Others had come in to see if she had anything suitable as going away gifts. 'My Annie's joining the navy as a nurse. I wanted a little locket for her.'

'I need some beer money. My Albert wants to go out on the razzle before he gets drafted – though I reckon it's only an excuse. I told him he was too old to be called up, but he won't have it.'

There were many others, all wanting money or items, their sudden needs caused by Adolf Hitler.

The last was Flossie Davies, her sleeping youngster clamped to her hip, his plump cheek resting on her shoulder. Although she hadn't been the first to arrive, she hung back. It was obvious she wanted to be last. Mary Anne wondered what she had to hock. Her husband drank more than Henry, and that was saying something. There were no mats on the floor in the Davies' house, only bare lino because anything they owned was continually being sold or hocked to pay the rent or put food on the table.

Flossie handed over the paper carrier she was carrying. 'Can you give me two pounds for this?'

'Two pounds!'

Mary Anne balked at the figure asked, but took the bag anyway and peered inside. What she saw surprised her.

'I didn't know your Frank played a trumpet.'

Flossie sniffed. 'Frank ain't musical. He brought it home one night. Next morning, I asked him where he got it, but he didn't remember.'

'So it's stolen.'

Flossie shook her own head vehemently, sending the baby's head jiggling like a rubber ball against her bony shoulder.

'No! No! I wouldn't say that. My Frank's not a thief. He got drunk and this thing got mislaid.'

Mary Anne sighed. 'You should know better, Flossie. Take it away. I don't deal in stolen stuff. Besides, what am I going to do with a trumpet round here?' She offered her back the carrier bag. 'Best for you to take it down to Uncle's. You heard me say he's back.'

The carrier bag swung on its string handles. Flossie's expression hardened and her pert chin quivered with indignation.

'I need this money, Mary Anne. My Frank's joined up, but he swears he won't go without a penny in his pocket. He reckons on buying a few rounds down at the Admiral Nelson before he goes, and swears he'll have a good send-off or stay home. And don't look at me like that, Mary Anne. Be in no doubt, I want the bleeder to go and the sooner the better. I can't go down Uncle's. I had a loan. I owes money there, and that new bloke might not be as obliging as his uncle.'

'Well, that's a different excuse to those I've been hearing. Women all around are bewailing the fact that their men are being called up and you, Flossie, can't wait for yours to go.'

Flossie was the picture of defiance. 'Can you blame me?'

Mary Anne eyed her for a few seconds only before shaking her head. 'No. I don't blame you. Won't you be worried about him spending all his army pay before you get any?'

Flossie smiled secretively and pulled her dingy blouse up from her breast so the baby could get at her nipple. 'Unbeknown to him, I've already looked into that. They'll apportion it so I don't go destitute. He'll get a bit of spending and I'll get the rest, which no doubt will be more than I'm getting from the drunken sod now. So you see, Mary Anne? I'll be better off.'

Mary Anne shook her head and smiled. 'Good for you.'

There were too many run-down women, she thought. Flossie had once been a good-looking girl, but she was thirty now and had a few teeth missing. Her hair, which had once been shiny and shingled, was now like rats' tails hanging around her face. Poor cow, thought Mary Anne, her gaze shifting between the bag and Flossie's face. It wasn't in her heart to refuse. Look at her, she thought, as she eased a few shillings from her purse. Straggly, greasy hair, no brassiere or vest, and God knows what the rest of her underwear was like. She had to agree that Flossie would quite likely be better off without Frank. It occurred to her that the war might change women's lives quite a bit if it was already changing the way they behaved, like Flossie being outspoken about what she would gain if Frank wasn't around.

'I must be soft in the head. Take this on account,' she said, thrusting five shillings into Flossie's hand. 'Like I said, it wouldn't be wise to hawk it around here. I'll take the trumpet down Uncle's for you. I can't promise two pounds, but you should get at least fifteen shillings for it.'

'Ooow, ta ever so much,' Flossie said, secreting the coins into the safety of her cleavage. What came next was barefaced cheek. 'As quick as you can, eh? I'm desperate, Mary Anne. Really desperate.'

'And cheeky with it! Be quick indeed!'

She smiled as she said it, though it struck her that Flossie was too saucy for her own good. She wondered how far she would go for the sake of her kids. To her mind, kids were the centre of a woman's world so she couldn't help but sympathise. There were too many husbands like Frank and, Christ knows, she had one of them.

Aggie Hill agreed to keep an eye on Stanley while Mary Anne went off to hock Flossie Davies' trumpet so long as she took the mother of pearl vase along too.

Mary Anne warned her. 'He's not to go out. Not in this fog.'

'I'll make sure he stays inside,' said Aggie. 'And thanks for this, Mary Anne. I'd go meself, but your legs are younger than mine.'

Mary Anne lifted her skirt a little, gazed down and was pleased with what she saw. 'They're getting older, but still stride out well and are still worth a look.'

Aggie winked. 'Never say die, girl, never say die!'

It wasn't until the next morning that she got round to doing it. A thick November fog choked the streets, dampened the daylight and deadened the sound of trams, buses and tradesmen on their rounds.

She wasn't comfortable doing the errand. The string handles of the carrier bag cut into her palms, not because of the instrument's weight, but because it was stolen – or might as well be. Frank Davies had a reputation for getting into trouble when he was drunk. Goodness knows where the trumpet had come from.

Aggie Hill's vase was just as heavy on her hands, but not on her conscience. Still, no point in dwelling on it, she thought, as she considered what she would say and what the pawnbroker would say to her.

She walked half the length of East Street, dodging the grey shapes of people, their faces half hidden with scarves, hat brims pulled tightly down, shivering hands shoved into deep pockets, all going places, though slower than usual because the fog had come.

In order to walk swiftly, it was best to look at the pavement, though it did mean bumping into people, but at least she could find her way. Intermittently looking upwards, she judged where she was by the shop signs: Reynolds Biscuits; David Greig, teas, fine hams; Stan Butts the butcher, the greengrocer's, the cockle shop, the shoe shop and the haberdasher's.

When at last she saw the sign of the three brass balls, they loomed out of the fog like black spots floating in a sea of grey. She paused outside, rehearsing what she would say. First, she would apologise for threatening him with the garden spade. It was the right thing to do.

But you did make amends, she told herself, fighting the urge to turn round and go home. You did save him from being beaten up because he was foreign.

She hadn't realised she was about to step into the road until the rattle of a tram and a shout from someone up top burst her thoughts.

'Got a lot on yer mind, luv?' shouted a costermonger, his barrel perched at an angle, partly on the pavement, partly on the road.

'We all 'ave,' said a woman he was serving with five pounds of King Edwards. 'We're at war with Germany. Ain't that right, luv? Can't keep yer mind on anything fer two minutes.'

'That's right,' said Mary Anne.

All this talk of war, she thought. What is it really to do with us? Why do we have to fight the Germans all over again?

So far nothing really concrete had happened except for the building of a communal air raid shelter at the end of the street and an air raid warden station at the other. Then there was all this talk of call-up papers and joining up. So far Harry had not received his; she hoped he never would. She hoped it would all prove a storm in a teacup, a bad dream from which they would all shortly awake – including Adolf Hitler.

The door groaned as she pushed it open. The shop smelled of beeswax and old paper. The sound of music came from the living quarters at the rear of the shop, loud enough to drown the jangle of the brass bell above the door. Mary Anne peered through the thick wire mesh running around the countertop towards the living quarters. There was a passage with stairs going off to the right. Straight ahead was a door. It was half open.

Leaning over the counter she shouted, 'Hello? Is anyone there?'

There was no response.

She tapped her foot and looked around. Surely there was another bell? She didn't see one and the string handles of the carrier bag were cutting ever deeper. It had been an ordeal carrying it here and she certainly didn't want to carry it back home.

She called again, more vigorously this time. 'Hello? Are you dead or just sleeping?'

It came to her then that it was gone one o'clock. All the shops she knew closed at one for a bite to eat. Perhaps the pawnbroker had forgotten to lock up before eating his meal.

No matter, she thought with a determined thrust of her chin. This trumpet is not going back and Flossie needs the money. So does Aggie.

There was a doorway in the wire that gave when she pushed it. The countertop was of polished wood, dissected halfway along with a lift-up lid and a bolted gate beneath it.

Lift up the lid and go inside. That was all she had to do. First she put the carriers down. By the looks of the countertop, she'd need both hands to open it. She was right; it was made of shiny wood, but one big heave and it was open. Retrieving her carriers, she passed through the gate and into a passageway where rugs of various colours and condition covered the floor.

Being behind the counter gave her a strange feeling of crossing a barrier between shop and owner, between the public face of the business and the private world of the man who lived behind it.

The smell of beeswax was left behind in the shop with its glass-fronted cabinets, deep drawers, cupboards and china knobs.

Mary Anne wrinkled her nose. The passage and the room it led to smelled of a man living alone, a man who thought he could cope. Clothes sat on a chair; more spilled from a suitcase. The smoke from a cigarette curled upwards from a full ashtray. Both doors of a green-painted cupboard at the side of the chimney breast hung open. Boxes of records, newspapers and dusty old documents cascaded in a jumbled heap from the cupboard shelves, the drawers gaped open and singed sheets of paper hung half-burned from a glowing coal fire.

The music came from a gramophone beside a chair in which lay its owner. Michael lay oblivious to music, his cigarette or the stale air that badly needed replacing. He was slumped in a chair, his head thrown back, eyes tightly closed.

The sleep of the just, she thought. She was struck by how good-looking he was, and no younger than twenty-five, no older than thirty.

Before her amusement had barely creased her lips, something struck her about his face. The tension around the lips, the strain of flesh over cheeks; it was as though he were holding something in, something that caused him great agony. If he had been a woman he would have been crying.

The music ended, replaced by the crackling whirr of the needle digging into the centre groove.

His eyes flicked open. On seeing her, he jerked upright in his chair causing her to jump back. '*Ja?*'

'I came to...'

He ran his hands nervously through his hair and looked embarrassed. There was a moment when he seemed to collect his thoughts, a sudden realisation that he'd responded correctly but in the wrong language.

He shot to his feet, his shoulders level with her head, making her feel small. He eyed her questioningly. 'What is it? What are you doing here?'

Suddenly intimidated by his height and presence, Mary Anne backed closer to the door. She raised the carrier bag. 'This, I brought you this,' she said lifting the bag in her right hand. 'And this,' she added, lifting the one in her left.

He glanced at the bags then back at her, his deep-set eyes unblinking and thoughtful. 'To hit me with?'

She winced. His eyes were too intense, surprisingly dark compared with his blond-streaked hair.

'Oh!'

Just as she'd expected, he'd brought up the garden spade, making her feel surprisingly foolish. Her cheeks burned like hot coals, but she remained defiant.

'You had no right to tell me to stop my business. I make pennies doing what I do. You make pounds.' She jerked her head at the shop behind her and the piled shelves, the glass display cases full of watches, necklaces and rings. 'Look at all that stuff out there. It must be worth a fortune, far more than the little bit I deal with. You must make lots of money.'

For a moment his stare held, though the tension in his jaw visibly slackened. He threw back his head and convulsed with laughter all the way down to the hands he rested on his hips.

'This place...' He jerked his chin towards the shop. 'It makes nothing. People bring in their valuables for money. The valuables stay here. It is a storeroom. Nothing else. Just a storeroom. My uncle was a fool.'

Mary Anne cocked her head to one side as though she hadn't quite heard correctly.

'That's ridiculous. Pawnshops have always made money round here.'

'Not any more. No one comes in – except to stare at me.'

Mary Anne eased her weight from one hip to another, both hands clutching the carriers now held in front of her.

'Well, I suppose it may have changed a little. Back in the twenties and thirties it did all right, when a lot of people were out of work, and back in Victorian times it was even worse. I know from my customers what it was like; women pawning their wedding rings on a Monday and redeeming them on Friday when their husbands were paid.'

'So your family were better off?'

'I didn't say that.'

'You did not need to. Your voice is different – the way you speak – not like others around here. And you did not mention the pawning of wedding rings as being your own experience. You heard this second-hand.'

He had a forthright way of looking at her, as though challenging her to explain herself. Admitting that he was right was difficult. Her own background had been different, but over copious cups of tea, her customers had told her some pretty grim stories of how it was; stories of the street, their families and times gone by. Tea was a great leveller. Yes. Tea. A brew shared could heal all manner of things – including the tension between her and this man.

'Are you going to offer me a cup of tea? It's a very English thing to do, you know.'

Something about his expression altered. He nodded and regarded her as though it was indeed a very civilised idea. 'Yes. I will.'

Turning his back on her, he made his way through the door and into the small kitchen. She could see a sink, a stove and a large table, a larder in the far corner.

Pipes banged and clanged as a tap was turned. She noticed he'd had to use both hands to turn it on. The old place needed pulling down, or at least a good lick of distemper.

Her eyes scanned the shabby room. The furniture was old, the dining chairs dating from before the Great War, horsehair-stuffing poking through worn velvet that might once have been quite luxurious. A black marble clock sat silently before a huge overmantel, its mirror pockmarked with rust. Another clock sat just as silently on the wall, its brass pendulum gleaming despite the gloom. On another wall hung a black-framed copy of Landseer's *Monarch of the Glen*, the same as she had in her own living room and just as dislikeable. Besides an ebony-legged side table, the armchair he had been sitting in and a chaise longue rested against the back wall. The wallpaper was dark and overly ornate – red flock and smelling of dust – another leftover from the previous century.

He came back and placed two teacups on the table.

'The clocks are stopped,' she said dispassionately, as though it had some bearing on his predicament.

'Ah! Does it matter?'

Her gaze was steady, her voice soft. 'I was just thinking, if we could turn back time, would we do things differently? I mean, would Mr Chamberlain have handled things differently and perhaps averted a war. Would I have done things differently in my life?' A half-smile playing around her mouth, she looked directly into his eyes. 'Would you have done things differently?'

For a moment, he paused and she wondered whether the tea he had just swallowed was too hot. It wasn't. Mary Anne could see from the floating tea leaves that he hadn't quite mastered the art of tea-making.

Averting his eyes, he put his cup back into the saucer. He couldn't answer her question in the general terms demanded.

He sensed the warm heart beneath her steely tenacity and couldn't help get the impression that the woman he saw had only recently broken out from a different person; like a butterfly escaping from a chrysalis. He wondered if she was always so different when her husband wasn't around. For now, being reminded of his own history stymied his thoughts about her. If he opened his mouth and gave the slightest hint of how much he would like to change things, everything, the whole story of what he had done would come pouring out. So he held his tongue.

'These are such difficult times, and are likely to get more difficult,' she said.

Michael leaped on the chance to change the course of the conversation.

'War! Difficult times! What do you know about difficult times, you living here in England? Nothing! Nothing at all!'

Mary Anne could hardly believe the change in the man, one minute amiable, the next downright pompous. When her face reddened now it was from anger, not embarrassment.

She got up from the shabby chair, a spring making a zinging sound as she did so.

'I am a mother. Mothers have difficult times bringing their babies into the world, difficult times watching them get sick, difficult times putting enough on the table to feed them, difficult times watching them grow up and make the same mistakes their mothers made. And now, in war, difficult times wondering whether our sons will be killed, our daughters made widows before they're barely wives! That's what women know about difficult times, Mister whoever you are... that's what they know! England is really no different than Holland.'

Holland!

Germany, he thought. If you could only see Germany. Mary Anne failed to see the consternation in his face, the fight between truth and lies, not because she didn't want to, but because walking the length of East Street carrying bags and in her present condition had sapped her energy. The details of the room swam before her eyes and her legs felt as though the floor had turned to water and was rising to her knees.

She reached for a chair. 'I must...'

He caught her before she hit the floor, saw the pallor and closed eyes, her hair tumbling out from beneath her fallen hat.

'What is wrong? Can you hear me?'

Of course, she couldn't.

He must bring her round. He pushed the small table away from the front of the old chaise longue. Far too big for the room, earlier in the week he'd thought about burning it. Now he was glad of its width and cumbersome detail.

He picked her up easily and lay her out on it. After placing a cushion beneath her head, he bent his ear close to her mouth and checked her breathing, then took her wrist and checked her pulse. As he did so, he found himself surprised at the slimness of her wrist and the elegance of her hands. He heard her give a little fluttery sigh and worried that she was having trouble breathing. What should he do? Unbuttoning her coat and the cardigan beneath, he studied her face, the fine cheekbones and the naturally arched eyebrows before peeling both garments away from her throat.

He thought about getting her a glass of water, but reconsidered. Would she choke on it while unconscious? Surely it was better to let her come round in her own time. He decided that was the best course, pulled up a chair and waited, watching as the colour returned to her face and her breasts rose and fell, her full lips parting slightly with each breath. He became mesmerised by her breathing, the gentle rise and fall of her breasts, the parted lips, the pale smooth complexion. She was at his mercy and all he could do was stare and become as familiar with her features as a lover watching his mistress sleep.

How would it be to sleep with her? he wondered. What did her laughter sound like? How would her fingers feel on his flesh?

His eyes followed the curve of her shoulder, the narrowing of her waist, the more sumptuous curve of her hip. And she had compassion; she had relented when it looked as though the workmen would beat him on her behalf. He liked that and seeing her coupled with that pig of a husband upset him. He suddenly wanted to show her how it could be. A woman of such classic good looks should know real passion at least once in her life.

She reminded him of Bronica and that summer – when was it? Nineteen thirty-three? He'd been twenty-three at the time and, having left university, was working as an assistant in a music shop. Not exactly the ideal profession, but he was in Berlin with companions of his own age, which meant he didn't have to live at home. The memories still discomfited him.

He hadn't died from his mutilation, but the scarring around the head of his penis was now very obviously the result of an accident, not a religious ceremony. 'I don't want to be a Jew!' he'd shouted when his stepfather had asked him why he'd done it.

'Don't be ridiculous,' the pastor had replied, his expression and tone of voice decreeing that all discussion about such a distasteful part of the anatomy was at an end.

He couldn't find the courage to question his mother, so the problem smouldered, his physical defect a mental barrier to him becoming a fully paid up member of Aryan society.

Bronica's red hair had glowed like fire through the smoke-filled haze of a beer hall, the atmosphere buzzing with politics, bravado and sexual attraction. A brass ensemble belted out the usual background noise until she had got up, whispered in the ear of the trombonist, then, with assistance from some male friends, stepped up on to a tabletop and belted out an American jazz number.

Sleekly sinuous, her body had entranced him, her hair flying around her shoulders, her voice as smoky as the air around them. Most people rolled with the beat, faces red with beer, sweat pouring from eyebrows and into drinks. Others, mostly Brownshirts, and less inclined by indoctrination to American jazz, began thumping table-tops, then stamping their feet.

His stomach had churned. He'd seen what they could do if they felt someone was undermining German culture. One or two, their sweaty faces masked with evil, got to their feet.

The singer, Bronica as he later knew her, did not see the danger until her eyes met his warning glare, the left jerk of his head alerting her to it.

Her voice had been strong before, but now it soared with new notes and different words.

In a flash, the band followed her lead. The whole gathering stood to the tune of '*Deustchland über alles*', sweaty faces bright with patriotism.

During the crescendo of applause led, of course, by the Brown-shirts, he followed her out of the door into the cool night air. She was leaning against the wall of the building, her eyes closed, breathless and quite pale.

'Very clever of you,' he said, careful not to startle her.

She opened her eyes and smiled. 'Thank you for warning me. You have expressive eyes and a determined chin.' She eased herself away from the wall, her breath still coming in quick, sharp gasps.

'You deserve a kiss.'

He'd had no time for protest, but then he would have willingly submitted to whatever she wanted.

Her lips moved against his. He'd never expected a kiss could feel so alive, so pliable. He'd also never expected that Bronica could ever be anything but the freedom-loving girl he'd met that night, but first impressions, he realised later, could be deceiving.

18

When she woke up, Mary Anne found herself lying on the ugly Victorian chaise longue with the cut-velvet covering of swirling greens and browns.

It came back to her where she was and why she was there. Although she wanted to leave right away, she forced herself to do things slowly.

The first thing she noticed was her unbuttoned coat and cardigan. Violation being the first thought to enter her head, her hand automatically went to her throat then lower towards her cleavage. No more buttons were undone.

Raising her eyes she saw him, the pawnbroker. Dark blond hair curled over the nape of his neck. He had a strong neck, a handsome profile, though there was something in his eyes she couldn't quite understand. Most of the time he had a guarded look. Only when he smiled did the barrier come crashing down, betraying the man beneath the guarded exterior.

He was gazing into the carrier bag that held the trumpet, his face seeming to reflect its brassy gleam, his eyes glowing with rapture.

Suddenly aware that she was conscious, he put the bag down, and leaned over her. 'You feel better?'

Hesitantly, she raised a hand to her cheek. It felt hot, yet inside she shivered – especially her limbs. 'I fainted?'

He nodded, put one arm around her shoulders and held her hand. 'Sit up slowly.' His voice was kind.

She saw the defensive look return to his eyes as she rechecked the buttons of her blouse and smoothed her skirt. 'I'm so sorry about this. I feel so embarrassed.'

'Are you ill?'

'No! No.'

She swung her feet to the floor a little too quickly and wished she hadn't. Her head swam. Rubbing her eyes with the heels of her hands, she willed herself to focus properly, and, when she did, caught him staring at her, saw his expression shift between openness and restraint.

'What time is it? I have to get home to my children.'

He shrugged.

She remembered the clocks. 'Oh yes.'

'So is my watch,' he said, glancing at his wrist. 'But I think it is about three o'clock.'

Mary Anne gasped. 'Three!' She rose too quickly to her feet. 'I have to go. I have a family to cook for.'

A good mother, he thought, admiring her sense of duty, though not quite able to discard the thought that she was a woman first and foremost. Being solicitous, he decided, would help overcome his attraction to her.

'How many children do you have?'

'Four,' she said, buttoning her blouse, then her cardigan.

He picked up her hat and passed it to her. It was a brown hat with a wide brim and a green feather at the side. He thought it suited her well, and found himself quite liking it, though of course, he couldn't possibly say so.

His eyes stayed fixed on the feather when he spoke to her. 'A nice size family. How old are they?'

Mary Anne pulled on a pair of knitted gloves. 'Harry's twenty, Daw is nineteen, Lizzie is eighteen, and Stanley – he's the youngest – he's almost eleven.'

He tried not to look surprised, not just that she had grown-up children, but that he was still attracted to her even though she must be at least ten years his senior.

'I must go,' she said, swiftly buttoning up her clothes as she made for the door.

The rugs in the passageway were limp with age and rumpled by the loose floorboards underneath. The heel of her shoe caught in one and she toppled. Michael caught her elbow.

She started at his closeness, pushed her hair back from her face, glanced at him then dropped her gaze to her feet.

'Damn these peep-toe shoes. The heels are too high, much too high for a woman of my age. I don't wear them very often, but they were such a bargain. The woman who pledged them was desperate for a few shillings for her old man's tea...' She stopped. Was he still angry with her for infringing on his business? 'Just a few shillings,' she said, almost apologetically. 'We all have to live.'

'Yes. We all have to live.'

She did not flinch when he put his arm around her, knowing it was meant kindly and without sexual intent. 'You must take things slowly. Give your head time to clear.'

All the same, it was pleasant. He was in his shirtsleeves, the warmth of his body permeating the thin cotton. It was good to feel the gentleness and warmth of a man. Henry never touched her unless as a preamble to the sex act, and even then he wasn't particularly gentle.

'I have to go,' she said again, and remembered the trumpet and Flossie Davies, the mother of pearl vase and Aggie Hill.

Michael pre-empted her question. 'Yes. I will take the trumpet.'

'It's not for me, it's for a neighbour of mine.'

'I will give you five pounds. Do you think she will redeem it at some time in the future?'

Her jaw dropped. Five pounds! It didn't take a minute to think about it and reply. 'No. I don't think so.'

'And ten shillings for the vase. It is very pretty, but...' He shrugged.

Mary Anne managed a knowing smile. 'But a bit old-fashioned.'

'Yes.'

They might have laughed together, but someone was coughing and thereby making their presence known out beyond the counter.

'Stay here. Sit a while,' said Michael and sprang into the passageway. 'Who is there? Can I help you?'

Her first inclination was to leave anyway, but that was before she glimpsed the man standing at the counter. She vaguely recognised the man as being one of Henry's cronies from the pub. Like Henry, he had also served in the forces, but hadn't done a day's honest work since. She'd heard rumours he did a bit for street bookies, loan sharks and the owners of dubious clubs with even more dubious clientele.

Instinctively, she slid behind the door, hoping he had not seen her, but she couldn't be sure.

Michael's features hardened on recognising the so-called caretaker he'd found warming the bed instead of running the shop. His expression soured.

'What are you doing back here? I thought I told you to get out and not come back.'

'Just passing. Thought you might have reconsidered and needed some help.' His crafty eyes slid past Michael and into the passage to the door at the back. 'Don't look like you do, though, do it? Already got someone to help you... or whatever.' He grinned. 'Well, there we are then. All needs a bit of company at times, don't we?'

Mary Anne pressed herself against the scratchy surface of the old flock wallpaper.

'Get out of here!'

She could hear Michael's voice turning angry.

'Now, now! Don't be too hasty. I can understand how you might feel, catching me as you did with young Daisy, but there, we all 'ave a livin' to make, even 'er. Could always get you an introduction if you like – she might do you a cheap rate if she likes you.'

'No thank you.'

'No?' He sounded genuinely surprised. 'Well, never mind. But I needed to dip me wick, so to speak, and besides, I was due a bit of time off. Now, as I was saying...'

Michael was having trouble keeping his temper, yet he knew he must. The man facing him, dishonest as he was, was a natural born Englishman. If he had a mind to, he could get him into very great trouble.

'I do not want any trouble. Now please... go.'

Thomas Routledge had a greasy complexion, small eyes that never stayed still, like beetles scuttling from one subject to another. He scratched his face, his mouth hanging open and lopsided.

'I think you should reconsider, at least, hear what I got to say... how it is... so to speak.'

Michael remembered the solicitor, Abner Crombie, had described Thomas Routledge as being morose, far wide of the mark in his opinion. Schemer, snake and charlatan were far more accurate.

'I do not think I will reconsider.' He knew he was going to regret saying it, that he might still be on the receiving end of this man's revenge, but he still had some pride.

Routledge leaned further forwards on the counter, elbows resting on the polished wood, fleshy face cupped in stubby fingers, the ends of which dug into his flesh, pulling the flaccid jowls upwards and displaying the hair in his nostrils.

'Hear me out, Mr Maurice – if that's yer real name – you be a foreigner, and even though you says you ain't German, you sounds German, no matter how careful you is with yer speech. That's why nobody's coming into yer shop. And it ain't gonna change. This war is gonna make 'em even more chary of foreigners. They'll go to 'er round Kent Street, rather than deal with you. So I reckon this, let bygones be bygones. Take me back on and I'll stand up front and do the wheeling and dealing, take my cut and you'll make yours. Fact is I'm English and you ain't. Puts me at something of an advantage that does. Now! What do you say?'

Michael gritted his teeth. In a way Routledge was speaking the truth. On the other hand, it was hard to be civil, but he made the effort. 'I will not be blackmailed.'

Thomas Routledge's loose lips sagged into a sneer. 'Is that so?'

Michael nodded. 'That is so.'

Routledge straightened. The beady eyes were like buttons on either side of his nose. He shrugged and a smattering of dandruff fluttered from his shoulders. 'Your choice, Mr Maurice. Your choice. But you'll regret it, I'm tellin' ye, you'll regret it.' Arm level with his sightline, he pointed his finger accusingly, his other hand jerking the shop door open. 'Just you remember!'

The door slammed. The brass bell above it jangled angrily and the glass in the display cases shivered in their loose frames. Once she was sure Routledge was gone, Mary Anne came out into the shop. 'He'll make things difficult for you. You know that, don't you?'

Michael's eyes met hers and he nodded.

He sighed. 'I suppose it would have been sensible to take him back on, but...'

When he shrugged again, Mary Anne could not resist the urge to take hold of his shoulders, looking up at him intensely, as though she would will him to be careful. 'It might have been more sensible. He's a bully. He'll be back.'

He glanced at the hands clutching his shoulders, wanting to lay his upon them, but not daring to do so. Instead he looked into her face. 'In my experience it is never good to give in to bullies.' Mary Anne suddenly realised just how close they were standing and how taut were the muscles beneath his shirt-sleeves. Her cheeks, so pale a moment before, now reddened with embarrassment. Flustered, she dropped her hands, shoved them into the patch pockets of her red and black coat, and took a step back.

'I'd better be going.'

'Yes.'

He didn't want to see her go. Once she was gone he'd have only memories for company. Some were good, some not so good, and some the most terrible nightmares that would be with him for the rest of his life.

He reminded himself that she was married and that he was still an honourable man, or at least he liked to think that he was.

Head bowed, eyes averted, he turned his back on her and headed for the private rooms at the end of the passage.

Picking her way carefully over the rumpled carpets, she tried to put her thoughts in some order. For a while back there she had forgotten her 'little problem', and indeed, a lot of her problems. He'd been kind and she still tingled at the memory of his touch.

There was something about him that stirred her, perhaps the fact that he was the exact opposite of the man she was married to. Her thoughts were confused. Michael's confrontation with Thomas Routledge had meant something. Thomas and her husband, Henry, were out of the same mould. They were both bully boys, both wanting their own way regardless of who they had to trample underfoot.

The fact that her hands were tucked into her pockets broke into her thoughts. Where is your handbag and purse? The answer came swiftly: In the chair.

The loose floorboards creaked beneath her feet, creasing the scattered mats as they moved.

Michael was sitting in the same chair he had been when she'd arrived, only this time he was not asleep and dreaming. This time his elbows rested on his knees, the trumpet clasped between his hands like a religious chalice for which he had great reverence. He glanced up as she entered.

'I left my bag in the chair.' She pointed to the deep cleft between seat and arm at his side.

Shifting his thigh, he dug down into the narrow void and brought it out and handed it over.

It was warm because it had been next to his body. The feel of it was strangely erotic and she hugged it close. Although their eyes met, their conversation was at an end; he seemed wary of saying anything else to her. She put it down to worry. Crossing swords with Thomas Routledge was enough to worry anyone. She couldn't quite come to terms as to why her heart was beating so quickly, but decided to express her gratitude on behalf of Flossie and Aggie.

'And thank you for the money.'

In her estimation it was far too much, but she guessed at his reasons. He wanted more customers. He also wanted friends.

Michael Maurice was lonely. That was the decision she came to as she let herself out and the haunting strains of a trumpet drifted out into the empty shop.

_____

19

Flossie Davies was tickled pink when Mary Anne presented her with four pounds ten for the trumpet.

'Five shillings I already subbed you, and five shillings for going,' explained Mary Anne.

Flossie's eyes stayed pinned on the money, hardly noticing that her baby was pulling the side of her mouth out of shape with sticky fat fingers and making her speak funny.

'Not that I'll tell that bleeder that I got that much,' she said. 'I'll tell 'im two pounds. He'll probably tip me half a crown from it for being so obliging – then expect me to be even more obliging once he gets back from the pub, if you gets my meaning.' She made a guffawing sound – somewhere between a laugh and a sneer. 'Fat chance!'

Once she was alone, Mary Anne pulled the loose brick out from behind the boiler and took out an octagonal tea caddy with Chinese figures along its side. This served as her cash tin. Due to the dampness of the environment it lived in, the lid had rusted slightly and was usually difficult to prise off. Today it was less so, but Mary Anne did not regard it as irregular until she looked inside.

The tin was divided into two layers. She kept the bulk of her money in the bottom compartment. The 'current' money – such as that the pawnbroker had given her for the trumpet and the mother of pearl vase – she'd placed on the top until such time as she'd settled with the vendors, Flossie and Aggie. It wasn't there. It occurred to her it might have fluttered out without her noticing when she'd put it away. She'd been in a hurry at the time. As was his habit, Henry had been hammering at the front door, shouting to be let in. He never ever went through the arch and around the back of the house, and in case he might discover that she did more than laundry in the wash-house, Mary Anne had never encouraged it.

Leaving the tin on top of the boiler, she got down on her hands and knees, peering into the gap left by removing the brick. She also probed behind the boiler's supports.

There was no sign of anything except cobwebs, crumbs of loose mortar and scurrying spiders.

'What are you looking for?'

'Ouch!' Mary Anne jerked up hitting her head on one of the boiler's brick supports. She came face to face with Lizzie, who had a puzzled frown creasing her forehead above her clear, greyish-green eyes.

Slapping the dirt from her hands and plastering a smile on her lips, Mary Anne got to her feet.

'My scrubbing brush. I can't find it. Never mind. It'll turn up.' Lizzie's attention had been diverted to the tea caddy. She was peering into its bottom layer where bundles of ten bob notes jostled with pound notes and fivers.

'What's all that money?' Her voice was touched with wonder.

Mary Anne opened her mouth to explain while racking her brain for a suitable excuse, and ended up stating the obvious. 'It's mine!'

She pushed the money down beneath the partition and closed the lid. It didn't alter the fact that money had been taken from her tin, but now was not the time to worry about it. Lizzie was still looking puzzled, her eyes going from the tin to the cupboards, one of which was presently unlocked, hanging open and exposing the items within.

This particular cupboard held china: teapots, tea services, tureens never used, gravy boats and even a Lustreware chamber pot, palm trees and a bright-blue camel etched into its honey-coloured surface.

Lizzie's face held a look of wonder. 'What's all this stuff?'

Mary Anne slammed the door shut and turned the key.

'Nothing for you to worry about.'

Prevented from peering into an Aladdin's cave of best china that had once graced many a front parlour in the neighbourhood, Lizzie's gaze went back to the money and from there to her mother, her head tilted to one side and the frown remaining.

There was no need for words. Mary Anne knew she was waiting for an explanation, something believable.

Mary Anne slammed the lid shut and put it back in the gap, ramming the loose brick in behind it. The simplest excuse came to mind. 'It's my Christmas money.'

'You saved all that?'

She sounded and looked impressed, but Mary Anne fancied the look in her eyes was at odds with her attitude, not so much disbelief, but as though she knew the truth.

'I did,' said Mary Anne, turning to the pile of washing waiting for the water to heat up, sorting it into whites and coloureds as a way of busying herself and not meeting Lizzie's eyes.

Henry never entered the washhouse, and neither did her sons and daughters. As children they'd wrinkled their noses at the smell of soap-suds and steam. It had always been her domain. That's why she had been able to run her business without any of the family guessing why so many women came and went, presuming perhaps that they merely gossiped and drank tea. Her family didn't question where the good tablecloths, fine china and excess indulgences in dress and food came from. They were accepting of the good things, living their own lives and leaving their mother to lead hers. Why had Lizzie chosen to come out here now?

'What are you doing out here anyway?' Mary Anne asked.

'I wanted to talk to you.'

Lizzie leaned against the boiler; her bright eyes, made brighter because her lashes were so dark, followed her mother's every move.

Although Mary Anne only glanced at her, she was aware of something akin to wonder in her daughter's eyes, but found interpretation quite impossible.

Lizzie had learned a lot of things since the 3rd of September. For a start she knew more about European politics than she'd ever cared to. She'd also seen another side to her father and brother, even a more selfish one in Daw, her sister. Daw, she'd decided, was under the impression that the world revolved around her or her and John. She'd never noticed before. And then there was Peter. It still irked that he hadn't told her he was going to Canada. It irked her that he never really took her out, only in the back of his car or to Clancy's Farm. Why had he never taken her dancing or to the pictures?

The world was altering, or perhaps it was her that was altering, seeing things differently – like her mother. The realisation that her mother, Mary Anne Randall, wasn't just her mother but a person in her own right had only recently come to her. She had lived her own life, fallen in love at one time, though it was hard to imagine her parents lusting for each other. It just didn't seem right.

We don't see them as people at all, she thought to herself. To her and her friends, parents were just 'them', the woman washing the dishes and the man sitting, smoking and reading a paper, or in her father's case pretending to read, picking out the words he did know and getting the gist of the news that way. They certainly couldn't see them doing 'it', though God knows how they would have come into existence in the first place. Chillingly, so chillingly that she shuddered, it occurred to her that Stanley could be telling the truth, that her father did actually strike her mother. The thought left her feeling quite sick, but the possibility was now undeniable. How much did any of them really know about their parents' private relationship?

'So what do you want to talk to me about?'

Mary Anne made a great show of folding the dirty sheets into neat piles. She didn't usually do that, but keeping busy was better than meeting the quizzical look in Lizzie's eyes. She couldn't recall Lizzie ever looking at her like that before. It made her feel like a child who's been caught with stolen chocolate around her mouth. In response to the thought, she wiped her mouth with the back of her hand.

'I don't quite know where to start,' said Lizzie, dropping her eyes to look sheepishly down at her toes as she wriggled them against her fleecy-lined boots.

Following Stanley's outburst, she had watched her parents more closely during the past few days and what she'd seen had surprised her. Her father's nostrils had flared and his eyes hardened when her mother dared to disagree with him. On one occasion, she'd seen her mother passing Daw ten shillings so she could buy herself something nice to wear. John was coming home for Christmas and Daw was frantic with excitement; she'd always been slightly vulnerable, a little anxious, not like Lizzie who had a tendency to go where angels fear to tread.

'That's it! Go and spend my hard-earned cash. Housekeeping money don't grow on trees, you know.'

Her father had said it jokingly, but a nerve had pulsed beneath one eye and his jaw had turned as stiff as cardboard, his eyes glaring with contemptuous anger, and that anger directed at her mother. The experience had alarmed her. She'd never seen him rise to anger, as he had with Henry. This war, she thought grimly, it's all down to this war. It's going to change all of us. Alone in the room she shared with Daw, she'd asked herself whether she had imagined it; was there really more to her father than met the eye, or had Stanley been dreaming?

Her question had been answered later that evening. Henry and Daw had gone out and Stanley was asleep when she passed the kitchen on her way to the outside lavatory. Only her parents remained.

Unseen, and feeling slightly guilty, she had watched and listened.

Her father's voice was low and rumbling and he was hovering over her mother as she cleared the dishes away, the front of his body almost pressed against hers. She couldn't hear what he was saying and didn't see him strike her, and yet he'd seemed intimidating.

'The beginning tends to be a good place.'

Her mother's voice brought her back to the present.

Lizzie sucked in her bottom lip, her dark lashes brushing her cheek as she lowered her eyes, searching for the right words to say, words that made sense.

'You and Dad; are you happy?'

Mary Anne stopped what she was doing. Her laugh was forced and short. 'Now there's a question.'

'Are you?'

Mary Anne covered her confusion with a concerted attack on Harry's dirty shirts. Regardless of the fact that he worked in the tobacco factory, he insisted on a clean shirt every day.

'We're no different than anyone else.'

'Our Stanley seems to think so. He said he saw Dad...' She paused, her mouth turning dry as her mind swiftly analysed the outcome of this. 'He said Dad hits you.'

Mary Anne felt her whole body stiffening, like the proverbial pillar of salt. Her poor boy! Her poor boy! She should have known. She *had* known, but had failed to face the problem.

She vowed to make sure he heard no more of his father's tantrums – though quite how...

'Our Stanley?' She blurted the words, not wanting to confront her own unease. Disbelief formed a better shield. She stared at Lizzie, her hands flopped on the pile of shirts.

Lizzie saw the look in her mother's eyes and it chilled her to the bone. 'It's true,' she said slowly. 'Don't deny it, Ma. I can see it in your eyes.'

The body that had felt like a salt pillar now turned fluid. Mary Anne lowered her eyes and shook her head. 'You don't understand.'

Lizzie's frown deepened and she folded her arms. Accusations could make one feel quite triumphant; but this wasn't quite that, thought Lizzie. 'Why do you protect him?'

Mary Anne thought hard how to smooth over this lump in her life. She couldn't think of anything and consequently turned defensive.

'Now that's enough of all this! Less of your lip, Lizzie. Just be thankful you have a comfortable home provided for you. I'd never let anything hurt you, you know that. What goes on between me and yer father is not your business.'

'Like your pawnbroking?'

Mary Anne's jaw dropped. It was the second time Lizzie had surprised her. Besides being a business, the washhouse was the women's place, like a club where they talked of their troubles among themselves.

'That's none of your business either.'

She attacked the washing with renewed vigour, stuffing it into the boiler though the water was not yet boiling and whites never did so well unless steam was rising. The way Lizzie, her own daughter, smiled and shook her head made Mary Anne feel like a silly little girl.

'I'm warning you!' said Mary Anne, suds flying from the finger she waved. 'You're getting too big for your boots.'

'That's because I've grown out of them. I'm grown up, Ma. I go to work. I've...' She had been about to say that she'd known love, but she wasn't quite sure she had any more. Her views on that were a bit distorted at the moment, so she took a different path. 'I know about the business. We all know about it to some extent, but as long as we're looked after and you're happy, what does it matter?'

If Mary Anne had been dumbfounded before, she was doubly so now. 'You know about it?'

'Of course we do – well, me and Harry anyway. We added up all the things we have including Dad's wages and ours, and found the figures didn't add up. So we sneaked out here, found your little book and made a few enquiries. John hinted at it the last time he was home. Thanks to you our Daw's got a whopping great ring on her finger.'

'And she knows too?'

Lizzie folded her arms and shook her head. 'Not Daw and not our Dad either.'

Mary Anne was tempted to ask why the two of them had never let on.

Reading her mind, Lizzie tilted her head to one side. 'Isn't it obvious? Me and Harry, and not forgetting our Stanley, are like you. We notice things. Dad and Daw don't. They do the things they want to do and most everything else goes over their heads. As long as they get what they want, that's it. They can't help it. It's just the way they are.'

Lizzie waited for her mother to respond, to unload at least some of her worries about her father. She dared to say what was on her mind. 'Does he only hit you when he's drunk?'

It might have been the child growing in her stomach, or it might just have been shock, because Mary Anne felt something tighten deep inside, as though she'd been kicked. All her life she had doted on her children, determined to give them a happy childhood and never, ever to expose them to the violence that existed deep in her husband's soul.

If only they hadn't grown up, but even so, they were still her children. She still deserved their respect. With that in mind she resolved not to let this go any further.

'Children should be seen and not heard,' she snapped.

Lizzie protested, 'Ma! I'm not a child.'

Mary Anne eyed Lizzie up and down. Her expression was stiff and guarded, but she saw the same hair and eyes as her own, the same girl likely to fall in love as she had, perhaps get in trouble like she had and being handed a way out that might turn out less than happy.

'Yes. You've grown up all right. I can see that,' she said regretfully, then turned defiant again. 'Though you don't always act like it,' she snapped, turning sharply back to her washing. 'Sometimes you act like a silly girl.'

Lizzie felt her face reddening. She knew exactly where this was going.

'I'm old enough to make my own choices, Ma.'

'Peter Selwyn is not for you.'

Feeling slighted and immature, Lizzie fidgeted before recovering her nerve. 'Hardly matters at the moment. He's in Canada. And Mrs Selwyn is talking about going to stay with her sister in Bournemouth. That was why I was thinking of joining the Wrens.'

'Well, you haven't done it yet, have you?'

'No.'

It had not been Lizzie's intention to turn the spotlight on herself. Despite her recent reservations, her passion for Peter Selwyn still gnawed at her insides. Off and on, she missed him and although she knew her interest would not be welcome, she had asked Mrs Selwyn when he was likely to get leave.

Mrs Selwyn had kept her glassy eyes fixed on the flowers she was arranging in a vase. Her voice had been as cold as glass, each word like a sliver of steel expressed through tightly clenched teeth.

'That is for his mother to know and not every nobody with whom he happens to have a passing acquaintance. After all, careless talk costs lives, as it says on the poster.'

Mrs Selwyn had left Lizzie in no doubt that she disapproved of her showing too much interest in her son.

'You are a nobody,' Lizzie had muttered while polishing the dining table with big, sweeping movements aggravated by anger rather than an overwhelming need to see her face in it.

It was also clear that his mother would disapprove of them marrying.

Peter had never mentioned marriage – not in so many words. Lizzie realised she'd been guilty of reading the possibility into the honeyed voice Peter had poured into her ear, while his hands explored her flesh, and her body had burned with longing.

It was a strange coincidence the following morning to find Mrs Selwyn was sitting at the breakfast table, reading a letter. She looked up beaming the moment Lizzie entered the room.

'Elizabeth! I have received a letter this morning from my darling Peter. Isn't that wonderful?' To Lizzie's surprise, she passed it to her. 'You may read it if you wish. After all, although not a member of the family, you are a member of this household.'

Crockery was in danger of being rattled to pieces as she put the tray down on the dining table.

Too surprised to speak, she took the letter, her eyes swiftly scanning the words, eating them line by line.

The letter gave details of what he was doing and hinted at where he was 'on-board ship somewhere in the Atlantic'. The letter was far less eloquent than the one Patrick Kelly had sent her, but she told herself it didn't matter. All she wanted to know was whether he had mentioned her.

At last it said,

Give my best regards to Elizabeth, and tell her to keep an eye on those butchers or they'll short change her and she'll have to do extra errands.

Dishes, dusting and polishing didn't require much mental effort, so as she scrubbed pots, dusted bookcases and polished the dining room table, Peter was there with her, hinting for her to give her usual excuse to meet him. She fairly floated around the house. She wanted badly to feel his presence, even if it was only to rub her cheek against his jacket or run her hand along the writing desk in his room. If his bedroom door had not been locked, she would have gone in there and lain on the bed just like they used to do when his mother was out. The door had been locked the day after he'd left for Canada, but, she reminded herself, the car was still here.

During that part of the day when Mrs Selwyn was having her after-noon nap, she crept out of the house and into the garage where Peter's Austin Seven was kept.

Lizzie stared at it. How many afternoons had she spent in the back seat, cuddled up to Peter, her underwear on the floor and her breasts exposed to his groping hands.

On opening the rear door, the smell of polished leather came out to greet her. Closing her eyes, she breathed it in. How wonderful it was; how much it reminded her of being half-naked against him. She guessed that his smell was still inside too. How wonderful it would be to imagine him there, beside her.

She thought about it, told herself no harm could be done, and slipped off her shoes. The temptation was too great. She climbed inside, lying full length along the back seat, closing her eyes and wrapping her arms around her own body. His smell was still here, mixed with that of the leather.

She stroked her shoulders and imagined it was Peter. A tingle of desire trickled down her throat, over her breastbone, down her arms, over her stomach and down to and between her thighs.

He mentioned me, she thought to herself, and was happy. He'd only said kind regards and to remember to order the right meat from the butcher, but that was enough. She might have been happy enough to believe that, except that she suddenly heard the sound of the letterbox. Second post! Was it possible for a second letter to arrive? They'd received so little.

She got out of the car, closing the door behind her, and made for the hallway and the letterbox. There were only two brown envelopes, but she could see through the frosted glass of the door that the post woman had stopped at the garden gate, possibly talking to someone else by the look of the other blob of colour she could see.

She opened the door. 'Is this second post?'

The post woman shook her head. 'No. This is the one and only post. Oh, and by the way, I'll be late again tomorrow. Midday post only. We've got a bit of a backlog.'

It wasn't until she'd closed the door that it came to her exactly what the post woman had said. There had been no first post this morning. All the day's excitement drained out through her toes as another thought occurred to her. If that was the case, when had the letter arrived? Surely not yesterday? Mrs Selwyn had been so anxious to show it to her, so surely she would have shown her it yesterday.

Thinking she could check the date stamp, she looked for the envelope in amongst the old newspapers and magazines they were saving. There was none. She shrugged. Perhaps Mrs Selwyn still had the envelope in her possession. Perhaps she'd placed it behind the clock on the mantelpiece, though she didn't recall seeing it. She had to accept it as fact and leave it at that.

20

The pawnshop and the storeroom behind it were an Aladdin's cave of unending discoveries. Personal items rubbed alongside hocked treasures, stuffed into cupboards regardless of tin scratching silver plate, or pewter amongst china.

The gramophone was the noticeable exception. No bits of underwear or china lurked in the cabinet beneath the green baize turntable. Obviously his uncle had enjoyed music. Wagner, Bizet, Schubert, Strauss rubbed shoulders with Puccini and Chopin, all protected in brown paper sleeves.

He searched through them avidly, his mouth almost watering with the delight of composer names, orchestras and recordings. Discarding Wagner, he found what must have been one of the first recordings of *Madam Butterfly*. The singer's name was unfamiliar to him, but it didn't matter. Only the music mattered. With something approaching reverence, he placed the record onto the soft felt of the turntable, wound the handle and carefully placed the needle on the record.

The initial scratchiness was drowned in delicate notes that tinkled like a fountain and pleased him. He would sit and listen. He'd made himself lunch – just bread and cheese. Camp coffee he found was more palatable when laced with cream from the top of the milk plus two spoonfuls of sugar.

Balancing plate and coffee on the arm of the chair, he heaped a few records onto his lap and proceeded to look through them, sliding some onto a keep file and some for discarding. Perhaps he would sell them in the shop.

Eight records down, his fingers found the edges of a brown envelope, creased and worn with years, which had been slid between the works of Beethoven and Handel. On the outside was written 'Summer 1912'.

Fingering the faded writing, he surmised what it might contain: family memories, photographs and birth, marriage and death certificates. Fearing what secrets it might contain, his first inclination was to destroy the contents without looking at them. Perhaps it was the music softening the residual savagery still lurking in his heart, or perhaps he was feeling more secure than when he'd first arrived, or braver, or stupid, or merely curious.

He sighed. It could be any or all of those things.

His fingers tapped the package. Do it, said a voice in his head. Do it!

Taking a deep breath like a diver before plunging headlong from the highest platform, he slid his fingers in and pulled out the contents.

They were a pile of sepia photographs, mostly what he'd expected: photographs of a man, a woman, a child. He recognised his mother and himself in some. There were dates and names on the back of each photograph.

On one he was four years old according to the notation on the reverse. He didn't recall it being taken. He didn't recall ever being with the man on whose knee he sat – the man he presumed was his father, his natural father, a man he had never known, but missed not doing so. There were so many truths he wanted to know.

The only father he had ever known was Heinz Deller, the only country Germany. He didn't even remember his short stay in Holland following his father's death.

The people in the photographs were very formal – hardly a smile between them, their clothes stiff and dark. On closer examination he fancied the corners of his father's mouth tilted upwards, as though trying to stem his laughter because the stiff poses amused him.

His mother, standing with her hand resting on her husband's shoulder, looked young and confident, even happy.

He caressed her image with his thumb. This was the Ruth Maurice that used to be, the young woman who had gone on to turn her back on her family, her roots and her religion and married a Lutheran pastor.

After eating the last of his lunch, he took the dirty dishes to the kitchen sink. His uncle's kitchen was very much like the rest of the premises; it had seen better days. There was a larder set into the wall, the door sawn in half at some time so that the top half opened onto a marble slab to better keep meat and dairy products. Above it were shelves holding tinned foods, bags of flour, jams and preserves. The bottom half opened on a storage space for vegetables.

Across from the larder was a deep sink with a wooden draining board. It had a single tap of indeterminate age, which was stiff and difficult to turn on.

Clamping both hands around it, he wrenched it on, promising himself that he'd fix it shortly, fit a new washer or whatever was needed.

Cold water poured first sluggishly then in angry spats as though resentful of being roused into action.

After washing it in cold water with a few lumps of soda, he took the fine Chinese porcelain into the shop, putting it back into one of the display cabinets from which he'd taken it. Using the items left in pledge had become something of a habit. Yesterday he'd used some items from a Royal Worcester set; the day before had been Coalport, today had been Chinese, and tomorrow? His eyes scanned the boxes, their contents scrawled in spidery writing.

He'd started making up an inventory a few days before that and, after discovering the most exquisite crystal glassware, had decided it was a great shame that these things were merely stored, and never used. They were like bones, merely the frame on which flesh is hung, just one part of the body or of life.

While shutting the cabinet door, he heard a sound from outside followed by a slight trembling of the front door, as if someone was leaning against it.

There followed a scuffling of many feet coupled with giggles and squeals of mischievous laughter, then a scratching noise, like a knife or nail down paintwork.

He shouted, heard running feet, and sprang for the door.

The local children! He'd had a few skirmishes with them when names had been called and faces pulled, but nothing he couldn't handle, and good God, he'd certainly seen and handled a lot more than name-calling and face-pulling back in Germany, but still, they were becoming a nuisance.

His uncle being a cautious man, there were three bolts securing the door, one at the top, one at the bottom and the largest in the middle.

Their stiff blackness fuelled his exasperation, each grating obstinately as he dragged them across, the latter proving the most obstinate of all. Eventually, using both hands, it grated back. Impatient to discover what was going on, he flung the door back so it slammed against the wall, sending the loose glass in the display cabinets shivering in their frames.

A winter sun threw the thin shadows of lampposts across the silent street, meeting the continuous shadow of the opposite terrace like sticks diving into a black pool. Apart from the shadows and a chill wind blowing the dust from the gutter, the street was empty.

He stayed looking this way and that for a few minutes more, thought he heard the giggling again, but couldn't be sure. If someone was still around, they were hanging about on the corner of Bottle Lane, a narrow alley of mouldering tenements. The lane divided the rank of shops from the rest of the terrace on this side of the street and smelled of dank cellars and rotting vermin.

Just children, he thought. Children playing.

He began to shut the door, when something caught his eye and turned his blood cold. The door was solid, heavy Victorian joinery, four panels set into a strong frame. On arrival, Michael had admired its strength, the careful workmanship and the dull blue paint that made it look even stronger.

Today he stared, his complexion paling at the sight of a white-painted swastika, a dribble of paint running from it like a demon's tail.

Sweat poured down his face and his body trembled as he slammed the door shut and squeezed the bolts home.

Leaning his head back against the door, he heard the hammering of his heart, the sweat turning cold between his shoulder blades.

Children! Just children, but children could be evil. Children could endanger his life and his freedom.

The chill memories returned, like dancing devils behind his closed eyes.

* * *

'The moment they see that uniform, the streets are yours,' said his friend Curt, his blue eyes sparkling behind a pair of wire-rimmed spectacles.

Michael ran his hands down the starched shirt and fingered the embroidered badges and insignia of the National Socialists and the senior arm of Jungsturm Adolf Hitler, the Hitler Boys Troop, of four-teen- to eighteen-year-olds founded in 1922. He was so excited he couldn't speak.

'So pleased to have you join us,' said Curt, offering his hand. 'It was about time.'

Michael shrugged. 'I would have done before, but... you know how parents are.'

Curt pushed his glasses back on his nose with one finger. 'I know. They don't understand. The Great War has a lot to do with it. So many of our brave men dying through no fault of their own, betrayed by the Western democracies and their Jewish bankers. But parents come round, though, of course, with your father being a pastor it must be even more difficult.'

'He's not my father! He's only my stepfather,' retorted Michael, displaying his contempt for the man who had denied him the companionship of his peers, other boys of his age.

'My real father died when I was a child.'

'Then he has no right to tell you what to do.'

'He could when I was younger. That was why I could never join you in the junior Jungsturm Adolf Hitler. He said that even the British Scout movement was based on militarism and he didn't approve.'

Curt laughed. 'The Scout movement was never like this! This is much more serious stuff. The Fuehrer makes great demands on our loyalty. Still,' he said, slapping Michael's arm. 'You're older now. It's up to you what you do. The worse your stepfather can do is to denounce you from the pulpit.'

Michael laughed. 'He can denounce all he likes. I won't be there to hear him. I've had enough of him and the church.'

Curt slapped him on the back. 'Good for you, my old friend! And give it no mind. We have our own church and Adolf Hitler is our God!'

21

Mary Anne counted the bus fare into her purse, noted that it also contained two half-crowns and a two shilling piece, plus two five pound notes folded into quarters.

It was the third time she'd checked it since getting herself ready to go out. Again, like she had on the previous occasions, she slid it back into her handbag next to the sanitary towels and the clean pair of knickers Mrs Riley had suggested she bring.

Closing her eyes, she wished that her periods would suddenly start, that all would be well and she wouldn't have to go through this. It hadn't happened so far. The foul-tasting stuff bought from Mrs Riley had not worked and her belly was getting bigger. She shivered as she remembered the point of the knitting needle sticking out through the rose decorating the side of Mrs Riley's bag, but she had to face it. She had to do this. The thought of worrying herself sick all over Christmas had brought her to the decision.

Once Henry and the family had left for work, she'd washed, changed and got herself ready. For no other reason than looking good might breed more confidence in herself, she had taken a great deal of care when choosing what she was going to wear for the trip to Old Market. She decided on a dark-red costume with a belted waist. It was cold so she'd have to wear her best coat, a navy blue Kashmir with patch pockets and turned-back cuffs. Her hat and handbag were black and matched her shoes. Biddy poked her head around the door at quarter to nine.

Even at that hour of the morning, she was wearing too much powder and red lipstick, a surplus smear of it staining her teeth.

'Just come to wish you luck.'

'Thanks.'

'How are you feeling?'

Mary Anne nodded stiffly. 'I've felt better.'

Biddy tutted in a sympathetic way. 'Never mind. It'll be over soon.'

Fear tangled with anticipation in her stomach, like barbed wire tightening into a huge ball.

She eyed her reflection in the mantelpiece mirror for one last time and swallowed.

'Yes.' Her voice sounded small and faraway. Eyes that looked too big and bright for her face stared out at her and, although she tried to tell herself that everything would be fine, she'd heard tell of women who hadn't been fine – afterbirth left inside, small limbs ripped from an unborn body...

'Do you want me to wait with you at the bus stop?'

Noticing that her face had turned paler at the macabre thoughts, Mary Anne dabbed rouge on her cheeks to add a little colour, licked her lips and shook her head.

'No. It might not look right.'

The bus journey to Old Market passed in a blur of buildings and traffic, though she could still detect wartime changes. Sandbag barriers had been built around buildings and amenities thought to be at risk of bombing, like the railway station, the docks and the city council chambers.

The clock outside the King's Cinema said ten thirty when she finally alighted in Old Market. Some kind of army post had been erected down the centre reservation of the wide expanse where traders used to sell everything from chickens to choppers, and men in uniform marched in and out of the barracks of the Gloucester Regiment.

Alighting from the bus, Mary Anne took a deep breath, ran her hands down over her hips as though the skirt she wore needed smoothing – which it did not.

Following the directions written down by one of her neighbours who had had occasion to use Mrs Riley herself, Mary Anne turned into Red Cross Lane then took a left at the bottom. She was thankful for the support of other women. That was the main difference between her business and the real one inherited by Michael Maurice. It wasn't just about making a shilling; it was also about mutual support. Inheriting that first bit of money from her mother had also benefited her neighbours as well as her own family, helping them as much as helping herself. And even more than that, she thought, and almost smiled. What pawnbroker had a shop where pledges were given and money handed out while gossiping over a cup of tea and a biscuit?

The feeling in her stomach was raw and empty, yet at the same time prickly and sickening. The closer she got to Mrs Riley's address, the more her legs turned to jelly.

Dark as a conker, Mrs Riley lived in a gypsy caravan in a yard bounded by dry stone walls and strips of corrugated iron, the ground stony and rough with weeds. In winter it was chock-a-block with carousels, dodgem car rides and even the big wheel, all broken down for winter storage. For the rest of the year, the brightly coloured caravan stood alone, the swirling colours of its bodywork in stark contrast to its grim, grey and empty surroundings. No horse being present, the end of each shaft rested on an upturned oil drum.

The early morning rain had been followed by a northerly wind that had swiftly turned the wet pavements to ice. The cobbles of the lane were dangerous to walk on, but once she had reached the yard that housed Mrs Riley's caravan the smooth ground turned to earth and stones so she ceased slipping and sliding.

The caravan was a riot of red roses, green leaves and the bluest birds she had ever seen, skilfully wrought in raised carvings. Green shutters sat either side of windows curtained with heavy Victorian lace, and a set of three wooden steps led up to the gaily painted door.

Mary Anne stood and stared, barely able to believe that such a shameful act could occur inside a place of such fairytale beauty. For a brief moment she thought about turning round and taking the next bus home. She would tell Henry, endure his anger and fully commit herself to caring for another child for many years to come.

She closed her eyes. The thought of it was too much to bear. The little independence she had would be at an end. No, she couldn't face it. She had to have some life before it was too late.

The biting wind chose that moment to squeeze through a gap between the roofs surrounding the yard. Mary Anne hugged her coat more firmly about her, pulling the astrakhan collar against her face, feeling its soft, comforting warmth, though her cheeks glowed pink with cold.

Hesitating before knocking, she turned her options over in her mind one last time, arguing herself out of it and at the same time urging herself to go on.

The top half of the door opened almost immediately to reveal Mrs Riley, her deep-set eyes glittering in her nut-brown face.

Mary Anne faltered in her speech; easy to do when faced with such a searching look. It made her feel like a pile of pennies being counted. Which is exactly what I am, she thought.

'Ah!' said Mrs Riley, her smile revealing a lack of teeth and traces of chewed tobacco on her tongue. 'I thought it were you. Come on in, me dear. Come on in.'

'I've come...' Mary Anne began, but couldn't go on. Licking the ice from her chapped lips, she tried to control her shivers.

'Bloody cold out there. Come on in.'

Although she sounded friendly, although her speech was common, Mrs Riley had a knowing look in her eyes.

Of course she knows why I'm here.

Mary Anne didn't like being regarded as vulnerable; she was determined to ensure that Mrs Riley knew exactly how she felt about paying for the brown liquid.

'The stuff you charged me two pounds for didn't work.'

Mrs Riley stood aside so she could pass between her and an upholstered seat to one side of the caravan and shut the two parts of the door, bolting each so they wouldn't be disturbed.

Despite the gravity of the situation, Mary Anne found herself standing open-mouthed, staring at the richness of her surroundings.

From the outside the caravan was richly carved but far smaller than the ground floor of a terraced house. Inside it was a palace of gleaming mirrors, lace covered shelves, a brass range, brass handles and thick Turkish rugs.

Seats were upholstered in red velvets; the wood-panelled walls shone and smelled of beeswax. Fine porcelain and cut glass blinked like stars from behind beautifully etched glass doors, and mirrors set into wooden panels sparkled with reflected light.

'Right!' said Mrs Riley. 'I don't say this ain't goin' to hurt, but I guarantee it'll work – and it'll cost ten pounds – payment in advance.'

'So I understand.' She wasn't the only one in Kent Street to have paid for the services of Mrs Riley.

She handed over the money, which Mrs Riley tucked into her bodice, nestling the notes between her meagre breasts.

'Now,' she said, turning her back and opening a cupboard from which she took out the infamous carpet bag that Mary Anne remembered having a rose motif on the side. 'Let's get started. Sooner started, sooner finished.'

Taut with nerves, Mary Anne continued to stand, harbouring the ridiculous notion that she'd snap in half if she sat down, from tension rather than cold. Besides, she hadn't been asked. Instead, she watched fearfully, the barbed wire ball in her stomach turning ever more taut as she watched Mrs Riley prepare for this sacred rite – the rite of ending life.

A piece of red flannel was laid out on a narrow table standing against one wall and on it she placed the knitting needle and a chunk of carbolic soap. Next, the kettle was placed on the glowing coals of a tiny cast iron range.

'I made meself a cup of tea before you came, so it won't be long before it boils.'

Mary Anne shook her head. 'I don't want one, thank you.'

'Goodness, me dear, you're more naive than you look. It ain't for that.'

It was as if a lead weight – like the ones inside a grandfather clock – had plunged to her stomach. Everything laid out and being done was for one purpose only. Suddenly, she weakened and sank onto a velvet-covered bench let into the wall.

'Aye! It ain't an easy thing to do,' said Mrs Riley, taking a puff from her pipe before putting it back on the hob. 'Shall I take yer coat?'

Mary Anne struggled to her feet, feeling naked after taking off her coat.

The coat was placed in what had looked like a ground-level cupboard but turned out to be a bed, sliding doors hiding it from the rest of the room.

She turned her back, her stomach growing queasy at the thought of what was about to be done to her. The less she saw of the preparations, the calmer she would be and the more likely to go through with it. And she had to go through with it, though it was against her nature. Her children were her joy. She had made sure they were well clothed, well fed and happy. She had protected them from the bad things and now they were grown. They didn't need such a high degree of protection as in the past. She was growing older and could concentrate on Stanley. Henry had not wanted any of the children, though no one would think so now. He'd been furious each time she'd reported herself pregnant. The way he had treated her, it was a wonder her pregnancies had gone full term. She couldn't go through that again. 'Did you 'ear what I said?' Mrs Riley's voice invaded her thoughts.

'What?'

'I said, now yer drawers.'

Sensing her shyness, Mrs Riley concentrated on taking a pinch of snuff from a small red tin before taking another puff of her pipe.

Blushing to the roots of her hair, Mary Anne did as she was told, pushing her knickers inside her handbag with the spare pair.

'I brought another pair,' she blurted without really knowing why – just that she wanted to say something, to hear her own voice, to know she was still there and really doing this.

'You'll need both pairs if it comes away quickly,' Mrs Riley said, wiping her hands over her hips to get rid of the surfeit of snuff.

The thought of what she was suggesting would have made the bravest woman reconsider. Mary Anne was certainly not the bravest, but reminded herself that those already in the world still needed her to make their paths through life run smoothly. 'Now,' said Mrs Riley, taking the boiling kettle off the coals and picking up the knitting needle in her right hand. 'I'm going to stand yur. I want you to roll up your skirt and put your feet up on the cupboards to either side of me.'

She did what she thought was being asked of her, feet braced against the cupboards to either side of Mrs Riley, who stood in between her legs, knitting needle in hand. Mary Anne turned her head to one side, unwilling to see Mrs Riley's face, let alone look into her eyes.

There was no way to describe how vulnerable and ashamed she felt, and age had nothing to do with it. No one, absolutely no one, should have to submit to such an ignominious procedure, she thought. She felt that she was no more than a lump of meat.

She wanted to cry out her despair; she wanted to tell someone just how bitter she felt about hopes she'd once cherished and shared with a man who had truly loved her.

She did none of those things but bit on a piece of wood given her by Mrs Riley, wincing as the needle probed her insides, piercing something soft and as vulnerable as her, and leaving behind a mix of pain, relief and a terrible surge of guilt that threatened to drown her.

22

Lizzie frowned and counted the eggs again. There were only two, but surely she'd bought six plus a free one. Mr Nixon at the corner shop had winked at her and slipped her one extra. She'd thanked him kindly but stayed on her toes ready to sprint out of range of his roving hands should he come too close.

Surely Mrs Selwyn hadn't used four in two days?

The most obvious explanation was that Mrs Selwyn had used it for visiting relatives but hadn't told her. Friday was her day for checking the larder, and it wasn't just about eggs. Lizzie didn't live in and Peter was in Canada, so only Mrs Selwyn counted as far as ration books were concerned. Provisions at the house in Ashton were being devoured at a rate of knots, according to what was left in the larder, and Lizzie was keeping such a close check nowadays. She could hardly accuse Mrs Selwyn of eating more than she should of her own food, and although well built, she wasn't fat and gave no signs of having put on any weight.

That afternoon she took in afternoon tea, the teapot, milk and sugar accompanied by a plate of bread, butter and the last of home-made strawberry jam sent up from the farm in Shepton Mallet by Mrs Selwyn's sister. As she set the tea tray down on the table, she scrutinised her employer as closely as she dared.

No extra weight being discernable, there was no alternative but to ask the pertinent question.

'Mrs Selwyn, I fear we won't have enough eggs to last the week – not if I'm going to make a cake and a Yorkshire pudding on Sunday. There were seven and now there are only two.'

As usual, Mrs Selwyn had her nose buried in a trashy romance, something entitled *Lord Ramsden and the Gypsy Girl*. Raising her head, her eyes met those of Lizzie.

'Then get some more.'

'I can't.'

Inwardly, Lizzie sighed. Mrs Selwyn had no idea about rationing. When the books had arrived, she'd simply handed them over to Lizzie who had studied the contents over toast and tea and duly reported back to Mrs Selwyn, who frowned in a very accusing manner.

'Do you mind repeating that?'

Lizzie obliged. 'I can't. Not until next week. And then there's the bread, the bacon and several other things...'

'Don't keep on so!'

Lizzie started, her expression full of surprise.

Like a wax tableau, both seemingly surprised by the other, they stood looking at each other, one awaiting an explanation, the other seemingly loath to give one.

'It's the cold weather,' said Mrs Selwyn. 'I keep feeling hungry. Just do what you can, will you?'

She immediately dropped her eyes back to the book, leaving Lizzie looking at the top of her head.

'Then I'll have to go out this afternoon. There's a few things needed—'

'Yes, yes, yes!'

Without bothering to look up from her book, Mrs Selwyn dismissed her with a casual wave of her hand. 'Take the rest of the afternoon off, if you must.'

Closing the parlour door behind her, Lizzie considered how easily she had acquired an afternoon off without even asking for one. Even after meeting Peter on those sweet summer afternoons, she'd still had time spare for shopping, but that was in the days before queuing had become normal.

There was a long queue outside the corner shop; women huddled against the plate glass window in an effort to escape the bitter wind, clutching ration books in gloved hands, shopping bags braced against their sides. Things had certainly changed. It occurred to her that she might as well head home and call in at the grocer's shop next door to the pawnbroker's just off East Street and see if he had any room on his list. Every household had to be registered. So far it was a pretty lackadaisical affair, people diving from one shop to another in a bid to escape the queues and get a bit more than they were entitled to, but it was worth a try.

It was after four by the time she got there and the worsening weather had driven all but the most hardy home to their hearths and a hot meal singing on the stove.

To her great relief, she found the queue was not so long outside this particular shop, and even though they didn't have exactly what she wanted, there were a few extras that weren't on ration.

'Wonderful,' she murmured, as she placed her purchases into the basket just below her now blacked-out headlamp.

Hearing a series of hoots and shouts, she looked up to see a group of boys on the corner of the street. One of them was a little smaller, a little slighter than the rest.

She narrowed her eyes. 'Stanley?'

No response.

Say it louder, prompted a suspicious voice inside. 'Stanley!'

Startled faces turned in her direction. She thought she recognised the cheeky little sods that had made faces through the butcher's shop window.

Like a flock of frightened starlings, they turned and ran, knocking Stanley to the ground in their effort to escape.

She propped her bicycle against a wall, ran to help her brother up from the ground and immediately began brushing the dirt from his clothes.

'Look at the state of you!'

Stanley wriggled his little body, but wasn't strong enough to escape her firm grip.

'I'm all right,' he grumbled. 'Leave me alone.'

'No. Look at the state of those knees. There's enough dirt on them alone to grow potatoes.'

Stanley continued to squirm. He suffered being fussed over when he was ill, but at no other time and Lizzie was unwilling to let him go. It was a matter of responsibility, and she had always been the most responsible in the family.

'Come on. Home with you!'

'Awww... Leave me alone.'

'No!' she said sharply, just as they were passing the pawnshop.

She was surprised to see Stanley's eyes grow wide with fear. *Now what?*

'Ssshhh!' he said, his eyes sliding sidelong as he raised his finger to his lips. 'He'll hear us.'

She frowned, thinking her little brother was quite consternating at times. 'Who will?'

'Him,' he whispered, pointing to the open door. 'That's where Mr Hitler lives.'

Lizzie shook her head in disbelief and laughed out loud. 'Mr Hitler lives there? I don't think so, Stanley. I think he's got deadlier things to do than run a pawnshop!'

The house seemed abnormally quiet and cold when she and Stanley got home. Normally, the smell of the evening meal and the warmth of a heap of glowing Welsh Steam coal would funnel down the passage like a welcoming arm, pulling them in. Music from the BBC Home Service would be floating on the air and Lizzie would feel every bone in her body relaxing because this was home, the safest and happiest place in the world – or it had been before Stanley had sown doubt in her mind.

This evening there was no welcoming smell and no sound except the rhythmic drip of the kitchen tap.

There's nothing wrong, Lizzie told herself, though in reality she sensed the opposite was true; something was VERY wrong.

* * *

Henry Randall had spent the day helping to repair an engine problem on one of the older taxis in the depot. The garage manager had made his presence known, urging Henry and the mechanic to mend it quickly, bleating that he couldn't afford to have it off the road for too long. The job had taken all day and at the end of it Henry's mouth was dry and the smell of hops hung over the brewery where the workers wore clogs and the women swore like troopers. The Red Cow beckoned!

'Wet yer whistle with that, Henry. A fresh barrel just tapped,' said Jack Skinner, landlord of the Red Cow.

Henry was about to take a swift sip, but being straight in such matters as paying on the nail, he first searched his pockets for the right money, dug his fingers in and found – nothing!

Frowning, he searched first one pocket then another, inside his coat, outside his coat, from coat to trouser pockets. Not a penny.

Jack saw his consternation. 'Forgot yer money, Henry?'

Never in his whole life had Henry felt so embarrassed as he did now. In the past he'd denigrated those who never stood their round or got it poured, took a sip then owned up to not having a penny on them when they knew all the time they were out of funds.

'I'm sorry, Jack,' he said at last, his face stiff with indignation. 'I ain't got a penny on me.'

Jack Skinner smiled and slung his bar towel over his shoulder. 'I trust you fer one, Henry.'

Henry shook his head. 'No. I don't drink if I can't pay.'

Luckily, someone else was standing next to him who *did* have the money and luckily drank the same bitter, but it did nothing for Henry's sense of pride.

Bitter and humiliated, his bristled chin tucked into his collar, he left the Red Cow long before he wanted to. For the first time in months, or was it years, he was going home sober and he didn't like it. It was like giving in to what everyday civilians were like – upright and sober, just like them who preached salvation and banged tambourines with their uniforms and their calling themselves an army. Well, he wasn't like them, and he didn't want to be.

When he got to Kent Street, Biddy Young was chatting to the workmen who had at last finished building the underground shelter in the middle of the street, but were lingering over Biddy's cups of tea. Biddy, always one to instigate a knees-up, had laced the tea with a liberal dollop of cheap sherry – 'To help the sugar ration go a bit further,' she'd laughed, her round cheeks matching the cherry red of her lipstick.

Biddy looked to the end of the street to see Henry Randall, her face registering surprise because he wasn't singing, shouting and staggering.

She hoped he hadn't seen her, but his angry eyes fell on her like a hawk on prey.

'Good evening, Henry.'

Even to her own ears, her voice sounded as though she had laryngitis.

He grumbled a good evening.

Biddy couldn't stop staring. Henry Randall sober. Goodness, was Mary Anne in for a shock.

All would have been well if one of the workmen hadn't swallowed too much of Biddy's doctored tea.

Recognising him as living in the same house he'd seen Mary Anne come out of, he shoved his cap back on his head, nodded a swift good evening and added, 'Still got that relative stayin' from Australia, have ya?'

Henry slowed his pace and frowned. 'What relative?'

Biddy nearly dropped her tea tray, her hand steadying the sherry bottle.

'Better have all yer cups,' she said, snatching her bits of mismatched china from the men's hands, aching to warn Mary Anne as swiftly as possible even if it meant smashing the china, though God forbid she dropped the sherry.

The workman, a bluff-faced man with ginger hair, kept going. 'That chap we thought she was arguing with. We was going to give him a pasting until she told us he was a relative and took him round the back for a cup of tea – or something,' he added with a smirk.

Henry looked stunned.

The workman misinterpreted his expression as that of a man wronged by a cheating wife. His face and voice were ripe with sympathy. 'Look, mate, I'm sorry. I just saw her with this bloke and she said he was from Australia, and we believed her. Sorry, mate.'

'I'm not yer mate,' muttered Henry.

Biddy didn't wait to hear any more, running into her front door and out of the back one, slinging the tea tray on the kitchen table on her way through.

She presumed that, as usual, Henry would go hammering on the front door, warning enough that he was home, and perhaps time enough for her to run along the back alley, and up Mary Anne's garden path.

Biddy was not built for speed, her breasts and belly wobbling as she puffed her way over the broken flags leading to the lane at the back of her garden. She'd just reached for the latch when she saw Henry, shoulders square and fists clenched, stalking along the alley, his face stiff as a board. Hoping he hadn't seen her, she ducked down, lost her balance and found herself wedged between the privet hedge and the rhubarb patch.

* * *

On investigating the cold, unwelcoming house, Lizzie found Mary Anne lying on Stanley's bed in the front parlour. Seeing her mother's face as white as the pillow, Lizzie was across the room in two strides and kneeling beside the bed, her face creased with terror.

'Ma! Ma!'

She touched her mother's face with only the tips of her fingers, fearful she would feel stiff and cold, and that she would never open her eyes again.

'Ma?'

She couldn't be dead! Why should she be? She hadn't been ill, had she? It occurred to her then that she didn't know her mother's state of health for sure. She hadn't asked and neither had her mother ever confided in her, more likely in fact to enquire about Lizzie's health.

'Lizzie? Lizzie?'

Stanley stood in the doorway, dark circles erupting beneath his blue eyes, a look of disbelief on his face.

'Has he killed her? Has he killed her?'

Lizzie frowned and glanced round at him. 'What?'

'Has our Dad...'

Her mother's eyes fluttered.

'Don't be stupid. She's fainted,' said Lizzie, as her own heart seemed to beat again, though she wasn't quite sure when she'd thought it had stopped.

'Go and fetch Mrs Young. She'll know what to do.'

She looked over her shoulder. Stanley still stood there, his face a frightened mask. In that instant his youth and his weakness were more apparent than they'd been for weeks. But this was no time for reflections.

'Well, go on then!'

Stanley sped off, his feet hammering along the passageway towards the back door.

Her mother's fingers folded over her arm. 'Help me up.'

Lizzie beheld the pale complexion and the dark hollows around the eyes as she helped her mother sit up.

'Did you faint?' she asked, her voice wobbling with emotion. 'Have you got a bad stomach,' she added as her mother bent forwards, arm thrown across her belly, and her face taut with pain. Her mother's eyes held hers. 'Lizzie, I've had a miscarriage. Before our Stanley comes back, get rid of that there.' She pointed to a bundle of bloodstained newspapers. 'Wrap more newspapers around it, then take it out to the dustbin; I'll burn it later.'

Lizzie rushed to do as asked. A baby! And this was it, she thought, narrowing her eyes and holding her breath, because if she saw or smelled too much, she would be sick.

Although her arms trembled, she worked quickly, finding more newspapers and laying them out flat, ready to wrap around the bloody parcel that she eyed warily, not sure whether she would scream with disgust or cry with despair when the time came for wrapping it up.

'What the bloody hell's goin' on?'

Lizzie jumped at the sound of her father's voice and turned cold as his shadow fell over her.

Henry Randall had a square jaw, angular cheekbones and a gaunt, overhanging forehead. It was easy to believe that he'd been carved from granite, like a primitive statue that moved like a human and looked like a human, but thought like a stone. 'Mum's had a miscarriage,' said Lizzie, barely able to keep her voice even, her eyes flitting between the ominous presence of her father and the equally upsetting parcel. 'I've sent Stanley to fetch Mrs Young.'

Mary Anne raised her eyes to those of her husband. He'd never been affectionate, except at those times when he thought he was losing her, like when she'd given birth to Stanley. It had been a difficult birth, and the doctor had hinted that he prepare himself for the worse. In the deep, dark hours of early morning, she'd heard him snivelling at her bedside. By noon of the following day he'd known that she would live. By evening he was his old self.

Stanley came racing back in, ducking under his father's arm. 'I've brought Mrs Young.'

A slightly dishevelled Biddy hovered in the doorway.

Mary Anne regarded them all with casual indifference until her gaze came to rest on Stanley.

'Henry. This is no place for the boy.'

At first it didn't seem as though he had heard her, and she couldn't understand why he was looking at her in such an accusing manner. Probably because he thought she'd inconvenienced him and the family. They expected her to be there for them: their meals on the table, the house clean, the laundry washed.

'I couldn't help it, Henry,' she said.

The look persisted, before he did as she'd asked. Placing his hand on Stanley's head, he wheeled him round about, heading him towards the door, throwing her an icy glare before he left the room.

She didn't understand his odd manner and at this point in time she didn't much care. The pain was too great, the loss of blood making her weaker than she had ever felt in her life. Once he'd left, she eyed Biddy through a blur of what seemed to be red mist.

'Biddy.' She pointed to where Lizzie was bent next to the bundle. 'You know what has to be done. Let our Lizzie go and do something else.'

Biddy's gaze met that of her friend in total understanding. They'd both been through similar at some time in their lives.

'Come on then, girl,' Biddy addressed Lizzie. 'You go and see to your dad and Stanley. I think yer mother wants the dinner put on before your Daw and Harry come home. I'll clean up 'ere.'

Lizzie looked at her with a dazed expression on her face. Biddy took hold of her shoulders and got her to her feet.

'Come on, come on. You heard me. Leave me to clean up here. You go and light the stove and the fire and get the dinner on.'

Wordlessly, Lizzie allowed herself to be helped to her feet. Why did she feel so afraid? It wasn't just fearing for her mother's health or that she might die. That couldn't happen, could it? Women miscarried every day, but there was something else. There'd been an unforgiving expression on her father's face and it worried her.

'I'll take this with me. My fire's blazing well. Alf brought a bit of coke home from the docks.'

Mary Anne thanked her, and would have said goodnight there and then, drifting off into a tortured sleep of sharp needles, prettily carved caravans and walls of mirrors whirling all around her. What Biddy then told her would ensure that her tortured sleep would develop into a nightmare.

'One of the workmen asked your Henry about your Australian relative that you had staying.'

At first Mary Anne couldn't quite grasp the implications, but as her mind cleared she began to plan a believable excuse. Everything will be all right, she told herself. All you did was to have a miscarriage, but still she had to smooth things over. Her family's happy home depended on it.

'I have to get up.'

'You're too weak.'

'I have to get up. I can't leave Lizzie to deal with him. I have to be there. Now help me get up.'

With Biddy's help, she managed to attain a sitting position accompanied by an increased flow of blood.

'I'll do it,' she whispered, placing first one foot then the other onto the floor. It made her smile to see she'd kept her shoes on. She hadn't realised it. Neither had she realised that her smile was more a grimace until she saw the expression on Biddy's face.

'Funny. I've still got my shoes on.'

She smiled again. This time Biddy knew what she was referring to.

Once on her feet, she concentrated all her efforts on putting one foot in front of another. 'I'll see you sometime tomorrow.'

Biddy paused, the parcel clasped in both hands and slightly away from her body.

'Yes. You'll be all right?'

'Of course I will.'

Mary Anne persuaded herself that all would be well. Henry wasn't going to query the workman's comment so soon after her miscarriage, though you never knew with Henry quite how his mind was working.

Slowly and bent almost double, Mary Anne followed Biddy down the passageway and into the kitchen where Henry sat in his favourite armchair staring into space, not even blinking as Biddy swept through, the bloody parcel held out in front of her.

Each step sharp with pain, Mary Anne felt her way along the walls. There was something comforting about the kitchen: the gas lit beneath the pans, the sound of cutlery and crockery clattering onto the table.

Stanley was helping his sister and looked up to see his mother hanging on to the doorpost. His face turned white with fear. 'Ma!'

She winced as his arms wrapped around her.

Lizzie, her face tight with concern, noticed and warned Stanley not to hold her so tightly.

Henry turned his head very slowly. 'So you got rid of it.' Mary Anne was filled with alarm. He couldn't know.

'I miscarried.'

''Cos you didn't want it.'

A surge of pain threatened to drive her into unconsciousness, but she overcame it. Her eyes fixed on the man she'd married, the man who had forced her to do anything to keep the peace. She knew then that he didn't know for sure that she'd had an abortion; he was presuming she had because the child wasn't his. She had to explain.

'I had to, Henry... I'm too old for babies... and so are you.' His look was as stiff and steadfast as ever. Before she had the chance to say anything more, he pointed at the table on which sat a small brown bottle.

'A Mrs Riley just called. She left that and said it would help clear out what the knitting needle might have left behind.'

Mary Anne blanched and sank into a chair, the pain wringing sweat from her body, weakening her legs and affecting her eyesight.

Without her noticing, he had got up from his chair and was hanging over her. Lizzie and Stanley looked on fearfully. Mary Anne's blood ran cold. Henry had never acted like this in front of them, not openly, not uncaring of appearances.

'I know what you've been up to. Mucking about with another man behind my back. What's his name? Tell me! What's his name?'

'Henry...' She rolled her head from side to side. This and the pain were too much to cope with. She opened her eyes and looked up at him pleadingly. 'There is no other man.' For the first time in years, she reached out for him, her hands touching the rough wool of his pullover.

Henry drew back as though he'd been scorched. 'Get off me! You slut! You whore! Bringing another man into this house! Did you expect me to accept the babe as my own? How many of the others are mine? How many of them did I father, and how many are by your lovers?'

The room spinning around her, Mary Anne did her best to focus on his face and, despite the pain gripping her belly, her anger grew.

Yesterday, she would have done her best to calm him, for the sake of the family, but something had changed.

What about me? What about me?

Perhaps it was the pain or the horrified looks on Lizzie and Stanley's faces, but the inner scream would not go away, screeching the truth until it felt as though her head would explode. The happy home she'd created for her children had been at the expense of her own happiness. The bare truth was uncovered; she could see it on Stanley and Lizzie's faces. The homely atmosphere, the sort children read about in sugary novels, did not exist. They were all different people living in a world that was becoming less homely every day.

'You are a wicked man, Henry Randall. A selfish, drunken bully and I hate you!'

His eyes turned black and his cheek trembled as though she'd slapped it, but he recovered quickly. Bullies usually do have one last attempt to prove their power before caving in. She feared what would come.

He raised his hand, but a blur of mauve dress leaped across the room.

'Leave my mother alone!'

Lizzie clung to his arm, but he flung it wide, easily throwing her aside.

Mary Anne gathered every ounce of strength she owned and struggled to her feet. Her eyes blazed with anger. 'Leave my children be, or so help me, I'll kill you!'

Rising onto her hands and knees, Lizzie wiped blood from the corner of her mouth. This was the kind of scene Stanley had described to her. She saw him out of the corner of her eye, frozen to the spot, his eyes wide and staring.

'And you're not only a slut,' Henry was saying, suddenly remembering his humiliation at the Red Cow, 'you're a bloody thief! That's what you are! Took the last penny from me pocket, you thieving cow!'

Just as he reached for her throat, she found a surge of inner strength and wriggled out from under him, kicking at his shins as she eased herself sideways. He toppled, tripped over his own feet and fell head first into his favourite chair.

Mary Anne gripped the back of a chair for support, eyeing the supine body. Was she safe now?

Her breathing steadied, then quickened as he started to rise.

Cowering against the wall, feeling weak, she covered her head with her arms.

Just as he raised his fist, a small figure sprang onto a chair and raised something black and solid above his head. There was a clang of metal on bone as Stanley brought a cast iron frying pan down onto his father's head.

'No,' cried his fearful mother as he raised it again, his pale faced flushed with temper.

The angelic face twisted with hate. 'I'll kill him.'

She wrested the frying pan from his hands, fearing for his life if Henry saw him with it.

'Get outside,' she murmured to Lizzie. 'Take our Stanley with you.'

'But...?'

'Go into the washhouse and stay there.'

Their eyes met. Lizzie didn't know when and how she'd come to interpret her mother's thoughts and actions, but she knew whatever she was up to was for the best.

Before he'd quite come to, Mary Anne saw the look in his eyes and feared for her son's life. The thing to do was to shift the blame. Only then would Stanley be safe, the home back to normal.

Gripping the pan with both hands, she summoned every bit of courage, product of the love she had for her family.

Henry's mouth curled into an ugly snarl. 'You—'

She raised the pan high above her head and brought it down on his, but he caught one wrist. She hit him but only a glancing blow. The backhander he gave her would have sent her spinning, but she stepped back.

But she'd seen the look in his eyes, and even though he was sober, she knew this was perhaps the defining moment in their relationship, the time when she had to make a more sombre choice than sexual submission or rejection. This was a matter of life and death – her life or her death.

Fear gave wings to her feet, the tearing pain still dragging at her insides, but her will to survive urging her on.

She ran out of the front door, along Kent Street and towards the corner shop. Every building in the street was in darkness, courtesy of the blackout. She stopped at the shop door, meaning to knock, to shout for help, but she could hear him calling her, threatening to beat her black and blue if she didn't come back immediately.

She ran out onto West Street, almost got knocked down by a blacked-out tram, then headed towards East Street, round the back of the London Inn, and still she could hear him calling.

The pain worsened; her clothes were drenched in sweat and blood; her heart hammered against her ribcage. She feared it would burst, but hurried on, determined to survive because even when surrounded by violence, there were still things to live for. As her strength ebbed, she no longer had any idea of where she was running and whether Henry was still pursuing her. All she could hear was the rush of her own pulse beating in her ears. Despite the darkness, there was something familiar about the dank-smelling alley, the sound of babies crying, people quarrelling, a plaintive voice singing '*Let me call you sweetheart.*'

The alley spilled out onto another road, just as dark but wider than the one she'd left behind. To her left, she felt the low curve of a garden wall. Across the road a chink of light showed from the side of a blackout curtain. She turned right, flattening herself against a wall that swiftly became a large expanse of cold glass.

She felt her way along it, turning her head so that her cheek took on the coolness of the plate glass. There was no way of knowing where she was; how did blind people manage? Her legs were crumpling, and although she listened for any sign of pursuit, it no longer seemed to matter. The pain was all consuming, draining her of strength and purposeful thought. If she died here and now on the pavement, then so be it. Oblivion was becoming quite attractive, and her eyes were closing, her body sliding against the glass though her feet still moved, sideways now until the window gave out and she tumbled into a shop doorway.

23

The atmosphere at number ten Kent Street the following morning was both strained and strange.

Although Lizzie had expected her father's anger to continue, Harry's intervention the night before had changed everything, especially once Stanley had told him the same things he'd told her.

'You bastard!'

Henry Randall's life as a soldier was far behind him, and although he tried to defend himself, Harry was younger and stronger. He was down on the floor in no time, his own son standing over him, glowering a warning.

'Lay a hand on any of these when I'm not around,' said Harry, sweeping his arm over the heads of his siblings, 'and I'll strangle you my fucking self!'

Daw had gasped to hear such language, but Lizzie and Stanley were accepting. They'd seen things their sister hadn't, and with Daw it was a case of seeing is believing, besides which, she took her world for granted, everything in its place including her parents, siblings and sweetheart. Home truths were too much to bear. Sobbing fit to burst, she ran upstairs crying that they were all horrible and that they'd ruined her life, and that John mustn't know, and neither must the neighbours. Nobody, nobody at all!

'She'll get over it,' Lizzie said to a puzzled Harry. For him, the sorting out of this whole scenario was cut and dried, though he wanted to know where his mother was.

Lizzie shrugged. 'I don't know.' She hugged Stanley against her side and ruffled his hair.

'Never mind,' said Harry. 'She's got to be better off than she was here. And you,' he said, addressing Stanley. 'Will you be able to cope until we find our mother?'

'Yes,' said Stanley, his triumphant smile leaving Harry in no doubt that if he'd been big enough he would have beaten his father himself. 'And you're the boss here now, ain't you, Harry?' Harry nodded, his eyes sliding to where his father was deftly investigating cuts and bruises and trying to catch his breath following the punches Harry had jabbed at his stomach.

'Right,' said Harry, the look on his face leaving his father in no doubt that he would hit him again if he had to. 'How far did you chase her?'

Henry winced, rubbed at his stomach then tentatively touched his bloodstained lip. 'I don't know. It was dark. Towards East Street maybe...'

Harry grabbed his father's shoulder and dragged him to his feet. 'Then get down the police station and report her missing. I'll go out and search the streets. I've got a few friends that'll help me – and take that look off your face,' he added, a warning finger jabbed in front of the contempt that suddenly appeared on his father's face. 'I can see from your eyes that you'd love to be right about what I am; I bet you don't sleep at night thinking about it. Well, I don't care what you think, but I do care about my mother.'

Lizzie and Stanley had stood with their mouths open as Harry pushed his father to the door. 'Get down to that police station. Report her missing. I'll deal with the hospitals. Let's hope we find her.'

Stanley's eyes shone with hero worship. His brother was everything.

The police came round to the house later that night asking if they could have a photograph.

Lizzie made tea while Harry handed them a faded black-and-white from a day at the seaside a few years before. The whole street had got up a charabanc outing. All but Henry had gone along, and Mary Anne looked happy on it.

Henry, the blood washed from his cut lip, sat morose and silent, more dejected than Lizzie had ever seen him. In fact he looked as though he had shrunk overnight – thanks to Harry.

'So what can the police do in such a situation?' Harry asked, his hands shoved in his trouser pockets, his eyes fixed on the sergeant and constable sent by the local police station. He stood immediately in front of the fireplace, like a ringmaster at the circus, demanding a lot from those around him.

Lizzie found herself admiring her brother's tenacity. He had a courteous way about him, a precise way of getting to the crux of the matter.

'My mother must be out there somewhere. She can't have vanished.'

The uniformed police sergeant mopped his forehead where the rim of his helmet had rubbed. He appeared to be gathering his thoughts and, once gathered, he addressed Henry, who he presumed was fretting over his wife's disappearance.

'Mr Randall, I sympathise and, rest assured, we will do our best to find your wife, but I feel obliged to state the facts as they are. Number one, accidents have increased tenfold since the blackout started. We've had more deaths from road accidents during the past three months than the previous two years put together.'

'If that was the case, we would surely have found her in hospital or the morgue,' said Harry.

Lizzie shivered and was glad an exhausted Stanley had cried himself to sleep, after telling her that he would be brave and was sure his mother was safe.

The police constable put his teacup back on the tray and got to his feet. 'Not necessarily. We've had occasion of motorists picking up their victims and throwing them in the river to avoid detection. And I wouldn't like to frighten you, sir, but there's some pretty rum characters taking advantage of the blackout.'

Harry stayed out until the early hours looking for her. Lizzie lay on the settee, staring into the darkness, desperate to stay awake in case she was needed, in case the worst had happened. Being needed would mean consoling Stanley and smacking Daw's face when she turned hysterical.

Her father had gone up to bed, but she knew he wasn't sleeping. And neither should he, she thought, her anger concentrated on a single spot on the ceiling. She hadn't been able to say goodnight to him, even to mop the blood from his broken lip. He'd had to do it himself. He'd looked at each of them in turn before going up the stairs, but no one acknowledged him, and the implications of it seemed to hit him hard. The strong man, who had regaled them over the years with brave tales of his time in the army, was now ignored by them, and for once there was pain in his eyes.

Even though she'd assured Harry she would stay awake until he got back, she started at the sound of his key in the front door.

The only light in the room came from a single candle she'd placed in the kitchen window. She'd read somewhere that in past wars women had placed candles in the window to guide their men home, and even though showing a light was breaching blackout laws, she didn't care. Her mother was out there and so was her brother and she wanted them home.

Harry flung his hat and raincoat onto a chair. He smelled of rain and hair lotion and she loved it. He was the only man she knew who wore such an exotically smelling lotion. In her opinion, every man should wear a smell that masked stale cigarette smoke.

'I like that lotion you're wearing,' she said, the words tumbling out and sounding stupid in the circumstances. 'It hides things.'

Harry ran his hand through his hair, pushing its dampness away from his temples.

'What?' He sounded totally drained and his tiredness had aged him.

Lizzie couldn't help herself. She rambled on. 'Biddy Young should wear that lotion. It would mask the smell of her feet.'

She laughed, a hollow, nervous sound, swallowing it as quickly as it came and guiltily biting her lip. Laughing was out of place at such a time, a betrayal of her love and concern for her mother.

To her surprise she heard a muffled chuckle from Harry, or at least that's what it seemed like at first, until she realised he'd choked back a sob.

Raising herself, she looked over the back of the settee. Harry had always seemed so sure of himself, so capable, but this upheaval in his home life had affected him just as badly as it had everyone else. There was little she could do to help. She felt pretty lousy herself. What could she do for him?

'Would you like a cup of tea?'

It sounded such a pathetic offer. Why was it always the first thing that came into people's heads when dreadful things happened? Your cat's run over, your boyfriend's ran away with someone else, your mother might have fallen into the river; never mind, have a cup of tea.

Negative thoughts about feeling pathetic disappeared when Harry smiled.

He sniffed and cleared his throat. 'I could do with one.'

She didn't need to ask him if he'd had any luck. He would have told her if he had.

The flickering blue of the gas flame under the kettle was reflected in the kitchen window, outdoing the gleam of the candle.

Lizzie eyed the reflection, a shadow of herself surrounded by light. Beyond the immediate darkness she could make out the stark edges of the washhouse. She remembered the tin box, the cupboards of pledges, the record book her mother kept under lock and key. To the women of the street, her mother's business had been more than a lifeline when times were hard. She could imagine them exchanging problems and asking advice on how best to sort out their children, their finances and their husbands. Unfortunately, Mary Anne had never managed to sort out her own marriage. Now when she looked back, Lizzie could see the tiny signs that should have warned her that her parents' marriage was far from being wedded bliss. Perhaps in that dark outhouse she might get some clue. Following a few hours' sleep she would go to work, but when she came home she would search out there for any sign of where she might have gone.

24

Mary Anne was aware of a terrible shrieking noise that set her teeth on edge and roused her from the deepest slumber she'd ever had in her life.

'Make it stop,' she whispered, 'make it stop.'

She felt a hand stroke her hair and a gentle voice soothed her fears. 'Ssshh. It will stop soon. It is—'

Whoever was smoothing her hair had been about to tell her the source of the sound, and then thought better of it; either that or she'd fallen back into unconsciousness. She was glad, wanting to return to the wonderful dream she'd been having. Edward had come home; he laughed when she told him a telegram had come saying he was dead. 'But I'm not,' he laughed. 'I'm here and I love you.'

* * *

For once her dream, one she'd had many times before, was not interrupted by reality. She was glad about that. She didn't want reality any more.She'd arrived bleeding profusely and Michael had fetched a neighbour who knew about such things. The blood had reminded him of what had happened one night in Germany. That's why he couldn't sleep, but sat here watching her.

He couldn't tell how long he watched her sleeping. She'd roused at the sound of the air raid siren, but then fallen back asleep. He hadn't a clue of how much time had passed. They might both be dead now if there had been an air raid, but there hadn't. Like many that had sounded since war was declared on 3rd September, nothing had happened, though he knew it would. He knew how ruthless those people could be.

Mrs Randall – he couldn't think of her as Mary Anne, though he'd heard her called that – reminded him of Bronica. Even asleep she had the same way of holding her fingers close to her mouth as though she were about to suck her thumb, but sensually, her lips slightly parted.

Bronica too had been a heady mix of girlishness and pure seduction. He remembered watching her lying beside him, a light film of sweat covering her skin, made silver by the moonlight streaming through the window.

At first he'd feared sexual relations, but decided to lie, telling her he'd had an accident and certainly wasn't Jewish but the son of a minister. Sons of Lutheran ministers could be trusted not to be pure-blooded Aryans.

He was about to join the army by then, proud to wear a proper uniform, the years of enviously watching Boy Scouts long behind him, as was his – mostly happy – years in the Hitler Youth.

It was through Bronica that he'd met Hans, a perfect example of what Aryan manhood should look like: blond hair, blue eyes and nearly six feet tall.

He couldn't recall all the details of why they had all gone out together that night, but the events were ingrained in his memory.

Hans had been one of Ernst Roehm's Brownshirts, but had been lucky enough to make a sideways move in time. He too had joined the army, but old habits die hard.

'I know a very good bar along here,' Hans had shouted, though they were already legless with laughter, beer and schnapps. 'Along here,' he'd shouted.

Bronica had been between them, purposely sashaying her behind, hitting first Hans's hip, then Michael's. The action was overtly sexual; Michael wondered, not without good reason, whether she'd slept with Hans, whether in fact she was still sleeping with him.

'Hey, Hans,' someone shouted.

A group of uniformed young men was gathered outside the Café Austria, boisterous and full of beer.

'My old friends,' Hans shouted back. 'Old Brownshirt friends,' he'd said, lowering his voice. 'But all in the army and suchlike now, of course.'

Their voices were loud; that was the main thing Michael remembered about them, and they strutted around proudly like young lions marking their territory. Some of them looked good in uniform; some of them looked more suited to slinging butchered cattle around in meat markets.

Another beer had been pressed into his fist.

'I think I've had enough,' he said, shaking his head and desperately trying to make eye contact with Bronica. He wanted to go to bed with her, even if sex was out of the question because he was too drunk. He wanted to feel her body close to him.

'Do you not welcome our companionship?' asked a red-faced man with shoulders the size of a garden gate.

Michael had smiled and shook his head. 'No offence intended, but I think I have drunk a whole barrel of beer to myself. I would not want to disgrace the uniform by being sick all over it.'

The refusal was frowned on. Other red faces joined the one glaring at him.

'Is he a Jew?' one of them said in a slurred voice. 'Is that why he refuses our hospitality?'

'Might be. Only one way to find out.'

They'd made a grab for his trousers. He heard no protest from

Bronica or Hans as he was swept into the air, just raucous shouts, laughter and demands to 'See what he's got.'

His humiliation would have been complete once his mutilation was exposed, and even if he did get the chance to explain, they might not believe him, they might see it for what it was – one mutilation piled on another.

'Look,' one of them said suddenly. 'Look.'

Whoever had shouted pointed to two men scurrying along in the shadows on the opposite side of the road.

Those about to yank Michael's trousers off turned and followed the gaze of their comrade. Relieved, Michael fell to the ground. Like a pack of wild dogs, they were off across the road. 'Come on,' said Hans, jerking him to his feet. 'You don't want to miss this.'

Probably because he'd drunk too much and his legs were like strips of India rubber, Michael found himself pushed to the front.

The two men flattened themselves against a wall, their eyes wide with terror.

Pig-face – for this was what Michael called the man with the red face – jabbed at the man's shoulder with the handle of a whip. 'Sir, you address me as sir.'

The man licked his lips. Michael imagined the dryness of his mouth.

'Home... sir... We are on our way home.'

Anticipating some bullying, Michael attempted to turn away. This was not the first violence he had witnessed since joining the army, and although he still adored wearing a uniform and having friends of his own age, his exhilaration was slightly tarnished. For the first time in his life he recognised the ring of truth in his stepfather's words.

There was a choice. He could go along with them or he could intervene and end up lying in a pool of his own blood.

He preferred a third option. He could turn away go back to Bronica's flat and pretend there was some glory in what was happening.

Hans's hand landed on his shoulder. He shot him a warning look. 'Come on, Michael. Prove your loyalty to the Fuerher.'

Between the devil and the deep blue sea... something his mother had once said, though in what context he couldn't quite remember.

Pig-face and his pals now surrounded the two men, one of who was braver than the other.

'Look, we are law-abiding citizens going about our business.'

'At this time of night?'

Pig-face adopted a disbelieving look.

'What is your business?' he asked, turning their lapels down, smoothing them with his thumbs, looking for ripped stitches.

Michael knew from this action that Pig-face suspected they were Jews who had torn off their yellow stars.

'We are just workers,' blurted the more frightened man. 'We have just come from a meeting.'

'A meeting?'

'Communists,' someone growled. There was a sudden surge forwards.

'Stop!'

Michael could barely believe the strength and volume of his own voice. Neither could he believe his own stupidity.

'Let them go. They're just workmen.'

'Communist workmen,' someone said. 'And perhaps Jewish.'

'Law-abiding workmen,' said Michael.

'Lying workmen,' said Pig-face, 'and I am certain I feel torn stitching in this fellow's coat.'

The smile that swept over those observing the scene was full of guile; like a stage magician or a circus clown, he was playing to the crowd.

'But I will not punish them if they confess. I think that is fair.'

There were groans of dismay, though some went along with him, their smirking lips at odds with the darker truths in their eyes.

The smell of fear had cleared his head. Michael watched warily, ready to flee if the need arose, regardless of whether they pursued him or not. As the alcohol diffused through his system, fear and an instinct to survive replaced courage.

'Do you confess, my friends?' asked Pig-face. 'Come, there is only justice for those who bare their souls and tell the truth.' The two men exchanged fearful glances. It was still obvious that one was more wary than the other. Unfortunately, it was the most trusting one who broke.

'Yes. We are communists, and we are Jews, but we only—' Laughter broke out among those assembled.

As his head cleared, Michael was filled with foreboding. His companions smelled blood and would spill some before the night was done.

'Then you will exact your own justice on each other.' Pig-face turned to those with him. 'Give me another whip.'

Someone obliged. Pig-face unravelled both whips and held them out to the two men. 'You will flog each other as punishment for lying. The first man down is the one who deserves to be punished and I will finish him off with a bullet in his brain. The one remaining standing can go free.'

Michael's blood turned to ice and his courage returned. He took a step forwards, his leg brushing Bronica's thigh, alerting her to his intention.

'No,' she said, clinging to his arm, her breath moist against his ear. 'No. I want you. You can have me where you like, in a door, up against a wall; wherever you like.

Bronica had saved him, draping herself around his neck, pressing against him so that he'd had to walk backwards, away from the sound of the whips, the catcalls and the smell of fresh blood.

That night he'd cried on her shoulder and told her everything about his family, the circumcision and that he'd made up his mind to get back to England.

She'd said nothing, but lain very still beside him. If he had been sober he might have questioned her silence and the way she'd kept a few inches of space between them. But he'd been glad to be there with her and soon he was snoring, the beer having dulled his senses both as far as the incident and Bronica were concerned.

The night he had told her everything! That night had changed everything.

25

Lizzie was finding it hard to concentrate on Christmas, and Daw wasn't much help.

'It's only shopping. Anyone can shop for food,' moaned Daw, as she teased her dark curls into greater fullness with the tips of her fingers.

'That was before the war. It's now about queuing,' said a grim-faced Lizzie, as she attempted to scribble a weekly menu down on a scrap of paper. 'I reckon by Thursday we'll be down to a crust of bread and half a pint of milk. Try making a meal from that, Potato Pete!' They laughed at her reference to the Ministry of Food character, the symbol of what wondrous meals could be made from next to nothing.

'I wish Mum was here,' said Daw, sinking down into a chair, elbows resting on the table.

'Well, she's not,' snapped Lizzie, who had ended up taking on the responsibility of running a household, plus continuing to work for Mrs Selwyn. 'We have to do the best we can.'

Daw pouted. 'It's not fair. Fancy running off and leaving her family in the lurch like that.'

Exasperated with her sister's complaining, Lizzie threw down her pencil and glared. 'And what would you have done if Dad was about to beat you black and blue?'

Daw lowered her eyes and shook her head vehemently. 'I don't believe any of it. Dad wouldn't do a thing like that. I know he wouldn't.'

Lizzie leaned across the table, her eyes blazing. 'You weren't there!'

Daw was the only sibling who had not accepted that their parents' marriage was far from perfect, mostly, Lizzie realised, because to do so upset Daw's rosy image of the world – her world – the one where she was the centre of attention.

Daw sighed. 'I so wanted this to be a perfect Christmas, what with John coming home. And Patrick will be with him,' she added, throwing Lizzie a sly look.

Lizzie was not unaffected by mention of Patrick. His letters had given her a deep insight to the man he really was. 'Hmm. I agree we need to make the most of it. Who knows when we'll see them again?'

Her thoughts went to Patrick's letters and how her mother had loved to read his poetry. Patrick had a way with words and a side to him she hadn't known existed, but then, she reasoned, a lot of people were showing their true colours since September. Her father, her brother, even Daw and Stanley. Even her mother had changed and she wondered what had caused it. Steadfast in her devotion to her family, Mary Anne had put up with her father for their sakes and would still have done so, but something had happened, perhaps she had suddenly realised that they *had* changed, her children had become adults, no longer dependent on her but pursuing their own lives.

The clock on the mantelpiece interrupted her thoughts, striking seven o'clock. The potatoes, cabbage and turnip she'd dug up from the garden were cooked through. The smell of stuffed breast of lamb filled the kitchen and she'd made thick gravy from scum left to cool and scooped off the surface of the lamb fat. There was even enough left over to spread on bread with a pinch of salt or to make a cake.

Stanley's face appeared at the kitchen door. 'I'm hungry. When's tea?' He was surly before his mother had left home; now he was running wild, independent and answering to no one.

One week had passed and nothing had altered, and despite

enquiries made by the police and Harry, plus their father out at odd hours searching the streets, there was no trace.

'Ten minutes,' said Lizzie in a matter-of-fact manner. 'Our Daw's just about to lay the table.'

Daw looked up from reading John's letter for the umpteenth time, uttered an exasperated sigh, and returned the letter to her handbag.

Henry Randall came in at around seven, his face grey and his lips as straight as a letterbox, his cheeks sucked in and forming deep hollows.

Daw was the only one to say hello.

Lizzie got up from the table and looked away, busying herself with getting the plates down from the rack ready to dish up. Little conversation had passed between her and her father since the day he had dared strike her and her mother had disappeared. Even though she knew that it had become his habit to go around the streets looking for her rather than spend his time in the pub, she hadn't yet forgiven him.

Daw, on the other hand, was desperate for everything to be as it was.

'No luck, Dad?'

He shook his head. 'No. I showed some people her picture, and they thought they'd seen her, but they said it was too dark what with no street lights any more.'

Lizzie gritted her teeth, displeased at the cosy father–daughter exchange. 'Daw? The vegetables.'

Ignoring Daw's angry glare, she returned her father's pleading look with one of pure contempt. All this was his fault, and so far she hadn't heard him admit his guilt.

The girls dished up while their father sat in his armchair staring into space, their brother Stanley sitting on the floor continuously winding the jib of a Meccano crane up and down.

Daw eyed the five dinner plates. 'Our Harry's late.'

Lizzie didn't acknowledge her. Something about Harry was bothering her, though she'd said nothing to anyone else. She'd made the beds that morning before going to work at Mrs Selwyn's, but found

Harry's not slept in and the wardrobe door slightly ajar. Meaning to push back whatever was preventing it from shutting properly, she opened it and found things were not as she'd expected. Clothes were no longer folded on shelves or hangers and at the bottom of the wardrobe was a tan case. She'd nudged it further in, but it was heavy and wouldn't budge. The obvious conclusion came to her – Harry was leaving home, but it hurt because he hadn't said anything to her. She didn't recall seeing any call-up papers. Whatever the reason for the packed suitcase, Harry was leaving, but where was he going and why? She decided not to mention it to anyone until she'd spoken with him face to face, and she'd wait impatiently until he came home.

The clock on the mantelpiece ticked more slowly, or at least that was the way it seemed to her. How dare he be late when she was bursting with curiosity?

The sound of next-door's dog barking preceded him coming up through the back garden. In her mind she rehearsed what she was going to say.

Not yet, though, she told herself. Not here in front of everyone.

His clear blue eyes met hers in greeting as he apologised for being late. 'There were some things I had to do.'

'Mother? Have you got any news?' asked Daw.

He shook his head mournfully.

'Leave him to his dinner,' snapped Lizzie.

She could have forgiven him anything. Most women could. Hollywood film stars were nothing compared to her brother. He was Heathcliffe in *Wuthering Heights*, Darcy in *Pride and Prejudice*, Laurence Olivier and Douglas Fairbanks all rolled into one. And he was leaving.

The meal was eaten silently, and even Stanley didn't grumble that it was only spotted dick and custard for afters, left over from the night before and warmed up over a pan of boiling water.

'We're not eating so much, and nothing can be wasted,' Lizzie stated, slamming the dish down in front of him. 'Now eat it. Mum would want you to.'

Cutlery stopped moving and scraping at mention of her mother.

'Well, she would,' snapped Lizzie, unrepentant, because if she did show any sign of regret she'd burst into tears. Someone had to be strong. Someone had to manage.

Later, after the dishes were cleared, she followed Harry upstairs. He was sitting on the bed and looked surprised to see her when she pulled back the curtain.

'I saw the suitcase.'

His eyes met hers, just as they had over the kitchen table, but differently, as though he were weighing up whether she could take hearing the whole truth.

'I'm leaving.' He turned back to untying his shoelaces.

'Are you joining up? I didn't know you'd received any call-up papers.'

'I haven't. I've got a flat.'

'A flat? On your wages? I know you were on about getting a place of your own, but won't a flat be a bit expensive?'

He didn't answer for a minute, taking off his socks, rolling them up and slipping them inside his shoes. Sighing, he bent his head over clasped hands.

'I've left Wills'.'

'You've left your job? Why?'

Lifting his head, he smiled at her, the creasing at the sides of his eyes making them glitter.

'Oh, sis. You know me and Dad could end up killing each other.'

Lizzie folded her arms and adopted a knowing look. 'What's that got to do with leaving your job?'

His smile broadened. 'You're a shrewd one, our Lizzie. Nothing. It's not really about family at all. It's about me. I'm ambitious. I'm going into business.'

'What as? Are you going to open a shop?'

He got to his feet and began unbuttoning his shirt. He looked amused. 'Not quite in the accepted sense, but along those lines. As I said weeks ago, I ain't going to get myself killed like them in nineteen fourteen who thought war was all a great big adventure. I ain't that naive. If this war's coming then I'm going to be one of the clever sods making money from it, and don't look at me like that, Lizzie. There's going to be plenty of people getting rich from the slaughter of others, though that ain't quite what I got in mind. I've got mates I'm going into business with. I'm goin' to take advantage of this war before it takes advantage of me.'

Lizzie couldn't pretend that she was glad for him. No matter that what he said made sense in a mercenary kind of way and was totally different to her father's attitude.

'Is there a woman involved?'

He smiled sadly. She tried reading the look in his eyes, but there was something guarded about it. It occurred to her that she'd never seen him with a woman; never heard tale that he'd had even a mild flirtation.

Another more worrying conclusion came to her, but no! Not Harry! Not the toughest boy in the street.

She wondered why he hadn't left earlier; the case seemed to have been packed for a while. He read her mind.

The sparkle went from his eyes and he looked sad. 'I can't leave until I find out what's happened to me mother. I can't leave until then.'

Mary Anne heaved herself up onto her elbows and looked around her. She was lying in a double bed in a bedroom at the back of the house. A shaft of sunlight from the single window highlighted a late-Victorian piece of furniture: two single wardrobes either side of a conjoined chest of drawers.

The bedding was clean and smelled of lavender. A row of dining chairs with spindly legs and finely carved backs lined one wall. A simple chest of dark oak sat beneath the window and a blue water jug with matching glass had been placed on a table beside the bed.

There was also a pile of newly washed clothes – her clothes – including her underwear.

And whose house was this? The view through the window over the rooftops gave her a clue. Could it possibly be true that she'd stumbled into the doorway of the pawnshop purely by chance? And if so, could it be that Michael had washed her bloodstained clothes?

The thought was unnerving, but in her present state of weakness, embarrassment swiftly gave way to indifference. Everything was down to practicalities.

Memories of the night she'd run away came back to her.

Henry had finally lost his temper in front of the children and had actually struck Lizzie to the ground.

Lizzie! She tried to get up, but was too weak. Instead she tried to put her thoughts in order.

The crisp cotton bed linen was cool against her head; perhaps that was why everything was suddenly so clear. Lizzie had told her to live more for herself now her children were grown. Continuing to live with Henry was like sacrificing what remained of her life. It seemed stupid now, but back in Kent Street it appeared the only choice she had.

But surely she couldn't stay here?

Lying without any demands on her time and services, she reviewed her options.

Number one option was to go home and try to paper over the cracks, try to make everything as it was before, for her family's sake rather than for herself.

My God, how were they managing? Dreadfully, she didn't doubt; they just weren't used to coping without her.

Number two option was not as clear cut as number one. Making a life of her own and on her own was all very well, but where did she start? She had no skills except running a house, plus the little sideline out in the washhouse.

Perhaps, she thought, her gaze falling back to the view outside the window, providence may have brought you to the right place. If indeed she was in a room above the pawnshop, she could offer to do exactly what Thomas Routledge had offered; accepted by the locals, she could deal with the customers. It made sense; she just needed Michael to see it her way.

She closed her eyes. All this thinking was making her tired, but she mustn't doze too long. She had to do *something*, and there was also Stanley to consider. No matter what happened, her main worry would be Stanley. He was only a boy. She had to know that he was well and not missing her too much.

He could live here, she thought, and almost laughed. Who did she think she was? This was Michael's place – at least she guessed it was. Who lived here was his decision not hers.

She pushed the bedclothes back and forced herself to drag her legs across the bed. Gradually, her circulation prompted by movement, she managed to dangle her feet over the side.

For a moment she paused, surprised to see that her legs were almost as white as the old-fashioned nightgown she was wearing. The gown itself was quite beautiful, but rather large. Holding up one arm she studied the long, billowing sleeve tied with ribbons around the wrist, musing that it might have once belonged to Queen Victoria, though she might have needed the hem taken up.

Wriggling her bottom closer to the edge, she launched herself. Her feet landed squarely, but she'd misjudged the height. As her feet hit the floor, her knees crumpled. Letting go of the mattress, she flung her hands forwards, in time to stop her nose bumping the floor, but landing with a loud thud on her hands and knees.

The sound of footsteps running upstairs preceded the door being flung open.

Gently but firmly, Michael lifted her, tucking the long nightgown modestly beneath her as he picked her up.

'You are too weak. Perhaps tomorrow?'

Because of her dizziness, she saw him as a blur, a figure tucking her in, fluffing up her pillows and pouring water from the jug. Gradually the dizziness passed.

'My children... Have you told them where I am?' She could tell by the look on his face that he hadn't. 'Why didn't you?'

He shrugged. 'I meant to. I went along to your house the next day, but the police were there. I came back here and told myself I would do it the day after that, but then I thought the police and your family would ask too many questions. I hoped that you might be on your feet and able to walk back. I would have walked part of the way with you. Perhaps we could do that tomorrow or the next day, but please, I do not want to be involved. I hope you understand that.'

She didn't answer straightaway. All her plans for running the shop cracked wide open. But no matter what, she resolved that things had changed; she had changed.

Perhaps it was resting or as a result of the trauma she had suffered, something to do with losing the baby. The guilt was unbearable, and so was the need for restitution. The answer was to live her life to the full in future, to live it both for the unborn child *and* herself. That meant she could not go back to being the downtrodden spirit who had lived through her family. She must not sacrifice her life as she had that of the child, but live it for both of them. Thanks to the gathering storm over Europe, all their lives would be different in future.

The inarguable truth was that her children were growing up and the outbreak of war had accelerated the process. It had first hit her when Harry had argued with his father, adamant that he would not join the forces until he absolutely had to. She thought of their last conversation. He'd always had ambitions. Shame he would never marry and she knew beyond doubt now that he never would.

Then there was Daw; aching to get married, and even though she wouldn't move that far away, it would leave another gap in Mary Anne's life. Last of all there was Lizzie, as dutiful as her mother, but channelling that sense of giving to joining the Wrens, not to a husband and family. She didn't doubt she would indeed join something.

That left Stanley. Hopefully, the war would be over before he got called up. He was the only one left who truly needed her, and even then he harboured an independence she herself could only dream of.

She looked at Michael, who had pulled up a chair and was watching her intently.

'You lost a lot of blood.'

She bit her lip, felt herself blushing again, and looked away from him. She didn't want to know whether it was him who had put her to bed, but he guessed the reason for her blush and had seen the sideways look.

His blush matched hers. 'I told Mrs Westerman, the tailor's wife next door, that you were my sister. She sorted you out and did the laundry.'

He hung his head, his hands still clasped before him. 'I will tell your family if you wish.'

She sensed his nervousness, but also she was very aware of her own reluctance, and not just because she was planning a new future. Someone was looking after her and it filled her with a sense of wonder. She was looking at her life and her family from the outside and the view was certainly different than from within. There had seemed nothing else to live for; even the pawning and gardening were a means to an end, making sure her family were well fed and looked after.

'Not yet,' she said thoughtfully. 'I need time to think.' She looked into his face and caught him looking back at her. 'Do you mind if I stay a while longer?'

He blinked then shook his head. 'No. No. Do you want to tell me what happened?'

Initially, she wanted to say no, because that's what she'd been saying all these years, denying the truth, hiding it beneath a veneer of 'Happy Families'. On reflection she needed to talk about it in full, not just moan and groan about the trivial things like the women who supped tea and traded treasures for six-pences in her washhouse, but never did anything because their lives weren't really that bad. They saw her as attractive for her age and being a bit better off financially than they were. They didn't see the bruises; they didn't cry her tears.

'Yes.' She looked at him almost impudently, surprising herself with her boldness. 'I have to tell someone and it might as well be you.'

'I can't think of a better Christmas present,' Lizzie said with a giggle, much to Daw's consternation, who couldn't see what the fuss was all about.

'It's a chicken.'

'No. It's a capon,' said Patrick, who had presented it to Lizzie on arrival.

'And a sack of vegetables,' said Lizzie who was suitably impressed. 'No wonder your kitbag looked a bit bulky. It must have weighed a ton.'

'I'm a big strong fellah,' said Patrick, flexing his muscles.

Lizzie laughed. 'Oh. So now you're Tarzan Kelly.'

'That's right. You should see me in a loincloth!'

Daw was the only one who didn't laugh. She was frowning at John, sending him silent signals that she wanted him to herself.

Lizzie ignored her sister. They hadn't been quite so close since their mother's disappearance, mostly because Daw's selfishness had become more apparent.

Patrick's comment had Lizzie blushing, and not just because of his jokiness. This was not the downtrodden Patrick Kelly that some in the street had looked down on because his mother was on the game.

'And just to prove it, will you take a gander at this.' He tapped the single stripe adorning his sleeve. 'Corporal Kelly, Armourer First Class.'

Stanley, whose spirits had been severely affected by his mother's disappearance, was hanging on to every word Patrick uttered, and was totally mesmerised by their uniforms and tales of what they'd been up to.

'What does that mean?' he asked Patrick. 'What's an armourer?'

'Someone who arms the plane. You know, makes sure it's got a full load of weapons.'

'To shoot down the Germans?'

'That's right. Shoot 'em all out of the sky when they come over here to drop their bombs.'

A shivering Daw moved closer to John, who immediately put his arm around her.

'Do you think they will?' she asked in a quavering voice. 'If Hitler has his way they will. They've taken enough of Europe, but I don't think it'll ever be enough for them.'

Animated by their conversation, Stanley stood up on a chair so he could better speak directly into Patrick's face. 'I know where Mr Hitler lives,' he said, his eyes shining.

'Is that right?'

Lizzie winked at Patrick.

'Lives down East Street and runs a pawnbroker's,' she said, barely able to contain her amusement.

Patrick nodded at Stanley, who didn't notice that his sister was poking fun. 'And there was me thought his sideline was house painting. But there, I ain't always right.'

'Yes. Mr Hitler lives there. Ollie Young said so.'

'Then it must be true, young Stanley.' Hiding his smile, he turned to Lizzie. 'Talking about the Youngs, how's Mrs Young's boy doing in the army?'

'Posted somewhere abroad, from what we can gather. We haven't seen much of Biddy since Mum...'

Up until that moment, everyone had avoided mentioning what had happened. They fell to silence. Patrick and John looked the most awkward despite their smart blue uniforms.

'I was sorry to hear about it,' said Patrick at the same time as holding his cup out for more tea. 'There's no news, I take it.'

Lizzie shook her head and pulled at the tea cosy, supposedly trying to make it fit the pot better, but really doing it because she didn't want to admit defeat. If she did that she would crumble altogether.

'That's why Dad's tea's drying up on the stove,' she said, indicating the boiling saucepan and the plate of food on top, covered with a saucepan lid. 'He goes out looking for her, though God knows he can't see much with all the lights out.'

'I told him he's likely to get knocked down by a bus,' said Daw, 'but he won't listen.'

Stanley snarled like an angry cat as he climbed down the chair. 'I hope he does get knocked down! I hope he gets killed!'

Daw condemned him. 'Stanley! He's your father!'

Lizzie couldn't forget that it was Stanley who had warned her, and she'd done? Nothing!

She rubbed his hair. 'Come on, Stanley. Time for bed. Don't want to tire yerself out, do you?'

Stanley's eyes were fixed on Patrick. 'Will you be here tomorrow?'

Lizzie recognised the hero worship.

Patrick thrust his hands in the deep pockets of his uniform, stretched his legs out in front of him and nodded. 'Unless the whole of the German Luftwaffe threatens to invade tonight, I will certainly be here tomorrow.'

'Great,' said Stanley. 'I'll see you then.'

'At reveille.'

'Reveille?'

'First light.'

'Right,' said John, rubbing his hands together and glancing at each of them in turn. 'Who's for a foursome for the pictures?'

'I thought you'd never ask,' trilled an excited Daw.

'I'm up for that,' said Patrick, rising from the table.

Lizzie shook her head. 'Count me out. I'll wait until Dad gets home. He's useless with hot plates and pots of tea.'

Patrick cleared his throat, holding his hat in front of him, passing it from left to right hand and back again.

'I could... um... keep you company, if you like.'

There was a grim intensity to his face, as though he'd stopped breathing while awaiting her answer.

'I suppose you could.'

'We're going to see the new Joan Crawford,' said Daw, poking her head around door before leaving. 'We'll let you know what it's like.'

'That would be great,' said Patrick. Turning back to Lizzie, he said. 'Then p'raps we can see it tomorrow.'

'Yes,' said Lizzie, intending to wipe the smile from Daw's face. 'Our Daw can wait in for Dad tomorrow night. It's time she took her turn.'

The look Daw threw her was pure venom, but Lizzie didn't care. Never, until this war and the events connected with it, had she ever felt so annoyed with her sister.

With the slamming of the front door and the softer closing of Stanley's door, the house fell silent.

Patrick helped with the dishes.

Lizzie felt rather than saw his frequent sideways glances. At last, he said, 'Thanks for writing to me.'

'Thank *you*. I enjoyed your letters.'

She decided not to tell him that writing to him was by way of substitution. Peter had written only one letter from Canada and that to his mother. It still seemed strange, but writing to Patrick had been by way of compensation, and yet she'd miss his letters if he stopped writing.

'Would you really come to the pictures with me tomorrow night?'

'Why not?'

Why not indeed. She needed cheering up. Working in a domestic environment all day and then coming home to another one, she was beginning to feel like a full-time skivvy. It came to her that her mother must have felt the same way, demands being made on her all the time.

'You haven't said how your Harry's getting on.'

Lizzie tucked in her upper lip. She'd promised not to tell anyone that Harry was leaving the minute his mother was found and, what was more, he seemed totally convinced that she would be found.

'Dad got angry with him because he refused to enlist.'

'He hasn't received any call-up papers?'

Lizzie shook her head. 'No.'

Patrick fell to silence. She noticed he was frowning when she passed him a plate to wipe dry.

'Is something wrong?'

'I thought everyone in our age group was being called up. Seems strange they've overlooked Harry.'

'He said he'll go when he gets his papers, but so far...'

She fancied she sounded defensive, but it wasn't just to protect her brother. She also felt she was protecting herself, or rather her own suspicions. No one knew where Harry spent his evenings or who he spent them with. Away from home and work, he had a secret life, one they were not privilege to.

'He's still at the cigarette factory,' she said, but didn't add 'though not for much longer'. Harry had confided in her. He was biding his time, trusting in the best news possible about his mother, whereas Lizzie was preparing herself for the worse.

She passed him the basting tin in which she'd just roasted five pigs' tails. 'You must come here for Christmas Day dinner.'

He beamed. 'That's nice of you.'

She smiled back at him. 'Not at all. I was afraid Tarzan might whip away his capon if I didn't invite him round.'

'Now there's a thought! Anything you need for the great day?'

'Holly and mistletoe.'

She wondered afterwards what had possessed her to say that, but answered her own question.

To cheer us all up. To make us believe that life goes on, and Mum wouldn't want us to be unhappy.

28

It seemed strange and totally selfish not being at home for Christmas, but also the world outside seemed stranger since war was declared. Mary Anne felt as though a book had fallen open at exactly the right page and she couldn't put it down. Looking back, living with Henry had been like being stuck in a quicksand with the tide rolling in. No matter how much she struggled to get to the shore, the waves kept washing over her, growing ever higher with the years.

They ate a Christmas dinner of forcemeat and vegetables followed by an apple strudel in front of the fire, all prepared by Michael. Madam Butterfly sang plaintively for her Lieutenant Pinkerton in the background. Neither spoke for a while, each cloistered with their thoughts.

'You are thinking of your family,' Michael said suddenly.

'And you are thinking of yours.'

Michael was silent. He'd felt privileged that she had told him so much about hers and by doing so he had felt part of her life. He had only hinted at his own.

'Are they still alive?'

Her question sent a jolt like electricity through his brain.

'I don't know,' he said, his voice barely above a whisper.

* * *

It began to snow just after Christmas, flakes blowing with a bitter wind from an overcast sky.

Mary Anne, recovered now, watched them falling and wondered if her children were watching them too, perhaps also Henry. Distanced from him, she no longer saw him in quite the same light as she had all these years. No longer a figure of fear, she now felt quite sorry for him. Her parents had wanted her married, and once Edward's child had been adopted and she was presentable again, they'd encouraged Henry to court her. Ordinarily, he would have been shown the door; they had been worlds apart. She had been well educated, and he had come straight from the army having served in Palestine and Egypt, then the dreaded trenches of Ypres, the Somme and Cambrai. Barely literate but good-looking, he had fallen in love with her. At first she'd felt protective towards him, and in the early days had attempted to teach him to read. Once he'd found out about

Edward's child, his attitude had changed.

Where was that child now? she wondered, as she watched the snowflakes fall.

A knock sounded at the bedroom door. Mary Anne smiled warmly. Michael was a courteous man, knocking at the bedroom door of his own house. So different to Henry, she thought, not a violent bone in his body.

'I have made some soup,' he said, and looked proud to have achieved it. 'There is not much meat in it, but plenty of vegetables and the bread is fresh.'

She nodded. 'That would be nice. I'll be right down.'

He nodded too and smiled. She fancied he had more colour in his face than when she'd first arrived and he did not hunch his shoulders so much as he had done when they'd first met, as though he were trying to disguise his height – or himself – trying not to be noticed.

The smell of the soup mixed with that of burning coals and the all-pervasive beeswax. Doors and windows were shut tight against the cold, the old-fashioned wooden shutters drawn, and the shop shut for the weekend. Michael had decided not to open up after Saturday lunch once he saw that few other people did either.

'Shall we have Schubert?' he asked, his palms gingerly curved around the outside edge of the record.

She nodded. 'Yes. Shall I pour the tea?'

'Just a minute...'

Bending his head and steadying his hand, he placed the needle onto the record. Once the first notes sounded, he was at her side, bending over her, cutting bread and pouring tea.

'You spoil me,' she said. 'In fact you make me feel like a child again. That was the last time anyone spoiled me, I'm afraid.'

The clocks now ticked together like a small orchestra all hitting the same notes but at different time sequences. She presumed he'd wound them up some time after her arrival.

'I am glad to have you here. I think you know that.'

She looked up from the very good soup. His smile was so like that of Edward. So were his eyes, his mouth, his hair...

She fought to drag her gaze away from him and back to her soup.

'Are you almost finished clearing the cupboards?'

'Just one more,' he said, finally sitting down at the table once he'd poked at the fire thereby releasing a shower of sparks from the bed of glowing coals.

'Just one more. I do not think there is anything of value there, just family papers.'

'You may find a treasure even amongst them.'

'I doubt it, just dusty old sales receipts and bills for the plumbing when it was first put indoors.'

Mary Anne smiled. 'We could do with a plumber now,' she said, referring to the incessant dripping of the kitchen tap.

Michael shook his head. 'No. We need a better one than him. That tap is no good and needs fixing properly. I think I will do it.' It was something she had noticed about Michael just days after she'd arrived; he preferred to mend things for himself, and that included his own clothes. He even ironed them himself although she had offered to do them for him.

'No. I must look after myself. When you are gone...'

It was rarely he referred to the time when she would leave, his eyes lowering at the thought of it; his dark lashes like smears of charcoal against his skin.

'When you are gone, I will have to look after myself.'

Mary Anne put down her spoon. 'That's what I want to speak to you about.'

His eyes met hers.

Resting her elbows on the table, she clasped her hands in front of her chin.

'I think Thomas Routledge's idea about having him serve out in the shop was a good one. You need someone to help you.'

Michael's jaw dropped.

She smiled. 'I didn't mean that you should employ him. I think I should do it.'

At first she mistook his silence and his frozen expression as disapproval.

A huge gasp escaped his mouth, relief lighting his face. 'That is wonderful.'

'It is?'

He nodded vehemently and took hold of her hands. 'Truly wonderful. Truly wonderful that you will be staying here.'

Both looked down at their clasped hands, then back up into each other's face.

'I am very pleased,' he said.

She nodded. 'So am I.'

29

Once her bicycle was safely stored in the coal shed behind the house she worked in, Lizzie went gladly into the kitchen, where she took off her coat and gave it a good shake before hanging it up.

She'd been queuing for hours both on Mrs Selwyn's and her own behalf, causing grumbling at the grocer's because it took twice as long to sort out *two* ration books as it did one.

As she'd waited, she'd read the latest letter from Patrick, smiling at his description of one of the officers, which brought to mind their last conversation before going back to base just after Christmas.

'I think you should keep an eye on yer dad.'

'He can look after himself,' she'd said begrudgingly. 'It was his fault that Mum ran off, him down the pub all the time getting drunk.'

'And he knows it,' Patrick had said softly. 'He's still drunk, only not with beer. He's drunk with regret.'

They'd fallen to silence, Lizzie a little huffy because she didn't want to even *think* about her father, let alone talk to him.

'Does he ever talk about the war?' Patrick asked.

'Oh, yes,' said Lizzie with undisguised impatience. 'How he won it single-handed.'

Patrick shook his head. 'I don't mean the bits he glorifies; I mean the bits he doesn't tell you. How long was it before he met your mother?'

Lizzie shrugged. 'I'm not sure. A year, I think. She didn't know him too well at all before that, only in passing. He never said anything. I think she said he was literally the strong and silent type; never said a word to anyone before they stepped out together.'

'Ah!'

'What's "ah!" supposed to mean?'

Patrick had clasped his hands together and gazed into the fire. 'That's what happened after the Great War. Men came home but hardly spoke for years. They were in a state of shock, you see. They'd seen too many horrors, terrible things that affected their minds more than they let on.'

Lizzie eyed him sceptically. 'And how come you know so much, Patrick Kelly?'

He'd smiled at her. 'Because I take the trouble to find out. I read a lot.'

Patrick had started to make an impression on her. He made her feel warm. Wish he was with me today, she'd thought, her face stung by snowflakes.

By the time she'd got back to Ashton, it was snowing hard. Mrs Selwyn was nowhere to be found. She usually had her afternoon nap on the settee in the front parlour, but not always. Upstairs snoozing, she thought, and went on unpacking and putting away the things she'd fetched for her employer.

There was a wireless in the kitchen and, after putting the kettle on, she turned it on meaning to listen to the music while waiting for the kettle to boil. Mrs Selwyn was bound to be down before long.

The kettle had boiled, the tea was in the pot and brewing nicely, and still there was no sign of her.

Lizzie sighed impatiently. As if she didn't have enough to do. There was nothing for it but to make up a tray and take it up to her.

Tapping lightly, her ear close to the door, she waited for the command to enter. There was no reply and, although the tray wasn't that heavy, she didn't want to take it back downstairs. After one more knock, she opened the bedroom door, fully expecting to see Mrs Selwyn fast asleep on the bed. If she had done she would have left the tray there and asked her if she was all right, but Mrs Selwyn wasn't there. The bed was as smooth and unruffled as when she'd made it that morning.

Back down in the kitchen, she poured herself a cup of tea from the pot she'd placed on the tray and took two of the biscuits. She pulled a chair up in front of the fire and slipped off her shoes, wriggling her toes in front of the old-fashioned range.

As she sipped the hot tea, it occurred to her that Mrs Selwyn didn't usually go out in the afternoon, but she presumed something had gone wrong at the store and someone had called round in a taxi to take her there. It was the only explanation, she decided, dunking the first biscuit into the tea.

Sultry music, something introduced as 'Hawaiian Romance', made her think of warm places, blue skies, golden beaches and waving palms. Toasting her toes, listening to the music and drinking tea while snuggled in a comfortable chair before the fire had a soporific effect. It was just too comfortable. She hadn't been sleeping well lately what with the extra responsibilities she'd inherited since her mother had gone missing, that and the extra responsibilities of looking after the house.

She began to doze and dream in that funny halfway place between sleeping and waking: a beach, a soft breeze... and someone calling her name.

'Elizabeth! Elizabeth!'

Lizzie jerked awake, turning in her chair and just catching the teacup before it crashed to the floor.

Mrs Selwyn was smoothing her hair back from her face and patting her cheeks as if she had only just woke up.

'Have you made tea?'

Lizzie slid her feet into her shoes and stood up. 'Yes. I couldn't find you in the living room...'

'I wasn't in there. I had a bit of a headache and had a lie down on my bed.'

'Oh, but I did take the tray up to your room.'

'That must have been while I was in the bathroom,' she snapped, her expression almost daring Lizzie to question her further.

Lizzie didn't recall hearing the pulling of the lavatory chain from the bathroom, but didn't say so. Mrs Selwyn was adamant, her whole attitude conveying that she would tolerate no more questions.

In Lizzie's opinion, it seemed a strange thing to be secretive about. She was in no doubt that Mrs Selwyn had been in the house, but didn't want her to know where, and she wondered why.

There was no point in pursuing the matter. She had more important things to deal with.

'I got you sausages, tea and sugar. You should have enough to last.'

Mrs Selwyn nodded. Her manner was stiffly formal. 'Good. Now perhaps you could bring me in a pot rather than drinking it all yourself.'

'Bitch,' muttered Lizzie once the kitchen door was safely closed between them. She put the kettle back on the gas.

Shopping, worrying and work had taken their toll. She was tired out and full of glum concerns. Thinking of Patrick Kelly, his poems and his company at Christmas were the only things that brought a smile to her face. She'd found herself missing him immediately after he'd gone. 'Write me if anything happens,' he'd said, and then added with a kindly smile, 'and if anything doesn't. Pretend I'm listening.'

Once the tea was delivered, drank, and the crockery washed, she carried out the last tasks of the day, one eye on the clock and another on the weather outside.

'Thank God for that,' she muttered once the clock had struck six. She went in to say goodbye before leaving as she always did. Mrs Selwyn was in the front parlour, looking with pursed lips out at the darkness.

'You may have to walk,' she said, just as stiffly as she'd spoken earlier. 'The snow is very deep indeed.'

'I'll manage.' She'd prefer to take her bike, but if the snow was too deep, she'd walk if she had to.

Mrs Selwyn gave a curt nod by way of agreement.

Well wrapped up against the cold, Lizzie closed the back door behind her, groaning on seeing just how bad the weather had become.

Hidden by darkness, the snow was deeper than she'd thought, coming halfway up her shins and up to her knees where it had drifted. The door to the coal shed faced the wind-blown blizzard causing a drift to form reaching halfway up the door, and her legs were aching by the time she got there.

'I want my bike,' she muttered to herself, digging at the snow with her bare hands, her woollen gloves growing soggier by the minute. 'I will have my bike!'

After a few minutes' hard work, she rested, her breath turning to steam on the icy air. She considered the matter carefully. If she had a spade, or even a garden rake, she could dig the snow away from the door and get her bike out. Unfortunately, they were kept in the coal shed in which everything was stored that wasn't for immediate use, and there was just too much snow piled against the door. There was no point in trying to get the bicycle. It made sense to walk.

By feeling the garden fence with her right hand and balancing with the other, she found her way to the back gate. It had occurred to her to go through the house to save time and energy, but that would leave a wet mess through the house. Mrs Selwyn would not approve!

On opening the garden gate she stepped out into the back lane and into a deep drift, the coldness of which took her breath away. She looked back at the house, to get her bearing before she tramped off through the drifts and darkness. The large square villa looked more intensely black than the night because no lights glowed behind curtains and threw patches of amber onto the snow. The blackout was total and the snow was making things worse.

Taking a step forwards consisted of hauling one foot up and over deep snow. By the time she reached the end of the lane, her legs were aching and her lungs straining to cope both with the effort and the cold air.

What if it was like this all the way home? It could be midnight by the time she got there – if she got there.

She struggled on. Getting from the back lane to the main road seemed to take ages. She tried to judge how long she'd been outside. Judging by the wetness of her clothes and the coldness of her face, at least thirty minutes had passed.

The darkness deepened. What was familiar by day had disappeared. Bare twigs of trees and bushes snagged her hat and hair: seeking support, her hands sank into soft snow that hid sharp stones upended on garden walls.

Slipping and sinking into a sea of freezing whiteness, she finally reached the end of the lane, where she stopped and caught her breath. The main road was not quite as bad as the back lane because some traffic had passed over it, but that was earlier in the day. It still came up to her shins. Stopping and pausing for breath, she thought carefully about what she was doing. A lot of effort would be needed if she were to find her way home in the blackout and this terrible weather and, what was more, she'd have to walk. It was quite possible she'd lose her way before collapsing from exhaustion.

She looked back through the blackness to the lane and along to where she thought was the front of the house. It was hard to detect its exact location; the drifts ahead of her were bound to be thick and it was desperately difficult to gauge distance. At least if she went back the way she'd come there were indentations left in the snow by her feet. If she followed them, feeling her way back along the same walls and fences, recognising the same trees and bushes that had scratched at her coming out, she would find the back of the Selwyn house. There was nothing for it but to stay the night.

The journey back was just as bad as the journey out; she was wearier now, the cold air paining her chest and snowflakes stinging her face.

Her woollen hat and gloves were clogged with snow; her stockings were like a crusting of ice against her legs, and more snow, melted by the heat of her body, seeped into her boots.

Struggling against the biting wind, she turned into the familiar gateway, groping her way back up the garden path. Where possible she placed her feet in the indentations she'd made on the way out. All the same, it was quite a struggle getting up the garden path.

The back of the house looked ominous, dark and unwelcoming. There was every chance the back door was unlocked. Mrs Selwyn never locked it before nine, though after that there was no chance of being heard. Once settled in the front parlour or the dining room, it was not possible to hear anything coming from the back of the house.

Lizzie prayed it was still unlocked so that she wouldn't have to go all the way back round the front, though she would if she had to.

The handle turned! Sighing with relief, she almost fell through the door, lying against it for a while once it was closed, her mouth closing and opening like a goldfish in a bowl as she fought to get her breathing back to normal.

A few minutes and she pushed herself forwards, heading for the kitchen and the warm fire she'd left in the range, the embers ready to be turned over in the morning.

Her clothes began to steam in response to the warmth, and she began to shiver as the snow stuck to her coat, hat, face and legs turned to water.

Hastily, she pulled off her woollen gloves and hat, folding them over the bar running round the front of the range. Her coat was sodden; she hung it over the back of a chair, pulling it forwards to get the benefit of the heat.

Her stockings were next. There wasn't much chance of Mrs Selwyn coming in once she'd eaten her supper, which Lizzie had left for her set out on a tray. She always ate her main meal at lunchtime unless Peter was home, mostly at weekends before he'd gone away.

Placing one foot on the chair that held her coat, she hitched up her skirt, shivering as she unfastened a suspender, began peeling it down her leg.

Suddenly, she felt a cold draught, looked up and... froze, though not from cold.

A door had opened. Someone had entered the room and was watching her.

She stared. She had expected Mrs Selwyn, but it wasn't.

Fingers still on her stocking top, foot balanced on the seat of the chair, her mouth dropped open.

'Peter!' Her voice was little above a whisper.

He stared back, gulping down his surprise like a glass of water to a thirsty man. He looked more surprised to see her than she was to see him.

His eyes travelled from her face to her leg, coming to rest on the bare flesh between stocking top and underwear.

Lizzie found her voice. 'I didn't know you were on leave.' Flushing slightly, she rearranged her clothes and dropped her foot back to the floor.

'Ah!' he said. 'Yes.'

There was something in his expression that didn't ring true. He didn't go into immediate explanation as to why she wouldn't have known, but merely confirmed what she'd suggested.

'It was a last minute thing,' he blurted.

To her ears it sounded more like an excuse than a bona fide reason, the sort of excuse that grows from a lie.

His mother appeared behind him, her face turning pale when she saw Lizzie, as surprised as her son, though not merely at finding Lizzie still in her kitchen – not even indignation. There was fear in her eyes and Lizzie wondered why.

30

If the snow were not so deep, you wouldn't be so worried about Stanley. That's what Mary Anne told herself as she surveyed the backyard behind the pawnshop, its grave lines softened by a blanket of blinding whiteness.

Enclosed by brick walls, an ugly square amongst more of the same all along the rank, nothing grew except weeds and a single sapling right in the centre. She judged it to be no more than thirty years old, its brave little seed originally dropped there by some migrating swallow: at least, she hoped it was a swallow. They were her favourite bird, nesting every year in the washhouse in Kent Street, their elegant tails poking out from a recess between the top of the wall and the tiles. She liked the way they swooped and soared, envying their freedom of movement. Every year they nested in the same place, just like her, the difference being that she never got to swoop and soar.

She'd been telling herself that soon she would visit Kent Street and inform her family that she would not be coming back and that Stanley could come and live with her and Michael if he wished. The attic bedroom was free. Michael had been agreeable when she'd suggested it.

'There is plenty of room here. You have a room, I have a room, and there is the attic room.'

They did indeed both have a room. Sometimes, lying awake at night, she heard him walking around, finally falling into bed after midnight. She imagined him lying there, still awake, alone with his thoughts. Flattening her hand against the wall, she imagined him doing the same the other side; their hands together, divided by only the thinnest of walls.

Last night another chapter of the book that had fallen open so propitiously had come to an inconclusive ending.

'Goodnight,' she'd said, loud enough for him to hear. At first there'd been silence, as though he hadn't heard.

'Goodnight,' he answered. He sounded surprised.

She'd turned over, snuggling against the pillow and closer to the wall. It was good to know he was there with just a thin wall between them, almost as if they were lying together, but not quite yet, not quite yet.

That evening they sat together on the old chaise longue. The room had turned chill so he'd pulled it closer to the fire, making toast and cooking jacket potatoes in the ashes.

Michael was the biggest surprise in her life. Since knowing him she had become more aware of herself and of an awakening in her own body. Telling herself that she feared it to be bloated by the miscarriage, she had eyed her naked body in the mirror and saw the sort of figure seen in the myriad paintings of grand masters.

I want him to see it, she thought to herself. I want him to know me.

Sometimes, when reading or even washing dishes, she felt his eyes on her.

'I feel I have always been here,' she said to him on one such instance.

'I feel this was planned,' he replied.

She understood. 'As though our meeting was prearranged.'

He didn't answer, but she could tell by the look in his eyes that he was feeling exactly the same unfathomable tingling beneath his heart.

She found him easy to talk to. There was an openness to his look, as if saying, 'Come on in. Tell me all.'

He was a good listener, patient as she tried to explain, seeming to share her emotions whether it was pain, fear, love or hope.

'I've made some big mistakes in my life,' she said. 'The biggest one was burying *me* beneath other people's lives. I pawned my identity in life, telling myself I was content to live for my children, to live *through* them.'

'Would you do things differently if you lived your life again?' he asked, his features a patchwork of light and dark made golden by the glow of the fire. 'I do not think you would.' He lowered his eyes. 'We all have obsessions in life. For you it was – and perhaps still is – your children.'

'And for you?'

At first he seemed reluctant to answer. Dark lashes brushed his cheeks as he blinked into the brandy glass cupped by both hands. He'd poured them both a measure of brandy. The liquid had hit the back of her throat with a burning tingle, and although she hadn't liked it at first, it became more pleasant the more sips she'd taken.

He looked at her sidelong, as though assessing whether he should say any more.

'I liked uniforms.'

She cupped the brandy glass as though the liquid within warmed her hands. Her hair hung loose down her back. 'What sort of uniforms?'

He shrugged, took in the look of her with just one glance, and answered softly, 'Any. At first it was the Boy Scouts. I desperately wanted to join them and learn to blow a bugle.'

'So why didn't you?'

'My stepfather did not approve. He was a Lutheran minister. He did not approve of any kind of uniform. Even the Boy Scouts, and he did not like me mixing with the local boys. He thought it best that I stay in the company of him and my mother.'

'Did you have any friends?'

'There were some, but they did not understand why I was not allowed to do the things they did. I desperately wanted to, but my step-father would not allow it and so I hated him.'

'You must have been lonely.'

'I was, but as I got older I did what many young men did – I rebelled. Eventually, I left home.'

'And joined the army?'

There was something in the sharp way he jerked his head round that made her think he was hiding something. The open look disappeared, replaced by a more veiled expression.

'As I said, I loved uniforms. More brandy?' he asked, reaching for a cut glass decanter with a silver top.

'A lovely thing,' she said, nodding at the decanter. 'And very good brandy,' she added, raising the glass and taking another sip even though she thought it very likely that she'd had enough already. She was feeling too relaxed, too comfortable in front of the fire and in this man's company. Michael was like Edward in that he'd rekindled physical responses she'd thought were dead and buried. The thought sent a thrill through her body, the sort of thrill she hadn't felt in years.

Her hand travelled to her throat, felt its heat then fell away.

What was she doing here? Her hand trembled slightly.

'Are you all right?'

His hand covered hers. It was the lightest of touches, and yet it felt as though lightning had shot through them both, binding them together.

'Yes!' she said breathlessly, raising her eyes to meet his.

They looked at each other. She chose to believe that he was as surprised as her that this had come about, and yet, deep down, she knew the seed had been sown that first day he'd come to complain about her business when she'd threatened to brain him with a spade.

He dropped his hand first, self-consciously dropping his gaze and rubbing his palms together.

Clutching the brandy glass more tightly, she gulped another mouthful and tried to forget that the memory of his touch tingled on her skin. His fingers were sensitive, she thought. Had someone once told her that sensitive hands betrayed a sensitive heart?

Wondering about its source was obliterated by her confusion; a euphoric tingling that raised goosebumps and made her forget that she was married, a mother and older than him.

It's the brandy, she thought, it's making me act strangely. 'I am going to need a lot of courage,' she said, her hair falling like a curtain around her face.

'The courage to go or the courage to stay?'

He'd worded the question oddly, but she understood what he was saying. She'd had to be brave to live with Henry and had done so for the sake of the children. She also had to be brave to stay with Michael – if that indeed was what he was asking her – to stay openly, in total disregard of what people might say, including her own family.

She gazed into the amber liquid as though it were a crystal ball that might tell her the future.

She did not notice that her hair was almost the same colour as the brandy – but he did.

She told him her main fear. 'The neighbours will call me a scarlet woman and that my place is at home with my husband.'

'It is not for them to say. You must be true to yourself.'

'I have to think of my children.'

'And forget yourself as you have done all these years?'

He said it almost accusingly, she thought, and it annoyed her.

'And is that so wrong?'

He raised his eyebrows in an offhand way, as though it was of no consequence to him, and yet, if she could read his thoughts, she would see that it was.

'Steering them through their lives? Protecting them by sacrificing yourself?'

'Is that so bad?' Her tone was sharp.

'You have answered both my questions with questions. "Is that so wrong?" "Is that so bad?"'

'Things could have been so different.'

'So you said.'

'I could have sung "One Fine Day" for Edward with all the emotion it requires. He was my Lieutenant Pinkerton who did promise to return. I could never have sung it for Henry.'

Her heart fluttered. He couldn't have moved closer, and yet she felt the warmth of his body more intently than she had before. She felt his eyes on her.

'Could you sing it for me?'

Slowly, she came out from behind the curtain of hair and looked into his eyes.

You are so much older than him. What are you thinking of?

The naked truth, tell him the naked truth. 'Yes,' she said, badly wanting to raise her hand and trace the lines on his face. 'I could.'

Gently, like the fleeting touch of a bird's wing, he wiped a tear from the corner of her eye. She did not protest when he went on to trace the faint lines radiating from the corners of her lips.

His breath was warm upon her neck and, although there were still inches between them, she felt the warmth of his body reaching for her.

Throwing back her head, she closed her eyes.

'You shouldn't be doing that.' Her voice sounded far away. Was it her voice? She thought it might not be, that it could be the old Mary Anne who had existed before the other war and Henry and the resultant children of that liaison.

'Do you like it?'

She didn't answer, mostly because she had got out of the habit of liking intimacy, but this was not sex with Henry. This was the kind of intimacy that opens the floodgate to the liberties only taken by those totally immersed in passion.

She started to open her eyes.

'No,' he said, touching them shut with his fingertips and then his lips. 'Keep them closed. If you can't bear to see yourself living, at least feel your passion, but make believe it is another woman enjoying it, perhaps the other woman you used to be.'

Had he read her thoughts? Or was it possible that two people could be that much in tune with each other?

More tears squeezed out from the corners of her closed eyelids. It's the brandy, she decided. Or perhaps not. Perhaps a door had been opened. How long had it been since she'd felt like this?

Softly, he traced the line of her jaw, the fullness of her lips, the slight dent in her chin. Even though her eyes were still shut, she could see those fingers – purely by feeling them.

She felt the cool air on her breasts as he unbuttoned her blouse.

'No!'

He stopped. 'No?'

'A feeling... just a feeling...'

She could explain it no further. It was just an exclamation of surprise for what she was feeling. She did not attempt to stop him. Neither did she stop him when his fingers slid beneath her underwear and the coolness of his palm cupped her breast.

They lay full stretch before the fire, relishing the warmth on their bodies, exploring, caressing and kissing, hugging each other and whispering delight in each other's ear.

Not until the act of love had run its course did she open her eyes and see the tears pouring from his, wetting his cheeks and running into his mouth. He was like a child.

'I have to tell you,' he said haltingly. 'You have to listen... to know... it is so terrible...'

'I know,' she said softly, not having the slightest idea of what he was about to say, but smoothing his hair back from his brow, just as she did Stanley, just as she would any child.

He told her about Berlin and her blood turned to ice.

31

'Off to see that delicious redhead again?' asked Brunner, a recent recruit from a small village outside Potsdam.

Michael smiled. 'Where else?'

'Give her one for me.' Brunner smirked, adding a lewd gesture and leaving Michael in no doubt of his meaning.

'I will.' He grinned broadly and ruffled Brunner's hair. 'Don't wait up for me, Mother!'

He left the barracks to the sound of ribald laughter and managed to keep a smirk on his face until he was beyond them and could concentrate on his true intention.

Bronica lived in a one-bedroomed flat above a tobacconist on a road off the Wilhemstrasse. It was at the very top of three flights of stairs, yet he took them easily, driven by a mix of exhilaration and fear at the prospect of what he was about to do. She answered the door, smoking from a cigarette holder held delicately between painted fingernails and dressed in a satin robe that left him in no doubt that she was naked underneath.

He dragged his gaze away from the prominent nipples thrusting like buttons against the satin.

'Did you get them?'

She stepped back and let him in, closing the door behind her, and nodded at a brown parcel sitting on the sofa.

She tilted her head to one side and a cloud of red hair fell over one shoulder. 'I did. Why do you want a load of smelly clothes?'

He sensed her disquiet. It occurred to him that he should not tell her why he had given her money to buy civilian clothes – old civilian clothes – but hell, they'd gone to bed together. Surely that meant he could trust her?

Love is blind, so they say, and he'd purposely blinded himself to her easy-going sexuality. Bronica slept with anyone she fancied and even though she'd whispered that she loved only him, there was no guarantee that she didn't whisper the same to any man who gave her pleasure.

All the same, he ignored his head and followed his heart – or more likely, his loins.

He began unbuttoning his uniform. 'I'm leaving.'

She gave a little gasp and her eyebrows arched above the pencil lines she favoured. 'You're deserting?'

He nodded as he sorted through the clothes: a shirt, a black jacket and dark-blue trousers, a brown hat and matching shoes. The shoes were scuffed, the trousers shiny at the knees.

'Call it that if you like.'

'But why? You were so proud of your uniform.'

He could hear the shock in her voice, but still chose to trust her.

'The other night – it wasn't the first time I've witnessed such brutality, but never as bad as that. I want no part of it. It sickens me.'

She eyed him through a cloud of smoke, a slight frown wrinkling her brow. 'But you're a soldier. Soldiers are brutes by nature.'

Throwing his army shirt to one side, he turned to her, his eyes blazing with intent.

'A soldier's duty is to fight for his country. To my mind, that means fighting other soldiers, not this... this... torture of innocent people. Didn't you see what they did? They intimidated; they instilled such terror that the victims actually had no way out but to do what they ordered. Both men were soaked in blood. One of them died there on the pavement. Tell me, Bronica, what sort of victory is that?' He shook his head and reached for the second-hand shirt. Ignoring the smell of camphor, he slipped one arm into the sleeve.

There was a moment's hesitation, a stiffening of expression before she seemed to relent and ooze sympathy.

'My poor, poor, boy,' she cooed, stroking his arm and gazing up at him with her cool, green eyes. 'Are you going to leave me without saying goodbye properly?'

His breath caught in his throat when he looked at her, because in looking he relived every sexual encounter they'd ever had. She was desirable, and he knew what kind of goodbye she referred to.

He was totally lost. 'I wouldn't dream of it.'

Shirt hanging by one arm, he drew her body against his. There was no resisting her. The sound of his blood pulsing with excitement rushed into his ears. The shirt was discarded along with his boots and his trousers. But wasn't he going to discard them anyway and put on the other clothes?

She let the satin robe fall to the floor, exposing her nakedness to his eyes and the grey daylight slipping through the window.

Her breath mingled with his, her lips gently brushing his mouth, her tongue dividing his lips. 'Say goodbye to me properly, my dear boy.'

They ended up in the familiar iron bedstead with the goose down mattress and feather boas hanging from the bedhead. Never had Bronica been so demanding and never had Michael been so encouraged to perform. Her body was totally open to him, inviting him to fill her, to take her and do whatever he wanted, though he knew that really he was doing what *she* wanted.

'More,' she said after he'd rested. 'I must have more. You have to leave me something to remember you by. I mean this moment, not a child,' she added, on seeing the sudden question in his eyes.

'Thank God. I wouldn't want to bring a child into this sickening world.'

For the third time he mounted her, astounded that she could

inspire a man to such sexual heights, and grateful that she had taught him so much.

After the third time, he sank back into the mattress, totally exhausted.

He didn't know how long he slept, but he awoke suddenly aware he was alone and vaguely remembering she had said something about going out to buy cigarettes.

'Bronica?'

There was no response. He thought about washing before she came back. He smelled of sex, and even though she might want it again, he wasn't sure he could rise to it. If he was dressed perhaps she wouldn't insist.

He decided to get up. She had sapped so much of his energy that it took a great deal of effort to swing his legs over the side of the bed.

Running his fingers through his hair, he smiled to himself, somewhat proud that he'd done her so well. How many of her lovers could satisfy her three times in three hours? he wondered. Hans had told him that it must be love as far as he was concerned, because Michael was the lowest-ranking lover she had. It was rumoured that the highest ranking was a general, and the rumour had made him jealous. He'd tried asking her about this general, but she'd refused to admit there was one.

'I take my pleasures where I will,' she'd said blithely.

He had chosen not to believe that she was so mercenary because it suited him to pretend that she was his alone, that her desire for men in uniform was just a fleeting fancy, that in his case it was the man beneath the uniform she most desired.

The bed was comfortable and Bronica's body was warm. He thought about staying here a little longer, having her again when she got back from getting the cigarettes... but he was looking at cigarettes. A full packet lying on the table next to the cigarette holder.

The blood that had pulsed through his body with arousal now ran cold. There were cigarettes on the table, and yet she'd told him she was going out to buy more. Why had she gone out, and if not for cigarettes, what for?

Facing up to reality was extremely painful, akin perhaps to having a gangrenous limb removed – if you could call a penis a limb. He'd been thinking below his waist. Now his eyes were open.

'You fool! You bloody fool!'

Despite being shagged out, he scrambled into the second-hand clothes. It crossed his mind to put his uniform back on, to pretend it was all a joke, but the purchase of the clothes was evidence enough. He'd still end up in the guardhouse, the butt of some pretty brutal behaviour if the stories he'd heard were true.

He knew for sure now that there really was a general she was having a relationship with, and that she had probably gone to fetch him.

Angry with himself as much as with her, he took the stairs two, sometimes three, at a time. He had to get away. He had to put all this behind him. He had to put distance between him and Berlin.

At first he wasn't sure where to go. Was it possible to be inconspicuous in a city of military, factory workers, and all manner of government informers?

He thought he heard pursuers at the corner of the street and ran. Giving chase had become a disease, swiftly passed from one ignorant soul to another. People dropped out or joined in the chase as they felt like it. He darted down alleys, pressed himself against walls, sipping coffee in wayside inns and all the time fearing he would be hunted down and now, as a true deserter, shot.

At one point, sure he was being followed, he ran into a chapel on the edge of the city, falling through the door, which shut noiselessly behind him as if pulled by an unseen hand.

There was no altar, no plaster saints, not even a crucifix. His first impression was of a meeting room rather than a church, very much like the one his stepfather preached in. Rows of benches sloped towards the lectern at the front where an altar should be.

Stumbling onto the end of a bench, he fell forwards, elbows on knees, hands covering his face.

The terrible things he'd seen reverberated through his body like a troublesome ague and it was a while before he regained any self-control. When eventually he came out from behind his hands, the quiet, peace and serenity of his surroundings calmed him. Sitting there a while longer, it was as if the world of uniforms, marching bands and cruelty had melted away. The stillness enveloped him and it became as though he could hear his own thoughts; or was it God telling him what he must do to gain forgiveness for his sins, to cover old ground, to make amends for past mistakes.

Days later he was staring across a field of straw stubble. Smoke rose in a feathery plume from the tall brick chimney of his childhood home. He'd never regarded the house so warmly as he did now. The child he had been was like a stranger to him, and the stepfather who had sought to control his love of all things military was no longer despised.

The smell of baking bread greeted him as he pushed open the kitchen door.

His mother was kneading dough, pushing and pulling it in all directions. She looked up, stared then smiled.

'I wasn't expecting you to be on leave just yet. Is it a special occasion?'

He nodded. 'Yes. I have left the army and I am not going back.'

She looked him up and down, frowning at the state of his clothes but not commenting.

After they'd talked more that evening, discussing what he should do with far more understanding and kindness than he deserved, his mother brought a letter out from the pewter box she kept for household letters as opposed to those received with regard to the church.

'It's from your Uncle Joseph's solicitors in England. It seems he has died and left his shop and some money to you.'

Michael had been staggered. 'But I hardly knew him.'

His mother shrugged. 'He and my sister Rosa had no children. He took to you when he visited. I expect you remember him visiting.'

Michael suppressed a shudder at the painful reminder, the vindictiveness of the Jungsturm Lieutenant, the taunts of the other boys, his creeping down to the cellar and passing out in pain.

Uncle Joseph had come to his bedroom once the doctor had been and he'd regained consciousness.

His dark eyes had crinkled up quizzically as though he were counting all the hairs on Michael's head. At last he asked, 'Why did you do this?'

Michael had stared at him, feeling funny because his penis was wrapped in a great wad of cotton wool and bandages and it throbbed like a stick beating on a drum.

Uncle Joseph had jerked his chin. 'I see. Or at least I think I see. You do not want to be me. You aren't me. You never can be me. You are yourself. No matter your roots, your politics or your religion, always be yourself.' He'd held up one finger as a schoolteacher stressing an important point. 'Better still... Unto yourself be true.'

Michael remembered the two men who'd been forced to whip each other until one of them fell dead. They might have been Jewish, they might have been communists, but it didn't matter. Being different should not be a crime. Their sheer helplessness had touched his conscience.

'He was Jewish,' he said suddenly.

His mother poured tea, her deep brown eyes glancing up at him and smiling as she answered. 'Yes. Your Auntie Rosa married him in a civil ceremony. Although she'd been willing to convert, Joseph would have none of it. He didn't think you could change what was in a person's heart just by going through a ceremony. He firmly believed that everyone should follow their own conscience – which I think is what you have done,' she said, finally placing the pot down on the table, her gaze steady and that same smile on her face.

On thinking back to his childhood, he realised that warm smile had always been there, it was just that he hadn't noticed. And he understood what she meant. Regardless of uniform, the thumping of drums and the blowing of bugles, it could not change the man underneath who would always be guided by his conscience.

'It will take time, but we must make plans for you to leave,' said his stepfather.

Michael had never considered him a brave man, but he did now. 'You could get into serious trouble just for harbouring a deserter.'

'I will assist any man who stands up for the rights of humanity!'

The table shook and both Michael and his mother jumped as his stepfather's fist hit the table, just as it sometimes hit the pulpit during a particularly passionate sermon.

'You have a British passport, it's just a case of getting you out of the country.'

Just?

It seemed an immense task, but the Lutheran minister knew more dissidents than Michael had ever thought possible, including a banker who had transferred to a Swiss bank once he'd realised that as a Jew he would be dismissed from his present job.

'Just a few days and you will be leaving us. Is there anything else needing clarification before you go?'

There was one other question that he would have liked to ask, but old habits and the respect of a boy for his elders is never quite overcome. It was respect for his mother's sensibilities that made him refrain from asking why he'd been circumcised. Somehow it no longer mattered.

'No,' he'd said. 'I think everything is clear.'

32

In the opinion of Thomas Routledge, Harry Randall was a good-looking gent, smartly dressed, and not at all the sort of bloke likely to punch your teeth down your throat. But Thomas Routledge was not a very good judge of character.

"Course I did think of telling yer father I'd seen 'er, cos as you might know, we did do service together in the war, but then Bonehead, who I sees on account of 'im taking me bets in the Red Cow, said that you was paying for information. Well, that was it. I stepped forward, didn't I. Never was afraid to volunteer information...'

Thomas Routledge made a choking sound as Harry's hands grabbed his collar, jerking him off his feet.

Harry glared into his face. 'Say anything to my old man and you're at the bottom of the river. Savvy?'

Eyes almost popping out of his head, Routledge nodded his agreement.

After letting him go, Harry brushed his hands together, a sign that the matter was finalised and also that he considered Routledge slightly unclean.

Routledge lingered, nervously shuffling his feet and coughing behind his hand.

Harry glared. 'Well? What the bloody hell are you waiting for? Fuck off!'

Surprised at the outcome of this meeting, Routledge took a step back.

'My money,' he said nervously. 'Twenty quid for information. That's what I heard.'

Harry narrowed his eyes. He didn't like Routledge's sort. It was hard to believe he'd served beside his father, though in one respect they were very alike. They both drank to excess, and both had a violent streak, though, judging by rumour, Thomas Routledge abused his children whereas Henry Randall abused his wife.

Harry peeled four crisp, white fivers from the wedge he kept in his inside pocket.

'There you are. Might give some of it to that missus of yours so the poor cow can put some food on the table for them kids.'

Routledge smirked. 'Come off it, 'Arry. You know how it is. A man's got to live.'

Harry clenched his jaw. 'Wife and kids come first, or at least they do in my book.'

Routledge hesitated, not sure whether to take his comment seriously. 'Aw come on...'

Harry's fierce look sorted things. Routledge was gone, scurrying out of the door of the Catnip Club as though his ass was on fire.

Mark came out from behind the bar and stood beside him, casually wiping the inside of a beer glass.

'You sleeping over tonight?'

Harry shook his head. 'Much as I'd like to, there's something I've got to do.'

Mark sighed. 'So when are we going to be living in this flat – I mean together.'

Harry leaned towards him and waved a finger in front of his face. 'When I'm good and ready, but first I've got to see what the score is with my mum. You can understand that, can't you?'

Mark smiled and nodded. 'Of course I can. We all love our mums.'

Harry nodded, relieved that Mark had so willingly accepted his excuse. Mark was besotted with the flat; he hadn't stopped painting the walls and hanging curtains since Harry had signed the lease. Luckily, he'd been there the night before when the geezer with the pink gin had sidled up to him, seemingly interested in the crossword he'd just completed, and even more intrigued at one of his word and number grids.

'How very interesting,' he'd said, languidly shifting his gaze between the crossword and the grid. 'What exactly is that?' he'd asked, a well-manicured finger jabbing at the word grid.

Harry had looked the bloke up and down, immediately recognising a left-footer when he saw one, and a well heeled one at that. The cut of the grey double-breasted jacket was literally more than a few cuts above the one he was wearing, and that hadn't been cheap. Was bringing up the crossword merely a smokescreen for a chat-up line?

'It's a secret code.'

'Ah. I see. A cipher.'

The way his jaw worked, and the way he said cipher, made Harry wish he'd called it that too. Secret code suddenly seemed so inane, so working class.

'Yeah. A cipher.'

The man's voice was as languid as his looks, the hooded eyes seeming to swim over the page like liquid lead.

'To what purpose?'

The question had taken him by surprise. There was no purpose, but it seemed a betrayal of his own integrity, his own class to say so.

'I do it for fun. Always have done. I change letters for figures and try to make the grids as difficult as possible, try to forget what the words were in the first place, then go back to them a few months later and try to interpret what I've created.'

'And are you always successful?'

The stranger's glib tone and fleshy face had seemed to harden up. It made him feel uncomfortable. Normally, he would have told him to sod off, but there was something about the bloke that made him think he wasn't as soft as he looked.

Harry had thought about it. Finally, he nodded. 'Yes,' he said. 'Yes. I always do.'

He left the club he ran for Charlie Knowles and got into his car. It never failed to make him smile when he got behind the wheel, mostly because he thought about his father's face when he'd first pulled up in it. Outright shock, and perhaps a bit of envy; after all, the cab Henry Randall drove did not belong to him, it was only his courtesy of the Blue Cab Company.

He hadn't asked where it came from and what kind of job he was doing where he could afford a car like that. He hadn't questioned what anyone did since Mary Anne had left. Because he no longer cares, thought Harry, and the thought had surprised him. Other sons might have given their father a more thorough pasting for abusing their mother, but Harry had restrained himself. That one time, he decided, was enough – for now. It was more satisfying to see a very subdued Henry Randall, a man who seemed a shadow of his former self. And now he knew where his mother was. He smiled to himself. He couldn't wait to see his father's face when he told him she was living with a foreigner, a man not much older than him, if what he'd heard was right. Well, he hoped the bloke was treating her right; if not he would answer to him.

He looked out at the roads. The main ones were fairly clear now, the snow mostly melted away.

Let the hound see the hare before we do anything else, he decided. He turned the wheel and swung the car into East Street.

* * *

Michael was surrounded by the contents of the last remaining cupboard. Mary Anne was sifting through yet another box of gramophone records.

'Why don't you sell some of these? There's far too many.'

At first she presumed his silence was because he didn't want to make a decision, but when she looked at him she could see that was not the case. He was holding a sheaf of dusty envelopes, and reading a letter he'd taken out from one of them.

'It is from my mother to my aunt,' he said quietly.

'Is it important?'

'To me it is.'

He looked up at her thoughtfully; she'd noticed he chewed at one corner of his mouth when he was making a decision. Having made it, he passed her the letter.

She read it quickly; there was nothing special about it from what she could see, but something here had affected him. What was it?

She looked up at him. 'I don't understand. Your mother is writing about a small operation you had when you were a few months old.'

'That is it.'

Mary Anne frowned. 'According to this there was a constriction in your waterworks and the doctor made an incision...'

Anger flashed in his eyes. 'Circumcision. He carried out a circumcision and all these years I thought I had been born a Jew.'

She remembered the incident he'd told her of. 'Children can be cruel.'

'They were encouraged by adults; that is what makes it so bad.'

Settling herself on the chair arm, she stroked the back of his neck where the dark blond curled into his collar.

'Try not to be bitter. You have the rest of your life ahead of you.'

To her surprise there was no trace of bitterness on his face, only a look of peace in his eyes, as though he had come to a conclusion.

'With all that is happening in Germany, I now feel privileged to have undergone such a baptism of fire. I thought I was one of the despised and sought to hide my shame in order that I could be as everyone else and accepted by my friends – those I thought were friends.'

Mary Anne hugged his head, hesitating before kissing his crown;

the action of a mother rather than a lover. She pushed the thought to the back of her mind.

'It's all in the past now.'

'It was. But now it is here.'

Mary Anne sighed. The war. Everything was changing because of the war; some things for better, and some for the worse; and even worse, she suspected, was yet to come.

Michael pushed the paperwork aside. 'I will open the shop now.'

Mary Anne bent and picked up the lunchtime crockery. They closed from one until two every day, except Wednesday, of course, when they shut at one for the afternoon.

So far Mary Anne hadn't chanced serving in the shop, in case she was recognised. She wasn't quite ready for facing the world just yet. In fact, she was still in the process of coming to terms with the arrangement herself, but was in no doubt that she would be condemned by her peers.

The bedroom wall was no longer between them. They'd shared the same bed for a while. Sometimes she lay awake at night listening to Michael talking in his sleep. Although she didn't understand German, she understood the emotions behind the words, the shame, the despair and the horror of scenes that would haunt him for the rest of his life.

There were times when she shed her own tears, her concern for her family, especially Stanley, making her think of running back home. Fear of what Henry might do when she got there, especially if he found out that she'd been living with another man, stopped her.

'Marianna! Marianna! Come out here.'

She loved Michael calling her Marianna. She'd tried correcting him, but he'd told her he preferred that name.

'It is my name for you. Only I will call you that.'

He was calling her from the shop, and yet surely the door must be open by now? Someone she knew might see her, but he sounded so urgent. She had to go.

Leaving the dishes in the sink, the tap running, she went through to the shop, the old rugs, soft with age slewing sideways beneath her feet.

Michael was standing with his back to her, silently facing another man, initially hiding his identity from her: until she stood beside him.

'Mum.'

It was easy to fall into his arms, to hug him in much the same way as she had Michael just a few moments earlier.

'I've missed you. We've all missed you.'

She couldn't believe the joy she felt looking up into her son's face. At first she was lost for words, and then she remembered Michael.

She turned to face him. 'My son,' she said.

It was difficult to read the look on Michael's face, but she guessed he was worried that Harry might cause trouble. She knew he wouldn't. Harry made up his own mind about everything. He would do whatever he wanted, or whatever she wanted. She knew in her heart that she was the only woman, perhaps the only person, he cared about.

She asked the most important question, the one that would settle all their minds. 'Have you come here to take me home?'

His brown eyes came to rest on her, totally bereft of judgement. 'Do you want to come home?'

Not willing to meet Michael's gaze, she dropped her own to the floor. 'No. This is where I belong.' She looked up suddenly. 'How's Stanley's chest? Is he taking his medicine and resting properly? You mustn't let him run about too much with those rough boys from Sydenham Street, especially when it's cold, and if he does, he has to rest after to catch his breath and—'

'Ma, Ma, Ma!'

Laughingly, Harry held her shoulders.

'Stanley is stronger than you think. He's getting to be a bit more streetwise than he was, and the boys he's with look after him fine, and at home our Lizzie makes sure he does all them things you want him to, not that he needs them half the time. Let him grow up, Mum. We all have to sometime, though we might not all end up exactly as you want us to be.'

He raised his eyes from her face, a harder expression entering them when he looked at Michael. 'I wouldn't mind knowing exactly how she came here.'

Michael did not flinch but met Harry's gaze headlong. 'She was bleeding, bruised and collapsed in my doorway. I tended her and called the doctor.'

Harry gave a slight jerk of his chin indicating that he was satisfied with the explanation. At the same time, his eyes swept over this man his mother appeared to be living with, might even be fond of. He was good at analysing a man's worthiness. Michael struck him as having integrity. There were few enough of them nowadays.

'I appreciate what you did, chum.'

His eyes swept between them.

Mary Anne felt a flush of embarrassment plus a need to explain. 'Harry, I think I should say—'

'No. You don't need to explain anything, Ma, and you don't have to feel guilty about anything. I'm glad you're being looked after, and if you don't want to come home at all, then that's all right by me.'

'Your father...?'

Harry shook his head. 'I'm not going to tell him I know where you are, not if you don't want me to, but I think you might let me tell our Lizzie. She's dead worried about you and don't even speak to the old man, so ain't so likely to let on. But it's up to you.'

Lizzie. Yes, she would be the one to take on all the responsibility and concern. Of course she'd be worried.

She nodded. 'Yes. Lizzie should know.'

Harry turned to go.

'Is Daw all right?' Mary Anne asked suddenly.

A half-smile cracked his mouth. 'Daw's the same as ever; too wrapped up in herself to notice what's going on around her. Never worry about Daw, Ma.'

The smile vanished. His shoulders stiffened as he shot Michael a warning look. 'Take care of her.'

Michael met his look with equal stiffness and an air of defiance. 'I intend to.'

33

Rising the day after Peter Selwyn had walked into the kitchen, Lizzie pinched herself just in case the whole thing was a dream. At Peter's insistence she had stayed overnight, much against his mother's wishes, judging by her astonished expression.

'The snow's too deep. She can't cycle home, and neither can she walk, and before you mention a bus or tram, I haven't heard one go past since four o'clock this afternoon.'

The electricity had gone off and they'd cooked and ate by candle-light and storm lanterns fetched up from the cellar. Peter had gone down there with her to look for them. The moment the door was closed behind them and they were at the bottom of the steps, he'd taken her in his arms and kissed her passionately, one hand immediately shooting up her skirt.

'My God, but there's something about that expanse of flesh above a girl's stocking top.'

'I'm not wearing any stockings. They're upstairs drying.'

'And your knickers?'

'Your mother will hear,' she said, doing her best to push him away, her eyes straying to the door at the top of the stairs.

'No she won't.'

She pushed down at the prying hand. 'I didn't know you were home.'

'Well, you do now.'

Something hard pressed against her thigh. 'And you didn't write very often.'

The one letter his mother had shown her didn't count. The paper had been as stiff as the sentiments it contained.

'I was busy.'

'You didn't write to me, only to your mother.'

'Didn't I? Oh, well, I'm here now. Let me make it up to you, just like I did in the field, and remember that day in the back of my car?'

'Oh yes...'

She closed her eyes in an effort to capture the passion of that moment, but something stopped her. Something about him being home and the way he looked worried her.

Patrick and John had benefited from their military training; they were leaner and fitter, even their face muscles were more toned than when they'd left. Peter had changed too, though not in the same way. He'd put on weight and had acquired a paler, smoother look, not the rugged, salty look of a merchant seaman.

'No,' she said, pushing him away. 'No. Your mother's waiting.'

Smiling, he stood looking at her, at the same time rubbing the front of his trousers. 'I can wait until later to show you how much I've missed you.'

Flushed and confused, she grabbed two of the storm lanterns, passed them to him and took two more.

After taking the simple stew she'd cooked into the dining room, she retired, leaving mother and son alone, for once glad to be eating her meal by herself.

There was bread and butter pudding for afters, sweetened with last year's honey in order to preserve the sugar ration. She reminded herself to ask Peter for his ration book in the morning. If he were staying for any length of time, she would have to get him registered with the local grocer.

Once the meal was completely finished, he surprised her by bringing out the plates.

'I'll be up to your room later,' he said, taking the tea tray from her hands. 'I'm stiff enough to stir tea,' he added, leering and patting the front of his trousers as he had before.

'I don't think that would be a good idea...'

'I won't take no for an answer.'

He didn't wait for her response, which was just as well.

Lizzie needed time to think.

Alone at last, she busied herself with the dishes, scrubbing at the plates as though they were thick with grime and grease, and eventually, lost in thought, she suddenly realised she was cleaning the same plates twice.

Up to her elbows in washing up water, she paused and asked herself what had changed between her and Peter. His frenzied groping and lascivious remarks had not aroused her. Was that how it had been before? If so, why hadn't she noticed it?

Love is blind. The statement came unbidden into her mind. She had been in love, her passion driven by her adolescent awakening to adulthood. She'd *wanted* to be in love, and Peter was so different to the young men she'd grown up with like Patrick Kelly. But now it was the likes of Patrick who were different. The war had changed him, just as it would change a lot of men and women, perhaps even society itself. She could not see herself sacrificing herself to a less than loving husband for the sake of her family, just as her mother had.

Thinking of her mother, she said a silent prayer, hoped she was still alive and, if she was, that she was happy.

She stiffened as the kitchen door creaked open behind her. Peter?

Taking her dripping hands from the sink, she grabbed a tea towel and turned round intending to tell Peter how she felt and that he was never to take liberties with her again.

Pale-faced and dressed in the same shade of green as the parlour curtains, Mrs Selwyn stood with her hands clasped before her, deep age lines radiating from her pursed, purple lips.

'Lizzie! I want to talk to you.' Lizzie faced her.

Mrs Selwyn straightened her already ramrod frame. A mixture of expressions came and went, as if she were trying on a series of masks, unsure which most suited.

Satisfied she now had Lizzie's full attention, Mrs Selwyn's pursed lips burst like a tulip in bloom.

'Lizzie, you are not to tell anyone that Peter is home.'

'But what about his ration book? I'm supposed to register him with a grocer. Surely he's brought it back from Canada?'

Mrs Selwyn's complexion seemed to glisten, as though she had broken out in light perspiration.

She blinked but swiftly gathered herself. 'No one is to know. We can manage. Buy food on the black market if you must. I hear there are plenty around willing to supply if they're paid enough. I'm quite prepared to pay whatever it takes, Lizzie.'

Lizzie eyed her suspiciously. 'You do know you're asking me to do something that's illegal?'

Mrs Selwyn's remarkable chest expanded over the top of her corset. 'I'm sure we can plead extenuating circumstances. You see, my dear,' she said, suddenly beaming as though everything was perfectly simple, 'he is very involved in secret work for the war effort. No one must know he is here, is that clear?'

Yes. It was clear, but not quite in the way Mrs Selwyn had intended. Peter had admitted that the sound of buses and trams ceased at around four o'clock yesterday afternoon. He'd been in the house then, but hadn't declared himself? It was odd. And also, four o'clock was about the same time as Mrs Selwyn had said she was asleep on the bed, but Lizzie had gone up there with the tea tray and found the room empty. If she thought very carefully, she vaguely remembered a slight creaking of the attic floorboards, and there was only one reason why mother and son might be up there.

Then there was the paper Peter's letter had been written on. Something about the stiff paper had suddenly come to her. There was a whole pad of it in the overly ornate bureau that sat before the window in the study. Doing shopping for Mrs Selwyn was a long-running habit; she'd bought the pad and envelopes herself, attracted by the watermark embedded into every leaf. It was exactly the same as the letter Mrs Selwyn said she'd received from Canada. It was a lie – it was all a lie. There was only one other alternative. Neither Peter nor his mother wanted him to serve in the services. He had never gone to Canada but, probably under cover of darkness, had gone back to the house just hours after she'd seen his mother at the station supposedly waving him off.

And why was she being allowed to sleep in a bedroom on the family floor rather than consigned to one of the attic rooms, which had once been the servants' quarters?

The answer was simple and hit her so badly that she could hardly believe it. Peter was living up there, out of sight – until the snow had come.

No wonder he wants his oats, she thought, as angry with herself as she was with him – and his mother!

Peter had waylaid her on her way up to bed, an old-fashioned stone hot water bottle wrapped in a towel and tucked beneath her arm.

His voice was hushed, not much above a whisper. He laid his hand over hers, his eyes sparkling with intent. 'I'll be up later.'

His mother had come out of the parlour just then, so there was no time to tell him not to bother. All the bedroom doors had locks and a stout bolt on the inside. Peter would not be sharing her bed.

Later, snuggled down beneath blankets and a thick eiderdown, she'd heard a soft knocking at the bedroom door.

Closing her eyes, she'd ducked down further beneath the bedclothes.

'Lizzie?' He'd knocked a little louder. 'Lizzie?'

She would not answer the door. She wouldn't answer him at all, but stay warm and comfortable beneath the bedclothes. Peter could go back to whatever hole he'd crawled out of. His mother was welcome to him.

34

Refugees were flooding out of Europe, and the British army were flooding in, according to the newspapers.

Lizzie had got up early, intending to use the day to get some baking done; the snowstorm and her overnight stay at Mrs Selwyn's had upset her routine.

She hadn't seen Peter on the day she'd left, but using the same notepad from the bureau, she'd composed a letter of resignation, leaving it on the kitchen table for Mrs Selwyn to find when she eventually came looking for her breakfast.

By four o'clock the table was laid, the smell of liver and onions hung in the air, and the pink rays of a late winter sunset streamed through the window.

Glad at last of some respite, she made herself a cup of tea and continued reading the papers, catching up on items she'd missed. Reading old news had whetted her interest in the war, questioning the truths behind the headlines; after all it was only a few years ago that people had applauded the upsurge in fortunes. Unfortunately, it didn't appear that they'd considered the reason behind rearming. Glancing at the clock, she judged the paperboy would be due with the evening paper, if he hadn't already been. She decided to check.

The passage running to the front door was far chillier than the kitchen, its brown paint and lino depressing enough without the drop in temperature.

At first the newspaper was hanging there, but just as she was about to pull it, it plopped through, pushed by someone on the other side of the door, a sheet of white paper falling in behind it.

Someone had pushed it through.

Her father! Back to his old ways and gone out without a key. Adopting a look sharp enough to cut glass, she wrenched the door open. A startled man half turned, watery eyes viewing her from behind thick spectacle lenses.

It occurred to her that he might want her mother's pawnbroking service. Most of the merchandise had been returned to its owners or sold off, the money saved for a rainy day.

'Can I help you?'

He pointed at the letterbox. 'The paper. For Mr Randall.'

She nodded and stood by the door until the little man, one foot encased in an overlarge boot, limped his way down the street and disappeared.

Lizzie shrugged, shivered, and then closed the door against the sharpening cold of the crystal clear day.

Picking up both the newspaper and the piece of paper, she returned to the warmth of the kitchen, put both on the table and poured herself another cup of tea.

The piece of paper delivered by the little man was small and official looking, but then, she reasoned, if it were official or private, surely it would have come in an envelope.

Curious as to why it was delivered by such a strange little man, she unfolded and read it.

Even the winter weather could not have chilled her more than the contents of that piece of paper. Henry Alfred Randall, her brother's name, address, date of birth were all written neatly enough, but what caught her eye was the heading and the final comment. The heading referred to a medical prior to being accepted into the army. The final comment referred to Harry as being FI – unfit for service.

The colour drained from her face. Harry was the fittest person she knew. Even Patrick and John, despite their new-found toughness at the hands of a Royal Air Force PT instructor, were incomparable with Harry's physical perfection.

Her suspicion that Harry had done something totally illegal and that it was linked with his plan to leave home would not leave her mind. Deciding it was better that no one else saw the notice of rejection, she went upstairs and placed it in his best shoe for safe keeping.

She dished up dinner, the smell of her cooking luring Daw, Stanley and her father to the table on time. There was no sign of Harry and no one asked if he was working late. Lizzie was still the only one to know of his plans; something of a burden but what was one burden among all the others that had got lumped on her? Directing her resentment towards her father was an easy option. Sometimes she did that; other times she found herself achieving a greater insight into her mother's life than she'd ever thought possible.

Harry arrived home just as Lizzie was forking her own food around the plate, wondering what would have happened if there had been no war. Would she and Peter still be seeing each other? Who knows! It had taken a war to bring out his lewder and more deceitful side, but she wished she'd been aware of it before.

'I don't want anything to eat.'

He looked directly at her as he said it. She thought she knew what he was going to say, but had second thoughts. He looked triumphant rather than ashamed.

His gaze swept over everyone else, that crooked smile lifting one side of his sensual lips.

'Dad! Daw! I've got an important announcement to make.'

As usual, Henry Randall, his father, barely acknowledged him, and Daw seemed more self-absorbed than usual.

Smiling, he ruffled Stanley's hair. 'And you, young Stanley. And you, Lizzie,' he added, giving her a cautious wink as though she above all others were privy to what he was about to say. 'I'm leaving home. I've got myself a flat and better money. Won't be too far away. No doubt be seeing you now and again, so no frets, eh? No crying over yer great loss, and I won't cry over mine.'

Daw's mouth fell open before she burst into tears and said that everyone was leaving her to her own devices and that it just wasn't fair.

Stanley demanded more details, and could he come and visit him, and was he going to take him on more car rides when the good weather came.

Her father lifted his head from the last piece of liver and stared at him. 'Who with?'

They were just two small words, and yet she fancied that her brother's handsome, strong face turned quite rigid, as though he had no wish to answer the question, and in fact guessed that his father already knew the answer.

'A friend. Just a friend.' His voice was uncommonly cold.

Turning abruptly, he muttered something about fetching his suitcase. Dropping her knife and fork, Lizzie followed him upstairs and behind the curtain forming the fourth wall of his bedroom.

Of course! He wanted a room of his own.

She was in time to see him grab the suitcase from the wardrobe and fling it onto the bed.

Folding her arms, she stood there watching his expression change as he picked up the shoes and saw the official form confirming that he was F1, unfit for duty.

His eyelids fluttered. She could tell he was uncomfortable and could not find the words to explain; not that she needed explanation. She knew the truth. She knew what he had done.

'Who was that man?'

He started. For the first time in a long while Harry's confidence was notably absent.

'What man?'

She could read from his expression that he knew perfectly well what man, but was hedging his bets, hoping she hadn't seen him perhaps.

'The man who pretended to be you. I saw your call-up papers, Harry. I know you had a medical to attend. And you and I know you would have passed with flying colours. The man who brought the notice was definitely an F1. I take it you paid him to go in your place.'

She could see by the look in his eyes that he'd realised lying to her was a worthless option.

The sound of Daw wailing and snivelling sounded from downstairs, for all the world like an echo of the air raid sirens, which so far, had proved to be false alarms.

His discomfort did not last. The old smile lifted one side of his mouth, his eyes seeming to change colour with his scent of advantage.

'You haven't questioned why I'm packing my last belongings into my suitcase. I'm leaving, Lizzie. Get it? I'm leaving.'

Lizzie frowned as she tried to work out the cryptic message he was sending her.

'You're leaving.' Then she remembered what he had said about not leaving until he'd found their mother. He'd found her! He must have found her!

She gasped and covered her mouth with her hand.

Harry lowered his voice. 'Not a word to anyone. She doesn't want anyone to know where she is except you – and me, of course.'

Still with her hand over her mouth, Lizzie shook her head, her eyes like saucers above the curve of her thumb.

'She said you can visit her, if you wish, that is. She's feeling guilty about leaving you with all the responsibility, but she's not coming back. Can't say I blame her.'

'Where is she? Tell me! Tell me now!'

He smiled. She sensed he was going to taunt her, just as he had when they were younger.

He took his gaze aside and shook his head. 'Couldn't believe it myself at first, until I saw them together, until I saw how he made her glow. She looked ten years younger and I'm glad she does. It's a bit late in the day, but she deserves to be happy; she deserves to live for herself not just her kids.'

At first she only heard the words, she wasn't really taking them in, but finally she flung her arms around Harry's neck.

'Harry, you're the best bloke in the world, even though you are my brother.'

He laughed then. 'Give over, Lizzie. I'd be the first to admit that I'm flawed.'

Clinging tightly to his neck, she looked into his eyes. 'Where is she?' she asked softly. 'Where is she?'

He kissed her forehead. 'Listen. Listen and I'll tell you.'

* * *

By the time they got back downstairs, Daw had piled the dishes in the sink and was eyeing the tea towel with jaundiced hate and still sniffing because Harry was leaving.

Lizzie followed him down, her feet seeming to float just above the stairs because she wasn't concentrating on where she was going and what she was doing. She felt like a child who's just seen fairies at the bottom of the garden and has been told that she'll turn into a frog if she tells anyone. Her mother was living with a man. She couldn't quite believe it and, as yet, she didn't quite know how to react. But she knew Daw would probably squirm with disgust. She knew how her father would react too; hence there could be no telling. Stanley, of course, didn't count. Anyone with any sense knew they couldn't tell a mere boy anything.

Henry was sitting in his chair, smoking his pipe, his eyes fixed on the glowing coals of the fire.

Harry, flamboyant and confident in his smart suit and navy over-coat, stood in the centre of the room holding his suitcase in one hand and his hat in the other.

'I'm off now, Dad.' Setting his hat on his head, he extended his hand. 'Will you wish me good luck?'

Henry's eyes fell to his son's hand. 'No.'

Harry's face hardened. 'Then I wish you none either.'

Lizzie watched him drive away, waving until he reached the end of the street, though he couldn't possibly wave back and perhaps couldn't even see her by then.

When she got back inside she looked for Daw.

'She ran upstairs still grizzling about something,' said Stanley who, despite having just eaten a plateful of liver and onions, plus rice pudding, was now buttering a large doorstep of bread. Daw was prostrate on her side of the bed, head buried in the pillow, and her arms thrown over her head. Her shoulders were shuddering, a jerky sob escaping the ones she was attempting to stifle with her pillow.

Lizzie smoothed the glossy dark hair that was swept back into a bun, nestling like a pigeon at the nape of Daw's neck.

'It's all right, Daw. You can bet our Harry will be back to visit. And you won't be alone. I'm here.'

She was almost tempted to tell Daw that she knew where her mother was, but she didn't dare. She had promised her brother Harry, and Lizzie always kept promises.

Nothing she said seemed to make any difference at first to Daw's outpouring of despair, but then she detected a change in the pattern and force of the sobs.

'I know he will. It's not just that.'

Lizzie continued to stroke. 'Tell me then.'

Daw rubbed at her eyes then peered at her through her fingers, spacing them like the bars of a cage.

'I'm having... a baby,' she said.

Since the moment Harry had given Lizzie her mother's address, she'd been rehearsing what she would say to her mother when she saw her. She'd decided to tell her everything that had been going on in her life and that of the family. This was something new, something she certainly hadn't counted on.

'I take it it's John's.'

'Of course it is.'

'Like a Christmas present,' she muttered, more to herself rather than for Daw's ears. 'Have you written to John?'

'Yes. He hasn't replied yet.'

Lizzie smiled. 'Well, he will. I bet you a pound note he will. I expect he'll be really pleased.'

35

Someone had daubed a swastika on the shutters of the pawn-shop. Michael, she presumed it was he, was scrubbing it off. Was this the man her mother was living with? He didn't look much older than she was. Strangely enough she felt no resentment. Michael, she decided, had kind eyes. Her mother could do with a large dose of kindness.

On coming level with him, she slowed down, brought her hands to the front, clasping her handbag – as if it needed two hands. Far from it: her purse, a comb and a tube of lipstick were all it contained.

Michael looked down at her, saw her hesitate before turning into the shop. 'I will be right with you.'

She sensed him following her into the dark interior where she became aware of being surrounded by polished wood and sparkling glass. Such attention to presentation, coupled with the smell of beeswax and watered-down vinegar, brought her mother to mind and she shivered.

'Can I help you?' he asked once he was behind the counter and facing her.

She met his gaze, but continued to shiver, not because she was cold; the day was milder than it had been of late. Hopefully spring would be early this year. Apprehension and a silly feeling of discovering her mother had become a stranger had haunted her sleep the previous night. Meeting her could not be put off, or she'd be too tired to function.

Licking the dryness from her lips, she readied herself to pronounce the words she'd rehearsed in front of her dressing-table mirror.

Swiftly she took in his details. Michael was no real surprise; Harry had primed her, told her he was younger than her mother but seemed a good person.

She was surprised to see how handsome he was, a good specimen of what the new Germany expected its citizens to be, if everything she'd read in the newspaper and seen at the pictures was correct.

'I've come to see my mother.'

The words were rushed and uncomplicated. What was the point in them being anything else?

For a moment, he stared at her, a fleeting fear entering his eyes before being replaced by realisation. 'Of course. I should have realised. You look so much like her. Please. Come this way.' He reopened the hatch he had entered through, closed it behind her and led the way down a narrow passageway that folded in on them, having no door to right or left and no steep stairs like the family home in Kent Street.

Lizzie stopped at the entrance to a small room at the rear of the shop and looked in. Off to her left a narrow doorway exposed an almost as narrow kitchen. Beside that was a window with a view onto an ugly yard; its only redeeming feature seemed to be a young tree showing the first signs of spring buds.

Her gaze was drawn to the heavy mahogany mantelpiece. To one side there was an opening exposing a set of winding stairs.

Michael went over to these, rested his hand on the fireplace and tilted his head back.

'Marianna, Marianna. You have a visitor.'

Marianna? Lizzie wondered whether she had made a mistake, that perhaps she was at the wrong address. But this must be the right place; besides, Harry had said so.

She felt Michael's eyes on her, reading her as he might the words written in a book, interpreting the confusion on her face.

'Marianna is my name for her.'

She nodded, but couldn't find her tongue and, even if she could, what would she say? That she felt like an intruder in a private world? These people had created a small intimacy in which she had no share.

The urge to leave became very strong, but her legs were like jelly, just like on the very first day at school when she hadn't been sure she would make a single friend, and had feared the look of the headmistress.

Footsteps thudded down the narrow staircase. 'Lizzie!'

Lizzie's jaw dropped. The woman before her shone in a way her mother never had. The grey-green eyes sparkled; her complexion had a peachy tone, as though she'd been sitting in sunshine, which was quite impossible. Spring was early this year, but the sunny days were still subject to chill air.

The green woollen dress she wore was perhaps a little old-fashioned, but it matched her eyes and hair, the latter of which seemed a more vibrant colour than she remembered, and yet it had been only a few months.

'Lizzie!'

There was no doubt in Lizzie's mind that she was glad to see her, and the feeling was mutual. She had fully expected to fall into her mother's arms, and yet there was hesitation, and that too, like their joy, was mutual.

Mary Anne indicated the old chaise longue, which she'd freshened with a sponge and soapy water, then added some glorious tapestry cushions and draped a wonderful silk scarf – large enough to cover a table or use as a shawl. According to the date on the label, whoever had pledged it had died long ago. 'Please. Sit down.'

Lizzie noticed the whiteness of her mother's hands, the way she tangled her fingers, clasped them together and then separated them again. Her eyes flickered between her daughter and the man she was living with as she sat beside her.

Michael, his attention switching between the two, sized up the situation, identified himself as the reason for their discomfort.

'I will make us some tea,' he said, closing the kitchen door behind him.

In his absence, the two women looked at each other. Mary Anne's shining eyes were the first to glisten with tears.

'Lizzie! Can you forgive me?'

Lizzie shook her head, not in a negative way, but because the question was not necessary. 'Ma, I was there. Remember? I heard and saw everything, and the worse thing is, I learned it from Stanley. You know he's been stealing, don't you? It was him who pinched money from Dad's pocket. I heard from Daisy – her father is landlord at the Red Cow – that he came in to buy a pint that day. There it was sitting on the counter, poured straight from the barrel, but when he came to pay for it there wasn't a penny in his pocket.'

Mary Anne hung her head, remembered the money missing from her cashbox. She'd accused nobody. Those with the opportunity to take it were either friends and neighbours or members of her family.

'I was so ashamed that he knew and saw so much. Not just that he saw things a boy shouldn't see, but also because I presumed he wouldn't be affected by it. I was so sure I was doing the right thing: making sure there was food on the table and a comfortable home; pretending that me and your father weren't so much a happy marriage as a stable one.'

Her own eyes welling up with tears, Lizzie took hold of her mother's hands, surprised to find them so cold and so smooth. 'Ma, you can't imagine how happy it makes me feel to see you looking so happy.'

Mary Anne smiled through her tears. 'Oh Lizzie.' Still clasping hands, they hugged each other.

Michael joined them with the tea. He talked of the business and how much her mother had helped him sort things out.

'She is better at this business than I am,' he said.

Lizzie hung on to his every word, not just because they concerned her mother but also because his accent pleased her. She addressed him directly. 'I hear you come from Holland. Is that right?'

There was an exchange of looks between him and her mother. Judging by the look on both their faces, they'd talked about how much of their personal life they would divulge to her.

Calmly and slowly, as though he were using every second to think carefully about it and choose his words, he put first his saucer back on the table, then the cup, turning it and placing the teaspoon so the handle pointed back at him.

'I was born here, but have lived most of my life in Germany.'

The swastika painted on the front door had slipped her mind.

'Ah! Yes,' she said stoically. 'Well, that explains that.'

'Explains what?' asked Mary Anne.

Michael put his cup down on the tray. 'Another swastika was painted on the front door. I did not like to worry you.'

Mary Anne sighed and shook her head, the calm retreating from her eyes. 'Thomas Routledge. I bet he's got something to do with it.'

'But you were born here,' Lizzie blurted.

Michael's smile made her feel terribly young and naive. The colour of his eyes, and the way they glittered in response to the creasing around them, made her heart skip a beat. He was older than her, younger than her mother, yet she could see the attraction.

'But I do not sound British.'

There was more talk about the business, the family and the war. Mary Anne mentioned Harry's visit.

'I was so pleased to see him, and so relieved that Stanley is full of beans.' Some fragment of the old Mary Anne flashed across her mind. Was Harry telling the truth? She had to have it confirmed. 'He is full of beans, isn't he?'

Lizzie smiled broadly. 'Of course he is, though a bit wild, but I think he'll grow out of it.'

Reassured, Mary Anne smiled and nodded gratefully. 'Our Harry said that he was doing fine. I just worry,' she said, gesturing with one hand before bringing it back on top of the other. 'At least our Harry and you are there to keep an eye on him – and his father of course.' She added the last comment in a more sober voice and there was no hiding the hint of bitterness. 'It'll be only me now. Our Harry's left home. I believe he's sharing a flat with a friend and he's gone into business with someone. He hasn't told me much about it, except that it pays better than making cigarettes and that I wouldn't understand even if he did decide to explain. But he will call in regularly. He reckons he can't help but do that. He worries, although he doesn't always show it. But at least he's around.'

'I am surprised he has not been called up.'

Michael's words had the same effect as cold water being poured down her back. She might have shrugged it off, but there was something about the way he looked at her that made Lizzie blush. She hoped to God he couldn't read her thoughts.

Mary Anne stacked the saucers in a neat pile, the cups lying on top, one inside the other like a large porcelain flower.

'No doubt he'll tell me more when he next calls.'

Lizzie managed a tight smile. She still hadn't come to terms with Harry's deception, although she'd admired him taking a stand for what he believed was right. But using a crippled man to attend the medical in his place stretched her compliance. Patrick and John hadn't hesitated to enlist and, even if he didn't want to fight, Harry could have declared himself a conscientious objector and served in the medical corps.

'I wouldn't be surprised if he's declared himself a conscientious objector,' her mother said suddenly.

It was an extraordinary comment, perfectly attuned to her thoughts. 'You could be right, Mother. Oh, and I had another letter from Patrick. He sends you his love.'

'And another poem?' Her mother's eyebrows arched in expectation.

'Of course.'

'And John, and Daw?'

'They're fine.'

No news yet about the baby, thought Lizzie. I can't tell her just yet.

Mary Anne cocked her head to one side and eyed her daughter appraisingly. They had the same colouring. She hoped they wouldn't have the same lives.

'And how is Peter Selwyn?'

Lizzie's look was steadfast, and this was one sentence she didn't need to rehearse. She knew exactly how she felt.

'I wouldn't know. I've left Mrs Selwyn's employ.'

Her mother leaned forwards expectantly. 'You're not going to join the Wrens, are you?'

Lizzie smiled. 'Don't worry, Mum. Someone has to stay and look after our Stanley. There's plenty of jobs on the home front. I might train as a full-time firefighter. There's a lot of jobs going with the fire brigade, what with some men preferring to fight the Nazis rather than fires.'

Her mother didn't go on to ask any more about Peter, and for that she was glad. Peter wasn't worth anyone's attention and she'd have no hesitation in shopping him to the authorities, if it wasn't for Harry. Oddly, Peter and her brother were two of a kind – though one was a coward and one was not.

'And now...' She got up to leave.

'I will get your coat,' said Michael and went ahead of them into the passage where a number of coats hung from a hallstand.

'He's very considerate,' whispered Lizzie. Mary Anne's smile lit up her face.

'He's very many things. You wouldn't believe... No,' she said, shaking her head. 'I won't tell you of the things he's been through and the things he's seen. Perhaps he'll do that himself in years to come when this dreadful war is over.'

After Michael held Lizzie's coat while she put it on, he slid the bolt back on the front door and waited patiently while mother and daughter said goodbye, rocking with emotion as they embraced.

'I miss you, Mum. You know that, don't you?'

Mary Anne bit her lip and nodded.

Lizzie went on. 'I'm not going to ask you to come home because I know you're happy here.' She threw a thankful smile at Michael. 'And we're old enough to look after ourselves, and perfectly capable of looking after Stanley, but I need to tell him, Ma, and I also think Daw should know. Dad isn't going to find out just yet, but you know how things go round. You can't stay indoors forever.'

Mother and daughter held each other at arm's length, Mary Anne biting her bottom lip and frowning slightly as she considered what she was being asked.

Lizzie sighed. There was nothing for it but to tell her the one thing that would decide her.

'Daw's expecting.'

36

Daw threw Lizzie a sceptical glare, inhaling her disbelief through clenched teeth.

'No!'

It was all she said. Her look said everything else, her eyes seeming to lock with the glassy-eyed remnants of her childhood sitting in a row on the chest of drawers.

As though she's blaming them for all her misfortunes, thought Lizzie, and not for the first time it occurred to her how self-centred her sister was.

'Mum's happy. That's what we have to bear in mind,' Lizzie said, presuming Daw would want to know how her mother was and convincing herself that although Daw's first priority was herself she did love her mother.

Daw shook her head in disbelief. 'No.'

'What does that mean?'

'I won't visit her. It's disgusting.'

Lizzie raised her eyebrows in surprise. 'Because she's living with a man who treats her well? It might be disgusting to the outside world because she's not married to him, but what's a marriage certificate anyway? Just a piece of paper. That's all.'

Daw screwed up her face in horror. 'Can you imagine the neighbours whispering when we walk past?'

Lizzie shrugged. 'Let them whisper. People who live in glasshouses and all that...'

Daw frowned. 'What's that supposed to mean?'

Older she might be, but Daw wasn't widely read, had hated school and didn't really care what the world was up to as long as it didn't affect her. A house, a husband and children were all she'd ever wanted. Lizzie folded her arms and regarded Daw as though she were twenty years older than her and not twenty months younger.

'They've all got their own dark secrets and shouldn't be so quick to condemn others.'

Tight-lipped and flushed, Daw shook her head, her dark hair bouncing around her cheeks. 'I don't care about their reputations. It's my mother's that matters and the way it affects me.' Lizzie tapped her foot impatiently as she sought the right words that might snap Daw out of her own little world. The wrong ones came instead.

'Stop being such a selfish little cow.'

'What will John say?' It didn't seem as though she'd heard.

Her hands were clenched, her eyes staring at the floor. 'About the baby or Mother?'

Daw shook her head. 'I don't know what he'll think.'

'He'll be so pleased to hear about the baby, I doubt what Mother is up to is likely to matter.'

Daw shook her head. 'I don't know. Living in sin is so shameful. She suddenly spun round on Lizzie. 'Have you told Ma about the baby?'

Lizzie nodded.

Daw covered her face with her hands. 'Oh, God!'

'She was pleased for you.'

Emerging from behind her hands, Daw looked up at her wide-eyed, the darkness of her pupils in stark contrast to her creamy white skin, her lips blood red because she'd been biting them. 'Oh God. It almost makes me as bad as her, doesn't it? I'm as much of a slut as she is!'

'Daw!'

Daw began to wail and scream.

'Daw! Stop it!'

She didn't stop. Aware of the noise carrying downstairs, Lizzie swung out her hand and slapped her face, hard enough to leave a vivid red mark.

Daw was stunned to silence. She sat shaking on the side of the bed, her eyes staring at nothing, her lips quivering as she rubbed the hot hand mark on her face.

Seeing her sister's round-eyed shock, Lizzie was suddenly overcome with remorse. 'Daw, I'm sorry...'

Her sister stiffened before her outstretched hand, sniffed and stuck out her chin. 'At least me and John will be married. There won't be any shame attached to this baby. If there was, I'd throw myself in the river!'

The statement was delivered with chilling resolve.

Lizzie turned away, telling herself that everything would turn out fine – or as well as it could be expected to.

But there was worse to come.

As she descended the stairs, her eyes met those of her father standing at the bottom. She could tell by his face that he'd heard every word.

Her abdomen tightened against the sudden urge to use the lavatory. 'Dad... I...' Whatever she might have considered saying froze in her throat. It was hard to read the look on his face, the darkness in his eyes, but she saw the way his cheeks flexed with tension and knew that he knew...

What he said next was not what she'd expected him to say.

'Tell our Daw to write to John right now. Tell 'er to marry the bloke now. Get 'im to put in for compassionate leave right now, not in a few months, not when he gets a chance at some leave, *now*!'

Lizzie looked back up the stairs and saw Daw looking down, her perplexed expression mirroring her own feelings.

* * *

Stanley was eager to visit his mother and Lizzie offered to take him there. 'Where does she live?' he asked eagerly, as she pulled his balaclava over his head and tucked his scarf into a firm knot beneath his chin.

'You'll know when we get there.'

There was more than one reason for taking him with her; it would keep him away from the bad company he'd fallen in with. She wasn't always there to keep him under control, her father had turned into himself since her mother had left, and Daw was too busy looking after herself.

Harry came by at least once a week and was the only one Stanley really looked up to.

'All my mates have seen Harry in his car. Do you think he'll take us for a ride in it when he's not doing secret things?' he asked her, as they walked from Kent Street, past the red brick of E. S. & A. Robinson, paper bag manufacturer, and into East Street.

Another one of his famous stories? she wondered. 'What secret things?'

'When I asked our Harry why he'd never had a car before, he said it was cos he couldn't afford it, and now he's doing other, *special* work, now he can, thanks to the war and all that. So me and me mates talked about it, and we reckon it's because he's doing *secret* things – you know – like a spy.'

'Like Beau Drummond or Richard Hannay.'

'Have they got cars too?'

Lizzie smiled. Spying was secondary in importance to an Austin Seven or a Morris.

Stanley continued to chatter, mostly telling her about his mates. Luckily, when he did ask more questions, only a simple yes or no was needed in reply, which gave Lizzie time to think. How was it going to be when mother and son were reunited?

She was very aware that on sight of Stanley her mother might resort to her old ways, putting his welfare and everyone else's before her own. She was determined this would not happen. This war was going to change quite a few things, including women's lives. Her mother had to be assured of this.

Lizzie half turned into the pawnshop doorway, when Stanley stopped dead in his tracks, a look of dark horror distorting his pale features.

'I'm not going in there! That's where Mr Hitler lives!'

'Stanley, don't be so ridiculous. This is where your mother lives now.'

Stanley was adamant. 'You don't understand. He keeps people there. He kidnaps them and keeps them there. Some of them he sends to Germany as slaves!'

Stanley's outburst began to attract attention. Lizzie felt her face reddening. This was ridiculous!

'Stanley. Do you want to see your mother?'

He nodded. 'But not in there. I ain't going in there, cos if we go in there, he'll kidnap us too and put us in a box and send us to Germany.'

Losing patience, Lizzie tried to pull him into the doorway. 'Now come on...'

Stanley's hand slipped from her grasp. 'No!'

Like a rabbit pursued by a pack of hounds, he was gone, darting off into the Saturday morning crowds, leaving Lizzie frustrated, her arms hanging loose at her side.

37

It was Wednesday evening, the time they'd agreed to set aside for cleaning and generally taking stock. The stocktaking had taken longer than they'd expected, so by the time it came to cleaning, a misty evening had settled, made darker by the rules of the blackout.

Mary Anne put more effort than usual into polishing the pawnshop counter and even tried putting some shine back into the brass grille dividing their domain from that of the customers.

Every so often, Michael looked at her sidelong, knowing what she was worrying about but leaving her to get it out of her system.

Lizzie had apologised for Stanley running away. Out of earshot of Michael, she'd reiterated Stanley's view of the pawnbroker to her mother.

'He's convinced that he's Adolf Hitler and that he boxes people up and sends them to Germany.'

Terribly disappointed, Mary Anne had sighed. 'It's those boys he mixes with,' she'd said, the old worries momentarily taking the newfound shine from her eyes. 'I should have been there...'

Lizzie had been firm, as though she were the mother and Mary Anne the daughter. 'You have your own life to lead, Mum. He'll come round. He's just a boy. Leave it to me.'

Later that evening, Michael, sensing she was troubled, gently fondled the nape of her neck. They lay naked together in the big bed that had come to represent the safest place she'd ever been in her life.

'You are troubled, Marianna?'

She closed her eyes. When he called her Marianna in that tone of voice, she could almost forget that she had ever been called Mary Anne. 'I have a headache. Just keep stroking my neck.'

'You were disappointed Stanley did not come?'

She sighed. 'He's mixing with a rum lot. They're filling his head with stupid tales.'

'About me?'

'Yes. They're the boys you suspect of painting the swastikas on the door.'

'Ah yes. They run away when they see me.'

He was silent for a while. Mary Anne lay with her head on his chest, listening to the beating of his heart as his hand stroked her neck. Bliss! She'd never felt such bliss, such a state of calm and being treasured. Henry had never made her feel anything but used. Making love with Henry was having sex. Having sex with Michael was making love. There was a distinct difference and made life worth living.

* * *

They planned to wash the black and white tiles in the portico once the shop was closed. The bolt was already slid back and the door unlocked in preparation. Unfortunately, it was now too dark, but Michael had left the door to the last minute – a last minute that had already come and gone.

Sudden scuffling at the door made them look up, exchange a quick glance, and spring into action.

Michael flung the door open, his athletic frame pouncing on the perpetrator with the paint can and brush, pulling him into the shop, slamming the door and slamming the man's body against it.

'Routledge!'

Routledge fought to prise Michael's hands from around his throat, his fingers clawing at his iron grip but making no progress.

Gentle, sensitive Michael; his face changed into a demon-like mask, inches from the face of Thomas Routledge, the man he'd thrown off the premises. His eyes were like daggers, his words spat like bullets.

'So you think you are clever, eh? You think it is clever to paint swastikas on my door, just like the fascists do in Germany. And what next? Force me to scrub lavatories with a prayer shawl? Rape my mother in front of my eyes? Send me off to be worked to death? *That* is what it means! *That* is what it means!'

The intensity of feeling behind the words was as powerful as Michael's voice, echoing around the little shop, taking hold of him so completely that he forgot he had his hands around a man's throat, didn't see his struggle for breath or the plum-coloured cheeks slowly changing to blue.

Mary Anne threw up her hands in horror. 'Michael! Michael!'

At the sound of her voice, a sudden moment followed when it seemed as though time stood still, the two men locked in a rigid, deadly embrace.

Michael's arms trembled as he came to, gradually loosening his grip. His hair fell forwards in wild disarray and the anger lingered in his eyes as his arms fell to his sides. He continued to stand in front of Routledge, daring him to move.

Spluttering and rubbing at his throat, Thomas Routledge rolled his eyes to settle on her. 'Ta very much, Mrs Randall. Foreign bastard would have bloody killed me...'

Michael made a move to grab him again. 'No!' Mary Anne moved to Michael's side.

'Ta again, Mrs Randall,' said Routledge breathlessly, licking his fleshy lips as though he was considering eating her off a plate.

'I think you should go, Mr Routledge,' she said, turning to Michael, clasping his upper arm against her with both of her own.

Gaslights hung at irregular intervals in the shop, their old-fashioned glow sending Michael's shadow to fall blackly over the cowering man, and yet there was defiance in Routledge's prickly face – a chin unshaved for days judging by the length of stubble. He smelled of damp earth and stale beer.

As he straightened, Routledge threw her a polite nod and she fancied there was even a little gratefulness in his expression, but she had no wish to dwell on his face, so turned away, leaning her head against Michael's arm.

'I can see why old Henry married you, Missus, especially all that happened in the war and 'ow it affected 'im.'

'My husband loves war, Mr Routledge. He's made it perfectly plain over the years that he loved the army and that it was the best time of his life; all comrades together.'

'Ah, no. That ain't 'ow it was. And I should know. We was in the same regiment, you see.'

'So I understand.'

Feeling her tremble against him, Michael interceded. 'I think you should go.'

Routledge's expression darkened. 'Everyone's shouting and hollerin' about war and they don't know what it's really like, not unless they was in the last lot, and we was, me and the likes of Henry Randall and his mate, Lewis Allen.'

Mary Anne looked up at the mention of the name of the other man in the photograph on the mantelpiece. 'Who was he?'

Routledge looked pleased that she'd asked. 'Lewis Allen? Well, he was yer husband's best mate, he was. They went through everything together, right up to nineteen eighteen, all the gut-wrenching horror of the trenches. Them places stunk of death and mud and the rats were as big as rabbits and if they 'ad been, we'd 'ave roasted them. Well, if I was honest, I admit we did roast a few now and again. Army rations weren't up to much.'

Mary Anne didn't need to look at Michael to know that he was listening as intently as she was.

'What happened in nineteen eighteen?'

There was a rasping sound, like a file going over rough metal as

Routledge rubbed at the stubble on his chin. The weasel-like look went from his eyes and for a moment something returned of the young man he had been before the brutalisation of war had changed him.

'Well, it was like this. Henry and his old friend Lewis Allen were always together, went through everything together, and made sure they backed each other up when needed, covering for each other in the heaviest of barrages. One day they got caught out in No Man's Land. They were trapped in a hole full of bodies and bits of bodies and legs and arms and what 'ave you, all rotting into the mud and stinkin' to 'igh 'eaven. There was an almighty artillery barrage goin' on and they were trapped there for twenty-four hours. Well, that, I can tell you, is a pretty penny to 'appen. By the time they got out, they was both in a bit of a state, but Lewis far worse than Henry. Poor old Lewis fell to pieces, jerking about like a puppet on a string. Shell shock they calls it now, but back then not everybody believed it existed. Cowardice said the commander, and poor old Lewis was taken out to be shot. The worse thing was that Henry was forced to be part of the firing squad. He was never the same after that, swore he would never care for anyone ever again. Couldn't face losing them, you see?'

* * *

Thomas Routledge counted himself lucky to have got off so lightly. If he hadn't heard the kids call the pawnbroker Mr Hitler, and then seen them paint the first swastika, he would never have got the idea. He'd bumped into Henry outside the Red Cow, and had voiced his surprise that he wasn't going inside for a beer.

Henry had shaken his head. 'No.'

'Just one? For old times' sake?'

As is the way of hardened drinkers, one pint became two, then three, then four. Eventually Henry told him what was troubling him.

Thomas had felt sorry for the bloke, but following the threat from Harry Randall, he didn't dare tell him where his wife was. Harry was gaining a bit of a reputation in a criminal underworld that had grown in influence since the onset of the blackout and, more especially, rationing of everything contributory to a comfortable lifestyle. Thomas wondered how much Henry's father knew of his son's business dealings. It puzzled him as to how Harry had managed to keep one step ahead of the call-up. Something smelled, and if he could find the source of the smell he could scupper Harry's rise to fame and fortune, perhaps even make a bit for himself.

'I'll think on it,' he muttered to himself, pushing open the door of the Queen's Arms to the warm fug of a crowded bar, something he might never have experienced again if Mary Anne Randall hadn't stopped the pawnbroker choking him.

He toasted her with his first beer. 'To the love of a good woman.'

A few regulars joined his toast. Someone asked him if he'd finally found the love of his life.

'Did that years ago,' he replied, lifting his beer and kissing the glass. 'She fills me with gladness... and deserves another kiss.'

* * *

Following Routledge's departure, Michael slid the bolt firmly across the door and turned the key. He was slow to face her, and Mary Anne thought she knew the reason why. They'd both been affected by the account Routledge had given them, but in slightly different ways.

'He might still be inclined to report me to the police,' he said.

'Why should he?'

'An enemy accent regardless of my passport.'

'They can't do anything.'

'I hope not,' he said, still facing the door.

When he did finally turn round, she saw the concern in his eyes and understood. 'It doesn't make any difference.' Reaching out, she lay her hand upon his cheek, feeling the heat of his pain warm the coolness of her palm. 'I understand now why Henry behaved as he did, but that doesn't mean I forgive him. I never will. His only saving grace was that he wasn't cruel to our children, only to me.'

'Do you think he might have been different if you hadn't given birth to another man's child?'

She lowered her eyes. She'd told Michael about Edward, how he'd died in the Great War and how the child of their union had been given up for adoption. She'd also told him how her family had connived to get her married off, introduced her to Henry and encouraged his courtship without disclosing anything of Edward or the child. Numbed by what had happened, Mary Anne had gone along with it. 'Much to my regret,' she'd told him. 'The early days were happy. Perhaps if I hadn't told him the truth...' She sighed.

'He would not have felt betrayed. He got close to you and then it must have felt like you were taken from him.'

Mary Anne looked at Michael. His sonorous voice worried her and his depth of insight was surprising.

'I won't go back, Michael, not even if you say I must, I won't. It's too late for that. Far too late.'

'We always think so,' he said, and this time she sensed that something else had been said that she hadn't recognised as being deeply significant. It wasn't until later when they were in bed that she found out it was due to Michael's outburst not the tale told by Thomas Routledge.

38

Lizzie had found a job in a munitions factory along Coronation Road. Previous to war being declared, Bawns Brothers had run a large car dealership and repair workshop from the site. The small showroom and large workshops were now given over to the production of artillery shells. She was regarding it as a short-term option until Stanley was sorted and she could join the Wrens. What she meant by Stanley being sorted, she wasn't quite sure. Who else would look after him? Everyone was working.

Before leaving for work, she read a letter from Patrick while eating a piece of toast lightly scraped with butter. Reading one of his letters had become one of the high spots of her day, especially the little poem he always included that never failed to raise a smile.

On this occasion, there was no poem, just as much news as the censors allowed him to write. He also urged her to consider evacuation, if not for her, then at least for Stanley. He also said he'd be home shortly, which could have been the reason he didn't include any poetry. Combining his lack of poetry with his warnings about leaving the city brought her to another conclusion: the war was about to get much worse.

Daw thudded down the stairs; the corners of her mouth turned down and there were dark circles beneath her eyes.

She fetched herself a cup and saucer. 'I'll just have tea.'

'It's in the pot,' said Lizzie, not attempting to pour it for her.

'Is Dad already gone?'

Lizzie frowned. 'If he did I didn't hear him go. He didn't do himself breakfast or a cup of tea.'

She got up and called along the passage for Stanley. 'Come on, Stanley. Off to school.'

Hearing no response, she went along and popped her head around the door. The body in bed had no head, it being safely buried beneath the bedclothes.

Fists on hips and a determined set to her jaw, she looked down at him.

'Off to school.'

A muffled cough sounded from beneath the bedclothes and was followed by a weedy voice claiming that he wasn't very well.

'Off to school!' Lizzie repeated in a firmer voice. 'Get yourself out from under that eiderdown before I do it for you.'

Slowly a cloud of near-white blond hair appeared, followed by blue eyes in a floury pale face.

'Mum used to let me stay home if I had a cough.'

Lizzie had promised herself that she would not be as soft with her brother as her mother had been. 'You had a bad chest infection at the beginning of last year, but that doesn't mean you've got it for ever.'

Snail-like, Stanley prodded at the bedclothes until they were down past his waist, then slowly, as though each leg weighed half a ton, he moved them one at a time to the edge of the bed.

'My mum wouldn't make me do this.'

Lizzie maintained her firm resolve. 'Your mum isn't here and I am.'

'No,' he blurted, tearing his pyjama top off and throwing it on the floor, 'she's not because that bloody German's got her!'

The bad language earned him a clip round the ear from his sister.

'His name's Michael and he was born here. And don't swear.'

Stanley pouted and rubbed at his ear. 'My mates do.'

'That doesn't mean you can.'

'And they smoke.'

'You're not to do that either.'

Lizzie glanced at her watch. She prided herself on running the house and looking after Stanley, but she did need to work and she had been enjoying Patrick's letter and also enjoyed writing back to him. Her patience was coming to an end.

'Come on, Stanley. I have to go to work.'

'That's right. Come on, Stanley. Get out of bed.'

She jerked her head round to face her father. His voice had come as a complete surprise and so did his presence. It had never been his policy to get involved in household matters, and she couldn't ever remember him visiting Stanley when he'd been lying ill with the chest infection he'd taken so long to get over.

'Go on,' he said, mistakenly thinking she hadn't heard. 'You go on to work. I'll get our Stanley off to school.' He looked tellingly back at his youngest son. 'I'll get him there if I've got to drag him there myself.'

'Right,' said Lizzie, telling herself not to look the proverbial gift horse in the mouth and hoping that it might be a permanent arrangement. 'I'll get off to work.'

Daw was coming in from outside, wiping her mouth.

'Sick again?'

Daw nodded.

Lizzie indicated the official-looking envelope on the table. 'You've got a letter from John. Patrick's coming home in a few days. I expect John is too.'

A hint of colour came suddenly to her sister's wan cheeks. 'I'll see you this evening. Put the potatoes on if you're home before me. And don't worry about getting our Stanley off to school. Dad's dealing with it.'

Daw gave no indication that she either heard or cared. Her fingers were busily ripping at the letter. She didn't even hear or answer Lizzie's shouted goodbye.

* * *

Henry couldn't remember the last time he'd taken hold of his son's hand, if ever. He frowned at the guilty feeling it gave him and also the sadness.

At first it seemed the experience was as strange to Stanley as it was to him. Every now and again he felt Stanley's eyes on him. Once or twice he'd looked down at him, surprised to see how blue they were. When had he stopped noticing the precious things of life? He liked to think it was when Mary Anne had torn his heart out telling him there'd not only been another man before him, but also a child. He could see now why her parents had been so keen for him to marry her, him with little education but a steady job and an upright character. In his heart of hearts he knew he'd been damaged before then, but what was one more damaged man among thousands of damaged men returning from the Great War?

'Are you going to get my ma to come home?'

His big hands clasped and unclasped over his knees. 'That's up to her.'

'Will you make her come?'

'I can't make her.'

'You can punch her and make her come. That's what you always used to do.'

Out of the mouths of babes and sucklings... Where had he heard that... the Bible... yes... of course. Another one was *the truth always hurts*. Both of them were true. He felt as though he'd been stung by a thousand bees.

Some folk confessed to a priest, but he wasn't of that religious persuasion. Perversely, he began to confess to his son.

First, he cleared his throat. 'Son? I have a confession to make.'

Whether Stanley even understood the word, he didn't know, but the blue eyes flashed and he looked as if he were concentrating.

Henry continued. 'I didn't treat your ma right. That's why she ran off.'

Stanley aped his father, clearing his throat and adopting the same sober expression. 'Did it surprise you, Dad?'

Henry sighed. 'Looking back on it, the only thing that surprised me is what took her so long, but then I know the answer to that anyway. It was you, son. You, and your brother and your sisters. She wouldn't leave you and I'm grateful for that. She's a good woman, a good mother and a good wife if I'd given her half a chance.'

* * *

Outside Rollos, a posh dress shop in West Street, a woman laden with bags flounced out of the shop, aiming for a taxi from Henry's own company waiting for her at the kerb. The fur coat she wore would have looked better on a leaner frame, and although the matching hat looked expensive and was decorated with curly brown feathers, its resemblance to a tea cosy was unmistakable.

'Mr Randall?' Her voice was as cutting as a nail scratching glass.

Henry frowned, trying to place where he'd seen the woman before. Seeing his consternation, she explained.

'I'm Mrs Selwyn. You brought your daughter Elizabeth to me in your cab sometimes. She left my employ recently. I must say I thought her method of leaving was quite impolite. It is not done to merely leave a letter on the table. She should have given me formal notice and told me to my face in order that we could consider any problems and have time to find a replacement. She did neither of those things. I must state my dissatisfaction, Mr Randall, indeed I must—'

'I'm sorry Mrs Selwyn, but I have an appointment...'

'It cannot be as important as hearing my grievances, Mr Randall—'

'Yes it is!' cried Stanley, his earnest expression matching the passion in his voice. 'My ma's living with a German pawnbroker in East Street, so get out of our way!'

Henry raised his hat to her horror-stricken face as he passed her and followed his son.

* * *

The tree in the backyard was breaking into bright buds, tiny leaves bursting out like flower petals or elliptical wings of lime-green butterflies.

Mary Anne saw them, and although she usually felt a great burst of hope when eyeing the tree's resilience in such drab surroundings, today she had other things on her mind. Yesterday, Michael had almost strangled a man. The occurrence had left a profound impression on both of them. She'd already learned from him that some very terrible things were happening in Germany. Last night he had told her one last thing, one happening that he had sworn he would never repeat to anyone.

'It was the day before I was due to leave. They were storm troopers, just as those that are marching all over Europe. Hide, my stepfather said, and I did. My mother had a very ornate piece of furniture, a credenza I think it is called. It was French and very ornate. The doors were emblazoned with porcelain panels decorated with nymphs and trees and flowers. It was huge... used for the storage of linens. Some-how, I hardly believe it now, but they squeezed me into this. I could only see out of it through a keyhole. I found myself looking at black breeches and boots. I could only surmise what was happening from what I heard. They asked where I was, that I was a deserter and traitor to my country. My stepfather said I was with the army, but that he did not know where. I heard the slap of his gloved hand on my step-father's face. He did not cry out. They asked more questions, beat him some more, but he still answered them in the same voice he used for a church service. Eventually, seeing as they would get nowhere with him, they started on my mother...'

His voice had broken. She'd cupped his face in her hands. 'You don't need to go on.'

'I must.'

He'd taken a deep breath and she'd realised just what a great strain this was.

'They started on my mother. I heard her cry out. My first instinct was to rush out and help her, but I knew I could not do this, that it would do no good. We would all be punished, but also the memories of the bloodlust I had seen in the eyes of men I had once regarded as friends were still with me. I was afraid. I admit it, I was *very* afraid.'

Her stomach had churned as the horror unfolded.

'There were six of them. Some were little more than boys – perhaps nineteen or so. On the command of the officer, they took their turn, and still I could not show myself.' His eyes had filled with tears. 'I was a fool. Blinded by my own fear, I led them there and still terrified, I did not help her. I am a coward.'

'What happened next?' Her voice was low and gentle. His throat pulsed in a hard swallow.

'They went away. I came out of my hiding place full of shame and apologising to them both for not helping. But at least we are alive, said my stepfather, my mother crying in his arms. He told me to go, to reach England and to prepare for their arrival for he felt sure that they would not be long in following me because he knew someone who could get him the proper papers.

'I must have looked dumbfounded because for some reason he explained further. "They are church members, committed Christians willing to help those unable to help themselves." He gave me an address in Hamburg. "We have been referring people to them... mostly Jews," he added, his stricken look switching between a hasty concern for me and a more intense one for my mother.

'I did not know what to say to her, to either of them. I remember I kept apologising. It was all my fault; I had been blinded by a childhood obsession with uniforms and of fitting in with my peers and, because of that, I had brought great pain to them. I had betrayed their love, blinded myself to understanding.

'I told them I could not leave them. My stepfather shouted at me to go. He would take care of my mother. He would take care of everything.

'There seemed no choice. For me to stay there was as dangerous for them as it was for me. I took the address they gave me and fled, came here and I wait, hoping they are still alive, hoping that they really do know someone who can get them the necessary papers so they can follow the route to Hamburg.' It was only then that she knew the full extent of the guilt he was carrying, now because she was sharing it with him. 'We must hope they will come.'

She looked at the tree and its sturdy new growth.

Hope springs eternal.

She certainly hoped it did. The war had seemed a faraway thing and there were plenty of people still saying that it was nothing to do with them. It had affected Michael very deeply and personally. Hope was indeed what they were all going to need in the years to come.

Her other concern was Stanley. Although Lizzie had stressed that there was nothing to worry about, that given time he'd accept Michael fully, she couldn't help being anxious.

For the second time in little under a fortnight, Michael came in from the shop to tell her that someone was here to see her.

'Harry?' she asked, her spirits lifting at the prospect of seeing her handsome, successful son yet again.

He shook his head. 'No. It is Stanley.'

She ran from the yard and into the living quarters where Stanley was waiting for her. Michael had given him a slice of some apple cake that he'd made; 'strudel' he'd called it and took great pride in baking it purely for Mary Anne, complaining the whole time that he couldn't get quite the same ingredients that his mother had used. He'd always referred to his mother in respectful, subdued tones. Now she knew just how much respect he had for her.

'Stanley!'

To her great disappointment, his exuberance did not match her own, his enthusiasm for the strudel outweighing his joy at seeing her.

Mary Anne swallowed her emotion almost as quickly as Stanley was swallowing the spicy mix of apple and pastry. 'Are you well, Stanley?'

He looked at her as though only just realising she was there and gave her a crumb-filled kiss before returning his full attention to his cake. 'I wasn't going to come here, but Dad said it would be all right. He said you wouldn't go off with anyone who wasn't a decent sort of bloke and that besides, I had to be brave, just like he did.'

Mary Anne's mouth dropped open. Oblivious to the surprise he'd caused by mentioning his father knew her whereabouts, Stanley continued. 'That pawnbroker do seem a nice bloke, Ma. If I'd known he could make cakes I wouldn't have run away the other day. It was Ollie Young who said he was Hitler and boxed people up to send back to Germany. He was lying, Ma, weren't he? He was lying.'

Mary Anne nodded. 'Of course he was lying.' She hugged him again.

'Dad wants to see you,' he said after swallowing the last bite.

Mary Anne looked over her shoulder, knowing Michael was standing there, and ready to support her in whatever way she needed.

Their eyes met in mutual understanding before she turned back to face her youngest son.

'Why does your father want to see me?'

Stanley shrugged. 'He just does. He let me take the day off school to come here and he took the day off work. He said it was important.'

The thought of seeing him again resurrected the same old fears. It had only been a few months since she'd left, and yet in those months she had lived a lifetime, learned more about herself, about the world, her children and her husband. She *had* to be able to do this.

'I must do this,' she said and, even though she didn't look at him, Michael knew she was saying it for his benefit.

'Do you want me to come with you?'

She shook her head and her eyes met his. 'Will you pass me my coat?'

He opened the closet door and handed it to her. 'Wrap up warm, won't you.'

She nodded. 'I will.'

There was a bandstand in the park, a brick-built three-sided construction looking out over the city. Immediately between it and the view were two artillery pieces from the Great War, said to have been captured from the Germans, but might just as well have belonged to the British Army: the truth had become obscure with the years.

Henry was sitting there waiting for her, his face raw from the cold wind that swooped up from the vale, pinching at nostrils and the first of the daffodils.

He blinked when he first saw her, looked away and then took a second look. Any other wife would have welcomed the obvious admiration that he desperately tried to hide, but not Mary Anne. No matter how he looked at her, she could only feel a deep-seated, loathsome fear. She had declared forgiveness would never come and that was an end to the matter.

'You wanted to see me?'

The firmness of her voice surprised her, and she could see from Henry's face that it did him too.

Stanley went off to play on the guns.

Henry's hands were clasped between his knees, his gaze fixed on the floor.

'I'm not going to ask you back.'

'Just as well. I wouldn't come,' she replied hotly.

'That's what I thought. What I did was unforgivable. I knew I was being wicked, but I couldn't seem to stop myself. It was as if the devil took me over, wearing me as easily as a preacher would wear a Sunday suit.'

He didn't mention the war, so she didn't either. What Thomas Routledge had said to her, she would keep to herself.

'I can't forgive you.'

'I'm not surprised. But we do have a family, and before long they'll have their own families and we'll be grandparents. We still have responsibilities to them, even though we don't to each other. You know our Daw's expecting?'

She nodded, her eyes fixed on the barrage balloons floating above the shunting yards in Midland Road. 'Yes.'

'I've told her to hurry up and marry the bloke while he's still alive. I think she understands, I think she'll do it.'

Mary Anne sat down on the bench, being careful to allow plenty of space between them.

'How did you find out?'

He shrugged. 'Your whereabouts?'

She nodded.

'Word gets around.'

'Thomas Routledge?'

'Let's say there's a lifelong brotherhood between them that's served their country.'

Mary Anne stiffened. She didn't doubt that the story about Lewis Allen was true, but could she trust him not to stir things up for Michael?

She turned the collar of her coat up around her face as she thought things through.

Henry was staring into the distance. 'Our Lizzie should be off before very long. She's still set on joining the Wrens. What with our Daw getting married, and Harry off on his own, that only leaves me and Stanley. There's a spare room there if ever you want it.' He held up his hand suddenly, pre-empting her protest that she wouldn't ever consider moving back under the same roof. 'In case of need,' he said. 'They bombed Warsaw you know, blasted people's homes to smithereens. Any time in the future, one of us might want a roof over our heads, and if Stanley wants to spend some time with you, well I've got no objection to that either.'

'I'm going now,' she said, getting stiffly to her feet, not wanting to feel sorry or, indeed, to feel anything for him at all, but she found herself feeling a whole whirlpool of emotions, some of which were quite surprising.

Henry also got to his feet. 'I'm a proud man,' he said. 'But I was never prouder than when I married a clever woman like you, but there were wounds in our past. You owned up to yours, but I never owned up to mine. Too proud. And all because of a bloody war. Let's hope our children don't get injured like we was.' He chuckled sadly. 'Oh well.

Kiss yer mother goodbye,' he called to Stanley, before turning for home.

Stanley did as his father ordered, his lips cold from the wind.

'Off to school now?'

A single frown line appeared on Stanley's shiny forehead. 'Do I have to?'

His father overheard and called to him, 'Only if you want to be a gunnery officer or a fighter pilot when you grow up.'

Stanley's face changed at the prospect of firing a gun or flying an aircraft, a thoughtful look coming to his eyes.

'Go with your father.'

She watched them walk up the incline past the park keeper's cottage, a tall man with stooped shoulders, and a young boy marching like a soldier at a victory parade. Her feelings were too confusing, too painful and too surprising.

39

Arm in arm with Patrick Kelly, Lizzie ignored the questioning looks of neighbours. No doubt they were wondering at the drama at number ten in the past months, a house full of surprises. First the mother had run off, and now here was Lizzie Randall walking out with the likes of Patrick Kelly. They were probably whispering that he looked good in a uniform. Who would have thought his mother was a strumpet who'd had more men than the Sally Army had tambourines!

As they walked along the pavement, they sidestepped a small woman with a nut-brown face. Those watching switched their attention as the woman headed in the direction of Kate Harvey at number sixteen; rumour had it she was pregnant again.

Kent Street behind them, she couldn't resist patting the buttons on Patrick's uniform as they walked to the bus stop to get the bus for the pictures.

He smiled with pleasure. 'Do you like my shiny buttons?'

'It wasn't them. You've put on a bit of weight since you joined the air force. Is that all you do – eat and drink?'

She fancied his face clouded a little and immediately knew why, her own smile vanishing. 'You're going off somewhere, aren't you? Is it France?'

He smiled nervously, but even so deep laugh lines appeared at the corners of his mouth. 'We're not supposed to say.'

'But I've guessed right.' Her stomach tightened, like it did when she was frightened or excited, but this was something different, this was anticipation of an uncertain future. 'Is John going too?'

Patrick nodded silently. She noted the concern in his eyes, but also pride. Patrick, she realised, had found his vocation in life, or rather he'd found a place where he was fully appreciated.

His expression turned even more serious. 'Have you thought any more about sending Stanley to the country?'

She shook her head. 'Life is very complicated at the moment what with my mum living in one place and my dad in another.' She looked up at him, suddenly aware of the implications of what he was saying. 'Are we going to be bombed shortly? We've had a few false alarms, but they came to nothing.'

He didn't meet her look. 'It's best to be prepared.'

'Ah!'

She didn't need him to say the words. His expression said it all. She'd read the papers; although the press was under strict orders to adopt an upbeat attitude, the reports coming in from the continent were not good.

'What does "Ah" mean?' he asked her.

'Spring's coming. Don't armies go on the march when the weather gets better?'

'I won't be marching. I'll be on the ground ready to rearm every fighter that needs it. John won't be marching either. He'll be flying.'

And what about Daw? Lizzie hesitated, but Patrick beat her to it.

'John and Daw are going to get a special licence.'

'I was going to be tactful and ask if you knew about the baby. Obviously, you do.'

He nodded and looked up the road for a bus, but saw only a blue cab.

Lizzie frowned. 'Not Dad's,' she said, reading his mind. The cab came to halt immediately opposite the bus stop, and even before she alighted, Lizzie recognised the forthright figure of Mrs Selwyn, her powdered face creased with rage, her angry looks shooting like arrows directly at Lizzie.

'You!' she shouted, eyes blazing and pointing the spike of an old-fashioned brolly directly at Lizzie's midriff. 'You little trollop! Don't think I don't know why you did this, leading my Peter astray with a view to getting your hands on the Selwyn money and business. Well, you don't fool me, Miss Randall. I know a gold-digging slut when I see one, but to betray him!'

Although her cheeks burned, Lizzie looked at her in amazement. 'I don't know what you're talking about.'

'Well, I don't believe that either. My Peter, my darling Peter has been taken away from me. You Judas, you told them he was with me. You told them where he was—'

'He hasn't gone back to Canada?'

The reference to Canada seemed to stop her in her tracks. 'No,' she said coldly, the wind momentarily seeming to have left her sails. 'He has not.'

'But then, he never was in Canada, was he? That's what this is all about.'

Mrs Selwyn's face turned a frightening shade of eau de Nil. 'This war is pointless. Germany was on its knees and has now regained its self-respect. What's wrong with that, may I ask, so I make no apologies for trying to save my son's life in a worthless quest for glory. That's all it is thanks to the warmongers in Parliament. And you, miss,' she said, the tip of her umbrella defected by a swipe of Patrick's hand, 'you turned him in. *You* betrayed him.'

Angered by the accusation, Lizzie opened her mouth to shout a few words of retaliation, but the woman with the nut-brown face interrupted their confrontation.

'Maude Smith. Is that you, Maude? Surely you recognise old Mrs Riley? Remember that tablecloth you gave me for doing you a turn when you were in service up in Clifton?' The glittery, small eyes swept over the handsome mauve two-piece Mrs Selwyn was wearing. 'My, but you've come along a bit since then, me dear. My word that was in the early days of me profession, when I was just starting out, and you nothing but a humble housemaid. Now how long ago was that?'

'Not a schoolteacher?' Lizzie blurted, unable to keep her mouth closed.

Mrs Selwyn did not wait for any more revelations about her former life, but rushed headlong back into the cab, falling full length on the seat in her hurry to get away.

They both watched the cab pull away. The woman with the nut-brown face, carrying a tapestry bag over her arm, joined them in the bus queue.

'I take it her son didn't respond to his call-up papers,' Patrick said.

'They pretended he'd gone to Canada, even to the extent of her seeing him off at the station. They were there when I saw you off. Something funny struck me at the time. She wasn't crying, but just standing there as though they'd only come to look at the trains. I realise now it was for my benefit. If anyone asked, I would have to admit I'd seen them at the station.'

'So where was he?'

'In the attic. I wondered where all the rations were going.'

'Well, being in Canada wouldn't save him. Certainly not now. Canadian troops and air force have arrived. She wouldn't have been able to use that cover any longer.'

'What will happen to him?'

'He'll get put in the glasshouse.'

'Glasshouse?'

'Military prison. It's pretty grim, double time all the time, even in the lavatory.'

'And then?'

'He'll join the ranks like everyone else.' He looked at her quizzically. 'Why so curious? There wasn't anything between you two was there?'

'No,' she said, trying to sound as though it had never been so. 'I was just interested in case I do get to join the Wrens.'

He laughed at that. 'I don't think they'll put you in the glasshouse. Too disconcerting for the blokes already in there.' Her laughter hid her concern for Harry. What if he got caught too, what would happen to him? It was obvious he'd been avoiding call-up for some time.

* * *

The man wore a brown felt trilby and a gaberdine raincoat belted at the waist.

Like an American gangster, Mary Anne thought wryly, but inside she was fearful. This was not a fictional scenario played in black and white to a mesmerised audience. This was for real and it was frightening. A uniformed constable followed him in, one of the old-timers dragged back from retirement to fill gaps left by those who'd joined the armed forces.

She dared a sidelong glance at Michael. His coolness amazed her. His voice was calm. 'Can I help you?'

The man in the raincoat nodded. 'You can.' His tone was terse. He gave only a cursory glance at Mary Anne, saving closer scrutiny for Michael's athletic frame, as though dissecting him piece by piece; either that or he was plain jealous.

'May I see your passport?'

No asking of name, no introduction of who he was or why he was there.

Michael showed no sign of protest but went to the glass-fronted cabinet at the side of the fireplace, opened it and took out his passport from a pile of other papers.

The man in the trilby hat opened it, studied the photographs, studied Michael and returned to the photographs yet again.

It was, thought Mary Anne, as though he's studying each facial feature in turn: nose, eyes, mouth, chin and hairline.

'I need to check this more fully,' he said, tucking the passport into the inside pocket of his raincoat.

'Michael nodded. 'Fine. I am not going anywhere.'

The policeman gave him a jaundiced look. 'I can assure you of that. You won't be going anywhere until I check who you say you are. In the meantime you're to report to the police station each week until I say otherwise. Miss one week and you'll find yourself inside. Do I make myself clear?'

Michael gave a jerk of his chin. Mary Anne fancied he wanted to say more but was not inclined to upset the system. But she was.

'Why does he have to do that? He was born here.'

The man's eyes flickered when he looked at her. She presumed he was weighing up the situation; what was she to this young man. Seemingly not old enough to be his mother, but not of the same age; good-looking and definitely not a relative, if he'd done any research, which she presumed he had.

He seemed to reach a conclusion. 'We can't be too careful.'

'Too careful! Michael was born here. What is this all about? Who's been pointing the finger?'

She felt Michael's fingers brush her hand, a warning not to say anything, but she had to. She couldn't just stand by and let this happen. This was England, for God's sake!

The man's face stiffened. 'And you are?'

'Mary Anne Randall, and I'm British and I'm not a Nazi spy or a sympathiser – in fact quite the opposite.'

The uniformed policeman, who up until now had just provided a dark-blue backdrop for the mud brown of his superior's gaberdine, bent his head in an effort to hide a smirk. His senior suppressed a tight smile. 'Ah! That explains a lot. A Mrs Selwyn reported that a young man told her that Mr Maurice shouted at him in German. The young man's name was Stanley Randall.'

40

Michael rubbed his face with both hands, massaged the bridge of his nose with finger and thumb, then pressed them into the corners of his eyes, anything to alleviate the glaring whiteness of the tiled walls.

He had not expected to be placed in a cell. He'd always believed the British to be a tolerant race and no one was incarcerated without trial.

Perhaps it will only be for a few days, he told himself. He certainly hoped so. He wanted to get back to Marianna, lie beside her in the warmth of his old uncle's big bed, and lock the door against the world and its troubles.

Instead... he looked over his shoulder at the grey blanket covering the thin mattress. It looked rough enough to bring the toughest skin out in a rash, and Lord knows how many other men had slept beneath it.

The sudden opening of the solid steel door heralded the arrival of a young constable, carrying a mug of something hot and steaming. He wore glasses and had the faint vestige of a ginger moustache on his upper lip. Michael presumed he was a new recruit, rejected by the military due to bad eyesight.

'I brought you a cup of tea. Didn't know how you like it, but put two sugars in. That be all right, mate?' he said, his casual manner betraying his lack of training.

Michael took the tea gratefully and smiled. 'How long will I be here?'

'Not long. Rees Jones, the bloke who brought you here, has got to get a few papers together.' He glanced over his shoulder before leaning closer and whispering. 'It's something to do with Germany.' He tapped the side of his nose. 'Mum's the word.'

It was about an hour later when the plain-clothes officer he now knew was named Rees Jones reappeared. This time he was alone and carrying a sheaf of papers, including Michael's British passport.

'Sorry about this,' he said, indicating the miserable surroundings. 'But we've ran out of room. Normally, I'd see you at my desk, but I have to share it with the ARP and goodness knows who else until they get their own base sorted out. This place gets more like Paddington Station every day. Still, at least we didn't lock the door on you,' he added, smiling reassuringly.

Michael was dumbfounded at the revelation that he hadn't been imprisoned at all. Why hadn't he checked? He could have walked out if he'd tried the door.

'Your passport checks out as do the details you've told me about your uncle leaving you the shop. Lucky you had a good solicitor.'

He handed him the passport, his joviality diminishing as he fished among the other official-looking documents. 'However, there has been a development, one of which you may not be aware.'

Michael leaned forwards, his teeth aching because he was clenching them so hard. One bright hope burned in his heart.

'My parents? Have you heard from them?'

He wanted to ask whether they were alive or dead, but he reasoned they couldn't know. No one could find out what was happening in Germany, even the people that lived there. It must be something else.

'We have.' Rees Jones looked him straight in the eye. His voice had a certain melodic quality. 'Your parents have arrived in this country.'

Michael let out an explosion of relief, flinging his arms in the air, letting them drop and covering his face with his hands. He wasn't quite sobbing, but when he finally emerged, his face was creased with emotion.

Rees Jones had waited politely until he deemed him ready for more information. 'They brought over a boatload of Jewish children into Holland and then by Dutch trawler to Harwich. They did it under assumed names and with clearance from various embassies. They were very brave and I think they were the last to get out.' Rees Jones's expression was as grey as November. 'With the worsening situation, it took time for us to check their details and let you know.'

'It doesn't matter! It doesn't matter! When can I see them?' Rees Jones drew his lips back from his clenched teeth, drawing his breath through with a hissing sound.

Michael waited to be told that it wasn't possible, but Rees Jones surprised him.

'It is possible for you to see them, either for a short term or much longer, depending on how you yourself wish to be treated.'

Michael remained silent, letting the other man continue, keeping his gaze steady as he digested the details.

'You can remain in your shop as a British citizen. However, this does mean that you might get called up. Or you can be incarcerated with them.'

'Incarcerated?'

'Yes. Not that your status would be changed as such, it's just that they're not in an ideal visiting spot, so if you go there, you stay there – well – more or less. You're not interned as they are, but your stepfather is a German citizen, an enemy alien. Your mother refuses to leave his side although like you, she can, though with reservations. It's up to you.'

It felt as though the blood had drained from his system. 'May I know where they are?'

Rees Jones made that hissing sound again followed by a low whine as he made up his mind. 'I don't see why not. I think everybody in Britain knows. They're on the Isle of Man. I don't know whether you've ever crossed the Irish Sea, but it's not always a pleasant experience – in fact most of the time it's most unpleasant.'

One vital question remained. 'How long do I have before I make up my mind?'

Rees Jones looked at his watch. 'There's a train to the rendezvous point at midday tomorrow. You need to be on it. Travel's going to become more difficult in future, so bear that in mind too. You might not be able to come back quite as freely as you go.'

'So I can go.'

The policeman nodded. 'Of course. Oh, and I think you might want this.' He handed him a letter. Looking at it he could see that it had been opened, resealed and stamped with a censorship mark, 'War Office'.

* * *

Walking back to the pawnshop, he stopped in the park, sitting on a seat close to the old artillery guns that children were playing on. Spread out before him was a city of over three hundred thousand souls, its buildings sharp as sixpence in the clear spring air. Following the gummed edges that had already been disturbed, he opened the envelope.

My dear son, Michael,

We both hope you are reading this note. If you are, then we thank God for his mercy. We acquired the correct papers and followed the route to Holland and then by Dutch trawler to Harwich. We brought small friends with us; children entrusted to us by their parents. On arrival in Harwich we were immediately interned, but do not worry for us. We are being fed and well treated. As we all know there are others far worse off than we are, some of them in camps from where they will never return. The horrors of this war will only increase. I recall something I read, that all it takes for evil to triumph is for good men to do nothing. Refrain from doing nothing, Michael. The world is depending on you. All our love.

Everything had seemed very straightforward up until he read the note. Of course he would join them, even if it meant being incarcerated. Following his heart rather than his head had seemed the right thing to do. People meant more than wearing a smart uniform or living in comfort, that's what he had told himself. The trumpet blowing and smartness now faded into insignificance. The *reason* for wearing the uniform was what counted.

Turning his collar up against the wind, he retraced his steps down the incline past the bowling green, the smell of wallflowers pungent on the air. He knew what he had to do and walked quickly back to the police station.

He wrinkled his nose at the prospect of once again smelling the disagreeable mix of carbolic, chalk dust and unwashed bodies in the square waiting room of Bedminster Police Station. On this occasion, he detected a more pleasant smell and it emanated from someone he recognised already sitting there.

Harry winked at him. 'Michael! Nice weather we're 'avin for the time of year.'

Michael nodded an acknowledgement. His demeanour was too fragile at present for trivialities. What he was about to do would affect a lot of people.

'Take a pew,' said Harry, moving up the bench a fraction so the new arrival could squeeze in. 'Move up a bit,' Harry said to the constable sitting next to him. There was no one behind the counter, so Michael sat down.

The young man obligingly moved up. Michael wondered what he was doing here, gave Harry a tight smile and nodded at the newspaper balanced on his knee, watching as Mary Anne's son filled each square with a letter in double quick time.

'You are very good at that,' he said.

'So I understand,' said Harry. 'I could do it even quicker if I had both hands free.' He lifted his hand and flexed his wrist. Being attached to the other half of the handcuffs, the constable did the same, but didn't look happy about it.

'What happened?' asked Michael.

Harry made a casual shrug. 'I got caught.'

Michael didn't ask what for. He thought of how it would affect Mary Anne. 'Will you go to prison?'

'Apparently not.'

The constable, his expression growing more concerned by the minute, intervened. 'Careless talk! Careless talk!'

Rees Jones came out through the door that led to the interview rooms and the cells. Michael got to his feet. Rees Jones looked surprised to see him.

'Ah!' he exclaimed. 'It seems you've come at the right time. I've got some very interesting visitors who I'm sure would like to meet you.' He turned to Harry and his handcuffed companion. 'You first. And then I'll sort you out,' he said to Michael.

41

Mary Anne had taken a chair out under the sweet-smelling sapling, hoping the fresh air would calm her nerves. The moment she heard someone knock on the shop door, she raced through, hoping it would be Michael, but opened it to see her daughter Lizzie and Patrick Kelly.

Her disappointment must have been obvious. 'Mum! What's the matter?'

She let them into the shop, Patrick bolting the door behind them.

'I should be open,' she said apologetically, 'but I just couldn't face anyone today.'

'I think she'd better sit down,' Patrick said to Lizzie.

Lizzie shrugged off her coat on the way to the kitchen to put the kettle on, though she needed Patrick to turn on the tap. Lizzie looked around the room, noted the fire had gone out, but apart from that, everything seemed exactly the same, except that her mother looked devastated.

Sensing the atmosphere was less than happy, Patrick took charge. 'You sit with yer mother. I'll make the tea.'

'What is it, Mum?'

Mary Anne sighed and closed her eyes as she attempted to collect her thoughts. 'Michael's been arrested.'

Lizzie's jaw dropped. 'What? What for?' Her mother told her all that had happened.

Lizzie shook her head. 'It couldn't have been Stanley. He wouldn't go near a police station.'

'But they mentioned his name. Someone must have really had it in for Michael to do that. After all, he is a British subject.'

Patrick watched them from the doorway. 'Perhaps it was you they had it in for.'

Lizzie's eyes locked with his. 'Mrs Selwyn!'

Patrick lifted his head in one simple acknowledgement. 'She said she'd get back at you for shopping her son.'

'You shopped Peter?' said Mary Anne incredulously. 'What for?'

'He dodged his call-up papers. She told everyone that he was in Canada, but he wasn't. She'd hidden him up in the attic. I happened to find out he was up there, but I didn't shop him, I merely left her employ because I didn't want him near me.'

Mary Anne smiled and looked from her to Patrick. 'Good.'

'Mum.' Lizzie gave her a warning look. 'My life is mine. I'm still going to join the Wrens when I can.'

Her mother's smile vanished. 'I know.'

'But where's Michael?' said Patrick, keen not to show his hurt as he poured hot water into the teapot.

Mary Anne looked up at him. 'What will happen to him?'

Lizzie looked from her mother to Patrick. It struck her that they were referring more and more to this new Patrick that had developed as an aspect of the war, like a butterfly emerging from a chrysalis.

Taking a cup of tea from Patrick, Lizzie sighed and stirred it until she was sure the sugar was totally dissolved. Stirring also gave her time to gather her thoughts.

'Our Daw is getting married. That's why we came round. She wanted us to tell you.'

She could tell her mother wanted to ask why Daw hadn't come round herself, her expression seeming to turn inwards as though she'd answered her own question.

'We thought you'd like to know what's been arranged. They've got a special licence. No printed invitations will be sent out, and there's no time for bridesmaids or a church, but John's aunt and uncle at the corner shop have donated a cake and a tin of ham.'

'And as best man, I've got extra leave,' said Patrick.

Dropping her gaze into the weak tea, Mary Anne cleared her throat. 'And she's allowing me to come. She doesn't have to. Tell her that. I quite understand. People gossip and my reputation must be at rock bottom at the moment.'

Lizzie exchanged a quick look with Patrick. He was one of the few people outside of the family who knew what had happened.

She didn't know when he'd first acquired such a mature stance or a deeper, more commanding voice, but he'd certainly acquired presence. It was his words that got through to them.

'We don't choose our families, and there isn't one family in Kent Street without secrets, much as they might pretend otherwise.' He grinned and flicked a finger at Lizzie's nose. 'At least my mother didn't pretend to be anything else. There were no secrets in our house, that's for sure.'

Patrick looked at his watch and then at Mary Anne. 'Do you want me to go to the police station and find out what's happening?'

At first she did not answer. She was listening to the ticking of the clocks.

'Do you hear them?' she asked, her blood coursing through her veins in time with the incessant ticking.

Lizzie tilted her head in the same manner as her mother. 'The clocks?'

Mary Anne nodded. 'Time is ticking by, and our hearts are ticking with it.'

Patrick shrugged his puzzlement at Lizzie, who could only look at him briefly, then look away.

'Do you smoke?' he asked, handing out the opened packet to Mary Anne and then to Lizzie.

Mary Anne shook her head.

Lizzie took a light from the end of the one Patrick had already lit.

Mary Anne heaved her shoulders in a deep sigh. 'Can we go outside? A little fresh air might clear my head and help me to think. After that, we'll go to the police station.' She turned to Patrick. 'If you don't mind.'

Lizzie wasn't stupid. She saw from the look in her mother's eyes that there was no point in talking about the wedding. Her mind was elsewhere. In the circumstances – in other words, Daw's piggy behaviour – it seemed quite just.

Lizzie led the way out into the garden. It was a fresh, clear evening, overpoweringly bright after the dark interior of the cramped room at the back of the shop.

Patrick followed. It was only after they were both out there that they realised Mary Anne had ran back inside in response to a heavy thudding at the front door.

By the time they got there, the door was already open. Both women shouted with glee. Michael was back, and Harry was with him. Less gleeful and far more worrying, behind them were two uniformed men in red caps.

Patrick nodded at the two men, and then the two behind. 'Military police. My God, what have you two been up to?'

Hardly acknowledging anyone else, Michael spread out his arms. 'Marianna?'

She ran to him, frowning and stroking his face, murmuring words of affection, not caring that her son and her daughter were watching. They were oblivious to those watching them. 'I am going away,' he said to her.

'Where?'

'Same place as me,' said Harry.

Lizzie's face turned white. 'Prison?' She looked at the two hard-looking men wearing the uniforms of the military police.

'They're for me,' said Harry, nodding at the two men. 'They're to make sure I use my railway pass correctly and get to where I'm going.

They're not so worried about our friend Michael here. He hasn't been such a naughty boy.'

Michael answered their confusion. 'I am a British subject who speaks excellent German. My skills are needed for a special assignment at a secret location.'

'So are mine,' added Harry. 'Same place, different skill.' His mother, sister and Patrick looked puzzled.

He shrugged. 'Unbelievable as it may seem, I do have a very special skill.'

They looked puzzled.

'I'm very good at crosswords. There's some place to do with code breaking...'

One of the men in uniform intervened. 'Quiet! No details.'

Harry sneered at the man, his lips curling with contempt in response to the barked order.

'Anyway, as I said to you, I'll fight when I have to and in my own way. From what I can gather that's just what I'll be doing.' He tapped his head. 'Using my brain not my brawn.'

Because the Ministry of War didn't quite trust Harry to get where he'd been ordered, they were given only a little time to pack. They'd gone round to Harry's place first.

'My friend Mark will take care of the flat while I'm gone,' said Harry, giving his mother a look that she knew meant so much more than anyone else could possibly know. She knew his secret.

Michael took Mary Anne's hand. 'We will talk alone before I go.'

No one made any comment or stood in their way. The military police stayed put, concentrating on staying close to Harry as though he were a consignment of gold bullion.

Silently, they made for the mossy area beneath the flowering sapling, its petals tumbling over them with every breath of the evening breeze.

Michael heaved his shoulders up and down and took deep calming breaths. 'They are alive.'

He knew by the rapture on Mary Anne's face that he didn't need to explain who he was talking about. He did explain about the choice he'd been given.

'I have a confession to make,' he said, making a conscious effort to avoid looking into her eyes. 'I was going to opt to be interned with them. I felt I owed them that for treating them so badly in my youth, but then I received this...'

He unfolded the letter before handing it to her.

She looked up at him, needing some sign that she had his permission before reading on.

He nodded. 'Read.'

He watched her eyelashes flickering over her cheeks as her eyes danced over the words. He refrained from touching them as he had once before, because once he did, he would be lost, he would not want to leave her.

'You have to go,' she said, refolding the letter and pushing it back into his hand.

'Keep it. Their address is on it. Should anything happen to me...'

She looked alarmed. 'Is it likely to? I thought you were going to this place...'

'Just in case, you have their address. Tell them I love them. Tell them that.'

They clung to each other, reliving in their hearts and minds each moment they'd spent in the big bed above the pawnshop. 'We are like the things in the cupboards,' he said at last.

'We are pledged in the hope of being redeemed some day.'

'Will that someday come?'

'We can only hope.'

She knew then that she would attend her daughter's wedding, but would never go back to Kent Street and Henry, but run the shop until Michael returned from wherever he was going. In the meantime, it would be a great comfort to know where each of her children was heading, and that even Stanley would have the benefit of both his parents. Hopefully, the war would be ended before his life too would be changed by it.

MORE FROM LIZZIE LANE

We hope you enjoyed reading *A Wartime Wife*. If you did, please leave a review.

If you'd like to gift a copy, this book is also available as an ebook, digital audio download and audiobook CD.

Sign up to Lizzie Lane's mailing list for news, competitions and updates on future books:

http://bit.ly/LizzieLaneNewsletter

If you enjoyed *A Wartime Wife*, *Wartime Sweethearts*, also by Lizzie Lane, is available to order now.

ABOUT THE AUTHOR

Lizzie Lane is the author of over 50 books, a number of which have been bestsellers. She was born and bred in Bristol where many of her family worked in the cigarette and cigar factories. This has inspired her new saga series for Boldwood *The Tobacco Girls*.

Follow Lizzie on social media:

f facebook.com/jean.goodhind
𝕏 twitter.com/baywriterallat1
📷 instagram.com/baywriterallatsea
BB bookbub.com/authors/lizzie-lane

ABOUT BOLDWOOD BOOKS

Boldwood Books is a fiction publishing company seeking out the best stories from around the world.

Find out more at www.boldwoodbooks.com

Sign up to the Book and Tonic newsletter for news, offers and competitions from Boldwood Books!

http://www.bit.ly/bookandtonic

We'd love to hear from you, follow us on social media:

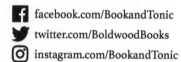

facebook.com/BookandTonic
twitter.com/BoldwoodBooks
instagram.com/BookandTonic